TIGRALLEF BOUND

"March!" is what they bellowed at us, but I would hardly call it marching. We staggered, mainly, the collection of fetters around our necks half-throttling us with every tortured step. The braces were special agony; we wore two, locking each of us into helpless partnership with the wretch ahead and the wretch behind.

"I won't go. I won't go. I won't go," the Gilman ahead of me was droning.

"He's right," muttered the man behind me. "He won't go. He won't live long enough."

"What's happening?" I whispered.

"What's happening? It's the slave levy, you pocketing fool, what did you think? We'll be well on the way to Sher this time tomorrow."

My heart turned into a kind of cold pudding behind my ribs. The quest was ending before it had even begun, my life would end in the salt pans of Sher, or deep in the killing mines near Iklankish, or high in the scaffolding of some pretentious new tower in the imperial warcourt . . .

LADY IN GIL

Rebecca Bradley

ACE BOOKS, NEW YORK

LADY IN GIL

An Ace Book / published by arrangement with
Victor Gollancz

PRINTING HISTORY
Victor Gollancz edition published 1996
Ace edition / March 2000

All rights reserved.
Copyright © 1996 by Rebecca Bradley.
Cover art by Fred Gambino.
This book may not be reproduced in whole or in part,
by mimeograph or any other means, without permission.
For information address: Victor Gollancz,
An imprint of the Cassell Group,
Wellington House, 125 Strand, London WC2R 0BB

The Penguin Putnam Inc. World Wide Web site address is
http://www.penguinputnam.com

Check out the Ace Science Fiction/Fantasy newsletter,
and much more, on the Internet at Club PPI!

ISBN: 0-441-00709-0

ACE®
Ace Books are published by The Berkley Publishing Group,
a division of Penguin Putnam Inc.,
375 Hudson Street, New York, New York 10014.
ACE and the "A" design are trademarks
belonging to Penguin Putnam Inc.

PRINTED IN THE UNITED STATES OF AMERICA

10 9 8 7 6 5 4 3 2 1

For K. N. Coutts

1

IT WAS THE sixth morning after my brother's accident. I was sitting peacefully in the archives, annotating a rare manuscript and minding my own business, when the door crashed open with enough energy to set the ink-jars tinkling on their rack. I marked my place with a finger and looked up.

A tall man loomed in the doorway. A black cloak swirled around him, a horned Sherkin helmet of quite overdone ferocity, mostly spikes and jutting brow ridges, concealed his face. He flourished a knife at me with one mailed fist and raised a lethal-looking club in the other.

"I think you have the wrong room," I said.

He roared at that. He flung the club past my head, charged through the door, vaulted over the table, grabbed my throat in one iron hand and lifted me half out of the chair. "Fight me," he growled.

"You mean me?" I was bewildered.

"Yes!"

The knife flashed in front of my eyes, then swung down to kiss my throat just under the chin. Groping, I managed to push the precious manuscript further along the table, to what I hoped was a safe distance.

"Let's be clear about this. You want me to fight you?"

"Yes! Fight, damn you!"

"But why?"

"Why? Why? By the Lady!" he exploded. The knife clattered into its sheath; the iron fist released my throat and gave me a shove that tipped the chair over backwards and sent me sprawling on the floor. Cautiously I raised myself on to my elbows. My assailant sat down on the edge of the table, pulling the Sherkin helmet off at the same time. I knew his face.

"You're one of my brother's training Flamens, aren't you?"

He nodded without speaking.

"I do hope," I said mildly, still from the floor, "that you're not sitting on that manuscript. It's very old."

He spoke one word. "Hopeless," he said, with deep scorn, and I thought at first that he was talking to me; but then I heard a swishing near the door, and peering through the legs of both the table and my ex-assailant, I could see a curtain of green robes moving sedately towards us. A second later, five pairs of old eyes under shaggy grey eyebrows appeared over the far edge of the table; five straggly old-man beards draped themselves over the tabletop as their owners craned to see me. They belonged to the Primate himself, the three most senior Flamens-in-Exile, and my good friend the First Memorian.

Hastily, I sat up straight and began a gesture of formal greeting.

"Don't bother," the Primate said. "You'll only get it wrong."

My greeting died in mid-waggle. I noted a slight curve of self-congratulation on the Primate's spotty old lips, as if I'd managed to live down to his very worst expectations. "My lord Tigrallef," he added, "do get up off the floor."

I scrambled to my feet, trying to watch all the Flamens at once. The First Flamen's face was gloomy, and he kept shaking his head so that his long grey beard swayed back and forth like a feather-bush in a breeze. The Second and Third Flamens looked awed, as if the spectacular failure they had just witnessed was something to build legends around. Their heads were also shaking.

I turned pleading eyes to the First Memorian and found him dutifully wagging his beard along with the rest of them, but with a gleam of muted approval, even relief, on his face. "You see?" he said, turning to the Flamens, "Lord Tigrallef is totally unsuitable."

"Totally," said the First Flamen.

"I quite agree," said the Second Flamen.

"Not to be thought of," said the Third Flamen.

The Primate's eyes narrowed. "He's a Scion of Oballef. That makes him suitable."

"But Most Revered One, you saw what happened when Clero attacked him. He hasn't the faintest idea how to fight; he has no heroic instincts whatsoever—"

The Primate silenced the First Memorian with one of his famous glares. "Lord Tigrallef can be trained. I'm sure Clero agrees."

Clero, the training Flamen, obviously did not agree, and was just opening his mouth to say so when he also caught the look in the Primate's eye. Armour and knife and bulging muscles and all, he quailed. "Oh, yes, Most Revered One. We can make a hero out of him—given enough time." Given a few decades, that's what his expression said, but the Primate was already turning to the door in triumph.

I coughed. "Most Revered One?"

The Primate swung back to glare at me, his great grey puffs of eyebrows raised. This was normally enough to make me shake like a jellydevil caught on a sharp rock, but a horrible suspicion was taking shape in my mind, and it steadied my voice.

"Most Revered One—does this have something to do with my brother?"

"There is nothing you need to know at this moment, Scion," said the Primate.

"But how is my brother? They said yesterday he was improving."

"Lord Arkolef will live," he answered coldly.

"Then what—?"

"Unfortunately," he interrupted, suddenly bearing down upon me, "his wound has begun to rot on the bone. The healing Flamens tell me the leg must be sacrificed, or he will die within a few days." The eyebrows knitted into a frown, daring me to speak again; daring me to accuse him.

For once, I didn't give a pick of the nose how the Primate was looking at me. The shock was lending me a sour kind of courage. "Well, that's a set-back for you, Most Revered One," I said. "Now you won't be able to send him to Gil.

What a shame. I know how you like to keep up your average—"

"Lord Tigrallef!"

"—and it's been four years since you sent poor Baraslef to his death—"

"We don't know that he's dead, Scion."

"—but I can't believe that even you would send a one-legged hero into the jaws of the appalling Sherank. If you ask me, the leg is a small price to pay for his life. Thank the Lady, Arko's safe."

"And thank the Lady," said the Primate coldly, "we have an alternative."

"An alternative?"

"Yes, indeed." He smiled, with a mouth like a narrow groove chipped in a block of ice. I knew that expression; I had seen it before, directed at persons whom the Primate planned to use, not necessarily with their whole-hearted approval, for some dangerous or distasteful task. "Someone who can take over the quest in Lord Arkolef's stead," he added.

"I trust you don't mean—"

"You will be told," he said, "when the Council of Flamens has made its decision."

"What decision?" I asked, but he was heading for the door again, sweeping Clero and the other Flamens with him. The First Memorian paused by the door, looking back at me with pity and regret, but when I mimed a question at him, he raised his hands helplessly and vanished after the others.

It was hard to concentrate after that. I rewrapped the manuscript in its leather envelope, cleaned my pens and trailed miserably over to the sickhouse to see if there was any news of my brother. I was not allowed to see Arko and the healing Flamens were too busy to talk to me, but the foetor of boiling herbs and bubbling concoctions was quite informative. I wandered disconsolately through the clouds of steam, identifying sleeping draughts, blood thickeners, flesh cleansers; when a little acolyte walked in carrying a cleaver and a saw, I left.

So, I remember thinking, Arko's leg would be lost, but his life would be spared. I knew Arko would not be pleased. The prospect of going to Gil and confronting the Sherank had meant everything in his life to him. He had been honed and polished for it from birth, immersed in the Ways of Combat, trained in the Arts of Valour, educated with patience and some difficulty in the Secrets of the Ancients, the Caveat and the Lesser and Greater Wills, and thoroughly steeped in the Heroic Code, which lays down the etiquette of combat and social behaviour for right-thinking heroes. He was tall, strong, golden-haired and handsome. He had muscles knit like chain mail, the physical fitness of a dozen athletes, the moral rectitude of two dozen saints, and the profile of a god—from both sides.

I was shortish, stocky, graceless, dirty-blond and as physically fit as half an athlete. Even my mother, who loved me, couldn't meet my eyes and call me handsome. As for courage, I suppose I'd be as brave as the next man, assuming the next man to be an abject coward; not even approximately hero material. This had been evident from such an early age that the Primate-in-Exile had despaired of me, and had not honoured me with the normal rigorous childhood of a Scion of Oballef. At the time of Arko's accident I was a memorian, obscure and largely unharassed, happily buried in the archives for most of my waking hours. I was a good one, too. It was all I ever wanted to be.

That day, however, roaming along Exile's rocky strand, I had a nasty feeling that my status was about to rise. My brother Arkolef had been ideal mission-fodder. He believed in the Heroic Code; he welcomed the chance to die for the honour of Gil. I never thought he was terribly bright. But he had somehow managed to buckle on his heavy leg-armour backwards, a feat requiring really inspired stupidity, and fallen over, breaking his left leg in three places, and then compounded this idiocy by ignoring the pain for several days, as per the Heroic Code. End of career.

But the Flamens still wanted a hero; with Arko out of action, they were left only with my cousin Callefiya, of the right age and training, but now the mother of two young children; six little Scions, including Callefiya's two and Arkolef's two, between the ages of one and fourteen; and myself. And the more I thought about it, the more ominous did that morning's performance in the archives appear.

The First Memorian told me later that the meeting called to discuss the ramifications of Arko's leg did not have the usual dignity of Flamen functions. One faction, the largest, held out for postponing the next mission until one of the children was of an age to go, a delay of at least seven years. The rest were split between those wanting to send Callefiya, although this would probably orphan her children (her husband Baraslef had been the last hero to depart); and the Primate, who wanted to send me.

Both the other factions thought the latter was about as sensible as setting a fieldmouse to nip a rippercat to death. I was well known to be of no use except in the archives, where my tendency to trip over even very small objects was not a fatal drawback. Furthermore, it was not customary to send a Scion to Gil before he or she had ensured the bloodline by producing another little Scion or two, whereas they hadn't even been able to arrange a marriage for me yet—and not for want of trying. No, they said, no indeed, even if Lord Tigrallef were the last of Oballef's line left in Exile, it would still be futile to send *him*.

Then the Primate took the floor—and kept it. The first argument he dismissed out of hand as unimportant; I was a certified Scion of Oballef, and I could be trained. As to the second argument, he said if they waited for me to father a child, they could very well wait for ever; and that was assuming my contribution to the Scions' lineage would be worth waiting for, which he rather doubted. He pointed out that their best attempt to marry me off so far had failed abysmally, although who could blame any discriminating peeress for rejecting me? He pointed out a great many things, none of them pleasant or tactful, and as he spoke he glared around the assembly with a face that promised endless grief to anyone who opposed him. By the end of the meeting, there was not a single dissenting voice. The First Memorian was the last to surrender.

That evening, the Primate sent an unhappy delegation to inform me. I suppose I could have refused at that point. Typically, I lacked the nerve. Anyway, we Scions were accustomed to doing what the Flamens told us, just as the Flamens were accustomed to sending us to theoretically glorious deaths at the hands of the Sherkin usurpers in Gil. The only note of hope was dropped by my mother, the Lady Dazeene, into the silence the delegation left behind.

"Strange," she said, "I'd resigned myself to the thought of losing Arko, and now you're to go instead. Of course, it's better this way."

"You mean, I'm not as much of a loss?" I asked, surprised and a little hurt. She had never given the impression that she liked my brother best.

"Don't be stupid, Tig," she said. "I mean that now I might keep both my sons—and by the way, if you happen to find your father, you can tell him I'm still waiting."

I sighed and kissed her. It was nineteen years since my father had taken ship for Gil, and she still refused to believe he was dead. As for implying that I might succeed where others and betters had failed, well—there was a fond mother for you. Of course, she was not of Oballef's line herself, but was a Satheli princess, born and bred in the Archipelago, and nobody expected her to understand these purely Gillish matters. I pushed her words to the back of my mind.

The decision made, the training Flamens descended on me, though without much conviction. I was put on a diet, given a crash course in the Heroic Code, the Ways of Combat and the Arts of Valour (I already knew the Secrets of the Ancients, the Caveat and the two Wills, forwards and backwards, from my years as a memorian), and browbeaten into a vigorous regime of exercise and physical education. A bare half-year was allotted to my training, six grisly, gruelling months that seemed endless at the time, but still passed far too quickly. At the end of that period, I was fairly fit, leaner than I'd ever been in my life, and could just about handle a weapon without endangering myself more than my opponent. On the other hand, my cynicism about the Heroic Code had deepened immeasurably, and my sense of doom had not abated one grain. I was a very unhappy hero.

My departure for Gil was attended by the usual ceremony and celebration, but it was easy to see that the Flamens' hearts were not in it. I felt bitter about this—if they had so little confidence, why send me at all? Surely a live memorian was more useful to them than a dead hero? I was within a skull's whisker of backing out when I glanced up and saw my cousin Callefiya standing between her children on top of the hills; her fatherless and potentially motherless children, I reminded myself. Knowing the Most Revered One, she'd be on a ship to Gil within the month if I refused to go. Behind her was Arko, with his younger child in the crook of one arm and a crutch under the other. His face was desolate, but he saluted me with the blessing for a departing hero. That clinched it. I directed a final despairing look at my mother, who smiled at me confidently from her place of honour next to the Primate, and then turned to plod through the arch of flowers and waving banners to the rowboat on the beach. As I stepped in, a hand clawed at my shoulder. It was Marori, the oldest Flamen of all, the last survivor of the Gilborn exiles.

"Beware, Child of Oballef," he whispered. He sketched in the air the old formal gesture of warning. "There are more foes in Gil than the accursed Sherank. The people of Gil have lived in bondage for seventy years and have forgotten the ways of our fathers. Trust no one—do you hear me, Scion? Until the Lady in Gil is found, even your countrymen are your deadly enemies." His grip tightened. I sighed.

"And hark to this, too! There are more perils in the Gilgard than those foolish youngsters would have you believe." Marori waved with contempt in the direction of the other Flamens, who bristled their grey beards irritably but made no move to shut him up. "Hark to me, Tigrallef, son of Cirallef! Before Fathan rose and fell, before Vizzath and Myr, before ever the Gilgard caves were carved out by Oballef, there was a maze under the rock—and do you know what was in it, Scion?"

"What, what?" I demanded. The tide was right, the ship was waiting. Since I was doomed to go anyway, I wanted to get it over with.

"Things!" he hissed. "Things of legend, terrible creatures of the dark, things older than Fathan, older than Vizzath, older than everything on earth except the Lady in Gil herself! It was indeed the Lady who forced them deeper into the mantle of the world and held them there for nearly a thousand years. But mark my words! It has been seventy winters and more since last a Priest-King ruled in Gil. Who knows what crept back to the Gilgard caves when the Lady's will was broken? Who knows, Scion, who knows? And hark to this too, Scion—"

But at this juncture the other Flamens moved in and had Marori carried off, still declaiming horrors and dark prognostications and other acutely uncomforting things. They assured me as I settled glumly into the boat that the old man was off his head, really, and was forever babbling gruesome nonsense about the ancient legends, when he wasn't boring them with the good old days in Gil. All right for them, I thought, as I watched their green-robed figures recede on the other side of a widening stretch of water; they'd be home safe in their beds while I stumbled about in those dark, sacred, unholy caverns—assuming I even got that far.

2

I WISH I could say that I was stirred by my first sight of the Gilgard, but it would not be true. I was seasick at the time. I was slumped in the bow, wishing from the bottom of my heart that the smelly little boat would be obliging enough to sink, when the captain bent and shook my arm.

"The Gilgard is on the horizon, my lord Tigrallef." I grunted, hoping he'd go away. He didn't. He seemed to be expecting some heroic and memorable saying, like those produced by previous Scions of Oballef on such occasions. I pushed my head briefly above the railing, blinked at the far-off misty outline of Gil, and retched. "Very nice," I mumbled. Thank the Lady, he left me alone after that.

There remain few other memories of that last day of my voyage to Gil. I know we were challenged at least twice by Sherkin patrol ships, great ugly hulks bristling with spear-chuckers and flame-slings and large heads in snouty Sherkin helmets, looming over the foredeck where I lay. The spectacle might have been terrifying if I'd been fit to appreciate it. I even have a dim memory of the fishing boat being boarded for inspection, for I recall hearing harsh voices and opening one eye to see a shiny black boot with sharp metal teeth set into the toes.

"One of your crew?" a deep voice growled above me.

"An apprentice," said the captain's voice smoothly, "and still finding his sea-belly."

The boot prodded my shoulder, then turned me over. "Great Raksh. Is he the best you can do? You'd be better to chop him into pieces and use him for bait." I listened dreamily as the boot-owner guffawed, kicked me light-heartedly in the ribs and disappeared. I was beyond caring.

It was not only the seasickness. It was also a deadly mixture of inadequacy, hopelessness, honest fear and shame. Arko would never have been afraid; and even if seasick, he'd have bitten the Sherkin bastard on the ankle. I permitted myself a moment of rage with Arko for getting his stupid leg cut off. After all, he wanted to be here, I didn't. I wanted to be safe at home in the archives, preferably reading.

And so, as the fishing boat lolloped its way towards the tall stone finger that marked a homeland I'd never seen, I thought neither of my mission nor of my heroic responsibility, but of cool, still air; of the musty smell of old books and flaking scrolls, the sour old-ink smell of the First Memorian, my friend and mentor, the whispering discourse between pens and pages; I dreamed of solid chairs on solid floors. The boat dipped, abandoning my belly in mid-air.

"Not long now, my lord," said the captain. This news was not good, though not entirely bad. In my view, the advantage to being on shipboard was that I wasn't yet on Gil; but just then the Sherank seemed the lesser of the evils as long as they were on dry land.

I hardly remember the approach to Gil harbour, only the sudden chill as we moved into the shadow of the Gilgard, shouts of greeting from nearby boats as we moored, the black prow of a massive Sherkin warship gliding past overhead; oh, and the smell. Dead fish and seasalt, as in any harbour in the known world, but borne on a shorewind of shit and decay, mouldering offal, sweat, dung-smoke and despair. My first whiff of Gil. The captain, seeing what was about to happen, draped me across the rail so that my head hung over the side.

"Forgive me, my lord Scion," he said, "but we've just swabbed the deck."

I was too busy to thank him. When I had finished losing whatever was left to lose (who knows where it came from; I hadn't eaten in four days) I rested my chin on the rail and focused blearily on the shore.

Rubble and smoke. No rosy stone villas, no spires, no fountains, no arcade of green trees sweeping the curve of the harbour. Rubble and smoke, that was all. It looked like the city had been sacked just that morning instead of seven decades before, and was still smouldering—in other words, like a typical subject city in the Sherkin empire. It was even uglier than I'd expected. I gulped and moved my eyes upwards, above the bleak urban jumble, to the mountain and the heights of Gilgard Castle.

Even sick as I was, that sight made me catch my breath. Gilgard Castle—the masterwork of Oballef, the seat of my ancestors, the sacred house of the Lady in Gil; also, more pertinently, the local Sherkin stronghold. Its turrets sprang from the living rock of the Gilgard, as if sprouted rather than built; its ramparts and buttresses, the tiers of the three palaces, the airy colonnades of the upper galleries, flowed easily up the mountainside like an ocean wave frozen in mid-break. It was impossible to see where the castle ended and the mountain began, so seamless was the construction. My ancestor had built well; his handiwork had defied even the Sherkin genius for vandalism, at least from a distance. It hung over the suppurating city like a dream of the shining past.

Oh, very nice, said the gloom-merchant in the back of my head. *Poetic, even. But what about the caves? What if they've found the secret ways into the mountain, where the Lady lies hidden? What about that?*

"What about it?" I mumbled out loud. I hung my head over the rail again, searching my stomach for something else to throw up. An object like a log bumped gently against the hull at the waterline—except that logs do not generally have shoulders for shreds of rotten cloth to cling to, nor faces like lumps of leavened dough. It had hands, too—one of them waved at me as it bobbed about in the ship's wash. *Welcome to Gil, lord Scion.*

"Thank you," I said.

The right eye seemed to wink as a small crab climbed up through the socket. *Come to find the Lady, have we?*

"Yes."

The head submerged for a moment, as if thrown back with laughter. *To free us? To rid us of the Sherank?*

"If I can."

You? You must be joking. What were the Flamens thinking of when they sent you? That was the lipless mouth-hole, grinning around a tongue that emerged waggishly—and emerged, and emerged, and emerged, until the eel pulled itself free and slid lazily into the murk below. The conversation was becoming unpleasant. I turned my face away.

"Captain," I said, "there's a body in the water."

He bent indifferently over the taffrail. "So? Don't let it bother you. You're in Gil now."

"Oh, I'm not bothered by the body," I whispered, "I'm bothered by the fact that I was talking to it."

But the captain had already walked away. I closed my eyes. Why should I fret over the opinions of a bloated

corpse? The deck was level for the first time in four days; I
stretched out and let the world grow fuzzy around the edges.
The captain told me later that I looked like a corpse myself—
certainly I slept like one, and had no dreams that I can recall.
He threw a blanket over me and kindly left me to sleep.

Thus it was not until the dark early hours of the next
morning that I was wakened, dumped respectfully into a rowboat and smuggled ashore. I remember curling up miserably
between the thwarts and half-dreaming about my ancestor
Oballef, who also came to Gil in a rowboat, and did rather
well for himself. In my daze, the rowboat was decisive in
his success.

That first rowboat came ashore about a thousand years ago,
when the unlamented Empire of Fathan had been dead for
less than a century, the nations were in their infancy and the
world was a hostile and unruly place. Who Oballef was and
where he came from were not recorded, not even in legend.
He arrived on Gil to find the island an armpit of a place,
infertile, unattractive, short of water, and torn by constant
petty squabbling among the factions of its tiny population.
The only impressive feature was the Gilgard itself, a great
flat-topped plug of volcanic rock some two thousand feet
high, dominating the dusty flatlands at the north end of the
island: on the seaward side, a sheer uncreviced cliff, too steep
to be scaled, too smooth even to provide nesting for birds;
on the landward side, almost as steep, but climbable in theory. In practice, nobody wanted to climb it. In the pre-
Oballef mythos of Gil, the Gilgard was both sacred and
unhealthy.

Nevertheless, carrying a small bundle over his shoulder
and ignoring the natives, Oballef immediately set off to scale
the Gilgard. The aboriginal Gilmen were confused by this
behaviour, but interested. They were also interested in the
contents of his bundle. Eventually, smothering their fears, a
small group banded together to follow him up the rocky landward slope.

They never exactly caught up with him. My ancestor
climbed steadily, easily, never faltering, never looking back;

the Gilmen scrambled unhappily a few score feet in the rear, not quite able to close the gap. Thus, when Oballef reached the flat summit of the Gilgard, his followers had an eagle's view of the extraordinary events that ensued.

According to eye-witness accounts passed down to us, my ancestor stood on the edge of the summit and took from his bundle a glowing object about the size and shape of his forearm. He held it over his head with both hands and commenced to chant in a tongue strange to the observers. As they watched, a golden mist emanated from the object, enveloping but not obscuring Oballef, and then expanded to roll down the cliffside towards them, a cloud spangled with motes of fire. It was past them before they could even think of being afraid—they turned to watch as it billowed to the foot of the Gilgard and across the sere lowlands, sweeping the entire long crescent of the island before dissipating at the far southern tip. The whole traverse, it was said, took no more than three minutes.

This cloud was spectacular enough in itself to ensure Oballef's reputation forever—and yet, it was only the beginning. As the astounded Gilmen watched from their vantage point high on the mountain, the island began a wonderful transformation. The tough yellow earth darkened to black, then to the tender green of sprouting shoots. Springs of clear water bubbled to the surface all over the island and began to cut meandering channels to the sea. Even the air seemed to warm and soften. Gil blossomed like a water-lily unfolding in the middle of a pond.

The Gilmen were impressed—so impressed that they failed to mark Oballef's descent until he was already among them, the bundle tucked securely under his arm. He paused, apparently noticing them for the first time. "Well—let's find something to eat," he is supposed to have said, before leading them down the mountain into the burgeoning new Gil. Those words, much analysed in later times, were to take on a huge burden of mythic significance; I believe that my ancestor was simply hungry.

However it was, this was the first recorded manifestation

of the Lady in Gil. The object in Oballef's bundle was said to be a figurine, the image of a woman, carved from a radiant amber-coloured stone veined richly with sapphire. Or, according to alternative versions, it was gold inlaid with lapis, or possibly with jade; in fact, its precise nature and how Oballef came by it in the first place were secrets long hidden in the fogbanks of time. From that first manifestation to the day of catastrophe, the Lady was never seen by any but the Priest-King and the most senior of the Flamens, who remained professionally secretive; the public statues, the little glazed figurines made for tourists, even the Flamens' insignia, were all based on popular fancy, and very beautiful they were. The actual records, however, proved only that the Lady was the focus of a power, flexible in its applications, mysterious in its workings—and only to be wielded with safety by Oballef and, in due course, his descendants, the Scions of Oballef.

Within weeks of Gil's transformation, the Lady had a large and devout following, which unanimously installed Oballef as Hereditary King of Gil and High Priest of the Cult of the Lady in Gil, a title that passed down intact through forty-odd generations of my forebears. In return, with liberal aid from the Lady, the people of Gil set about becoming the most cultured, peaceable and artistically brilliant race the world had known since the days of Fathan's innocence, and very likely the richest too.

Gil's next nine hundred and twenty-seven years could be described as happy, rewarding and blessedly uneventful, the Bright Ages, an extended golden summer in which the seeds planted by Oballef blossomed and bore fruit. The crops never failed, the fishing boats never landed empty, the Gillish argosies never sank. War was unknown. Combat was ritualized into a kind of athletic competition governed by strict rules of etiquette; under the matronage of the Lady, violence seemed irrelevant, even quaint. Gil became the wonder of the world, and the Gilmen a race apart. It lasted a long time—but no good thing, it seems, can last forever.

3

THE WATER MADE oily sucking noises around the nose of the boat. We seemed, strangely, to be gliding in the dark down the centre of a garden arcade, one of those long, dim, vine-ceilinged passages between two rows of columns that are such a feature of the grand Satheli villas; curious place, I thought, to put a garden. Then heavy footsteps thundered overhead, the columns turned abruptly into wooden pilings, the trailing vines into rank streamers of sea-growth, and I realized we were under a jetty in the harbour of Gil City.

The oars were muffled and slipped soundlessly in and out of the water. My belly calmed with the stillness. I sat up in time to feel the keel grate on to pebbly sand, with a noise that seemed shockingly loud. After a few moments, while I held my breath and waited fearfully for more footsteps above us, one of the oarsmen shook me by the shoulder and helped me over the side. We crept out from under the jetty on to an open beach, littered with crates, stinking of sewage and dead fish and bordered by a high sea-wall silhouetted spikily against the first lightening of the dawn.

The fisherman motioned for me to follow. Keeping to the cover of the crates as far as possible, we worked our way a fair distance up the beach, bypassing the first three flights of stairs set into the sea-wall. At the fourth, my companion patted me pityingly on the back and waved me upwards; a second later, like a spirit, he had vanished into the shadows. I was alone.

I stood for a moment, tamping down a fierce desire to follow the man back to the rowboat; or, failing that, to walk into the sea and start swimming. Then, sighing, I scrambled up the stairs and found myself for the first time on the streets of the city of Gil, former pearl of the world. Fortunately, there was no one there to meet me.

I hovered shivering by the sea-wall, completely at a loss. The gaunt buildings looked down at me with wide, dark eyes—except they should not have been there at all. I should have been facing a broad strip of garden running along the corniche for the whole arc of the harbour. To my right, where the harbour-master's villa should have been, was a small market; to my left, where the grand avenue leading to the Gilgard Gate should have met the corniche under a soaring arch of white stone, was a massive brick-and-rubble wall at least thirty feet high. And yes—the limp sacks dangling from hooks at the top of the wall were indeed human, or had been; there was little left of them by then.

The instructions given by the Flamens-in-Exile were extraordinarily vague when it came to practicalities. Go to Gil, find the Lady and destroy the accursed Sherank; that was clear enough. They were not very helpful, however, when it came to the middle bits.

Certainly they equipped us well enough in some ways. I had a little pouch of lead tokens, sufficient for a few days' food and lodging; I had a sword in a scabbard, disguised as a walking stick; I had a knife concealed in a sheath sewn into one of my boots; and I had a dart-tube and ten little darts, although these were not actually part of my official kit—the Flamens didn't think such a sneaky weapon was really in the spirit of the Heroic Code, so I had packed it myself on the sly. And I had one other weapon unblessed by the Flamens, in fact scorned by them as unworthy of any civilized person: my fair fluency in Sheranik, the language of Sher, acquired along with a few other so-called lower tongues in my dear dead days as a scholar. I think their idea was that I should defeat the Sherank without ever deigning to speak to them; or, at most, that I should set them cringing with a choice few words in Ceremonial Old High Gillish. Such was my trust in that theory that I spent my last night in Exile reviewing Sheranik plurals.

But there was no guarantee that I'd ever come to use any

of this equipment, sanctioned or not, since what the Flamens had never armed us with was knowledge—detailed practical knowledge of the conditions, customs and physical set-up of the new Gil. Yes, I had memorized the maps of Gil as it was before the catastrophe, and pored over the paintings that Marori and others had made while Gil was still fresh in their minds. Dropped in the middle of my great-great-grandfather's city, I'd have known exactly what to do, precisely where to go. But by the Lady, the old place had certainly changed.

Change came suddenly to Gil, seventy-two years before I did, when the Sherank, a race of murderers and thieves with the most abhorrent national habits since the latter days of Fathan, swept out of the desert-continent of Sher bent on conquering the world. Their first stop was Gil—partly to rape the island of its wealth in order to finance their ambitions, but mainly to capture the Lady in Gil herself, in the belief that her power could make them invincible. In the first aim, they achieved a notable and tragic success. In the second, they failed.

Had my great-great-grandfather, Oballef the Eleventh (may his bones bring forth flowers), had access to the Lady, the outcome might have been different—but Kishr, High Prince of Iklankish, capital of Sher, knew perfectly well what a hazard the Lady represented. He and his hordes approached stealthily, cunningly, and took Gil by surprise. The thunderbolt of their arrival was timed to coincide with the Festival of Harps at Malvi Point on the south end of the island, trapping the Priest-King and most of his court away from the safety of Gilgard Castle. Gil was helpless, plucked like an apple from a tree. The Priest-King and Queen were among the first to be butchered.

Prince Kishr did not pause to celebrate, even though oceans of the peerless Vintage of Gil had just come into his hands. He swept through the shattered gates of the Gilgard, past heaped corpses of castle guardsmen, past piles of looted treasures, into the violated sanctuary of the Temple Palace, searching for the one object he had really come to capture:

the Lady in Gil. He was very disappointed. The pedestal was empty. The Lady was gone. The few surviving Flamens were unable to tell him where she was, even when asked in Kishr's most pressing manner. The last one had scarcely stopped screaming when more bad news reached Kishr's ears: several younger members of the royal family (among them my great-grandfather) and a small number of Flamens could not be accounted for, and were presumed to have left the island.

Kishr's anger was terrible. First he eviscerated the messenger, by way of soothing his feelings. Then he ordered the castle and the island to be scoured—no traces were found. In time he gave up and proceeded to further conquests, but without the Lady (and a Scion of Oballef to conjure her for him) his success was only partial. Calloon fell messily, and Storica, and Kuttumm; Tata and Glishor surrendered and suffered anyway. Koroska, that nest of collaborating rumplickers, welcomed Kishr as a hero, and prospered. The others, profiting from the period of Kishr's distraction, banded together into the League of Free Nations and managed to strike an armed truce with Sher and its new slave empire. That uneasy balance of power still held at the time of my arrival in Gil—but the Lady in Gil, depending on who found her first, could tip the scales either way, or so the theory went.

This is what had happened with the Lady: when news of the Sherkin invasion reached the Gilgard, the Primate of the Flamens made a rapid and largely correct decision. He packed the royal children and twenty Flamens of various ranks into a fishing boat, along with whatever archives could be quickly assembled, and told them to take refuge in Sathelforn, in the Archipelago, three days' journey across the sea. This was a precaution in case the worst happened and the Gilgard fell. According to eye-witnesses in the party, something, probably the Lady herself, was hidden under the Primate's cloak as he waved the boat off at the harbour. That was his mistake.

Why he did not send the Lady to safety with the royal children was debated among the Flamens-in-Exile for decades. If he had done so, the first little Scion to mature could have returned to Gil in triumph within a matter of years. It is possible the Primate did not know that the Priest-King and his brothers were dead, and was waiting for them to return to the Gilgard. It may be that he himself attempted the Will that would work the downfall of Kishr's armies, but failed to control the Lady—he was not a Scion of Oballef. In any event, the Primate and the Lady both vanished.

On the other hand, the fishing boat managed to reach Sathelforn with its royal and priestly supercargo, followed by pitifully few shiploads of other Gillish refugees, all that were able to escape the Sherkin net. They were given sanctuary on a small island in the Archipelago, which the Satheli royals courteously, although not very tactfully, renamed Exile. The Archipelago, as a charter member of the League of Free Nations, managed not to be overrun by the Sherkin empire-builders. The little colony of exiled priests and princes remained safe, and so able to turn their entire energies to training up the royal children, and latterly their descendants, to penetrate the Sherkin security system, find the Lady and retrieve the fortunes of Gil.

This proved somewhat more difficult than it sounded. And, I am forced to say, I never thought the Flamens' approach was at all intelligent. Nineteen of my close relations embarked on the mission over the years, starting with my great-grandfather, in the seventh year of Exile, and continuing with my great-great-uncle, great-uncles and a great-aunt, uncles and aunts, cousins and second cousins, and also my own father, whom I could just barely remember. None succeeded. None was directly heard from again.

This, you might think, should have made the Flamens suspect the fitness of their strategy. Not so. The Flamens blithely continued to train their royal heroes in the old, formalized ethics of warfare and combat, firmly believing that what had been honourable and sufficient in the old Gil would be equally effective in the new; the Scions of Oballef continued to sail off to messy or unknown dooms in the Gilgard caverns, or on the swordpoints of the appalling Sherank. As far as I could tell, this worried nobody but me, and perhaps my mother. It certainly did not worry my brother Arkolef.

•   •   •

But it was not Arkolef who hunkered miserably by the parapet of the sea-wall in Gil that morning; it was I, Tigrallef, and I had no time to contemplate the ironies of history. I heard voices and footsteps approaching down the street, and hid myself behind a stack of barrels. It was a party of Gilmen heading towards the quays; they muttered as they walked with hunched shoulders and bent heads, like men accustomed to frequent beatings and precious few hot dinners. A greater shock was how they were dressed—britches, tunics and cloaks, like my own in design, but horribly different in state, so ragged, begrimed and worn that only the filth seemed to hold them together. My own clothes had been carefully dirtied and aged by a team of Flamens-in-Exile who fancied they were being very clever, but the cloth was basically sound. I would stick out like a boil.

That realization determined my strategy for the whole of the first long, long day. Not for this Scion the tactic of striding up to the Gilgard and demanding a champion from the Sherank—that approach was quite counter-productive, as one of my great-uncles had discovered. He was posted in the great marketplace, in small pieces, over a period of several years, with the compliments of Lord Kishr. What the other Scions had done, I had no way of knowing. Nobody knew. Me? I hid.

I crept first along narrow tortuous alleys where only a few early fires added their smoke to the general stink. It looked like a whole section of the city had been razed to the ground and built over with sticks and straw and broken masonry, hovel against hovel, into one sprawling continuous honeycomb of squalor. I saw few people at that hour, and every one I saw sent me scuttling into the nearest shadow. One figure in particular, hunched and hooded, kept appearing behind me, or on one of the little cross-alleys, or even ahead of me; it took me some time to realize that nearly everyone in Gil looked like that.

As the dawn progressed dangerously, I found myself wandering into a sector where the makeshift hovels gave way to stone buildings towering as many as six or seven floors above street level, really very impressive until I realized the state they were in. They were the the sordid wreckage of the ancient Gil; the scars of old damage might have been unrepaired since the invasion, and the rare rebuildings in brick and wormy wood were also on the point of collapse. The streets were deeply puddled, scummed with raw sewage. Rubbish lay everywhere in blankets and mounds. All of the landmarks I had carefully memorized had disappeared. I was lost.

There were more people moving about this quarter, which worried me, but there were also more possibilities for concealment. Many of the buildings looked deserted; screes of rubble blocked the alleyways here and there, in front of promising cavities in the thickness of collapsing walls. Under stairways, inside abandoned yards, deep in the shadows of half-exposed cellars—it seemed one could hide an army here, not to mention one short hero. After a hasty scout around, I chose a prime spot near the mouth of a dark alley, where a rockfall from one of the buildings had partially demolished a tiny shed. It was cramped and mucky, but by sitting against the rear wall I could see out into the main street without being seen myself.

I felt sick enough, and my covert felt secure enough, that I actually curled up in the rubble and slept. Around midday, I was wakened by a commotion in the street. Someone had obligingly parked a wain in front of my hiding place, but I crept forward and peered cautiously through the slatted side. A Sherkin patrol was riding by, and the Gilmen were either scattering or flattening themselves against the house-fronts. Over their bowed heads, I could see a caped and helmeted man on horseback and could hear others calling to him in the rough consonantal growl of Sheranik; he was the first Sherkin I had seen above ankle-level.

After he rode out of sight, I crept back into the furthest corner of my shelter, grinning to myself. So this was fear, true fear, the genuine stamped-in-the-selvedge, scratched-in-the-wet-clay article. I had been afraid before, many times— you do not survive six months of the Flamens' training pro-

gramme without a number of bad moments—but this was
different. This was the real thing.

By Oballef, the rest of that day passed slowly! I entertained
myself by working on my attire, attacking it with handfuls
of muck, abrading my cloak with a rock, rubbing mud and
dust into the pores of my face—but I didn't enjoy myself. I
was cold, and desperately hungry after four days of seasickness; I was also depressed by everything I saw. When at last
the drab day limped to a close, I waited until the darkness
was complete, and then waited a little more. Finally, too
hungry to put it off any longer, I emerged cautiously from
my hiding place. A few Gilmen trudged by, but nobody
looked at me. Down the black street, a dimly-lit sign announced an inn.

It was not prepossessing, but cooking smells battled
bravely with the stench outside and drew me in. The door
opened on to a large smoky room filled with long tables,
dismal but warm, and already crowded. Nobody looked up.
The other customers hunched over their bowls, muttering
drearily to each other or spooning stew into their mouths
with no appearance of pleasure. When I sat hesitantly down
at an empty table, the innkeeper slapped a bowl of stew and
a mug of beery-smelling liquid in front of me, then left me
alone. That cheered me up—until I tasted the stew.

While I picked at the clots of unidentifiable gristle floating
in my bowl, my eyes were caught by an old man crouched
in the opposite corner. He was staring at me fixedly with one
bloodshot eye; where the other used to be was an empty
socket rimmed with sores. Deep gouges ran down both sides
of his face, lifting the corners of his lips into a permanent
smirk. He was drooling.

He waved at me with an arm that ended in a pucker of
scar tissue instead of a hand. I looked away. Of all the de-
moralizing objects I'd seen that day, he could well have been
the worst, with the notable exception of the Sherkin patrol.
When I looked again, he was stumping in my direction on a
crude wooden leg and a twisted real one, head lolling on his
shoulders. He sat down at my table and leaned that ghastly

face close to mine. He smelled very bad, even for a Gilman.

"I've been waiting for you," he croaked.

I sighed and moved minutely along the bench. He followed.

"I thought you'd never come," he added, spraying generously into my dinner. I stared at the bowl and pushed it away.

"You're mistaken," I said politely, "we're strangers."

"You're no stranger. It's been a while since the last one, though."

"What are you talking about?"

He screwed up his face as if calculating where to bite. "You know."

I was suddenly afraid that I did know; either that, or the cross-purposes we were talking at were uncannily well matched. "Tell me what you mean," I whispered.

He glanced around and leaned even closer. "I mean—that I know who you are."

4

I FROZE INSIDE —the old man continued to watch me with that jugular-first look on his face.

"All right," I whispered. "Who am I?"

He didn't answer. Silently, he delved through layers of rags at his neck and brought out a small object on a tarnished chain. He held it close to my eyes, cupping it in his palm so that it was hidden from the others in the room. It was a tiny silver figurine, a woman, the only beautiful thing I had seen all day. Moreover, it was a miniature of the Lady—something worn only around the necks of the Flamens in Gil. It was brightly polished, unlike the chain, and gleamed against the setting of his dirt-encrusted palm. He chuckled soundlessly and pushed it back into its hiding place.

"Who are you?" I whispered.

"Come with me and I'll tell you—Scion. It's up to you."

He jerked his head towards the door, then heaved himself up from the bench and hobbled out without looking back. Nobody's eyes followed him except mine; he may as well have been invisible. When the door had closed behind him, I settled thoughtfully back on to the bench.

Marori's words came to me. *Trust no one. Everyone is an enemy.* It was true, I told myself, the old man's appearance was not one to inspire confidence; also, he had recognized me immediately for who and what I was, which made him a source of potentially terrible danger. However, he had shown me the unique insignia of a Flamen of the Lady in Gil, a turn of events that nobody, including Marori, could have predicted. As far as the Exiles knew, the Sherank had wiped out the Gil priesthood entirely within a month of the invasion.

I could see only two options: to take the chance of betrayal and listen to what he had to say, or to kill him quickly, before he had a chance to expose me to the nearest Sherkin patrol. Still undecided, I rose and headed for the door.

The street, hazily lit by the one smoking lantern on a pole, appeared at first to be empty, but then a shadow moved by a heap of rubble. It was the old man, beckoning impatiently. I hesitated on the doorstep.

The old man deplored my indecision, judging by the disgusted noise he made in his throat before he turned and plunged with surprising agility into the mouth of an alley across the way. That settled the question—whether I'd need to silence him or not, I could not risk letting him out of my sight.

Heart in mouth and hand over nose, I followed the old man's grotesque lead into a labyrinth of narrow, winding lanes, becoming steadily more miserable. The night was freezing, and stank with the pools of filth in the road. Rickety tenements loomed above me on both sides, their dark windows watching me with the eerie, intent stare of the blind. The alleys were utterly empty of people; only the shadows seemed alive. The old man flitted silently ahead of me like a dark spirit.

At last he stopped before a cavernous entrance lacking a door, looked back to make sure I saw him, and vanished inside. I followed him, but nervously, worried that he was leading me into a trap, half-convinced that I should kill him while I still had the chance. Caution demanded that I do so; compassion—and curiosity—suggested not. I hesitated on the threshold, hand on the hilt of my swordstick.

The old man took no notice, but went on as if confident I would follow. I followed. He led me up a staircase, perilous with age and rot, into a darkness blacker than I believed possible. Up and up I climbed, guided only by the laboured breathing a few steps above me and the wall at my right hand; there seemed to be no banister at all on my left. Once I thought I heard a soft padding of feet in the dark chasm behind me; I assured myself that it was an echo, but the skin of my back itched with dread.

Finally I sensed that the old man had stopped. There was a scratching, like a key in a reluctant lock, and then a door swung slowly open to allow a dim wedge of light to creep on to the landing. I followed the old man inside.

And stopped short in surprise. The room was not the filthy, sordid chaos I had come to expect after one day in Gil. By lamplight I could see that the floor was clean and polished, and scattered with thick-piled carpets. Tapestries covered the walls, heavy with metallic golden traceries separating woven scenes of life in the old Gil. The air was warm and blue with incense. From behind a gilded screen came a tentative plucking of harp-strings and a soft tenor voice humming a phrase of music. The old man hushed me with a finger on his lips, and beckoned me towards the screen.

"No, no, no!" cried a voice behind it. "Melody with the first finger, harmony with the fourth. I've told you a thousand times! Try it over from the half-mark. And if that third finger gets in the act again, I swear by the Lady I'll bite it off!"

The old man coughed gently and disappeared behind the screen. The music broke off and was replaced by a shrill chorus of welcome. Shyly, I stepped around the edge of the screen.

A middle-aged man in a clean but much-mended green robe was sitting on a carpet in the centre of a circle of children, all with harps in their hands. It appeared to be a music class. The teacher rose to greet my guide, giving me a hard look at the same time. "Is that the one?" he said to the old man. "Are you sure?"

"Quite sure."

The music teacher surveyed me sceptically, up and down, and shook his head. "Shorter than usual, wouldn't you say?"

"By a span, at least."

"Not very tidy in his habits, either."

"Filthy as a Gilman, as the Sherank would say."

"I mean, the others have all been so—so—"

"Impressive?" the old man suggested. The man in green nodded. They reviewed me again, point by point, with cool, critical eyes.

I scuffed my toes in the pile of the carpet. The children were giggling by now, and I could feel a blush reddening my neck. Arko would never have blushed, nor would he have let himself be baited by this low-grade two-clown comedy team. Arko would be off fighting the Sherank by now. That made me feel worse.

"Have you finished?" I enquired.

Neither of the men answered, but the children's enjoyment became louder. The man in green turned to frown at them, and they subsided. "Well, then," he said, "never mind what he looks like. Did he pass the test?"

The old man shrugged. "He made no move to kill me, but I believe he thought about it. Didn't you, young man?"

"Well—" I said uncomfortably, thrown off my guard. The old man, despite his appalling mutilations, was now exuding an authority that made me feel like a guilty child. No adult reply sprang to my lips, so I shut them.

"Not very talkative," said the man in green.

"Quiet, Namis. You, answer my question," said the old man more sharply. "Did you think about killing me?"

I realized with bewilderment that both men were hanging

on my reply. Even the children had developed an air of breathless expectation. Something strange was happening here, something serious, and I did not understand it, but it was clear that my answer was important.

"Well, yes, actually, I did sort of think about it at one point, but, you see—" I began, with as casual an air as I could manage at such short notice. True, I could see no weapons, but there was nothing to stop them from bludgeoning me to death with their harps.

To my amazement, they were delighted. The children cheered; one of them struck a few chords on his harp in a painful rendition of the Paean of Praise. The old man nodded as if satisfied, and the man in green clapped me on the shoulder.

"Thank the Lady for that, anyway!" he cried. "At last! You have no idea how frustrating it's been!"

I stared at him, smiled weakly, and swallowed. It seemed they were all quite mad. "I'm glad you're pleased," I said. "Mm—what if I'd actually killed him?"

"You would not have been given the chance." The voice, low and menacing, was behind me.

So it *was* a trap. I leapt around, startled, tugging at the hilt of my swordstick. The damned thing stuck halfway out of the scabbard, so I lunged for the knife in my boot, but the serrated tip snagged in the seam of my britches. I pulled at it desperately; the fabric ripped, and the knife flipped out of my fingers to land point-down in the floor, an inch or so from the old man's only foot.

"You could hurt someone, you know," said the newcomer flatly, retrieving the knife and holding it out to me. The voice was female and faintly husky, but its youthfulness was in curious contrast to the apparition that produced it.

She was a collection of rags knotted loosely on a broomstick, then dipped into a puddle of mud. Her face was thin and deeply wrinkled, half-hidden under a hood so old that the cloth seemed translucent under the dirt. On the other hand, her back was straight, and the filthy paw with my knife in it was steady inside a cocoon of disintegrating fabric.

"Who are you?" I asked. I took the knife from her, gingerly, and tried to work it back into its sheath.

"Never mind who I am," she answered. "It's more important who you are. A Scion of Oballef, unless Bekri missed his guess. Right?"

I gaped at her for a moment, then closed my mouth. So much for the Flamens' assurance that I would fit right in. Since the masquerade seemed to be over, I decided to impress them, or try to.

"I am Lord Tigrallef of Gil, of the line of Oballef, son of Cirallef, grandson of Arrislef, second in line to the throne of Gil, and sent by the Flamens-in-Exile to recover the Lady in Gil and restore the kingdom of my forefathers," I said all in one breath, making a last attempt to sheath my dagger. The pocketing object still refused to fit. I shifted it to my other hand, trying to give the impression that it was there for a purpose.

"Cirallef's son, are you? I remember Cirallef passing through," said the old man. "He was very good with knife and sword; not that it helped him in the end."

I stared at him, my embarrassment forgotten. My father had been one of those who simply vanished, and had been presumed dead by the Flamens. I was four when he left, and now I was twenty-three. Arko and I hardly remembered him.

"What happened to him?" I breathed. "Is he dead?"

"Most likely—may his bones bring forth flowers," replied the old man.

"How did he die?"

"I'll tell you all we know, but later, my lord Scion, if you please. For now, before we go on, we must know one thing: will you give us your trust, and accept our help?"

They were all hanging on my words again, even the children. I bounced the knife thoughtfully in my palm. *Trust no one*, Marori said. *Trust us*, the old man said. "You'll cut yourself," the female said. Strangely enough, it was that which decided me.

"I suppose so—" I said hesitantly. This time nobody cheered, but the two men and several of the children raised their hands in the Gillish gesture of thanksgiving. The female only nodded under her hood.

"Good. We'll start by feeding you and putting you to bed," she said firmly. The old man began to protest, but she took his hand and pressed it to her forehead—the old gesture of a subordinate seeking to overrule a superior. "Forgive me, Revered Bekri, but our Scion appears to have been ill. There will be time to talk in the morning. Come with me, Lord of Gil." She took my arm in a grip of granite. With one startled and probably pleading glance at the old man, I suffered myself to be led away.

She marched me to a curtained doorway beyond the circle of children and pushed me into a cold little chamber containing nothing but a pallet, a pisspot and a candle. A few minutes later, a jug of water and a reasonable supper were pushed under the curtain. Nobody disturbed me while I ate; I pictured the female creature on guard outside the door, armed quite adequately with nothing more than her personality. The excited buzz of voices in the outer room died away. I laid my belly down on the pallet and was asleep within seconds.

And thus, bemused and uncertain, but at least fed and within four walls, I ended my first day in Gil.

5

THE CHAMBER WHERE I awoke from confused dreams the next morning was clean, nearly bare, and achingly cold. I tried to wiggle my frozen toes inside the tight-fitting boots, which I had been too tired to take off, but the effort defeated me. Shivering miserably under my cloak and the one blanket, I mused over the day's prospects. Not one of them attracted me.

First, of course, there was danger. That went without saying, given that I was squarely in the middle of a Sherkin stronghold, a snakehole of vice, crime, violence and general desperation, according to the few reports that reached us in Exile.

Second, I was less certain of my new friends than I had been the night before. They were all too familiar as types, despite our short acquaintance. They, especially that harridan in the grey cloak, showed every sign of being zealous, enthusiastic, committed. I could well imagine them urging me into unappetizing situations, on the assumption that I was the heroic sort and would thrive on danger and difficulty.

My training Flamens, back in the Archipelago, belonged to that type. They *liked* doing horrible things like swarming up slimy ropes, and climbing sheer rock faces, and bearding wild creatures in their lairs, just for the fun of it. Moreover, they expected me to like doing such things too, and were always puzzled and a little hurt when I didn't. They never failed to point out how well Arko had done all those things, before his unfortunate accident.

Just as I was deciding to stay in bed all day (although I was frozen and hungry, at least I felt fairly safe), the curtain twitched aside and a young woman with long dark hair entered. She seemed somehow familiar. She was carrying a tray in one hand and a pottery bucket of gently steaming water in the other.

"Breakfast, Lord of Gil," she said briskly. "Up you get."

I groaned and rolled over. With one efficient movement she snapped the coverings off my body and flung them to the far end of the room. I groaned again and sat up. It seemed less trouble than defying her, and also safer.

"Here's water for washing, and some breakfast. When you're ready, Bekri Flamen and the council will see you." She slopped the bucket down beside the pallet and deposited the tray on my lap. It held a bowl of nasty-looking cold porridge and a beaker of hot liquid that my nose informed me was even nastier.

"Thank you very much," I said. I tried to sound like a person to whom physical discomfort was nothing. The girl watched me as I took a sip from the beaker and spluttered at the heat.

"It helps if you blow on it first," she said. Something in her tone made me look up in recognition. Of course! She was the female creature from the night before, the one with the wrinkles and the talent for bruising my self-esteem; only now her face was smooth and her gauntness had been transmuted into slenderness, pleasantly relieved by well-placed curves. It was such a complete transformation that I immediately doubted my eyes.

"Um—have we met? Or perhaps not—" I began.

"Of course we met. Last night. Bekri and I brought you here from the inn. At least, Bekri brought you and I followed. I'm Bekri's great-granddaughter, Calla." She smiled with more than a touch of smugness. "You didn't recognize me, did you? I do my own street-kit. The older and uglier you can look, the safer you are."

I nodded, thinking of the Sherkin reputation for taking or destroying anything of beauty, human or otherwise, virtually on sight. This might explain a lot of things, for example the fact that everyone and everything I'd seen since landing in Gil had been ugly to the point of ostentation. Perhaps there was more purpose in the squalor than I had imagined. The food, however, was fully as awful as it smelled, as my first spoonful proved.

Calla's smile stretched to a grin. "Eat up," she said, "it's good for you." She was past the curtain before I could argue the point.

I choked down as much of the glutinous muck as I could, alternating it with mouthfuls of the ghastly liquid. Washing seemed pointless. I pulled off my boots and used the hot water to defrost my feet. Last of all, I unpicked several stitches from the sheath in my boot and practised getting the dagger in and out of it a few times. At last voices in the outer room warned me that my new associates, whoever they might be, were waiting. I poked my head through the curtained doorway.

In the wan morning light, the room looked drabber and more threadbare than it had the night before. There were

large eroded patches in the carpets, and it was clear the tapestries had been designed for other chambers, some being
too long and others too short, and none forming a complete
set. All had been mutilated to some degree, and loving at-
tempts at repair had failed to disguise the damage. The effect
was somehow touching.

Five men in green robes stood in a rough semicircle by
the screen, watching me appraisingly. The music teacher of
the night before was not there, but the old man, Bekri, was
reclining on a low couch in the centre of the group, swathed
in a rough blanket. Underneath the blanket I could see the
neck of a green robe, and the tarnished silver chain of the
Lady. His scars were as horrific as I remembered, but a green
eye-patch hid the empty socket and he was not drooling. He ·
regarded me steadily for a moment, then bowed deeply and
sketched a familiar symbol in the air.

Suddenly he was a Flamen to his fingertips, making respectful obeisance to a Scion of Oballef, and he made me
feel like the Flamens always made me feel: that is to say,
unworthy and inadequate. I returned his gestural greeting
correctly on the second try. He sighed.

"Let's hope he has hidden talents," whispered one of the
other men, grinning, or more likely sneering. He was tall,
young and wretchedly handsome, and carried his worn green
robe with the air of a better man than I. Bekri looked irritated. "That's enough, Hawelli," he said sharply. "Remember
the respect due to a Scion of Oballef." Hawelli inclined his
head gracefully, but managed to pack more sheer insolence
into that than into the original snigger. Bekri sighed again
and turned back to me.

"My lord Tigrallef," he said, "what is the situation among
the Exiles in the Archipelago? Why did they send you? Are
there no other Scions of the royal house to take up the search
for the Lady?"

Hesitantly, I explained about Arko and his accident, and
my consequent promotion to royal hero. The others, even
Hawelli, looked profoundly depressed, but Bekri only nodded.

"So you are the last hope of Gil," he said thoughtfully.

"Oh, no," I said. "There are the children."

Bekri flung off his blanket and sat up, suddenly furious. "Yes," he repeated, "there are the children. And in ten years from now, another generation of princes and princesses will be thrown away, like their parents and grandparents and great-grandparents, and like the generations to follow them—unless the Sherank find the Lady first. Useless, pointless waste! No, my lord Tigrallef, I repeat: *you* are the last hope of Gil."

I realized my mouth was hanging open, and closed it. However ambiguous, this was the first time anyone but my mother had expressed even the faintest hope that I might be worthy of this mission, and my mother could be regarded as biased. Bekri threw himself off the couch and stumped to the window, muttering under his breath. "Come here, my lord," he said. "Come and see your birthright."

I went to the window and stood beside him. We were high in one of the aged tenements, looking over the rooftops of lower buildings stretching raggedly towards the Gilgard. Here and there I could see sad traces of noble architecture, vandalized and filthy, like flowers in a dungheap. Wooden and wattle shacks crowded the rooftops and spilled into the streets. Graceful raised plazas that had once held hanging gardens were squalidly packed with lean-tos and rubbish tips, browsed by scrawny beasts and scrawnier children. A thin river of ordure flowed sluggishly down the street from the market square at the corner, where a strident crowd surged about a litter of shoddy stalls. It was dirty beyond belief, tawdry beyond imagination. Even at this height, the stink was sickening. Only the topmost spires of Gilgard Castle, catching the mid-morning sun, remained beautiful—and only if you managed to block out the foreground. I turned blankly from the window.

"You don't like what you see," Bekri said softly. "Look there—that way, up the street."

I looked. A small group of Sherank were riding towards the market, prancing along on brightly caparisoned horses. A grey figure slumped in a ruined entry across the street evidently caught their eyes, for one of them leaned across his saddlebow to poke at it with the point of his sword. The figure pulled itself slowly erect and started to limp inside, but the Sherkin skilfully snagged his sword in the grey cloak and pulled the Gilman out into the street.

"One of their little amusements," said Bekri. "I don't imagine they'll kill him, but they'll surely give him a bad time before the fun palls."

We watched without speaking as the riders chivvied the man from one side of the street to the other, ripping at his cloak—and within it—with their swords. Their laughter reached our window clearly. The Gilman danced in silence from one swordpoint to the next, collapsing at last in a little ball, covering his head with his arms. I saw blood from a score of gashes run down to mingle with the foul stream on the cobblestones. His tormentors whooped with glee and rode their mounts over him and down the street, the game finished. Only when they were gone did two furtive figures, one a woman, creep out of the entry and half-carry the injured man inside. The shreds of his cloak still fluttered in the road.

I felt my stomach stir at the incident's casual brutality. It may have been mild compared with the legendary atrocities of the Sherank, but I'd led a curiously sheltered life—it was the first time I'd seen such a thing with my own eyes.

When I looked at Bekri, I found that he was watching my face intently. "A very small sample of life in latter-day Gil," he said drily. "Tell me—how does that make you feel?"

I assayed the lump in my throat. "Angry," I said. I looked at the floor. "Useless." And, more softly, "Frightened."

"Very good," said Bekri. "My hopes grow by the minute. Let us rejoin the others."

The circle had grown. I counted another dozen men beyond the five in green, a like number of women, and at least twenty children. About half were in what I was coming to recognize as street camouflage: dirty, ragged, stringy-haired and powerfully smelly. The woman Calla was among them, transformed again into an unsavoury crone. The others were clean, and decently dressed in old but meticulously mended robes and britches. A few even wore boots. Bekri motioned me to sit beside him on the couch, but the others spread themselves about on the carpets.

"This, my lord Tigrallef," said Bekri, with a sweep of his maimed arm, "is the centre of the Web. These are the servants of the Lady in Gil. We are eager to help you if you will allow us, and I would remind you that you agreed to this last night."

I made a gesture of acknowledgement, bewildered. What, in the Lady's name, was the Web? Why didn't the Exiles know about this? Surely my predecessors had also come into contact with this weird band—and what had happened to my predecessors? My suspicions clawed their way back above ground, uglier than ever.

"You're right to be suspicious," said Bekri. I wondered if the old man could read minds. "Also, it's a very good sign. Listen to what I have to say before you make your final decision; and then, if you decide to have nothing to do with us after all, you may leave here with our good will—as others have done before you."

I signed agreement with a slightly shaky hand. The motley audience shifted into comfortable positions, signifying that the story about to begin was a long and familiar one. Pulling his blanket back about his shoulders, the old man cleared his throat.

6

"AT THE TIME of the invasion, I was fifteen years old. I was a novice of the Flamens—fifth rank, very junior, but already entitled to wear the Lady at my throat." He touched the tiny pendant reverently. "I was with the Primate when news of Kishr's armies reached the Gilgard, in the middle of our lesson in divination. Ironic, when you think about it.

"Can you imagine our disbelief? After nearly a thousand years of peace, to be plunged without warning into such horror? I laughed in the beginning, along with many others, but the Primate went alone into the sanctuary, and when he returned to us his face was grave and he had a bundle tied under his cloak. It was then that he gave the command to provision the ship, and to take the royal children and the cream of the archives to the harbour. And he chose twenty Flamens—but that part you know.

"With my own eyes—I had two then—I saw those who were to become the Exiles make their departure from the harbour. When the ship was safely away, the Primate led the rest of us back to the Gilgard and gathered us in the Lady's antechamber. He knew the island was lost. We all knew by that point. We could hear the battle coming; Lord Kishr and his army of murderers had entered the suburbs of the city, and nothing in Gil could stand against them, except perhaps the Lady herself. There was still, at that moment, a desperate hope that the Priest-King was alive, and would reach us before Kishr did.

"But when the messenger came—a harpist, the only survivor of the royal party, and he delivered the news with his dying breath—the Primate only sighed, as if the Priest-King's death were no news at all, and ordered us to join the defenders in the towers. Before going to my post, I saw him and two others, the First and Second Flamens, enter the passage to the sanctuary. As far as I know, they were never seen to come out. When Kishr battered the door down, the sanctuary was empty. The Primate had vanished, taking the Lady with him. There was no other exit from the chamber, and none was ever found, even though the hangings were torn from the walls and the stones sounded over and over again for hidden doorways. Those of us who remained knew nothing of the Secrets of the Ancients."

Bekri's voice trailed away. He sat in silence for a long moment, his twisted slice of mouth set, his one eye clenched shut. One of the men in green leaned forward to touch him on the shoulder, and he started, then relaxed and continued in a stronger voice.

"They interrogated us—all the Flamens they could find, of whatever rank—for several days. I shall not describe their ways of asking questions, Scion: you can see the results for yourself." I looked at his scars, and turned my eyes away. "In any case," he continued, "whatever they did to us, we had nothing to tell them; but even when that became clear to Kishr, the torture went on. It was vengeance, I suppose; Lord Kishr was a very disappointed man."

He pulled the blanket up about his shoulders. I looked around at the others and saw that all their faces were grave and hard, cast in a mould of remembered pain and old bitterness—even those of the children. Dimly, deep inside, I felt the same feelings stir.

"Kishr spared no trouble in wiping the Flamens out. Those who were not tortured to death in Gilgard Castle were herded into the Great Garden for a victory bonfire around the statue of the Lady. The priesthood, of course, provided the fuel."

I nodded, feeling sick. That story, reaching the Flamens-in-Exile, had become part of the official memoirs of the catastrophe. As far as we knew, no Flamens at all had been left alive in Gil—and yet here was Bekri, with the figure of the Lady at his throat.

"Revered Bekri," I asked cautiously, eying his phalanx of supporters, "I do not wish to seem discourteous, but—if all the Flamens were killed—?"

"How did I come to be here? Why am I not dead too?"

"Yes."

"Chance, Lord of Gil, or perhaps the Lady's doing. When my interrogation was over—that is, when my questioners believed me to be dead—I joined a stack of my brother Flamens awaiting our last phase of usefulness. Adornments for the lower castle walls. The festoons of carcasses remained for years—but enough of that. One of the Gilmen who was forced to load the bodies into wains noticed that I was still bleeding, and realized I was alive. Ignoring his own danger, he managed to smuggle me out of the city, where those with the spirit to resist Kishr nursed me back to strength. They realized my importance, you see; however young, I was the sole survivor of the Flamens left on the island of Gil."

"So these others—?"

"—were trained by me, in as much of the lore of the priesthood as I had learned and could remember. I call myself First Flamen; taking the title of Primate-in-Gil would, I think, be pretentious. We are not many—only thirty feel entitled to wear the green—but we have a large body of support all over the island."

"The Web?"

"Yes, the Web, my lord Tigrallef. Think of what a web is like—how gossamer, how subtle, how nearly invisible, but how strong, out of all proportion to the strength of its member filaments." He grinned lopsidedly. "I named it myself. A good name, don't you think?"

"Oh yes, very apt. How many of you are there?"

Bekri waved his stump vaguely. "It's hard to say exactly, but between three and four thousand—almost one in every hundred." I nodded, both impressed and saddened, remembering that the population of Gil before the Sherkin invasion had been in the order of eight hundred thousand. "Almost weekly we lose one to the Sherank, and gain another or two from among the people of Gil," Bekri went on. "The Sherank know that we're here, but there's not much they can do about us. They would have to put the whole population to the sword to be sure of suppressing us altogether. It may come to that someday, of course."

Cheerful, very cheerful. From what I'd seen and heard so far, they were just the sort of doom-laden lunatics who would happily get themselves killed, and me along with them, just so long as they could get up a few Sherkin noses beforetimes. I shut my eyes and comforted myself for a few moments with my new favourite fantasy—that I was safely back in Exile, in the archives, reading about the exploits of Tigrallef the Great, Saviour of Gil, Finder of the Lady, Bane of the Sherank . . .

"My lord Tigrallef?"

"Yes, just thinking. Revered Bekri, I need to hear more before sealing an agreement with you. I am the twentieth

Scion of Oballef to come to Gil. What happened to the other nineteen?"

Bekri's ruined face twisted again. "Dead, most of them, may their bones bring forth flowers," he said flatly. "That is, we can confirm the deaths of most, and have seen some of the bodies. There are a few whose fates are unknown to us, though it seems a safe guess that they are also dead."

"Like my father?"

"Yes, like your father. I'm sorry." Bekri hesitated for a moment, then went on. "We know he was taken by the Sherank, captured as he tried to scale one of the towers of Gilgard Castle from the outside. Very brave; still it was a mad thing to attempt: we tried to dissuade him. No Gilman ever saw him again, alive or dead, but we assume he was tortured to death in the south dungeon, as—as others were, before and after him."

I choked back the grief and certainty that was filling my throat. Of course he was dead; my mother was simply reluctant to be a widow. "Did you offer him your help?"

"Naturally. We have made the same offer to every Scion of Oballef who ever reached Gil. Each decided not to accept our help, and to follow the quest alone."

"Why?" That is, what did they know that I didn't?

Bekri grimaced horribly. "The Heroic Code."

I waited for more, but he had slammed his mouth shut. I sighed. "All right. What about the Heroic Code?"

"Think about it, Lord of Gil. You know the Code?"

"Yes, of course."

"Then tell me—what is a hero?"

"The strong and good matched against the strong and evil," I answered promptly.

"And what must the hero do?"

"Defend the weak and combat evil through the strength of his own sinews and the power of his own pure motives."

"You've memorized it well. But what do you think of its teachings?"

I shuffled my feet. It was an embarrassing question. "Good in theory, I suppose, but it rather assumes that the opposition is playing by the same rules. And, to tell the truth, it seems to put less weight on succeeding, or even surviving, than on behaving as the ancients thought a hero should behave."

"Exactly!" Bekri turned to shoot a triumphant glance at Handsome Hawelli and the others. "It was not fitting, according to the Code, to accept the aid of the 'weak' against the strong; therefore, with varying degrees of reluctance, all your predecessors turned down our offer. We could not force them to accept our help, although we helped where we could without them knowing, as we did for you yesterday." He brushed off my surprise. "And they, poor murdered fools, threw themselves away in strict accordance with the Code which those murdering fools of Flamens-in-Exile had drummed into them. Now tell me, my lord Tigrallef, why are you different?"

Hesitating, I had a flash of pure recognition—what he was saying was precisely the heresy I had always held about the Code myself, but was unable to say. Afraid to say, rather, such was the hold of the Flamens-in-Exile over the Scions of Oballef. The look of Arkolef's putrid, gangrenous leg came to mind, an apt metaphor for the practical implications of Heroic theory. I fumbled for words. "It—it never made much sense to me. I always thought that the quest should come first, and bugger how you do it."

Bekri began to laugh, and continued until the others in the room picked it up and began laughing as well, slumping against each other, men, women and children, holding their aching sides. They roared helplessly until their laughter faded to hoots, and the hoots to giggles, and the giggles to a silence broken by hilarious hiccups. I sat morosely through the whole outburst. I didn't think it was funny at all.

"Forgive us, Lord of Gil," said Bekri at last, wiping his eye, "but those may be the first sensible words to be spoken by a Scion of Oballef since the day of catastrophe. I'm happy to see you're a fullborn sceptic. In fact, we had high hopes of you yesterday, when you wisely hid yourself and worked on your camouflage instead of striding about the streets of Gil looking for trouble."

I gaped. "You saw me? You know about that?"

"Of course. We first spotted you on the corniche and

trailed you through the streets to your hiding place. Not badly chosen, by the way, though you needed extra cover."

"The wain?" Pieces were starting to fall into place.

"Yes, we rolled it in front of your hole. And had our people ready to provide a diversion if any Sherkin patrol came too close."

"I'm grateful." And stupid, I added to myself, and blind.

Bekri gestured graciously. "Our hopes rose even more when you admitted thinking of killing me," he went on. "A proper hero, in true thrall to the Code, would never think of killing one weaker than himself, no matter how dangerous. We'd come to think of it as a kind of test."

I stared at him. It was true. It was the sort of thing that would never have crossed Arko's well-trained mind.

"And another thing," Bekri said, leaning forwards, "a few moments ago, you confessed to being afraid. Good. Properly used, fear is a potent tool, for there are dangers which it is better to face with respect than with blind courage. In the Web, there are no heroes—but there are many frightened men and women who do brave things."

"I see." Well, well, I said to myself, maybe they were my kind of people after all; and if what they wanted was a careful coward, that was precisely what I was equipped to give them. I dredged another gestural sign out of my repertoire, the one that meant acceptance of help from esteemed inferiors. Anyway, that's what I thought I was gesturing. Bekri stirred with surprise.

"I don't think you mean that, exactly," he said. Behind him, Hawelli, whom I was beginning to dislike intensely, barked with laughter. I realized, horrorstruck, that I had sketched the sign of blessing for a new mother on the birth of male twins; the old gestural system was full of subtle pitfalls. Blushing, I corrected myself. Bekri signed the appropriate reply. A sigh went round the room.

"All right," I said, "I've agreed to accept your help. Now what happens?"

7

"How do I look?"

"You look filthy, my lord." Mysheba scanned me critically, pulled a noisome cloak out of a chest, and draped it around my shoulders. I wrinkled my nose at the waft of ancient armpits. She seemed pleased with the result though, and turned away to wash her hands in a pottery bowl. She was Bekri's granddaughter, Calla's aunt, and one of the Web's greatest experts in the smelly art of camouflage. Bekri and the Council of Flamens, as the men in green called themselves, had insisted on sending me to her for one of her famous make-overs before setting me loose on the streets of Gil.

Calla appeared at the door in her street clothes, looking twice the age of Mysheba. "Aren't you finished, aunt?" she said impatiently. "He looks quite foul enough already. The council wants him back."

"Almost done," said Mysheba. "We don't want the Lord of Gil to stand out, do we?" So saying, she used a small bellows to spray some kind of rancid grease over my head, and energetically worked the resulting mess into authentic but itchy strings. In the large square of polished bronze that hung on the wall, I looked villainous, famished and grimy—a typical Gilman. My boots, with the troublesome knife-sheath, had been replaced by worn leather sandals; my clothes, which the Flamens-in-Exile had thought so clever a disguise, were in a heap on the floor.

"Very good," said Calla. I looked at her glumly. What would the Primate have said if he could see me? I bet myself that Arkolef would never submit to being mud-streaked, greased-sprayed, daubed with artificial pus and stuffed into stained and stinking old clothes; but then, Arko was a proper hero and I was not. Which was, of course, the whole point.

As a final touch, Mysheba bandaged my dirty hands in strips of yellowing cloth. "There," she said proudly. Calla nodded her head. "He'll pass," she said. "Come on, my lord Tigrallef, the council is ready for you."

Together we trudged through the empty corridors of the vast, gloomy tenement. It was like a warren, full of branching hallways and odd little staircases that wound up into darkness or down into darkness, and an endless series of doors, some shut, some hanging open to show empty rooms with faded, cracking walls. Dusty light fought its way through a window-sized hole at the end of each corridor; there were old candle-brackets spaced along the walls, but all of these were empty. I wondered how many of the closed doors hid surprises like the council chamber.

"Does the Web own this building?" I asked Calla.

She shrugged. "No Gilman owns anything in Gil. But we control the building at this moment, and some others like it. The council never stays in one place for very long, though, because it's too dangerous."

"Why? Do the Sherank come searching?"

Calla caught my arm to guide me past a hole gaping in the floor in the centre of the passage. "Yes and no. They make random raids, mostly for entertainment when they feel bored—for example, when they haven't executed anyone in public for a while. We don't worry about those too much, because the raiding parties are easily distracted from anything we don't want them to see." She stopped and swung me to face her. "But be warned, my lord—we can never be certain. Sometimes it seems that they're looking for someone or something in particular, and there's no distracting them then. That's when they're most dangerous."

"You mean—?"

"I mean they have their spies. Even the Web is not completely immune from treachery, though we try to be careful. Watch out for that hole, my lord."

I walked along behind her, wishing she would stop treating me like an idiot. She was as bad as the worst of my old teaching Flamens—perhaps even more talented in constructive humiliation, I thought, faultlessly picking my way through a rubble of fallen bricks. She wasn't even watching.

She stopped by the foot of one of the little winding staircases, dark as the middle of the night, and lit a candle out of her pocket with one expert swipe at a flint. Motioning me to follow, she started up the stairs. "Watch yourself, Lord of Gil," she said, "some of the treads are broken."

"Oof."

"I warned you." She sighed deeply and groped for my hand, but something snapped inside me. I pulled away, straightened myself and sketched a sign in the air: a brusque and rather insulting instruction to an inferior to shut up and get going—and I got it right first time. For once, for a few seconds, Calla seemed unsure of herself; then she shrugged, turned on her heel and led on up the stairs.

I followed silently, being very careful with my feet and enjoying the savour of triumph, though it was already tinged with guilt. How could I honestly object to this woman treating me like a clumsy oaf? I *was* a clumsy oaf. Being treated like one had never bothered me before. By the time she stopped on a landing in front of a solid-looking door, I was feeling humble and had reached the point of berating myself for my rudeness to her. She knocked on the door in a complicated rhythm, then opened it and motioned me past her. Haughtily, she avoided my eyes.

We were back in the council chamber, entering through a door hidden behind one of the tapestries, which was now looped back. Bekri and about a dozen others were there, all wearing the green. I recognized Handsome Hawelli, Jebri the Second Flamen, and a few others who had been there the previous day, plus Namis the music teacher and, to my surprise, the keeper of the inn where Bekri had picked me up.

I walked to the centre of the room, acutely conscious of my hideous street camouflage. The council, however, looked pleased, and most lifted their hands or whispered approvingly—except for Hawelli, who was sitting on the edge of the group with his arms folded and a sulky look on his face.

"My lord Tigrallef," said Bekri, "we've been discussing

some ways in which the Web can assist you. First, we propose that you spend a few days exploring Gil, to see with your own eyes the state of the land and how the Sherank operate. We also propose to send Calla with you as your guide, since she's among the best of our street people—you can learn a great deal from her if you choose. Does this meet with your approval?"

I hesitated for a moment, thinking of my gaffe on the stairs, then signed acceptance with the most formal possible gesture. Calla shifted beside me, obviously surprised, but whether at the council's choice of guide or my acceptance of it, I could not guess. I caught Hawelli's eye, and was startled by the flash of virulence across his face. A second later, I was not sure—was that hostility for me, or for Bekri?

"Of course," Bekri went on, "there will be others of the Web with you at all times. It may amuse you to try and work out who they are." He smiled horribly, but I was getting used to his face by now, and recognized the goodwill behind the scars. I signed a gracious farewell, and followed a silent, thundery-faced Calla out of the door, leaving a soft murmur of voices behind us.

Calla led me down the main staircase, the one that Bekri had led me up two nights previously. Observing it in the light, I was thankful I had not seen it properly before—I might have given up altogether on the idea of following Bekri. It was a souvenir of the old Gil, for it had once processed grandly around the sides of a large square stairwell, lined by an ornate banister. Only the carven stumps of a few newel posts remained, on the brink of an abyss carpeted with rubbish, a sheer drop of thirty-odd feet from the level of the landing. Calla flounced down the stairs with careless confidence; I went cautiously, hugging the wall. When she was halfway down, she turned to look up at me.

"Hurry yourself, Lord of Gil," she said. "Or am I not allowed to speak to you?"

"Of course you can speak, Calla. I'm sorry I was rude to you back there."

She humphed, and the corners of her mouth turned down.

"You should be sorry—I was only trying to help you."

I sighed. It seemed to me suddenly that I had been apologizing all my life, and I was getting tired of it. "Let's forget it, then. But just stop trying to be my nursemaid, all right?" I'd have said more, but I was concentrating on my footing on the rotten treads.

"But a nursemaid is just what I feel like," Calla sniffed, hovering impatiently on the lower landing. I could see I was not forgiven, and her indignation was starting to break out. "Look at you, *Lord of Gil*, you can barely walk two steps on level ground without falling over." She turned and bounded lightly down the rest of the stairs, stopping at the bottom to watch my descent with critical eyes. "Why did they have to choose me?" she muttered, just audibly.

"Because you have so much to teach me," I answered bitterly over the groaning of the stairs, "and I have so much to learn. By the Lady, I'm sick of being a meal for teachers! It wasn't my idea to be a hero, and it's not what I'm good at, and you're not helping matters much—oof." I subsided into mutters while fishing my foot out of a brand new hole in the stairs.

Calla was quiet for a few moments. She did not even leap to take charge of rescue operations. Instead, when I had extricated myself and was stumping on downwards, I found a new and even more sceptical expression had appeared on her face.

"So you're telling me, my lord, that there is something you're good at?"

"Of course."

"And what's that?"

"I'm a memorian—or was, until I got pushed into this madness." I reached the bottom at last, and sighed with relief.

"Oh. Books." Her tone was contemptuous.

"Yes, books. Reading and writing, and remembering the past. Can you read?"

She lifted her chin. "Only as much as I need to. Anyway, what use is remembering the past? Look at the mess your Flamens-in-Exile made by remembering the Heroic Code. What good did the past ever do anybody?"

I sighed and sat down on the bottom step to pick the splinters out of my ankle. "You're wrong, except for one thing—simply remembering isn't enough. I've always thought the Flamens remembered too much and thought too little. But don't judge all learning by the Flamens-in-Exile, Calla."

"Shall I judge it by you, then?" she asked cruelly. I did not answer, did not even look up from my search for splinters. After a few moments of silence, Calla sat down beside me.

"I'm sorry."

"Don't be."

"It's only that—I'm worried."

I looked across at her, pleased. "About me?"

"No, I didn't say that. I mean, if you don't mind me saying so, I'm worried you're going to make some awful blunder that'll bring the Sherank howling down on us like a winter storm."

"Ah." I tried to keep my voice light. There was a brief pause while I calculated what line to take that might put our fellowship on a different footing. Apologies only seemed to annoy her—humility would make her despise me even more. Her anger might be easier to tolerate than her contempt. Maybe a bit of a shock? I thought it over, and at last I said, "Tell me, Calla, shall I go back upstairs and ask Bekri for a guide I can trust?"

"What?" Calla looked at me disbelievingly, then shot to her feet, her hands fisted. "What did you say?"

"You heard me. This mission is too important to be endangered by your arrogance."

It was the first time I'd seen anyone's nostrils actually quiver with rage. "Endangering your mission, am I? *Arrogant*, am I?" she spat. "How dare you, you miserable mutton-arsed—"

"Gilwoman, you are addressing a Scion of Oballef." I stood up to my full height, which was maybe half an inch greater than hers.

She stared at me, her lips turning down with scorn. "So? You're not the first Scion I've seen. Here in Gil, you're just another beggar, only less useful than most."

That was true enough to sting, but I let it pass. I waited long enough to put her slightly off balance, then lifted my hand in the most imperious admonitory gesture in the Scions' entire repertoire. Calla grimaced, but there was only one possible reply. Grudgingly, she signed respect. "I beg my lord Tigrallef's pardon," she said formally through stiff lips. Then her anger burst out again. "But how can you expect me to take you seriously when all I've seen you do is play the fool—"

"I'm not a fool." I said this with such conviction that Calla stopped again and looked at me with surprise. "I may be a coward, a clown and a weakling, but I'm no more a fool than I am a hero. A hero only knows how to behave as a hero, but I know how to learn like a memorian. Never call me a fool again."

She signed agreement with a twist of the hand. "I understand. I can call you coward, clown or weakling, but never fool. I shall remember that, my lord."

"Be sure that you do. Shall we go now?" I grinned at her angry back as she stomped through the door. What I had just said to her, I had never before put into words, even inside my own head, but suddenly I believed it. I was not a fool. Not a complete fool, anyway.

8

IN THE STREET, my elation died. A small boy sat picking at his sores in the portal across the way, wrapped, as far as I could tell, in nothing more than a length of filthy cloth. The sores were disturbing enough, especially on such a little body, but I was more upset by how strongly he resembled my cousin Callefiya's younger child, back in Exile. It was a poignant reminder that this was my country, these were my people. When he saw me looking at him, he scurried inside on all fours like a frightened beetle.

Calla caught my look. "It's unwise, my lord," she said flatly out of the side of her mouth, "to look too long or boldly at anyone, even a child."

"Was I staring? Is that why he ran away?"

"Naturally."

"But why was he frightened? I don't look like a Sherkin, do I?"

Under the dirt on her face, she grimaced. "In Gil, it's wise to be wary of everyone you don't know, Gilman or Sherkin. He's a wise child, that one. There, that's your first lesson. Come along, clown of Gil."

I grinned again at that, and caught up with her as she moved down the street in a sidling, creeping fashion that nevertheless carried her along at a spanking rate. I tried to imitate her, even though it hurt my back.

"Can't you slouch a little more?" she muttered, glancing sideways at me.

"I'm trying, I'm trying. Remember, I spent the last six months learning to stride like a hero. You'd have loved my scholar's stoop."

"Well, stoop like a scholar then. Now, keep a few steps ahead of me, and go straight towards the bread ovens at the corner of the market. See them? But don't look at anyone."

Resignedly, and trying to keep my shoulders hunched, I followed her orders. Our street was almost empty, but a score of paces before the market square, a larger street joined it at an angle, and this was full of people. I slopped miserably through the thick of the crowd, heading for the bakery. Though the sun was shining, it was still the rump end of winter and the afternoon air was bitterly cold. My feet in the scurfy sandals had got wet through almost as soon as I stepped outside. I could hear Calla's sandals flapping behind me. When I reached the corner near the bakery, I stopped and looked around in horrified fascination.

I had been taken many times to the market on Sathelforn, the chief island of the Archipelago. Markets are chaotic almost by definition, but in Sathelforn it was also clean, well-swept, and laid out in a pleasant labyrinth of stalls and little eating compounds. The market of Gil was a cesspool scummed with garbage.

There was hardly a straight line in the whole stinking concourse. Gimcrack stalls of rotten greyish wood leaned against each other in clusters of four or five, ready to fall at the push of a breath, a few decorated in dubious taste with daubs of peeling paint. The sellers, hunched or squatting in the open mouths of their stalls, and the restless, ragged mob of customers regarded each other with deep mutual suspicion and haggled without dignity or good humour, the shrill voices of the women slicing through the gruff voices of the men. I recoiled as a tall thin creature, definitely a man but scarcely human, naked except for the coating of dirt that blackened him from crown to sole, danced to a stop in front of me and peered into my face, gibbering, the foam around his mouth flying in all directions. Suddenly, Calla was at my side.

"Here, little one," she cackled in a very old voice, tossing something into the air before the lunatic's eyes. He snatched it out of mid-air and vanished instantly into the crowd. No one else took any notice of him.

"Poor soul," I whispered to Calla. "He's mad, isn't he?"

"Actually," said Calla coldly, "he's my cousin. He looks better with clothes on. My lord, keep your face down—try to see through the top of your head."

I grumbled, but I knew what she meant. The technique was being demonstrated all around me. I pulled the horrible cloak up around my ears, as I saw others had done, but I lacked the knack of keeping it up. Calla sighed deeply.

"Just stay close to me," she said. "I'm going to show you proper market manners." She hobbled off obliquely towards the first cluster of stalls; I slogged unhappily in her wake. The first stall she stopped at, a weathered lean-to with crazy sloping sides, seemed at first to contain nothing but a sullen tradesman squatting on a hairy brown mat, picking at his toenails. Squinting into the shadows behind him, I saw a coarse sack filled with what looked like ordinary dirt. Calla hunkered down on the ground in front of the trader and began a long, sour dispute that ended with her contemptuously tossing a small cloth bag knotted at the top on to the ground at the trader's feet, and holding out a larger, empty bag of indescribable rottenness. The trader reluctantly stood up, fished a pottery beaker from the depths of his cloak and used it to transfer several measures of the dirt from the sack into Calla's bag. He flopped down again on his mat, sulking. Calla moved off, muttering. I was beginning to get the idea.

"What did you buy?" I asked curiously when we were clear of the stall. "It looked like ordinary dirt."

"Maggots," she said. "They last longer if they're stored in dirt. They taste like dirt, too, but they keep the children alive when there's nothing else to eat."

"Oh."

She rounded the corner of another cluster of stalls and moved across the trampled mud and dung surface to a large open-sided hut, really a thatched roof supported on a complex of rickety poles. If it were possible to say that any section of this pisspit market smelled worse than the rest, this was the place. Under the roof, a row of ten or twelve traders, perhaps a little less scrawny but no better dressed than anyone else, stood behind a long trestle table. In front of each was a brownish pyramid; as we got closer I saw, with a queasy stir of the belly, that each pyramid was a pile of small corpses, perhaps as big as my two fists together, covered with patchy brown fur matted with blood and excrement.

"Shulls," whispered Calla. "Quite tasty if you ignore what they feed on. You had some last night."

"Oh."

Shulls. Perhaps the only Sherkin contribution to the economy of Gil, vermin that travelled everywhere the Sherank did, swarming out of their ships, breeding in the grainbags of their caravans; in Gil, I knew, where there had been no indigenous vermin to compete with the newcomers, the shulls had flourished and happily bred famine and disease and lots of little shulls throughout the first decades after the catastrophe. I should have guessed that so desperate a people would find a use even for shulls, but my stomach was slow to appreciate the economic logic. Gagging, I hung far behind Calla as she negotiated her purchase.

"What other delicacies are you looking for?" I asked when she drifted back to me, tucking the late shull into a pocket of her cloak.

"Nothing in particular. Shall we just wander through the market, my lord? Perhaps you'll see something you like—a souvenir of your first visit to Gil." I detected a mocking note.

Of course my expectations could hardly have been lower; even so, the Gil market failed to rise to them. Most of the food stalls seemed to sell either maggots packed in dirt, sickly roots and vegetables, bluish milk, lumpy yogurt, or little malodorous cubes that Calla told me were pressed and salted fish. At one end of the square was the fuel section, untidily strewn with piles of dried dung, sacks of charcoal, a few stacks of logs chopped into short lengths and a great many bundles of faggots tied up with lengths of vine. Behind the crowded shull hut was another, smaller but similar in construction, where the fly-covered carcasses of a few goats and sheep dangled over rough cages filled with live, dour-looking chickens. There were fewer customers here than in the shull hut, and the tone of the bargaining was even more bitter.

One whole side of the market was taken up with dry-goods stalls and artisans' workshops. I fingered the rough cloth of ready-made cloaks and britches; discreetly watched one group of tinkers battering old pots into new shapes, and another of cobblers stitching the ubiquitous shull-leather sandals; and narrowly avoided bringing a display of exceptionally ugly clay cooking pots crashing around my feet. In one corner was what Calla sneeringly called the "fine goods"—two stalls of shoddy needles, misshapen candles, blunt metal knives, and other manufactured goods of a pitifully poor quality.

"The manufactories of Gil still turn out some of the finest work in the world," Calla commented in an undertone, "but of course we never see it after it leaves the workmen's hands. Just as we never see the best of the crops, the cream of the milk or the finest of the animals we're forced to raise. The

Sherank take them all, and allow us only the leavings. Did you wonder why we feed on maggots and shulls?"

"No, I didn't wonder. I'd already figured it out." There were other things that I'd figured out, but it was hardly the right time to broach them with Calla. Covertly, I watched the action around me, certain I was right—there was much more going on than showed on the surface.

We were cutting diagonally across the market by now, towards some kind of tall soot-coloured monument standing in a clear space in the centre. Clouds had been gathering, blocking out the late afternoon sun. I looked up as the clouds parted and a shaft of sunlight drifted across the square. Gasping, I grabbed Calla's arm.

The monument was not the broken pillar on a pedestal I had vaguely perceived it to be, but a figure: a stone woman, more than life-size, stretching towards the sky with a great stone bowl upheld in her hands. Flooded by the sun, she briefly managed to be beautiful, even through the filth that thickened and obscured her shape; then the sunlight moved on, and she was in shadow again.

Choking, I stumbled over to sit on the low stone parapet that ringed her pedestal. I recognized that statue, which meant that suddenly, for the first time since leaving the corniche two days before, I knew exactly where I was.

Calla sat down beside me a moment later. "What's wrong, my lord Tigralleff?" she whispered anxiously. "Are you ill? This isn't a clever place to sit."

My eyes were wet. I wiped my sleeve across them, taking some of the dirt off along with the tears. "Oballef's Fountain," I murmured. "This is the Great Garden, isn't it?"

"No, my lord. It's the central market."

"But that's the statue of the Lady—"

"Yes, I knew that," said Calla, "and I really think we should be going now."

"In a minute—"

There was a long silence while I struggled for control and Calla sat nervously poised at my side. When I closed my eyes, I could see Marori's painting of the Great Garden as it used to be, in a Gil that had vanished utterly. In the foreground was the same statue of the Lady, rose-white marble quarried from the veins of the Gilgard, clear water cascading from the stone bowl in her hands. Children splashed in the pool within the parapet; graceful men and women strolled among flowering trees in the background. I did not want to open my eyes again, to see what had become of them all.

But at last Calla shook my arm urgently. "Come on, my lord Tigrallef," she whispered. "They can't hold the wrong eyes off us for long. But take another look at the Lady as we go, and you'll see why the Sherank left her standing."

I set my face and stood up. A few feet away, a small knot of Gilmen were squabbling over a dead chicken, effectively screening us from all other eyes. I followed Calla to the shelter of the nearest stalls, then turned to look back at Oballef's Fountain. The Lady's nose was a leprous hole; a lewd leer was painted on the perfect lips. The body had also been decorated—obscene, graphic additions incised into the marble and tricked out with paint. Around the pedestal, in the bold barbed Sheranik script, was written this legend: *The Whore in Gil.*

Calla was pulling at my arm. "You must come now. Wake up, my lord! Tigrallef, listen to me. If the Sherank saw your face now, they'd peel it off. Please, my lord!"

I shook myself. Deliberately, I hunched my back and pulled the cloak over my head in approved Gilman style. It stayed. I hobbled a few steps, and looked back. Calla was still standing there, amazement showing through the filth and wrinkles on her face. "Call me Tig," I cackled, in a very old voice.

9

WE TALKED, CALLA and some of the council and I, late into that night. Calla was unnaturally quiet—I suppose I had either impressed her or frightened the britches off her beside Oballef's Fountain. Whichever it was, the few words she said were helpful rather than hectoring, and she watched me much of the time with a meditative look on her face. Bekri, who was sharing his sofa with Jebri, the Second Flamen, seemed encouraged by her report.

"My lord Tigrallef," he said after Calla finished speaking, "I congratulate you. You've not only survived three days in Gil, which is half a day longer than the best of your forebears, but you seem to be making progress."

"Yes, well, thanks," I said apprehensively. In my experience, praise from a Flamen was usually a prelude to something less pleasant.

But Bekri only signalled to Jebri to pour me out a beaker of wine. "Have you any questions about what you saw?" he asked.

"Oh yes, quite a few." I hesitated, putting my thoughts in order. "Calla's transactions in the marketplace—I had a strong feeling there was more to them than would show to, say, any Sherkin spy who happened to be around. Am I right?"

There was a small stir among the other Flamens, but Bekri simply gestured for me to go on. I took a gulp of wine.

"First, I think messages were being passed: the alms that Calla threw to her cousin the beggar; and I suspect the maggot seller and the shull merchant were also more than they seemed."

"That's correct," said Bekri. "Information, orders and

small items of contraband were being passed both ways, in the goods and in Calla's payment. What else?"

I drew a deep breath. "I think the surliness of all the business in the market is a blind. Whatever is said aloud, the real conversations happen like this." I moved my fingers in a small-scale version of the Gil gesture of greeting, followed by a polite enquiry as to the Revered Flamen's health. Bekri smiled—I had less trouble reading his face now—and answered in similar fashion that he was quite well, thank you very much, and how was I? Then he laughed out loud, and leaned forward to slap me on the back. "What was it you said, Hawelli? That perhaps the Scion has hidden talents? So you have, my lord. You have eyes and brains, and know how to use them."

"The Flamens-in-Exile would be very surprised to hear that, Revered Bekri."

"And what do they know? How many Scions have they sent to their deaths? Just think, my lord Tigrallef, they very nearly didn't send you!"

"Yes," I agreed dolefully, "just think of that."

Hawelli had been prowling the council chamber restlessly throughout this exchange; now he strode into the centre of the circle. He could be only a few years older than I, but he was built like a hungrier version of Arkolef; clean and in the garb of a Flamen, he was so physically impressive that I wondered how even Mysheba could disguise him for the street. His chiselled face was dark with hostility.

"So Lord Tigrallef can recognize fingerspeech when it's right in front of his nose. So what? Are we training him for a career as a shull merchant?"

"Hawelli—" Bekri began, but the younger Flamen cut him off.

"You're all fools," he said contemptuously. Calla's face, caught in the corner of my eye, became watchful. "Look at him! A weakling, a bumbler, a memorian, by the balls of Oballef. Less street-sense than the newest Gilborn baby, yet you tell him the secrets of the Web, and propose to send him off to the Gilgard to hunt for that damned pinchbeck figurine, like all the fools before him. Why don't you simply deck him out as a sacrifice and send him straight to Lord Kek-ashr?"

There was a general gasp at Hawelli's blasphemies. A few Flamens, including Jebri, jumped angrily to their feet, but Bekri raised his voice in a sharp call for order. When all had reluctantly seated themselves bar Hawelli, who remained defiantly upright, Bekri turned to me.

"Hawelli is our resident hot-head, my lord Scion. Are you surprised that he wears the green robe of a Flamen?"

"Well, yes," I murmured, conscious of Hawelli's hostile eyes.

"He is qualified, and he chooses to wear it. We've learned to live with his unbelief."

"You need me, old Bekri," Hawelli broke in bitterly. "The time will come when you realize how much."

Bekri continued to ignore him and to address himself to me. "Our brother Flamen believes the quest for the Lady is a fool's chase—that even if she were found, and by a Scion, she would be useless against the Sherank."

"Legends," Hawelli growled. "There is no magic, there never was. The Lady would be no more potent than those toys used to throw about in the marketplace, before they were all sent to the salt-pans in Sher."

A furious hubbub of voices broke out, but I jumped up and motioned for silence before I realized what I was doing. To my great surprise, everybody shut up, even Hawelli. I had a moment of panic. I was not used to being heard—for twenty-three years I had never expressed myself on any issue more controversial than a new cataloguing system for the archives. In the dead silence, I cleared my throat.

"Thank you," I said. "Hawelli Flamen, I gather you don't believe in the power of the Lady in Gil."

"It's a gutload of superstitious nonsense—my lord," he added insolently. "My brothers in the Web despise the Flamens-in-Exile for their blind trust in the old ways, but aren't the Flamens-in-Gil just as bad? Look at them! Waiting on their arses for seventy years for a miracle that will never happen—pinning their hopes on a bauble that, for all they know, was melted down for its gold content decades ago.

Magic!" he spat, "there is no magic in this world but the edge of a good blade."

"Ah," I said happily, "you're what we memorians would call a militant corporealist. How very interesting. However, I think you're wrong. There are four great validated magics in the world, and the Lady in Gil is by far the greatest and best-documented, and the only all-purpose one. I see no reason to doubt that she'll do the job. Then there're the Healing Bones of Medioch, of course, and the Zelfic Crystal, and—"

"Stop!" he thundered. I shut my mouth and looked at him enquiringly. From the look on his face, I inferred he was not interested in academic discourse. I sighed.

"What's your idea, then?" I asked.

He stepped closer and bent his head down to mine. "We must fight, my lord Tigrallef," he said fiercely. "We must rise up, the Web leading the rest, and slit the throat of every shull-arsed Sherkin on the island. We have the manpower, all we need is the will!"

"How about the weapons?"

"What?"

"Weapons. You know, swords, knives, flame-slings—"

"Yes, yes, I know. Of course we need weapons, but that's where you come in, Lord of Gil."

"Me?"

"Yes!" He was excited now, his handsome features alive. "You're the first link with Exile that hasn't walked straight off the boat into the jaws of the Sherank. Go back to Exile, my lord Tigrallef—tell them about the Web. Bring us back the weapons we need, and join us in the uprising." He stepped forward, I stepped back. His eyes were little flames of bloodthirsty zeal, burning into mine. I cleared my throat again.

"Yes, well, a most interesting idea, Hawelli Flamen. I especially liked the first part, where I go back to Exile. But it wouldn't work."

His face darkened again. "Why not?"

"Well, first of all, the Flamens-in-Exile are rather set in their ways, as you may have noticed. I might persuade the other Scions to join ranks with me, but without an actual Priest-King we have little say in what happens."

He muttered something involving the word "feeble." I ignored him and went on. "Then there are the difficulties of smuggling back enough weapons to make a difference. You know very well how tightly the Sherank have the island sewn into a sack—why, it's a chancy business landing one little Scion every few years, let alone a boatload of weaponry. And even if we could launch an armada from the Archipelago, fight our way past the Sherkin patrol boats and help you to overcome the garrison, there would still be the real problem."

"And what's that, Lord of Gil?" His voice was heavy with contempt.

"Sher itself. Do you have any idea what would happen if Gil did rebel successfully, with the world as it is? I can tell you exactly: the warlords in Iklankish would send a thumping great punitive force to retake the island, and our sufferings would double on the instant."

"Not if we showed them we will no longer wear their yoke!"

I sighed. "Don't be stupid, Flamen. Do you know how strong they are? They're the most powerful empire to rise on earth since the fall of Fathan. The League of Free Nations can only just hold them to the treaty. And they'll never free us if they can avoid it—Gil is their showplace, their greatest prize. They'll punish Gil for ever for how wonderful it used to be."

There was applause from Bekri's direction, a rapid snapping of fingers. Hawelli and I jumped; I think both of us had forgotten that others were present. Bekri leaned back on the sofa, his own strange version of a smile broadening across his face.

"I like you more and more, Scion," he said. "I'm afraid Hawelli lacks that wider view. Tell me, do you really want to go back to Exile?"

I thought about it. "Oh yes," I said, "but I can't."

"Why not?"

"I've been sent here to do something." I thought of the Great Garden, superimposing Marori's lush, lyrical paintings

on the dreary midden of the marketplace; of a child like
Callefiya's child, covered with running sores and shivering
with fear; of Calla—why in Oballef's name was I thinking
of Calla? I glanced at her, and saw she was watching Hawelli
with a deep frown creasing her forehead. "That is to say," I
finished, "I have a mission to carry out."

"Then you're as stupid as you look, Lord of Gil," said
Hawelli stiffly. He turned and strode through the door, which
he slammed behind him with such force that one of the tapestries slid to the floor. Calla half-rose, then settled down on
her haunches again. She looked more thoughtful than ever.
The Flamens, including Bekri, seemed to be waiting for me
to say something.

Slowly, I gestured the blessing for the stout-hearted in the
direction of the closed door. "Hawelli Flamen may play the
part he desires someday," I said, also slowly. "In the meantime, honoured Flamens, Revered Bekri, I need your ad-
vice—how can I gain safe entry to the Gilgard?"

"Ah," said Bekri. "We've been working on a plan."

"Already? Oh." (Long pause.) "Good. What is it?"

"It's really quite simple. The Gilman in charge of the castle scullery is one of ours—from the Web. His name is
Calvo. He can arrange a job for you within the next few
days, which will get you safely inside the Gilgard; when the
time is right, you can start off from the scullery using the
old between-ways."

I goggled. "The scullery?"

"Yes, the scullery. As a crocker, to begin with."

"Crocker?"

"Crocker. Someone who washes dirty crockery."

"But—I don't know how. I've never washed a dish in my
life."

"It isn't hard to learn, my lord, and bear in mind that it's
safer than scaling a wall."

"That's a point," I said, after a short, reflective pause.

"You agree, then? Good." He settled back and looked at
me steadily. "There is one more small thing: in a meeting of
the council this afternoon, we agreed that you should not go

alone into the Gilgard and the Caves. We want to send one
of our people with you."

I hesitated. It took me a few moments to absorb the idea.
In even my most hopeful imaginings I had seen myself
searching for the Lady alone, carrying the burden of my heritage in the approved and traditional solitude, like all the
Scions before me. Other figures had never intruded, except
perhaps those of the Sherank or of Marori's terrible creatures
of the dark, even though I didn't believe in them. "That's
stretching our agreement a bit thinly, even for me, First Flamen," I said finally. "Accepting your help is one matter, accepting a companion is quite another."

"Is that the Heroic Code talking, my lord Tigrallef?"

"The Lady forbid," I exclaimed, insulted.

"Then why not?"

Why not indeed, except that a hero was expected to go by
himself? I looked past Bekri's head to the tapestry on the
wall. It showed a hero from one of the old tales, gloriously
alone, waving a short sword in the face of a rippercat three
times his size. In the next panel, he was standing victori-
ously—and rather smugly—on a mound of bleeding catflesh.
No, not my style at all. "Now that I think about it, First
Flamen, it's a sensible suggestion. A companion would increase my chances of surviving to find the Lady, which is
the whole point of going. But how can I ask anyone to share
that kind of danger?"

After a moment when nobody said anything, there was a
voice from near the floor. "You don't need to ask. I'll go
with you."

I turned to stare at Calla, who was picking casually at one
of the fake boils on her cheek. She looked up. "With your
permission, my lord," she added in the same calm voice.
Suddenly and impenetrably, she grinned. I was even more
bewildered. I was sure she loathed me.

"Excellent!" said Bekri. "A volunteer—and we couldn't
ask for a better one. That's also agreed?" He took my stu-
pefied silence for consent. "Corri, make sure the scullery is
informed. Calvo will need a few days to set things up. Perhaps, Jebri, you could tell the Scion what he needs to know."

Jebri, old, pompous, and a bit fat for a Gilman, proceeded to talk at great length, but I was too busy puzzling over Calla to pay him much mind. As it happened, this did not matter at all. Another factor was already at work.

10

DARK EYES SHONE *through a slit in the helmet, a helmet snouted like a shull, inlaid with golden traceries and toothed with gold in its snarling mouth-orifice. It towered over me, loomed closer as the rider leaned forward on his prancing, circling horse. A sword slim as a snake lashed out, caught itself in my tattered cloak, jerked me out and down, my feet sliding on the muddy cobbles. A deep voice above me: "Welcome to the Gilgard, Scion." I screamed and scrambled backwards, pulling him off the horse with his own snagged sword—the helmet tumbled, showering me with dirt that wriggled with maggots, filled my mouth, clogged my nostrils. The sword was a snake writhing to free its fangs from my cloak. It struck, deep in my belly—*

I awoke, sweating. And leaned over the side of the pallet to vomit again, coughing frantically afterwards to clear my air passages. There was nothing dreamlike about the pain in my gut. It stabbed again, and I lurched urgently off the pallet to scrabble for the pisspot in the corner. A lamp appeared in the doorway and I dimly heard whispers. The lamp advanced into the room, underlighting Mysheba's motherly face.

"I've been poisoned," I moaned from my strategic position on the pot.

She put the lamp down and felt my forehead. "Feverish," she muttered. Then to me she said, "Not poisoned, my lord Tigrallef. Just a touch of the Gil-gut fever. We should have

expected it—why, even the Sherank get it when they first
arrive, or so we're told."

"How about the other Scions?" I asked through gritted
teeth.

"Who knows? None of them survived long enough to find
out. Anyway, there's nothing to worry about. We know just
how to deal with the old Gil-gut."

A healing Flamen named Faruli, whom I already knew
slightly, arrived at that point and poured something almost
as vile as vomit down my throat. Whatever it was knocked
me out, right there on the pot—and when I awoke, clean but
smelling of babyshit and herbs, thin sunlight was filtering
through the dirty slats on the window. Calla was cross-legged
on a cushion beside my pallet, stitching industriously at a
pair of tattered britches. In a clean yellow robe, with her face
washed and her dark hair spilling abundantly over her shoulders, she was as demure and pretty as any of the well-reared
maidens I'd ever seen in Sathelforn. When she saw I was
awake, she stopped sewing long enough to feel my forehead
and cheeks.

"Fever's down, Tig," she said, picking up her needle
again. "Are you hungry?"

"Ravenous. What time is it?"

"Mid-morning."

"Only? I feel like I've been sleeping for days."

"You have—three days. Faruli's tincture has that side-
effect. It makes you helpless and fairly disgusting to nurse,
but it does save your life."

Fairly disgusting to nurse. Damn it, I thought, betrayed by
my own bowels. I lay back on the pallet and turned my face
away out of pure shame. "Who nursed me, Calla? Did you?"

"Among others. Don't worry, Tig, the belly-rot is all part
of living in Gil. I'll get you something to eat."

She laid down her mending and disappeared through the
curtains. Wisps of memory floated through my mind—
wrenching pains, cool hands, foul tastes and smells; yes, I
could easily believe three days of disgustingness had passed,
witnessed at close hand by Calla, of all people. She reappeared with a bowl of soup, looking so fresh and flowerlike

that I groaned with humiliation. Calla took no notice.

She raised me expertly to a sitting position and propped her cushion behind me. I felt weak and tearful, and the bottom dropped out of my head. "Dizzy?" she asked, spooning soup into my mouth. "Don't worry, that's normal. I've told the Flamens you're awake—Faruli will be along to see you shortly."

The Flamens. That reminded me. Urgently, I tamped down my embarrassment and struggled to evade the spoon. "Calla—what about the scullery? The council's plan?"

"It's been put off until you're well again. Next month, probably. Don't think about it. Eat."

I swallowed another spoonful. "But Calla?"

"Yes?"

"There's something I have to know." Another spoonful. Calla was almost too efficient a feeder. I pushed her hand weakly aside. "Why did you volunteer to go with me?"

"Why not? Stop talking and eat."

"No, that's no answer. You hated being assigned to me as a guide; you've made it quite clear from the beginning that you think I'm a bumbling idiot. And I suspect you agree with Hawelli about the quest, anyway."

"Eat, Tig," she said.

"No. Tell me why."

"Well," she said casually, holding the spoon to my lips, "maybe I think you're not such a total fool after all. And if you really are such a fool, you'll need my help even more. Open wide."

It was an endorsement of a sort. Anyway, it sufficed. I relaxed against the cushion, wondering why I felt so pleased.

"By the way," Calla went on, "Faruli says you'll need a couple of weeks to get your strength back. We're going to use that time to our advantage."

I mumbled a question through the soup.

"How? Why, we're going to teach you some things you might want to know. You're a memorian, Tig, you'll enjoy yourself. Maybe you'll write it all down someday."

I nodded—unwisely. Calla reverted to her normal impatient self as she wiped the soup off my chin. But I felt even happier; it seemed that at last I might be taught something worth the learning. And it had suddenly dawned on me that Calla was calling me Tig.

Bekri took personal charge of my training programme, although he did not himself teach me. My pallet was moved to the outer chamber and we lay side by side, he on his sofa, I on my bed, while this instructor or that imparted wisdom from a cushion on the floor. Mysheba taught me many tricks of disguise, drafting a trio of bored, initially clean children as models. The Third Flamen, a grizzled giant named Corri, took me street by street through a detailed hand-drawn map of the city, stressing danger zones, escape routes, safe houses, rendezvous places, strategic viewpoints, and the odd inn where a beaker of reasonable brew could be had if you mentioned the right name.

It was Calla's job to teach me street theory, which kept me spellbound and happy. Things which I had observed and wondered about were suddenly illuminated: the ways of not drawing attention to yourself, for example; or, conversely, of creating a diversion if a Sherkin trooper approached too closely to something he was not meant to see. Methods of sabotage, of message-leaving, of thieving, of evanishment, of smuggling people and things past sensitive Sherkin noses—a whole street-lore, in short, beautifully adapted to the special and terrible needs of Gil. It seemed to me also that Calla enjoyed these lessons almost as much as I did, perhaps because I was such an avid pupil; I couldn't, of course, flatter myself that it was my company that she enjoyed. That would be expecting too much.

Jebri taught me the fingerspeech, not a difficult task for either of us, since it was rooted in the ancient gestural system. In the old days, and in Exile, the gestures had become ritualized and restricted to use on formal occasions. I had mastered the syntax as a child, but was always too clumsy or rattled to perform it well. This was different, more exciting, a genuine means of communication, at once subtler and more direct than the original motions. Its use was not limited to the Web—many of the things I was learning were used

by all Gilmen in their secret battle for survival—but Jebri
also taught me the special coded twitches and waggles that
only another member of the Web would understand. By the
end of a week, I was able to carry out longish conversations
with Bekri between lessons with never a word being spoken
out loud.

"You learn fast, Lord of Gil," Bekri said over our bowls
of soup on the eleventh day after my illness. I returned his
smile—when I looked at him now, I hardly saw the scars,
only the face of a good friend.

"I have good teachers. But there's still so much to learn,
Revered Bekri. The more I hear of the Web, the more I
marvel at it."

"It didn't happen all at once. The first years were grim,
Tig, very grim, before we learned what we had to do. Sometimes I wonder . . ." His voice died away.

"Yes?"

"I wonder what will happen when you find the Lady at
last, and free us from this kind of life? How will we cope
with real freedom? What will our street-wise children do
when there's no more need to hide?"

I shrugged, and signed with my fingers that life would go
on. "You may find freedom an easier lesson," I added aloud.

"I don't know," he said thoughtfully. "I suppose it's possible." Then he shook himself, and smiled at me. "At any
rate, I hope I will live long enough to find out. A month ago,
I had no such hope."

I put my spoon down and looked closely at him. He
seemed to be aging in front of my eyes; it was hard to believe
he was the same man who, only a few weeks before, one-
legged and all, had led me a fine chase through the dark
streets of the city. At that moment he looked all of his eighty-
odd years. I was suddenly frightened. Here was a new kind
of burden—his hope was like a sack of lead on my back. I
leaned across the gulf between sofa and pallet and took his
hand in mine. There was nothing sensible for me to say.

The time came when Faruli no longer looked at me with
pursed lips and a frown. He poked at my body, not nearly

as well-fatted as before; prodded my sunken belly, peered
into my pupils, nodded sombrely. He was a very tall, thin
Flamen, lugubrious to an extraordinary degree, whose very
appearance should have been enough to scare his patients to
death. Still, his tinctures were famous and his treatment the
best that could be had in the shadowy underworld of Gil.
"Your condition pleases me, my lord," he said in his deep,
funereal voice. "You may go outside this afternoon if you
wish, but nothing too energetic for the next few days."

He glided out through the curtains. I dressed slowly in a
clean tunic and britches, a confused mixture of feelings. Now
that the pleasant educational interlude was over, I was afraid
again; but I was also eager to get started, and that surprised
me.

Mysheba peered through the curtains, tense with excitement. "May I come in, my lord? Faruli says you're better.
Good, because there's something Bekri wants you to see."
She came in and drew me over to the window, pointing
through the slats in the direction of the market. "You'll have
to look from here, the fountain isn't visible from the council
chamber. Can you see it?"

"Yes." I saw crowds gathering; knots of distant workmen
streaming laden out of the marketplace, like ants carrying off
crumbs; others straining in teams to erect a framework like
a glittering gibbet, close to the fountain. "What is it? What's
going on down there?"

"Oh, the Sherank are laying on a bit of public entertainment. They do, now and then, though we're never very entertained." She laughed sourly.

"But what's happening? Why are they tearing down the
market?"

"They aren't, just the stalls within a certain distance of
Oballef's Fountain. Can you see the man on the white
horse?"

"With a red crest on his helmet? Near the gibbet?"

"That's the one. He's Lord Shree, Governor Kekashr's
nephew, second in command in Gil. A strange one, Shree.
We're told even the Sherank think so."

"How do you mean?"

"It seems he's not quite vicious enough for their liking. I don't know, Tig." Mysheba shrugged. "It's hard to tell one monster from another. Calla exchanged a few words with him once, and she didn't notice any difference. Anyway, he has no qualms about erecting the Gilman's Pleasure. Do you see it?"

"That gibbet-thing?" I squinted at the marketplace. The details I could make out suddenly made sense. "Does that do what I think it does?" I whispered, shocked.

"Are you thinking something awful?"

"Very awful."

"Then you're probably right."

"Great Lady in Gil," I said slowly.

"Never mind that now. The Flamens think you should go, for the experience. Calla's waiting to take you out. Better get changed, then I'll do your face." She threw a bundle of street clothes at me and hurried out of the room.

11

THE CROWDS SURGED towards the marketplace, not entirely of their own volition. We were goaded on by patrols of glee-ful Sherank, rearing their horses, prodding and smacking with their swords for more speed, more terror, more urgency. I got hit on the rump myself with the flat of somebody's sword, moments after Calla and I stepped into the street.

Calla heard the thwack and the hooves behind us. "Don't look back," she muttered. "They like it if you do."

"What's their hurry?" I panted.

"They want the audience in place well before the show begins."

"Oh." I hustled along beside her for a few paces. "You

speak of this like a juggling show, or a harp concert—but no Gilmen are depraved enough to enjoy it, are they?"

"You'd be surprised," Calla answered shortly. "But you're right, most hate it."

"Why do they come, then? Why not just stay in their houses?"

Calla sighed patiently. "Because if the Sherank aren't pleased with the turnout, they come and chivvy out everybody they can find, including the sick and the children. Now don't talk, Tig, just remember what I taught you."

I shut up, but not just because I was told to. Where the street joined the market, a Sherkin was sitting on horseback watching the crowds eddy past him. From the red crest on his helmet, I recognized Lord Shree. His visor was pushed up, unlike all the others—and so, for the first time, I looked on the real face of the enemy. It was a lean and dissatisfied face, youngish, leached-looking, as if it spent too much time behind metal; the eyes, which caught mine briefly and then passed on, were deep-set and underscored with purple smudges. It was not really a face to be frightened of—I could imagine my mother clucking over him and sending to the kitchen for a bowl of mutton broth. Then, when I was closest to him, he knocked his visor down and all semblance of personality vanished. He pulled at his reins and rode slowly through the parting crowd towards the mass of horsemen at the fountain.

"Quit gaping," Calla whispered furiously into my ear.

"Was I gaping? Sorry."

"It isn't safe, you know that."

"I said I was sorry," I answered mildly. Under cover of picking my nose, I added a rude twitch of the fingers that Bekri had taught me on the sly. Calla smothered a gasp of laughter. "Sorry," she whispered, "I always dread this."

"I understand. Is it really necessary for us to go?"

"Bekri thought so. It is something you should see—once. And you should see the Sherank in action before you go wandering into their fortress."

"Our fortress," I reminded her.

"They've made it theirs, haven't they? Come on."

We edged our way through the crowd, a little nearer to the Gilman's Pleasure than I really cared to be. It loomed over the marketplace beside the desecrated Lady, a scaffolding about twenty feet tall with a platform at the top, and a second platform about halfway down, reached by a set of stairs. The tall posts and stairs were of dark wood, carved with cruel Sherkin motifs; the platforms were grids made of iron bars, polished to a cold grey brilliance. In its way, it was a beautiful structure. But welded to the nodes of the upper platform were metal spikes about three feet in length, slim and viciously sharp, pointing downwards; and that platform was not fixed, but floating in vertical grooves in the posts, grooves that extended as far down as the lower platform. Its weight was counterbalanced by four enormous leather sacks, attached to the platform by four heavy hawsers running through pulleys. At that moment, the sacks were hanging just below the level of the lower platform.

"Calla?"

"What now?"

"Are there shackles on the lower platform?"

"Yes. Strong ones. You can't see them from this angle, but you'll see the poor shullbait in them soon enough."

I opened my mouth to ask another question, but she shook her head. "Hush now, it's not safe to talk in this crowd."

I closed my mouth and looked around in quick, sidelong glances. There were some faces I recognized within a few armlengths, a couple of the junior Flamens, some Web functionaries I had seen in the council chamber but never directly addressed—and, to my surprise and discomfort, Hawelli, miraculously sunken and ugly. Our eyes met; he lifted one hand to adjust his cloak, and flashed a quick greeting with his fingers. Then he was gone, sliding through the crowd towards the bakery. I nudged Calla.

"Hawelli's here."

Her body stiffened. "Where?"

"He went back through the crowd. What's wrong?"

She relaxed. "Nothing, if he's headed for home. The council banned him from attending these executions—the last time he came, he made some stupid trouble that could have endangered the Web."

"That sounds in character. But doesn't the audience ever protest?"

"Yes." Her whisper sank so low that I had difficulty hearing. The mob pressed around us.

"What did you say?"

"I said, yes, once, about sixty years ago, the crowd tried to rescue some poor wretch from the points of the Pleasure. That was the first and last time."

"The Sherank were angry?"

"No, they were delighted. Gil learned its lesson, right enough."

There was a shifting in the crowd like wind through a cornfield. A long parade of Sherkin horsemen, glittering in crimson and polished iron, charged into the square four abreast, parting the crowd with all the courtesy of a butcher's cleaver. They joined Lord Shree and the horsemen at the foot of the Gilman's Pleasure, milling about, waving their swords in the air, roaring bloody war-cries in the Sheranik tongue. A chorus outside the market answered them, and I saw that scores more had surrounded the square and were jocularly charging the fringes of the crowd. One old woman went down under their hooves, then another, then a man—this only seemed to increase the horsemen's pleasure, for there were howls of hilarity behind the snarling helmets.

Lord Shree raised his arm. The shouting cut off abruptly, the riders quieted their mounts. Down the aisle left by the horsemen marched a large body of Sherkin troopers, their boots thudding in unison into the muddy ground. Midway along the array, in a cage carried on a wain, came the object of this terrible exercise: a naked man, bearded and matted and filthy, crouching in a corner with his face pressed to the bars. The crowd was so quiet now that his keening could be heard as an eerie descant to the rhythm of the boots. As the wain pulled up by the Gilman's Pleasure, he fell silent. I caught a glimpse of his face, and looked quickly back at the ground.

Lord Shree dropped his arm. The square was perfectly,

weirdly quiet for a moment or two. Then a quartet of troopers marched to the cage and dragged out the wretched occupant. He struggled weakly; small noises came from his throat. I glanced around at the crowd—there was not a flicker of expression visible in the whole marketplace. Choking back despair, anger, compassion, I tried to be as stolid as the rest, but I lacked the experience. Calla nudged me sharply in the ribs.

They half-carried, half-dragged the prisoner up the stairs, threw him down on the lower platform, and busied themselves securing fetters around wrists, ankles, waist and upper arms and legs. The evil snicking of the shackles echoed through the marketplace. When the prisoner was fixed to the platform, the troopers turned and stepped smartly down the stairs, taking up positions beneath the leather sacks.

Lord Shree raised his arm again. "People of Gil, beloved subjects of the Dynasty in Iklankish in Sher, we present to you a dangerous criminal, a traitor who sought to defy the benevolent rule of Kekashr, Governor of Gil."

He spoke in a pleasant, well-modulated voice, in reasonable Gillish, with only a trace of the atrocious Sheranik accent. He paused for a moment, as if pondering the ironies of his own formulae—I wished that he would raise his visor again, so I could see if he was keeping a straight face. Suddenly he roared, "Make no mistake, people of Gil! Any ingratitude, any treachery, will bring any one of you to the same end! Watch this traitor die, people of Gil, and learn to love the justice of Sher. Let the Pleasure begin!"

Again he lowered his arm. The four executioners reached upwards, pulled at something dangling from each of the leather sacks, and stepped aside. From each sack, a thin stream descended. Sand, just as I expected. The heavy upper grid stirred as its equilibrium shifted. Ever so slowly, it began to move downwards in its grooves.

The prisoner jerked in his fetters. His profile was visible from that angle—I could see his mouth stretch wide in a silent scream, his eyes bulge up at the slow, smooth, inexorable advance of the glittering points. When I shut my eyes, I could see it too: the swelling squares of sky through the bars of the grille, the points of light sliding closer, as slowly as the dribble of sand through a small hole, so slowly that their approach was almost imperceptible; and at last, the first gentle touch of the spikes, sure and unhurried, minor as the prick of a pin, but insistent, inescapable, sharpening to agony as the sand drained from the counterweights and the heavy grid sank lower. Calla poked me again and disentangled her fingers from mine. (I could not remember taking her hand.) I opened my eyes.

The grid was visibly lower, the points only a span or so from the prisoner's straining body. One could trust the Sherank to position the spikes so that no vital organ would be pierced—the poor wretch was doomed to writhe for some time, perhaps hours, a quivering envelope of flesh around the hard shafts of metal, until at last he died of blood-loss, shock, or simply of pain. Under the Heroic Code, I thought bitterly, I'd be halfway to the Pleasure already, swordstick drawn, panting to slash my way through the Sherank to free him— and a second later, judging by the bloodthirsty faces of Shree's honour guard, I'd be mincemeat. The prisoner would still die, and I with him, and probably many innocent people; and also, of course, Bekri's hopes of the Lady. One grim death against four hundred thousand grim lives. No choice, really. But I found I was shaking with impotent rage.

I forced myself to look at the prisoner again—he was in the same posture precisely, mouth open, eyes wide, body arched; he seemed rigid with fear. Or—with something else? It was very odd that not a muscle had moved in all that time; and then the first gleaming needle-tip touched his belly, and I braced myself for the first flinch, the first scream, but he remained frozen, silent. I nudged Calla and she looked up and saw the same thing. After a second while she figured it out, she signed frantically for me to look anywhere but at the Pleasure.

I glanced around at the crowd, and saw that others had noticed as well, and were quickly turning their faces towards the ground. Only the Sherank, who were watching the crowd instead of the Pleasure, had not yet realized. The prisoner was dead—had been dead well before the spikes even touched him. I breathed a prayer of gratitude to the Lady. However, there was no relief on the faces around me; if anything, there was more terror.

Lord Shree caught my eye, and my heart lurched. Alone of the Sherank, he was looking up at the corpse shackled to the platform, impaled now at cheeks, belly, thighs and shoulders, and bleeding suspiciously little. The Sherkin prince was sitting straight and tense in his saddle; it was obvious that he understood. Any second, I expected him to bellow with rage and disappointment—after all, the Gilman had cheated by dying so soon and so painlessly; but Lord Shree only sat on his horse. Eventually, he looked away.

He shared the joke with us for several minutes longer. At last one of the honour guard, possibly wondering why the screams were so long in coming, looked up at the prisoner and shouted furiously in Sheranik.

"Bastard's died on us!"

His comrades whirled, outraged, and drew their swords with a great clattering and many curses. But Lord Shree roared for silence. He growled at the troopers who were already halfway up the stairs, and they stopped, uncertain, and then scrambled hastily down. At another word from Shree, they caught at the lines dangling from the counterweights and hauled until the spikes shook themselves free of the Gilman's body and jerked to the top of the Pleasure. Lord Shree himself dropped gracefully from the saddle and ascended the stairs alone. He bent over the fettered corpse for a few moments, then turned to address the crowd. The air in the marketplace was crackling with tension, like the air before a thunderstorm.

"People of Gil," Shree cried, "the criminal has paid for his treachery and is dead. I regret he was denied the full pleasure of the points—but the next among you to climb these stairs will not be so unfortunate." There was a corporate shudder throughout the crowd, but nobody moved. Shree paused and looked around. Then he shouted, "Go now! Go to your homes!" He stilled a Sheranik outburst with one raised hand. I was fascinated—but on Shree's last word, the crowd had begun a stampede out of the marketplace, and I was buffeted by moving bodies, nearly knocked down, separated from Calla within seconds. I turned and ran with the crowd, but when I reached the shelter of the bread ovens I crouched behind them and looked back. Lord Shree was still at the top of the stairs, watching the exodus, loftily ignoring an altercation among the honour guard below him. I saw him look down once, and heard him bark a short command—a mounted Sherkin holding a Gilman off the ground by the scruff of his neck threw the man down and watched dourly as he scrambled away. At that moment Calla found me and grabbed my hand.

"Quickly, Tig," she panted, "before Lord Shree changes his mind." We joined the stream of people flooding from the square. As we reached the mouth of our alley, I realized the man pounding along on my other side was none other than Hawelli.

12

CALLA WAITED UNTIL we were inside the doorway before she grabbed Hawelli's arm. She pulled him past the staircase and into a narrow corridor, half-blocked in places with brick rubble and carpeted with shull droppings. She stopped for a second to glare at the tall Flamen, then marched on ahead, swiping at the cobwebs. Without a glance at me, Hawelli followed her. I grimaced and took up the tail.

The corridor was gap-toothed with uninviting doorways. By the time I had finished crawling over the third or fourth heap of debris, the others were already waiting by the least inviting of all, a black hole distinguished by a sagging lintel and a powerfully cold draught from below. There was angry silence between the two of them, reminding me of Callefiya and Arkolef in one of their cousinly tiffs. I fought the impulse to turn back and leave them to it.

"Are you actually intending to go down there?" I asked, squinting into the blackness.

"It's safe and it's private. I have some questions for this esteemed Flamen here before I make my report to the council. You don't have to come if you're afraid."

I sighed at her tone and peered at Hawelli. Even in the near-darkness I could tell he was uncomfortable, that his forbidding façade was very slightly cracked. That alone made it worth tagging along. "Afraid? Me?" I said.

Calla humphed and led through the door on to a descending flight of stairs, of a decrepitude that made the main staircase seem positively youthful. She did have the sense to strike a light on a candle-end taken from a pocket in her cloak. And while she bounced down the stairs in her customary carefree fashion, I was pleased to see that Hawelli was testing each footfall and flinching at the groans of the rotten wood, just as I was.

The stairs landed in a cellar, cold as a mountaintop, with a cavernous feel—Calla's light barely scratched the darkness. A bitter faecal smell fouled the air, no doubt the legacy of many generations of shulls. Calla led surely across the hazard-strewn floor, with Hawelli and I stumbling in her trail, to a wooden door in the far wall. "In here," she snapped.

It was a small room, stone-floored and freezing, that might once have been used as a root-cellar. Calla stuck the candle-end to the floor with melted tallow and straightened up. "Sit down where I can see your face, Flamen."

He sighed heavily and obeyed. I was fascinated. "Is that how you talk to Flamens around here?" I asked. "I wish you'd teach me."

"Hawelli and I are—old friends," Calla said through tight lips. She sat down on the floor on the other side of the candle from Hawelli, looking anything but friendly. I hovered.

"Flamen," she began, "I was the council's designated observer at that Pleasuring."

"So?"

"So what were *you* doing there?"

"Standing around like everyone else, watching some poor sod get murdered," Hawelli said coolly.

"You should not have been there." There were marked overtones of the Primate in Calla's voice. "You deliberately defied the council's ban."

Hawelli warmed his hands at the candle. "So?"

"I'll have to include it in my report."

"I'm trembling with fear."

"Stop it, *Flamen*. This is serious. Did you have anything to do with what happened?"

"What do you mean?"

"I mean the Pleasurebait dying before the points reached him."

"Oh, that." Hawelli spread his hands. "How could I?"

"A dart-tube." I joined them on the floor. My buttocks instantly turned to globes of ice. "I was watching; I think I saw it happen, not long after the sandbags were unplugged."

"What did you see?" Calla frowned at me fiercely. So did Hawelli. Their breath made silver clouds in the candlelight.

"I saw the poor man jerk once and then go rigid, and he never moved again. I think he was hit with a poisoned dart."

Calla looked at Hawelli. "Is that true?"

Hawelli smiled. "Well done, lord Scion. One little pin-prick, a broken second of pain, and then a quick death. I used concentrated parth-asp venom and aimed for the neck."

"Beautiful shot," I said admiringly, "I mean, I'm not bad with the dart-tube myself, but I know I couldn't—"

"Be quiet, Tig," Calla snapped. She turned on Hawelli, furious. "You pocketing idiot! How could you? You know what the council said."

"Yes, I know."

"And you know what might have happened."

"Yes, I know that also."

"What might have happened?" I interjected. They ignored me.

"And in the face of the council's orders, and all common sense, you went ahead and did it anyway."

"Yes." Hawelli sat back on the floor, still smiling. Calla, speechless with outrage, glared at him.

"What might have happened?" I asked again, taking advantage of the lull.

Calla turned to me. "It's like this, Tig. Often, if the Sherank feel the first Gilman has not had enough Pleasure from the points, they will take his body out of the shackles and put in a second Pleasurebait, chosen at random from the crowd. But if Lord Shree had realized, or even suspected, that the prisoner's death was hastened by some *misguided well-wisher*," she raised her voice and glowered at Hawelli as she said this, "he would certainly have ordered a massacre. Scores, even hundreds, might have died—possibly even you, my lord." She shot to her feet and stomped around the room, stopping to bend angrily over Hawelli. "You should never have taken that chance, especially when you put the Scion at risk!"

Happy as I was to watch a Flamen being abused, especially that Flamen, I had to intervene. "You missed something, Calla," I said mildly.

She whirled to face me. "And what's that?"

"Lord Shree did know."

That stopped her cold. She looked at me thoughtfully as she lowered herself to the floor at my side. "What makes you think so?"

"I was watching him. He knew the prisoner was dead almost as soon as the crowd did."

"What did he do?"

"Nothing much. He looked away, that's all."

"You're only supposing that he noticed."

"Perhaps. But there's another thing I thought was interesting. Later, he made sure he was the first Sherkin to get close to the body. It's even possible he disposed of the dart himself—palmed it or dropped it through the grille."

"And then," Hawelli spoke up, "he let the crowd go, which was something I could never have foreseen—" He stopped abruptly.

"Something you could never have foreseen?" Calla repeated. "You mean, you were waiting for Lord Shree to order a massacre?"

"Hoping for it, maybe?" I added. I had a theory.

He cast me a poisonous glance, and I could see that he wished he hadn't spoken. "Who would hope for a massacre?" he said at last.

Calla stared at him. There was a silence while she seemed to be working out the obvious, and another while she forced herself to believe it, then she said, "It's true. It's *true*. You were *trying* to set off a massacre." Her voice was low and grieved; anger had temporarily deserted her. "Why, Hawelli? What kind of treachery—?"

"Not treachery, Calla," he began, but she made a sharp gesture for silence. There was pain in her face.

"Don't tell it to me. Explain yourself to the council."

"No, never again. I've wasted enough breath on the council; I'm finished with the Flamens."

"You still have to answer to them. You'll come up with me now."

"And if I won't?"

Calla answered by reaching into the apparently bottomless pockets of her cloak and producing a shiny, long-bladed knife. I saw tears in her eyes. The heretic Flamen saw them too.

"You couldn't," he said softly. "Not to me, Calla. Don't hurt yourself by trying." He held a hand out to her, but she knocked it away. Despite the tears, her own hand was steady. She used the knife to point to the door. Hawelli didn't move.

"Traitor," she said miserably. The knifepoint moved closer to Hawelli's throat.

This was rapidly getting too serious for my liking. "Calla, put the knife down. I really don't think he's a traitor."

"What do *you* know?" The knife remained steady.

"Well, think about it. For one thing, I'd wager there was more than one dart-tube in the marketplace today. Eh, Hawelli?"

His face was wooden. "Yes," he said.

"And you weren't after a massacre at all, were you? An uprising, more like. You were hoping to force Bekri's hand. And mine."

"In a way," he said grudgingly, "but there was more to it than that."

"Tell us."

He shrugged. "The prisoner—whoever he was—happened to be a countryman of mine. Do you know what his crime was? He spat. In the direction of a Sherkin he didn't know was there."

"So?" Calla said coldly. She was recovering her anger. "Real criminals never get sent to the Gilman's Pleasure. Real criminals are the nails on the fingers of Sher—they get used against us. The point is—"

"The point is," he broke in, "that we've become so bent on keeping our miserable lives that we've forgotten there are things worth dying for. The Sherank use that against us, too."

"That's not so—"

"Of course it is! What's happened to you, Calla? You used to agree with me. They know they can do anything, and all we'll do is look at the ground and smear a little more dirt on our faces, and thank the damned Lady that it's not our turn yet—"

They burst into a confused babble of argument, more and more like Callefiya and Arkolef before the Heroic Code made them too stately to squabble. I was not warm enough to tolerate it for long.

"Stop it!"

They both turned furiously on me. I reached out, took the knife from Calla's hand and laid it beside the candle. "You're both right, and you're both wrong," I said firmly. "Let's keep to the main issue. What was your plan, Hawelli?"

He scowled at the candle. "I had fifteen comrades positioned throughout the marketplace, plus myself, each with five or six venom-tipped darts. That was all the poison I could get hold of."

"Go on."

"Nothing complicated. We were going to kill as many of the bastards as possible. Lord Shree was to give us our signal, though he didn't know it."

"The order for the massacre?"

"Yes. Lord Shree was *mine*; I had my dart-tube trained on him from the moment he started up the stairs. Then—" Hawelli paused. "I'm not sure, but I think you may be right. I think he dropped the dart through the grille. And when he didn't give the signal, just told us all to go home, well—"

"Well?"

"Well, we went home. That wasn't a contingency we'd planned for. Scion, what are you grinning at?"

"Nothing. But I'd love to know why Lord Shree held back."

"I still don't believe he saw the dart," Calla said flatly. She picked up her knife, contemplated it for a moment and then stowed it back inside her cloak.

I shook my head. "Don't be so sure. The rumours may be true, that he's not as bloodthirsty as the rest, or—"

"Or what?"

"Or he figured out what was brewing when he saw the Gilman die, and decided to let you build yourself a bigger fire to burn in. That might be your real error, Hawelli: alerting Lord Shree to trouble. He could be very dangerous now."

"Speculation," Hawelli growled. "Calla, what are you going to report?"

"Everything," she said, prying the candle off the floor. "It's my duty, Hawelli, you know that. It's up to the council to decide what to do with you. You'll come with us willingly?"

He shrugged again—a habit of his—and led the way back through the cellar, up the stairs, and into the corridor. At that point, he seized Calla in a hasty embrace, kissed her hard on the lips and raced out of the door. Calla squawked and started to give chase, her arm thrusting for the knife in the folds of her cloak, but I caught her shoulder.

"Better to let him go," I said.

13

BEKRI, FOUND CONFERRING in the council chamber with Jebri, was less disturbed by Hawelli's insubordination than I expected. He hardly even seemed surprised; as Calla gave her report, stony-faced and flat-voiced, he listened with a serene absence of reaction. He simply nodded when she was done, and turned to me. "Have you anything to add, my lord Tigrallef?" he asked.

"No. Well, only that I would like to know more about this Lord Shree. He's at least as interesting as Hawelli."

"Oh, at least. Hawelli's not the first to rebel against the council, but Shree stands alone. We've never had a Sherkin lord before who missed a chance for bloodshed—they're more apt to create their chances out of dry clay. What are your thoughts on the matter, my lord?"

"Oh, I don't know." I was feeling worn by Bekri's assumption that I had meaningful insights for all occasions; flattered, yes, for nobody had ever taken me so seriously before except my mother and the First Memorian, but I was tired and I wanted the luxury of being as puzzled as everyone else. Bekri's single eye regarded me keenly for a few seconds. Then he turned to the Second Flamen, who was sitting on the other end of the sofa.

"You heard the Scion's request, Jebri. Send a message to Malviso—tell him to go to his contacts and find out all he can about Lord Shree's history before coming to Gil—two years ago, was it? Rumour as well as fact, tell him, but we must know which is which."

Jebri bobbed his head importantly. "And Hawelli?" he asked.

Bekri motioned let's-wait-and-see. "Calla was right not to

oppose his going; he will come back to us in his own good time, if the Lady wills it. Meanwhile, there's no treachery to fear from him."

"Oh, of course not, no treachery, no question of that. But what if he takes action again? Another foolhardy plot like today's?"

"A chance we'll have to take, Jebri Flamen. Anyway, how could we stop him? Web or not, he's a free man—if he chooses not to accept the council's authority, what are we to do? Lock him up? Cut his hands off, in case he disobeys again? We are not the Sherank, Jebri."

I opened my mouth and closed it again. Was Bekri really in touch with what was happening in the further reticulations of the Web? I had thought so, but now I was not so sure. What unwelcome duty, for example, had Calla been intending to carry out with that knife? I stole a glance at her. Her hood was pulled forward to hide her face. Jebri, looking very unhappy, had still not moved from the sofa.

"But he could endanger us all, Revered Bekri." Jebri was almost whining. "These wild ventures of his—suppose the Sherank traced him back to us? Suppose they caught him and tortured him?"

"That's not a new risk. We run it every day, every one of us."

"But we don't invite it, do we? Hawelli does. For his own good as well as ours, Bekri, we should—"

"What, Second Flamen?"

"We should restrain him. Or at least find out where he is and—and ask him to restrain himself," Jebri finished weakly.

Bekri laughed. "That hardly sounds like Hawelli."

"Revered Bekri, he's endangering the future of the Web," the Second Flamen wailed, nearly in tears. His podgy little hands were twisted together. Bekri closed his eye.

"Rest yourself, Flamen," he said.

It was then that I understood. Bekri was not worried about the future of the Web. He was not worried about Hawelli. He was not even worried about the Sherank. He had developed a touching faith that I, Tigrallef, the two-left-footed, the burrower-in-books, the despair of the training Flamens, the coward, the weakling, the clown of Gil, was going to saunter into the Gilgard and out of it again with the Lady in my britches' pocket. And soon. I cleared my throat.

"Revered Bekri?"

"Yes, Lord of Gil?"

I hesitated. Don't abdicate yet, is what I wanted to say. I'm not a good peg for your hopes to hang on. I could be caught or killed at any moment, I could fail abysmally in my mission. Don't neglect your other options. Don't depend on me. But what I did say was: "I think Jebri is right. You must make every effort to contact Hawelli and restrain him from doing anything impulsive."

Calla pushed her hood back and glared at me as fiercely as she ever had. Bekri's reaction was far more disturbing; he opened his eye slowly, and sat up straight. He looked ancient again. He lifted his one whole arm and sketched decisively in the air the formal acquiescence of a Flamen to a Scion of Oballef. This was the disturbing part: the variant he used should only have been signed to a reigning Priest-King in Gil. Jebri did not react, and I did not recover in time to return the gesture, or to protest against it, before Bekri spoke out loud.

"You heard, Jebri Flamen? Lord Tigrallef's intention is quite clear. So—we must then try to find Hawelli; and also, I suppose, to find out who his confederates were in today's escapade. Is that your wish, my lord? Jebri, start by finding out who is especially skilled with the dart-tube; also, check with whom Hawelli has been spending time lately. Corri may be able to help. Or Sibba. Calla?"

Calla shook her head stiffly. "I've seen very little of Hawelli. If you'll remember, Revered Bekri, I have been assigned to duty with Lord Tigrallef for some weeks now."

He transferred his sharp eye to her. "Yes, of course. Well then, do your duty. Take him down for supper. The shull's rather tasty tonight." He smiled, closed his eye again and leaned back on the sofa. The scars put on his face by the Sherank were suddenly less notable than those left by time, age and years of sorrow. I pulled at Calla's arm and we walked softly to the door, as softly as if Bekri were sleeping.

Jebri went out with us, leaving the old man alone in the council chamber.

We trooped down the stairs, the three of us, without speaking. On the landing that led to the communal kitchen, Jebri stopped us. "Are you sure you knew nothing of Hawelli's plot, Calla?" he asked.

Calla shrugged. "Nothing, Second Flamen," she said. "It was a piece of foolishness. I'd never have been party to it."

He nodded too many times, looking like an officious little gold-merchant I'd seen on one of my visits to the Sathelforn market. Then, with a respectful sign of leave-taking in my direction (though not, thank the Lady, one for a reigning Priest-King) he continued down the stairs. Calla lingered meaningfully on the landing. When Jebri was out of earshot, she turned on me furiously.

"Why did you do that, Tig? You were the one who stopped me going after him. Now you've set the Web in motion against him. Why?"

"You mean Hawelli?"

"Of course I mean Hawelli, you fishbrain. Who else could I mean?"

I began to pull the door open, but she slapped my arm down and put her back against the jamb. "Why?" she repeated.

I sighed. "Calla, I have nothing against Hawelli. I must admit that I like him for what he did today, even if it was complete madness."

"What do you mean, madness?" she flared. I caught my breath at the inconsistency of it. "Is it madness to keep hold of a few grains of dignity? A rag or two of pride? Maybe we need more of madness then, and a little less of this." She slumped dramatically into the blows-expected posture of a Gilman on the street.

"Stop it, Calla. You know that we're not ready to take on the Sherank."

"We'll never be ready," she said bitterly.

"That may or may not be so," I said, "but are you hopeless enough that you're ready to get yourself killed?"

"Of course not," she began, flaming, but she stopped short.

There was a pause while she looked through me, then she closed her eyes. She leaned her head back against the door-jamb, tilting her chin upwards so her face was foreshortened. The skin of her throat was stretched tight; for the first time since I had known her, she looked tired and vulnerable. "Sometimes," she said softly.

"What?"

"I said, yes, yes, sometimes. Sometimes I'm that hopeless. Anyway, there are things you don't know. Things I can't tell you. Sometimes I get confused."

"Oh." Now I was confused. This was not the abrasive, competent Calla of most days, nor the Calla who nursed me tenderly through a disgusting illness, nor yet the Calla who laughed with me at our lessons and treated me, now and then, like a comrade. This was a despairing stranger with Calla's face and eyes that wouldn't meet mine. I wondered if this one was the real face, the real face that hid behind the others.

"Growing up under the Sherank—it's a hopeless business, Tig," she went on. "The Web gives us a measure of pride, makes us feel like we're fighting back in a small way. But what do we really do? We survive, some of us. We manage to fool the Sherank in little things, which makes us feel clever. But in the end, nothing changes. Nothing will ever change. I know that, better than most."

"But Hawelli—"

"Hawelli thinks things can be changed; the problem is, he thinks any change will be for the better, even if it's for the worse."

"What?"

She sighed impatiently, with a fractional return of spirit. "I mean, he would rather get the entire population of Gil slaughtered in the course of some grand heroic gesture than to have us go on like this. Something about our dignity. Most of the time, I think he's a lunatic. Sometimes I think he's the only sane Flamen on the island."

"What do you feel right now?"

"Tired, just tired. I shouldn't be saying these things any-how. Let's not talk any more."

"Wait a second." She dropped her chin to look at me as I hesitated. "How about the Lady—and me? Don't you feel there's any hope there?"

"I don't know, Tig. I follow my orders because that's part of the game that keeps me alive. That's all. The Flamens say a Scion is the only thing that can save us, so I believe them. Sometimes. At any rate, it's worth a try."

"And if I fail?"

"Then we've lost nothing. To be honest, we have nothing to lose."

I sighed. "I suppose that's as much enthusiasm as I deserve. But about Hawelli—"

She shut her eyes again and let the corners of her mouth droop, as if mortally exhausted, and bored as well. "All right, go ahead, for what it's worth."

"I stopped you going after him because I think you were prepared to kill him. Is that correct?"

The eyes remained closed. "Maybe. If I could. And if he wouldn't stop."

"Well, I couldn't let you. Bekri's right about that: how can we hope to destroy the Sherank if we start by destroying each other?"

She opened her eyes at that and spoke with terrible sadness. "You've led a sheltered life, Tig."

"As for sending the Web after him," I ploughed on, "it's because I do believe there is hope for Gil. The Lady is real, Calla; the magic works. If we find her, we will win. There is hope. It's just a pity that so much depends on me." She seemed about to comment on that, and I hurried to cut her off. "So I have to try—and I need time. I need Hawelli to defer any of those grand heroic gestures of his until I've tried and failed. Then it doesn't matter what happens."

She grimaced. "Really. What would Bekri think of that?"

"Bekri thinks the same."

"How do you know?"

"I saw it in the council chamber. Haven't you seen how he's aged in the last few weeks? He's only holding on long enough to see how I do. He thinks nothing else matters."

"That's not like Bekri," Calla scoffed. "The Web is his life."

"His life is nearly over. In any case, I think he designed the Web as a tool to help the Scion when the right Scion came along, nothing more than that. And he thinks, bless his heart, that I'm the right Scion. He thinks that if I fail, Gil is finished. You saw the gesture he gave me?"

"Yes, but—" Calla began, then stopped short. A little of the burden I was feeling appeared in her face. She slid away from the door and pulled it open. "Don't talk of this to any of the others," she whispered fiercely as she drew me into the warm kitchen. "They still think the Web is worth something."

14

I WAS ARRESTED two days later.

This was not due to any real mistake on my part, nor on the Web's. Treachery was not involved. Nor was I even arrested in my role as Scion of Oballef and dragged off to a private audience with Lord Kekashr. It was nothing so dignified. Nevertheless, it could have been fatal, and I did not understand until much later the reason why it was not.

My main problem in those days of waiting was restlessness. It was not comfortable being poised on the brink of a quest, and I was at the point where, having accepted the Web's help, I also had to accept the Web's timetable. The scullery scheme was a good one, I knew that very well; so good that, had the Flamens-in-Exile possessed a feather's weight of sense among them, they'd have thought of it decades ago and put dish-washing high on the heroic curriculum. This was the scheme's great beauty: assuming the old palace plans in the archives were still accurate, there was a passage on the other side of the scullery wall that would give us direct access to the between-ways, with an absolute minimum of danger. That was a long way from finding the Lady, but it was a good, efficient start.

Still, the final stages of preparation demanded patience. Calvo, the scullery master, was unobtrusively moving trustworthy people on to the shift that Calla and I would join; plans were being rehearsed to give us the few moments we'd need to reach the passageway door unobserved, and to cover for us afterwards. These things took time and occupied the attention of my erstwhile teachers, and none of them provided anything for me to do with myself. As my companion-elect, Calla was also supposed to be resting; it didn't suit her either.

"Faruli says the delay will do you no harm," Mysheba said to comfort me. For want of anything better to do, Calla and I were sitting bored in the kitchen, pulling maggots out of a pot of fresh dirt from the marketplace. "You're not long over the Gil-gut, my lord, you're still looking drawn."

"The better to pass as a Gilborn," I said grumpily. I had hoped to start at the scullery within a day or two; Jebri had just informed me it would be six at the earliest, and we'd have to work in the scullery for at least one full day before striking out for the between-ways. My training programme in the Web's kitchen had taught me, among other things, that I hated washing dishes.

Calla sniffed irritably and said, "Perhaps you'd like to try a different entry to the Gilgard? The main gate, for instance?"

"No, thank you, I can wait." I flicked a few maggots off my fingers into the writhing contents of a large colander. Proportionately speaking, those maggots were probably the fattest creatures in Gil, except for the Koroskan mercenaries. Mysheba knew a hundred ways to make them edible. This lot was destined to become a kind of pâté. I buried the thought of lunch.

It was then that Mysheba made her fateful suggestion. "Why don't you go on a picnic, my lord? See a bit of the countryside? I'm sure Faruli would approve—he said you needed exercise and fresh air, and you're not getting either of those in here, Oballef knows. Calla, why don't you take Lord Tigrallef out along the Malvi Road?" She picked up the colander and poked a few climbers back down among their brethren.

"It might improve his temper," Calla said thoughtfully.

"Is there any risk?"

"Not if we're careful. Don't worry, I won't let anything happen to you."

"Thank you so much." I hated it when she dropped back into being my nursemaid. But the time was weighing on both of us and the inaction was giving my imagination, overly fertile at all times, too much poisoned compost to grow on. A day in the countryside might be a pleasant leafy distraction. "All right," I said, "we'll go."

An hour later, dressed for the street and armed with a bag of bread and soured-milk cheese (the maggot pâté wasn't ready yet, bless Oballef), we set off. My spirits were already higher, especially since Calla was also in a better mood and disposed to be friendly. It was not easy to hang my head and shuffle along like a beaten old man; spring had followed me to the island.

This is not to say that the suburbs of Gil were any prettier or more salubrious than the centre. The Malvi Road, once broad, paved and tree-lined, had become a sort of linear mud-flat, where the ruts from the morning wains were slowly congealing in the sun. The trees and pavements were gone, the hovels had encroached on both sides until in places the road was just barely wide enough for two wains to pass each other without their wheels locking. Here and there it broadened again into a small market, where peasants from the country-side peddled pallid vegetables from the tailgates of their wains. They looked no healthier than their urban counter-parts.

Eventually, however, the hovels thinned and trees began to appear. The air became fresher, or at least the stink light-ened; there were even a few early spring flowers by the road-side. Just before the old Swan's Neck, where the road curved around what had been an ornamental lake, Calla pulled me over to the verge. She glanced about. No one else on the road was paying us any attention.

"There's a Sherkin checkpoint just around the corner. To be safe, we'll have to leave the road here." She led me between one ramshackle cottage and the ruins of another, evidently used as combination rubbish dump and pisspit. Beyond these was a random sprouting of little huts, most of them cobbled together from weathered planks and disparate bits of garbage. Some of them were quite ingenious.

I stopped to look with fascination at one made entirely of sherds from large water pots, cemented with a kind of lime plaster into a bee-hive shape. Bits of metal glittered like jewels here and there in the plaster. Through a round hole in the wall, an indistinct face peered out at me suspiciously.

"Don't slow down," said Calla.

"But it's rather good," I said, looking back. "I like the mosaic effect over the door-hole."

Calla grinned. "The best things in Gil these days are made from garbage."

"A new art form," I said, struck by the idea. "A whole new architecture. Look at the roof on that one—an old rowboat. This is exciting, Calla; I wish I'd brought a notebook."

"You're strange, Tigrallef," she said.

Now this had been said to me many times before, including by Calla. The odd thing was, for once it was said with neither resignation nor scorn, but as if strangeness were one of my better points. *You heard her wrong,* said the usual voice in the back of my head, but suddenly the sunshine, the trees, even the grubby hen-scratched vegetable patches among the dilapidated hovels took on a peculiar bright intensity, a kind of glamour. I trailed happily along behind her, resisting the impulse to pick her some flowers. They were scruffy little flowers anyway.

She made a sudden sharp turn behind an abandoned cottage and dove into what looked like an impenetrable thicket. I followed her on faith, and found myself at the beginning of a path winding through the undergrowth, almost a tunnel. The branches met over our heads, lined with gravid buds;

they would be in leaf soon. The air was warmer and full of
fresh earthy smells. Calla took my hand and drew me along.

"There's a place on the hill where it's safe. One of the
ghost places. The Sherank haven't been there since they destroyed it, which means a long time ago, and the local people
are afraid of it. Come on, I'm hungry. It's not far."

"Not far" translated into almost an hour's energetic scramble. Although the path had charm, it was not easy going, and
it disappeared altogether after a while. We pushed on through
a sward of waist-deep grasses, up crumbling terraces of rubble where a hamlet had once clung to the hillside, on to an
upland of dense brambles and scrub cut by an indistinct trail,
by which time I was feeling all the effects of my recent
illness, and halfway sorry we had come; but when we pushed
through the last of the brambles and found ourselves on a
massive stone podium, mossed and shaded, my malaise vanished. We were in a dimple between two peaks of the hilltop,
with a view towards the Gilgard to the north and Malvi Point
to the west. Beyond the far edge of the podium, we could
see the ocean stretching tranquilly to the horizon. Everything
was familiar.

"I know this place," I said wonderingly.

"How can you? You've never been here before."

"But I know it anyway. I've read about it. It's the Contemplation Gardens—built by Oballef Third, I think it was,
and renovated by Tallislef Second about four hundred years
ago." I walked to the centre of the podium and rotated
slowly, fitting the details of the ruins into what I remembered
from the archives.

"The minstrels would sit there, Calla; there was music
from sunup to moonset, every day of the year. Over on that
side there were stone benches under an arbour, and over there
a colonnaded court where you could sit quietly and look at
the sea—" I broke off and skated excitedly across the mossy
stones. There had been a famous mosaic pavement inside that
court, chrysoprase and alabaster and polished coral, one of
the great art treasures of Oballef Third's reign. Gone now,
of course, although a few fragmentary tesserae still lay

among the shattered column drums. I squatted down and rooted in the dust.

Calla followed and sat down on the ivied stump of a column. Smiling up at her, I put into her hand an alabaster tessera, whole except for one crushed corner. "That might bring something on the black market," I said.

"Doesn't this bother you? Seeing it now and knowing what it used to be?"

"It doesn't, somehow. I've accepted what happened. Does it bother you?"

"How could it? We've never known it any different." She shivered and looked dubiously around as if she found the solitude menacing. "There's a strange feel about this place. I'm not sure now we should have come here."

"Don't worry. The only ghosts here would be gentle and contemplative ones. And anyway," I expanded my chest dangerously, "I'm here to protect you."

She laughed at that, not very tactful of her, but it broke the sombreness of her mood. I was glad to hear a real laugh from her, and didn't even mind that it was at my expense.

We ate our lunch sitting close together on the edge of the podium overlooking the old ornamental lake, which Calla referred to, with contemporary accuracy, as "the slough." I could not remember ever being happier, which was in itself curious; a greater curiosity was that Calla was happy too. It also occurred to me that she seemed rather more like a girl than usual, and was warm towards me to an extent that another man might have found encouraging, even seductive. Fortunately, however, I had the voice in the back of my head to tell me not to be a fool; no woman, especially a woman of Calla's spine and fibre, could possibly feel anything for me except tolerance, or friendship at best.

And so I enjoyed the warmth of the illusion, and was happy with her company, and instructed myself very firmly that whatever hopeless nonsense was starting to stir in the depths of my own heart must on no account be allowed to expose itself. I was just starting to realize that I would accept any kindness Calla was prepared to offer me, no matter how small, and be humbly grateful for it.

We finished our lunch and lay flat on our backs on the soft moss, looking up at the sky. After some desultory talk and a long drowsy silence, Calla said, "Tig?"

"Mmm?" I yawned.

"You've not had much to do with women, have you." This was a statement, not a question.

"Only my mother and my cousin Callefiya," I answered truthfully, "and you, in a way. Oh, I was supposed to be affianced a few years ago, some minor peeress in Sathelforn, but she didn't like the look of me, or didn't think a memorian was much of a match, even if I was a Scion of Oballef. If it had been Arko, now—but never mind that. No, I don't know much about women, except what I've read."

"You should have read less and done more," she said, rather sharply.

I turned over on my side to see her face. "Are you angry about something?"

"No. Not at all," she said. "Idiot," she added. She jerked herself upright. "There are clouds moving in—rain before evening, I shouldn't wonder. Come on, Lord of Gil, we'd better be going back."

We retraced our path in silence. Her gaiety had evaporated; mine had been smothered in bafflement. These sudden turnabouts of hers were intriguing, but you could hardly call them restful. I put a hand on her arm as we pushed through the thicket into the settlement, where the hovels were already casting long shadows across the mud. "There is something wrong, isn't there, Calla? Tell me what I said that upset you."

"It's nothing you said," she began impatiently. Then her eyes moved past my shoulder and widened with horror. I spun around.

A Sherkin patrol, at least ten-strong, had emerged from between two cottages. Trailing after them was a long queue of ragged Gilmen, linked together with chains and wooden neck-braces. They were silent, but their mouths were open with the strain of breathing; they stumbled corporately along like a wounded and many-legged beast.

"The levy!" Calla gasped. "Run, Tig!" She grabbed my hand, but an iron arm locked itself suddenly around my

throat from behind and hoisted me almost off my feet. Calla
clawed ineffectually at the gauntlet, then raised her talons
higher, aiming no doubt to knock off the helmet and go for
the eyes; but another trooper appeared behind her, lifted her
bodily and threw her off to the side. I saw her land hard,
very hard, and roll under the thicket, a limp bundle of clothing. Then the arm released me and I fell to my knees, gasping; something hard and cold snapped into place around my
neck.

"Twenty-seven," said one of the troopers in Sheranik.
"Another three, and we can go home. Get him on to the
string." Then, in bad Gillish, "Move on, you lazy louse-
ridden sons of cockroaches. In Iklankish they'll teach you
how to work."

15

"MARCH!" IS WHAT they bellowed at us, but I would hardly
call it marching. We staggered, mainly, jerked almost off our
feet by the stumbles of our neighbours in the string, the collection of fetters around our necks half-throttling us with
every tortured step. The braces were special agony, each being a thin hardwood plank about an arm's-length long with
a hinged neck-hole at each end; we wore two, locking each
of us into helpless partnership with the wretch ahead and the
wretch behind. As well, there was a narrow iron neck-band
linked to a chain that ran the length of the queue, which was
used rather light-heartedly by the troopers to control our
movements.

We were led like cattle all the way to the Gilgard, into
something like a stockpen erected in the courtyard just inside
the main gate of the castle; there were at least a dozen strings

of Gilmen already there and others trailed us in. Our guards allowed us to slump down on to the hard pavement, but the neck-braces linking us were left in place, which forced us to sit as upright as if we were proud and healthy men. Impassive Gilwomen passed along the lines, handing out lumps of bread and ladling tepid water into our mouths.

"I won't go. I won't go. I won't go," the Gilman ahead of me was droning. He knocked away the bread and water when it was offered to him. The woman glanced around hastily, then bent and whispered in his ear. He turned his face away; his chant gained slightly in volume. She shook her head sadly and passed on.

"He's right," muttered the man behind me. "He won't go. He won't live long enough. Brislo, shut up!" His voice was more disgusted than pitying. I snapped my fingers over my shoulder to get his attention.

"What's happening? Where are we being taken?" I whispered.

"What's happening? It's the slave levy, you pocketing fool, what did you think? They'll march us to Malvi tonight, we'll be well on the way to Sher this time tomorrow. That's where we're going."

My heart turned into a kind of cold pudding behind my ribs. I had been hoping that I'd misunderstood that reference to Iklankish, or that the Sherkin had been speaking figuratively. It was a stupid thing to hope—the Sherank were notoriously literal-minded.

And so, we were being carried off to Iklankish: the quest was ending before it had even begun, my life would end in the salt pans of Sher, or deep in the killing mines near Iklankish, or high in the scaffolding of some pretentious new tower in the imperial warcourt. Lords Kekashr and Shree would win this battle without even knowing it. Despairing, I put my head in my hands.

"I won't go. I won't go, I won't go." The monotonous chant in front of me went on and on.

"Hark at Brislo," hissed the man behind me. "No wife, no children, two brothers to make sure his mam doesn't starve— what's he complaining about? What's he got to lose? He'll

die before Malvi, and they'll hoick him out and pull some
other poor sod off the street to make up the levy, maybe
some poor sod with a wife and three children and ailing
old folks and not another soul in the world to take care of
them—"

I understood. "Like you, you mean?"

"Yes, damn you, like me." His voice broke on the final
word.

We sat without speaking for what seemed like a long time.
The last of the light bled out of the sky; the rain Calla had
predicted was still holding off. A group of Sherkin troopers
moved up and down the lines of prisoners, escorting a fat
man in a long healer's robe, who prodded and kneaded and
pulled back unresisting lips to inspect teeth as he went along.
I don't know why he bothered; although a good third of this
miserable company looked too frail for hard labour, and the
others none too healthy either, not one Gilman was released
as being unfit. They approached us from the rear of the
line—the healer gave me a cursory glance and walked on,
paused by mindless chanting Brislo in front, walked on
again. One of the troopers stopped long enough to deliver
the threnodist a kick in the teeth, which had only a temporary
effect. Immediately the Sherkin was gone, the chant picked
up again, slightly slurred. "I won't go. I won't go. I won't
go." By this time I wanted to kick the poor fool myself.

When the inspection party was out of earshot, the man
behind me hissed again. "You. You ahead. What about you?"

"What?"

"Who are you leaving behind? Who's going to starve
without you?"

"Nobody in particular," I said. Perhaps everybody in general, I thought, although there was no cast-iron guarantee I'd
have found the Lady anyway. I thought of Calla: was she
still under that hedge? Had they broken her neck, like a twig
on a branch that just happened to get in their way? You'll
never know, I told myself—and the spasm of pain at that
realization was so sharp through the dull ache of my despair
as to astonish even me.

"Nobody," I repeated out loud.

"Then you're one of the lucky ones," he said bitterly.

We waited. The moon rose from behind the Gilgard and was blotted again by clouds; the rain arrived, dripped morosely on to us for a wretched half hour or so, and then wandered off. Brislo continued to sing his doleful song, the man behind cursed or coaxed him now and then, but eventually lapsed into silence. We were counted several times and inspected once more, this time by a hard-faced Sherkin in civilian dress who made no comment beyond the look of distaste on his face. For an assemblage of perhaps four or five hundred men, we were strangely quiet: apathy, I suppose, resignation to the inescapable. Plus, of course, the fact that anyone who spoke above a whisper was promptly sought out and kicked in the face by one of the guards, all except my tireless chain-mate. "I won't go. I won't go. I won't go." Him, they left alone.

The levy, I found out later, was enforced at irregular intervals and never announced beforetimes. It was like one of those seasonal floods that erupts without warning down the dry watercourses of the desert, sweeping everything before it into oblivion. One moment, a man could be walking innocently down the street with his mind on his own business; the next, staggering under the weight of his chains and gasping for breath, cut off forever from home and friends, destined to be worked to death in Sher with no right of appeal, no hope of escape or rescue. We had heard of it in Exile—the Sherank used the levy system to recruit labour throughout the empire—but I had always imagined that some sort of selection was carried out, based on more than simply being in the wrong place at the moment the levy gangs passed by. It was, I now think, one of the crueller of the many cruelties of Iklankish, and I had walked straight into it.

The thought of rescue did cross my mind, but I discounted it at once. The Web's strength was in its deviousness, not its muscles. And I suspected, rightly, that it had been a very long time since any man had escaped the levy's neck-brace. Anyway, how would any potential rescuers know what had

happened to me? Calla was dead, I was becoming surer of
it. If I closed my eyes, I could see again with what terrible
force she was tossed aside, the awkward angles of the bundle
under the hedge. I ached for Bekri, for Gil, for the Web, for
crazy Brislo, for Callefiya's and Arko's children who would
someday follow me into this desperate madness; I even ached
a little on my own account. Above all, I ached for Calla.

At last something seemed to be happening at the gate. I
could not turn my head to see, but I could hear the jingle-
and-swish of horse trappings and the thunder of many booted
feet. A couple of troopers appeared at the head of each string
and hauled mightily on the chains. Perforce, we staggered to
our feet, most of us. Brislo did not.

"I won't go. I won't go."

The chain tautened with a jerk that nearly took our heads
off and yanked us forwards a pace or two. I stumbled on
something soft, but the neck-brace, now pulling downwards
at a choking angle, prevented me from seeing what it was. I
could guess. The chanting had stopped abruptly with the last
pull on the chain; I suppose Brislo's neck had been broken
instantly. I was being strangled by the weight on my neck-
brace, and couldn't even cry out.

"Easy, now," whispered the man behind me, sounding a
little strangled himself. "Hang on till they come. Keep
breathing."

Why bother? It was friendly of him to suggest it, I told
myself, but why bother? It seemed that bales of fleecy cotton
lint were packing themselves around my head, muffling his
voice, working into my nostrils and mouth and down my
throat, not unpleasantly. I started to float—and then, with a
monstrous click, the pressure fell away, air scalded into my
lungs, the bales lifted off. "This one's still breathing," said
a rough voice in Sheranik. "Hook him up again, we're wasting time."

Gasping, I stumbled forward with the rest. The archway
of the great castle gate passed overhead. "You're lucky," said
my friend behind me. "The poor bugger on the other side of
Brislo was dead before they reached him."

Lucky, I thought. Some luck.

• • •

The streets were deep with mud, dark and deserted. There
was nobody to watch us go by, unless the black squares of
the tenement windows held covert eyes; nobody to hear our
groans, the varied and imaginative threats of the guards, the
maddening chorus of the chains. The rain returned as a
steady cold drizzle.

Right foot, left foot, right foot, left foot—there was no
feeling left in either, but my legs kept on labouring to shift
them. I believe I even fell asleep without breaking the cor-
rosive rhythm of that march, for I seemed at one time to be
flying free of my body and soaring high above the tenement
roofs, watching a long, blind black worm coil its way
through the rain-glossed labyrinth of the city. I tried to pick
out the dark head that was myself, but the procession was
too long, there were too many to choose from.

"Wake up, son. If you fall over, you'll throttle us both."

I blinked and was back again in my raw-necked, leaden-
chested body, wet to the skin. "Thank you," I said ungrate-
fully to the man behind me; right foot, left foot, right foot,
left foot.

At a bend in the road, the troopers stopped each string in
turn and mercifully struck off the long chain. It was a token,
I suppose, that they wanted us to survive at least as far as
Malvi. Lightened by that much, I was able to look around—
and recognized the Swan's Neck, where Calla and I had left
the road only that morning. Behind those hovels, I told myself, Calla's body might still be lying. The rain on my face
turned salty.

They marched us all the way to Malvi that night. Right foot,
left foot, right foot, left foot. The last stretch was done in a
dream, not so pleasant as the flying one, wherein the houses
rising on the outskirts of Malvi became pitchy maws opened
on some sort of terrifying chaos—the details were hazy. I
wakened fully only when the road ended at a broad fortified
square, already striped with the queues that had arrived before us. The air was fresh and tangy; I raised my eyes and
saw the ship that would take us to Iklankish.

Great Lady in Gil, I said to myself. My mission in ruins, Calla probably dead, failure behind me, slavery and death ahead of me, and now they wanted to put me on a ship. Dire memories arose of my journey to Gil: the wretchedness, the tempestuous gut, the inexhaustible supply of vomit. It was finally too much. I rested my chin on the neck-brace and began to laugh.

"Oh, damn. You're not going mad too, are you?" Through my whoops, I barely heard the man behind me. "Quick, son, tell me your name."

I laughed harder. "My name? I'm Lord Tigrallef of Gil," I bubbled, "Son of Cirallef, Scion of Oballef, second in line to the throne of Gil."

"And I'm the Queen of Callon," he said acidly. "*What is your name?*"

I sobered a little. "Call me Tig."

"Tig, then. Stop laughing. They'll beat you bloody if they notice you, but they'll never let you go. Get that through your thick skull. Now tell me about yourself."

His tone was commanding enough to clear my head. I stopped laughing. "I have a brother named Arko," I said, "who lost one leg in an accident. My father died long ago, but my mother refuses to believe it. There was a woman I was very fond of, but I think she's dead too. I'm not a hero, and I get terribly seasick."

I felt his hand on my forearm. "An infusion of calfgrass is good for that—too bad we haven't got any." He was quiet for a moment and then began to talk in a low voice: home, wife and children, old parents, a brother taken in the last levy, three years ago. Tragic, but listening to him was oddly calming, and I have no doubt that he saved my mind that morning, although at the time it hardly seemed like a favour. We talked on in murmurs until a sudden horn-blast brought a hush to the concourse. The next moment, the guards were among us, beating us to our feet.

"Here we go," muttered my friend.

Our string was the fifth to be herded towards the quay. The ship was a big wind-galley, black and forbidding in the sickly moonlight, two banks of oars, masts like towers. At the foot of the gangplank stood a Gillish clerk with a writing palette, an officer with a squad of troopers and, off to the side, a tall still figure enveloped in a hooded cloak. Right foot, left foot, right foot, left foot; the gangplank approached. I looked up and saw the ship's black mouth swallowing the last men of another string. Our turn next.

"Tig!"

A trick of the ears, surely, but very clear. Startled, I snapped my head around in the neck-brace. The officer by the gangplank caught the movement and pointed at me. "That one!"

He approached with the clerk. Both of them peered dubiously into my face. I lifted my eyes and looked at them squarely with the last of my strength.

The clerk said in Sheranik, "He fits the description well enough, sir. And it's a string that was levied near the slough."

"Well, all right, they all look the same to me, the buggers, but if he fits the description—"

They turned to look behind them at the hooded figure. It nodded.

Rough gauntlets on my shoulders; a wrench, and the neck-braces fell away, one after the other. I staggered, unaware until that second how much I had depended on their support. Hands seized me from behind and dragged me out of the string, shoved me towards the cloaked figure. The string moved on. I could see the back of my friend's head as he stumbled away from me up the gangplank. I never saw his face. I never knew his name.

"Wait," I cried, but I was spun around by the hooded man and frogmarched through a small gate at the near end of the compound. We came out into the narrow streets of Malvi, still deserted at that hour; my companion, whose fingers dug into my arm, said nothing. A fresh terror took me—why was I, alone of five hundred, excused from the levy? They knew my name, they knew who I was, that was the only possible explanation: Lord Kekashr was claiming another Scion. Suddenly I knew I would far rather be on that ship, anonymous and puking my belly up, than back in the Gilgard in the governor's personal care.

My companion pulled me into an alleyway that looked blind, between a warehouse and a high stone wall. Without warning, halfway along the alley, he gave me a shove that sent me sprawling face-down on to the muddy ground. I braced myself for the first kick. None came. When I turned on to my back, the moon was in my face and the alley was empty.

Almost empty. A grey figure like a ghost materialized in the blind end of the alley and drifted silently towards me. My jaw dropped when I recognized it. I sat up and made the Tatakil sign of greeting for a revenant from the dead. It stopped, gazing down at me. "Oh, Calla," I whispered, "I knew they'd killed you."

The ghost hunkered down at my side. "But I'm not dead, Tig," it said.

16

CALLA MADE A mystery out of what was already a miracle. She cut through my joy at seeing her alive and brushed away my questions. "There are things you don't need to know." That was the sum of what she told me.

Sunrise was coming. Glancing at the sky, Calla pulled me to the supposedly blind end of the alley, through a gap just wide enough to squeeze past, into a yard beside the warehouse. Beyond that, I lost track of where she led me, retaining only an impression of dark lanes and dirty narrow passages like tunnels, steep stairways between overhanging buildings, hidden entrances into cavernous cellars with hidden exits—also an impression that the entire population of

Malvi was blind, since nobody seemed to see us, not even when Calla's route took us through a cellar room where at least a dozen men were at breakfast. We fetched up at last in the attic of what had been quite an imposing villa, though its airy chambers were now cut by a multitude of thin partitions and the garden I could see through a hole in the wall was a maze of lean-tos dotted with smashed statuary.

A Flamen was there, one of Faruli's pupils in the science of healing. He tutted over the weeping sores on my neck and applied a dry poultice that stung mightily at first, but deadened all feeling after a few moments. A child came in with a large bowl of broth, to which the Flamen added some herbs. Calla prevailed on me to drink every drop, though my stomach felt like a clenched fist and the herbs left a bitter, bilious taste.

"Now you must try to sleep," she said firmly. "We're leaving for the city tonight by a roundabout way and you'll need all your strength."

"Tell me first," I said.

Calla glanced at the Flamen, who discreetly glided out of the room. "Tell you what?"

"Why the Sherank released me. Who the hooded personage was. What you had to do to get me out."

"There are things," she repeated, "that you do not need to know."

"That won't do."

"It will have to." She looked at me gravely. "How could I have faced Bekri if I let you be taken to Sher? It would have killed him. You were with me, and I led you straight into the hands of the levy. So I did what was necessary—you don't need to know what that was, nor does the First Flamen." She paused. "Did you really think I was dead?"

"Yes. But that has nothing to do with—"

"Were you sad?"

The question pushed me off balance. "Of course I was sad." My internal censor stopped me at that point, before any nonsense emerged about how particularly grievously sad.

She sighed as if suddenly very tired. "Go to sleep, Tig.

Maybe someday I'll tell you. Until then, don't ask." She
turned to leave.

I opened my mouth and shut it again. When she was gone,
I lowered myself like an old man to the pallet and obediently
shut my eyes.

Though I felt like a piece of chewed string, sleep was a long
time coming. Apart from the mystery Calla had left unan-
swered, the main reason was guilt. Guilt at lying on what
felt like the softest pallet in Gil, while my levy-mates still
sweated upright in their neck-braces; guilt at being on dry
land; guilt at having a full belly; guilt at being free. My
rational side explained patiently that those men would gain
nothing by having me share their suffering, whereas Gil
would gain everything if my mission succeeded, which it
couldn't possibly do if I were off panning salt in Sher. Very
true; but, however persuasive this was, it did little to blot out
the image of my nameless, faceless friend trudging up the
gangplank to slavery and death.

We left Malvi that night using Calla's roundabout route,
which roughly doubled the distance. My limbs felt like they
were tacked on by a bad tailor; the sores on my neck started
to bleed through the poultice. Therefore we stopped fre-
quently to rest on the mazy paths and at the edges of freshly
ploughed fields, sipping from a gourd of bittersweet tonic
which the healing Flamen had given us. Once, while we were
resting on a slight rise that overlooked the Malvi road, several troops of Sherank passed below us headed for the city,
close enough so that we could hear the clinking of their
weapons. At their head was a small group on horseback. I
stretched my neck cautiously to see over the bushes.

"Isn't that Lord Shree? The one with a crest?"

"Maybe," said Calla. She didn't sound very interested.
"Better keep down."

I craned again. "I'd wager those are the troops that took
us to Malvi last night. There're certainly enough of them."

"Maybe," Calla repeated.

"I don't remember seeing Lord Shree at the harbour, though."

She shrugged without interest, and said, "Malvi's a big place now. We'll wait till they're well past before going on."

Just after sunrise, and without further incident, we arrived at the headquarters of the Web. We slept the rest of that day.

I expected Bekri to be on my side; that is, I expected him to extract from Calla, forthwith and with no mucking about, exactly how she had talked the Sherank into letting me go free. He disappointed me.

"There are things we do not need to know," he said.

I was getting tired of hearing that. We were sitting in the council chamber and Mysheba was trying valiantly to make me eat something nourishing but horrible. I waved the bowl away. "I need to know."

Bekri shifted his eye to Calla, who was sitting impassively on a cushion by the end of the sofa. Jebri hovered by the door. For a change, he was not wringing his little hands; he glanced at me from time to time, but mostly he watched Calla. He looked thoughtful, and not very happy.

"Calla?" said Bekri. "I can't blame the Scion for being curious, and I'm rather curious myself. Are you able to tell us anything?"

"No, Revered Bekri." She repeated it with her fingers—a firm and final no.

"You see, Tig? Calla, you may go. Mysheba, I really don't think the Scion is going to eat that. Perhaps you could bring up some of your lovely pâté?" He waited until aunt and niece had left the room, and then continued, "Tig, there are questions we do not ask in the Web."

"But surely for something like this—"

"A remarkable achievement, I agree," he broke in. "The first time in Kekashr's rule that anyone has been forgiven the levy. But I can't press her."

"Why not?"

"Because she doesn't wish to tell us, and I trust her to have a good reason."

"I don't understand. She's in the Web—you're the First

Flamen. What reason could be good enough?"

"I can think of one," he said dryly. "Many of our people have secret contacts in the Gilgard—some so secret and so valuable that the Web at large cannot be trusted with their names. We do have the occasional traitor, you know. Isn't the right, Jebri?"

"Alas, yes." The Second Flamen sat down beside Bekri.

I watched them both narrowly. "But she could trust you two, couldn't she—and me? We're hardly about to turn traitor."

"Even the most loyal can be tortured, Tig. Could you guarantee your own silence? I couldn't."

I looked at his scars, tried to imagine them raw and bleeding, tried to imagine the process that carved them into his body all those years ago. It was an illuminating exercise. "I suppose I couldn't either," I said grudgingly.

"Well, then."

We sat in silence for a few moments; I was more than halfway convinced, but still feverish with questions. Finally I said, "If you can't require Calla to tell us, at least give me your opinion. Do you think she has a contact in the Gilgard?"

"Probably. Almost certainly."

"What are we talking about, then? Bribery? Blackmail?" I paused, not liking the next word. "Seduction?"

"One or another, maybe all three, maybe some other form of collaboration."

I was shocked. "Calla's not a collaborator. She couldn't be."

"Why not?" He leaned forward earnestly. "Collaboration and resistance are fingers on the same hand. Think of Calvo—scullery master for the Sherank, rich and fat while the rest of us are poor and thin; who could be more of a collaborator than Calvo? He's hated by those who don't know what he does for Gil. Without Sherkin protection, he'd be dead in a day. And yet he's a loyal member of the Web, and more valuable than any of our firebrands."

There was a brisk knock at the door, breaking the mood. Mysheba peered in with a covered plate in her hands and such determination on her face that she looked like Calla's twin. "My lord?" she said.

Bekri grinned and settled back on the sofa. "There's no escape for you this time. Take him and feed him, Mysheba. Tig, put yourself in her hands—she's had her instructions from Faruli. You need to be well on your feet in four days from now."

"You mean—?"

"The date was fixed before we knew you'd been taken in the levy. Calvo can't change it now, except by moving it back by another month. Will you be strong enough?"

"I'll be strong enough." I took the plate from Mysheba, shut my eyes, and began to eat. But after a few mouthfuls, I paused with the spoon halfway to my lips. "There is one thing, Bekri. There was a man behind me in the levy who was kind to me. He must have lived somewhere near the Swan's Neck; he had a wife, three children and ailing parents, and his brother was taken in the last levy. Can we find his family and help them?"

Bekri and Mysheba exchanged a glance that was partly pity. Jebri rubbed his hands officiously. "His name?" he asked.

"I don't know. I've told you everything I do know."

Jebri shrugged. "We can try to find them, my lord; but remember how many families are left destitute every time we're levied. We haven't the resources to help them all."

There was a flash of anger inside my head. Not at the Second Flamen, though he was irritating enough; not even directly at the Sherank, but at our helplessness, at the fate that placed us in a lifeboat with a limited number of ropes to throw to the drowning. "Help these ones," I said curtly.

Three days passed. Calla was friendly but distant, like an amiable stranger, except during the mock battles that Faruli recommended for (ha!) gentle exercise. At those times, she badgered me and lectured me, and occasionally swatted me comfortably on the back when I scored a point or got past her guard. That was the most warmth I had from her, but it was satisfying enough. For the rest, I choked down everything Mysheba put before me, swallowed Faruli's most dire potions without a murmur and blocked everything except the moment from my mind. Suddenly, without my taking much notice, the days were gone and it was the eve of my new career as a washer of dishes and a saviour of nations.

Mysheba sent me to bed early that night, but her good intentions were wasted. I tossed on my pallet for what seemed like hours, wide-eyed and freezing. Images of Calla mixed with images of Lord Shree in his crested helmet, of Brislo, of leisurely death in the Gilman's Pleasure; and then fragments of Exile began to intrude, Arko's stump of a leg, Marori's dark warnings, the resigned faces of the training Flamens as they watched me, time after time, bungle my lessons. It was impossible to believe that I would do any better when the real test came. At last I flung myself off the pallet and went to the little window—it was a more pleasing view by night, the darkness masking the squalor, and the lights of Gilgard Castle, no matter who lit them, still beautiful. I was watching a thin horned moon lift itself off the summit of the mountain when someone slid quietly through the curtain and padded to the bed.

"Tig?" Calla's voice.

"Here, by the window."

"Is anything wrong? Mysheba was worried about you. She said you hardly ate any supper."

"I wasn't hungry."

"Oh, weren't you?" Mild disbelief. "You should have been. And why aren't you asleep?"

"I can't sleep. I think I'm afraid." I turned back to the window, embarrassed by my own frankness.

"Me too."

"You, Calla? Afraid?"

"Terrified." She crossed the room softly and stood close beside me. She was telling the truth. Even from a few inches away, I could sense the tension in her body. There was a long silence while we looked out together over the dark rooftops of Gil. Calla broke it at last.

"Tig? You've done well in the past weeks. I'm starting to think you just might survive." For a moment I thought she was trying to reassure me; but a tremor in her voice gave me the mad idea that she was reassuring herself. Very kind of her to care, I thought. I said, "Of course I'll survive."

She looked at me gravely—I could just make out her face. "You'll find the Lady."

"I'm sure I will." I wasn't, actually, but the lie was rewarded. Calla's eyes closed and her face relaxed. She moved closer, until our bodies touched; her dark hair, brushed and smelling lightly of soap and woodsmoke, came to rest against my cheek. Awkwardly, I put my arms around her. Warmth filtered through the rags dividing us.

We stood so for a few moments. I could feel the firmness of her body, and was ashamed of my own soft and flabby frame—until I remembered that the Flamens and the Gilgut had conspired to pare my fat away. Then it occurred to me that it didn't matter a flea's-weight what my body was like— this could only be a kind of comradely embrace, however nice it felt. She would move away in a second and give some tart instruction for the morning; she would look at me coolly and remind me, though not in so many words, that I was a clown, a coward and a weakling; she would—

She kissed me; her lips tasted of some aromatic herb. Certain pleasurable sensations, not unlike those experienced while transcribing the *Erotic Mistifalia* in the archives, began to stir in parts of my body that I generally ignored. We regarded each other, our faces on a level and only an inch or two apart. I coughed.

"Well, I—I suppose we should say good night," I stammered.

"Why?" she said. She kissed me again.

17

SOMEONE WAS SHAKING my shoulder. My other arm was being pressed down by a warm and pleasant but unidentified weight. I lifted myself on the free elbow and blinked sleepily into Mysheba's candlelit face. She smiled down on me.

"You must get up now, Lord Tigrallef. I've brought you some breakfast. Oh, and Bekri wants to see you before you go. Hurry now, get dressed!" She patted my head and vanished through the curtain. Muffled from the council chamber, there came the sounds of feet and low voices.

I freed my shoulder and sat up, yawning, aware that something was different this morning, something momentous and wonderful and not terribly well-understood, but completely beyond me for the moment. Of course I realized that this was to be the day I first entered the Gilgard, the seat of my ancestors, the fortress of my enemies, more or less in the footsteps of my father—though he wouldn't have dreamed of entering through the scullery—but that wasn't it. It was something much happier than that. I sneezed and gave up, and peered at the tray Mysheba had left on the floor. There were two beakers of broth on it. On the pallet beside me, Calla stretched.

The mists cleared. "Great Lady in Gil," I said faintly.

Calla reached over me to pick up a beaker, briefly exposing bare shoulders, a flash of white breast. "Sleep well?" she asked. "Come on, drink up, it's nearly sunrise. We want to make a good impression on the Koroskans, don't we?"

"But Calla—" I stared at her. She blew on the broth, sipped it as she climbed nimbly over me and started rooting about in the scatter of our rags on the floor. "But Calla—"

I repeated stupidly. Her back was narrow and very smooth, and the sight of it robbed me of speech. She pulled a grimy vest over it. "Your breakfast is getting cold," she said.

"But Calla—" I said for the third time.

She paused with her britches at her knees, and looked at me curiously. "What is it, Tig? Are you feeling all right?"

"No. Yes!" I groped among a thousand things to say, some of them rather eloquent. "But Calla—"

A lovely, tousled smile. Fully dressed, she sat down on the bed beside me and continued calmly with her breakfast. "Never mind, Tig," she said. "What happened, happened. Think of it this way—we were finally able to sleep."

"Sleep!" Memories were flooding back now, none of them involving sleep. My hands shook when I tried to pick up the second beaker, and a few drops of broth splashed on to my chest, which was naked—as was the rest of me. "How can you be so casual?" I demanded. "Was that all it meant to you? A way of putting yourself to sleep?"

"What? No, of course not."

"Then how do you feel?"

"About what?" She looked at me innocently over the beaker.

I slammed my own beaker down on the floor, untasted, grimacing as hot broth slopped over my hand. "About me. About the fact that you shared my bed last night. About the fact that we—"

"I feel fine, Lord of Gil," she interrupted coolly, "but there's no time now for talking. Just drink up."

I took an angry, unwise gulp of broth. While I was still gagging at the hot grease in my throat, she padded to the door. Without another word, she looked back at me, her face in shadow, and then was gone.

"Calla! Wait!" I cried. I threw off the blanket and stumbled naked after her through the curtained doorway—and halted. The whole Council of Flamens was there, solemn-faced, hugely dignified, tactfully silent, decked out in ragtag green regalia and arranged in a ceremonial semicircle with Bekri at the midpoint. I squawked with horror and dived back into the bedchamber. A few moments later, I stepped out again to receive, fully clothed, the honours for a departing hero. Calla might have warned me.

We filed out, Calla in the lead, all silent, all shivering in the early morning chill. There were four of us: myself, Calla and Sibba and Beliso, the two youngsters who would be our watchdogs in the scullery. The streets were empty between the looming tenements; the Great Garden was a pool of darkness, rustling with dogs and shulls feeding on the dross of yesterday's market. We cut across it past the white glimmer of the Lady, on to a broad thoroughfare that was the remnant of the Scions' Ride, linking the Great Garden with the south gate of Gilgard Castle. The seven stone arches that once spanned the Ride were gone; at the castle end, where the Silver Gate used to stand, was an ugly rampart of reused masonry, broken by a massive gate inset with a small door. I could guess where the arches had gone.

"They tore down the arches to build that," Sibba whispered, unconsciously confirming my guess. She was a small girl with a plain, pleasant face, who had sat with me playing finger-sticks a few times during my recovery from the Gilgut. As far as finger-sticks went, we were evenly matched; anything else, I couldn't say. Beliso was even smaller, with beautiful white teeth and terrible skin. He was said to be the only Webling who looked better in street camouflage than out of it, because the dirt covered his pimples. The two of them seemed more typical of the youth of Gil than Calla—cheekier, lighter in manner when no Sherank were about, and somehow less honest; they reminded me of beggar-youth I'd seen in Sathelforn. Calla had more of the Heroic Code in her design, though I would never have dared to tell her so.

We slogged through the mud of the dark streets, Sibba and Beliso a few paces ahead. I took advantage of that distance to whisper to Calla, "Bekri knows, doesn't he?"

"About what?"

"Stop it, Calla! About us, about last night. Does he know?"

"Well, what of it?"

That was an impossible question. I trudged along by her side trying to work out a sensible answer, then gave it up.

Anyway, I told myself, the entire council probably knew, given the disastrous start to my ritual send-off, and not one of them had lifted an eyebrow. And what, I demanded, was the etiquette of sex? I hadn't the faintest notion. The Secrets of the Ancients were mute on the subject, and all the Heroic Code held was a section on cold showers. All I could be sure of was that seduction by Calla had been astonishing, illuminating, revelatory and exceptionally pleasant, and had pushed fear firmly to the back of my head.

The sky was greying in the east as we neared the rampart gate, casting the graceless lines of the rooftops, warty with penthouse hovels, into silhouette. An array of Sherkin footsoldiers trooped towards us, turning my stomach to water, but they passed without a glance. Ahead of us, I could see a small crowd gathering at the door; above them, just starting to catch the dawn, was the soaring miracle of the Gilgard. My heart thumped painfully against my ribs and I almost forgot about Calla for the moment.

We joined the mob at the little door as the light grew. A few of the hooded figures eyed us listlessly. Most ignored us. They stood in the muck of the street in apathetic clusters, not speaking, hands tucked into their armpits for warmth, chins drooping almost on to their chests. I glanced furtively around, trying to work out which of them might be members of the Web, until Sibba, who was closest, elbowed me discreetly in the side—eyes were safest when they didn't leave the ground for long. Which seemed to hold true even when no Sherank were in sight; which led me to wonder, in turn, who the Gillish traitors in our midst might be.

At last the small inset door opened and a pair of Sherkin troopers stepped out, followed by the fattest man I had ever seen in my life. He was bald and chalky-skinned, and a long sharp Koroskan nose thrust out between his plump cheeks. His little pouched eyes surveyed the crowd irritably. From Jebri's description, he had to be Flax, the head underchef, one of the Koroskans imported to run the Gilgard kitchens. He was not quite fat enough to be the chef.

"Come on, you lazy pack of shulls," he growled in heavily accented Gillish. "Where are the new ones? You two? You wait here. The rest of you to your places!" He disappeared inside.

Sibba and Beliso, who had taken their jobs several days before, shuffled in with the rest of the crowd. Calla and I waited, heads subserviently hanging, until the street was empty but for us and the two impassive troopers. I examined them covertly: well-fed, well-armed, well-cloaked against the cold. Beside them, Calla looked small and helpless, like a child flanked by giants. After some time, Flax's head appeared at the door again.

"Get in here! Shirking already, eh? We'll teach you how to work, you ugly piles of dung, but first I want to see your hands."

We followed him through the door into a dark tunnel through the thickness of the rampart, leading to a musty, flagged courtyard. We stuck our hands out. He inspected them with disgust, fully justified, and spat on the paving stones.

"Crusted with filth, like the rest of your dirty little country. Oh well, a few hours in the scullery will peel you of a layer or two. Take that corridor, and report to Master Calvo."

We started past him, but his fat hand shot out and grabbed Calla's shoulder. She stiffened. Appraisingly, he pushed her hood back, peered into her face, lifted her mass of stringy hair. "The men of Koroska," he remarked, "have more discerning eyes than those louts from Sher. There's something young and tasty under all that grime, isn't there, my petal?"

His hand moved slowly down her body, kneading here and there; her lips tightened, but she stood her ground. My hands twitched for a knife, for a club, for the feel of his fat throat. Calla saw me start to move, and warned me with a flick of her fingers: *do nothing*. At last he shoved her away, but not ungently.

"Too skinny, like all you bitches in Gil," he said. "Still, a few weeks in the kitchen may fatten you up if you make the right friends. This dirty little cockroach here, is he your man?"

"No," she said firmly, just before I could shout yes, I was, and I would kill him if he touched her again with his flabby paws. I caught the look in Calla's eye, and shut my mouth.

"It's as well for him he's not," Flax grinned. "Play the proper game, my flower, and you may find yourself a softer job." He slapped her playfully on the bottom, then roared at us to go. As we walked down the dark steamy corridor to the scullery, I was choking on anger and frustration.

"I wanted to kill him," I spat. "I swear, Calla, if he mauls you again, I'll—"

"I'm grateful for the intention, Tig," she interrupted calmly, "but you'll do nothing of the sort. You have a mission, remember? Anyway, I can take care of myself."

"Against that lump of oxlard?"

"Yes."

I stopped and swung her to face me. "You wouldn't—"

"Let him touch me?" She shrugged. "I suppose I'd have to. It happens all the time, though not yet to me. Anyway, he's probably just pimping for the Sherank."

"And that makes it better?" I stared at her, horrified.

"Well, it makes it no worse. Forget it, Tig, with luck we'll be in the between-ways tomorrow, and it will never come to anything." She started to walk on, but I stayed where I was.

"No. It's off, Calla. We'll have to think of another way to get me in. I can't—I won't let you—"

She faced me with her hands on her hips. She looked more pitying than impatient. "What are you worried about?"

"You know, that he'll—that they'll—" I groped for unfamiliar words. She laughed.

"Look here, Tigrallef, every woman in Gil takes that risk every day. Are you going to protect us all? Of course not, because you can't—except, perhaps, by finding the Lady."

"But—"

"As for what's happened between us," she added severely, "it is nothing to do with that. Do you understand?"

I bit back the words I really wanted to say, and surrendered. "All right. But I still don't like it."

We proceeded in silence to the door of the scullery, where wisps of steam eddied outwards in the draft. More than ever, Calla confused me; how could she be so proud, so fierce at times, and yet stand still for that fat Koroskan's touch? And last night—I buried the thought of last night, but not before an aftershock of that rushing, flooding delightfulness shook my vitals. I glanced sideways at Calla and found her smiling at me affectionately.

"Good luck, Tig," she said.

I leaned forward and kissed her quickly on the mouth. Then, together, we stepped through the great door and into the scullery.

18

GREAT TANKS OF water bubbling above a furnace the size of my bedchamber; sweating crockers, dim beyond fogbanks of steam, elbow-deep in vats of dirty dishes. That was the scullery, or as much of it as I could see. Through an archway at the far end of the room I could make out a red, smoke-filled cavern, which I knew was the first of the kitchens proper. There was a powerful smell of baking bread in the air, underlaid by the rich reek of grilled meat. After several weeks on a diet of shull and sand-biscuit, it was maddening.

"Here comes Calvo," Calla whispered.

I followed her eyes. If I had not known Calvo was a Gil-man and in the Web, I'd have taken him for a Koroskan, and a nasty one at that. Not that he was particularly fat—but he was clean and sleek and wore the white robe and red sash of a Koroskan mercenary cook, and he scowled ferociously at us as he approached.

"Move, you dirty little layabout sewer-lice," he growled. "I'll have you know right now there's no room in my scullery for any nose-picking, arse-heavy slackers." His fingers signalled: *Welcome, my lord. You do us a great honour.*

Calla and I cringed appropriately. On the edge of my vision, I became aware of a hulking Sherkin guard in full battledress, with the beak of his helmet pointed our way. "Come along, come along, why are you standing there like a pair of witless chickens?" Calvo went on irritably. He cuffed me on the side of the head, a hard, honest blow. *Apologies, my lord. It has to look real. I'm sorry.*

My blurred eyes barely caught the fingerwords. *So am I*, I signalled. I coughed and quavered, "Where do we—?"

He cuffed me again, not quite so hard. "Speak only when I tell you to, snot," he growled; and added: *follow me, my lord. I've set aside a place where you'll be safe while you get your bearings.*

He turned and marched through the roiling steam towards the far corner of the room, on the other side of the water-furnace. I felt, or imagined I felt, the Sherkin's dark eyes boring into my back through the slit in his helmet. Calvo led us to an empty vat and turned the spigot to start it filling from the tank of boiling water. He glowered around at the nearby crockers and they all looked away. The Sherkin guard was mistily visible where we had left him.

Calvo leaned close to us and spoke in a low voice. "I've assigned Sibba and Beliso to this vat as your feeders, and I've placed you close to the hidden door, as Bekri asked, but I understand you won't venture anywhere today. Is that correct?"

Calla murmured, "Yes, today we'll just be crockers. But you're arranging cover for tomorrow?"

"No problem about that. But I'm glad you're making no move today—our masters are feasting this afternoon and the scullery always seems to be short-handed. Tomorrow will be a lighter day." His voice changed suddenly. "Do you think you can manage that, you skittle-headed oaf?" *Watch out!* his fingers flashed.

I gulped. A menacing Sherkin silhouette was gliding towards us through the steam. "Oh yes, sir, I can manage that, sir," I said fervently. Calvo stalked away to rant at the cowering crockers by the next vat. The Sherkin moved on. I sighed and tested the water with my finger. It was scalding hot.

• • •

It seemed odd to me that the Sherank, notoriously horrid in their habits, could be so finicky about their tableware. Sibba and Beliso trooped back and forth from the maw of the dumbwaiter, hauling an endless supply of greasy trenchers, plates, beakers and *krishank*, the multiple-spouted drinking bottles shaped like fat-bodied spiders. Everything had to sparkle before it left our vat; particular care had to be taken to clear the delicate spouts of the *krishank*, which were plugged solid with dried lees by the time they reached us. The skinny bottle-brushes provided for this task left our fingertips scored and smarting; our eyes ached from peering up the tiny apertures. There came a bad moment when Calla nearly dropped one, and caught it just in time.

"Stupid design for a bottle anyway," she grumbled, cradling the vessel in her arms until Sibba could take it from her. "Look at it, as soon as you pour something in the top, it runs out these little spouts around the bottom. What use is that?"

"The fith-beer ceremony," I said, scouring away at a trencher. "Eight Sherank sit in a circle, with that thing in the middle. When the beer gets poured in the top, they have to drink together from the spouts as long as the supply lasts. It's supposed to signify brotherhood—suckled by the same beer-pot, something like that. Apparently it can get quite messy, so be glad we're not working in the laundry."

Calla looked at me curiously as Sibba bore the bottle off. "How did you know that?" she asked.

"I read about it. I read everything I could find about the Sherank. There's a fair amount in the archives in Exile." I passed the clean trencher over to Beliso, who had just arrived with another armload of dirty ones.

Calla plunged her hands into the water, looking profoundly thoughtful. "Well, then. Do you speak any Sheranik?" she asked in a guarded voice.

"Yes, not badly. I can read it, too. What about you?"

"I know some obscenities and insults. That's all we ever hear from them in Sheranik. Anything else gets said in Gillish."

"There's not much to Sheranik beyond that," I grinned.
"There's no literature as such, just some folklore, mainly
military and dynastic traditions. The grammar is simple once
you get used to the tenses, though I admit I had difficulty
with the vocabulary. Did you know they have seventeen different adverbs to describe the way blood exits from a wound?
And thirty-three technical terms for positions on the blade of
a sword? And twenty-six different words for—"

"Hush," Calla hissed.

"Huh?"

"I said, you still owe me three tokens, you scrounging
bastard, and I want them back today." *Don't look behind you.*

My shoulders instinctively hunched. "I already paid you
your pocketing tokens," I snapped. "And anyway, it was only
two tokens."

"It was three—and you borrowed them back again the next
day."

"That's shullshit! I never did!"

"You did so, you pig-son."

"Did not, bitch."

"Son of a shull."

"Hag."

We let our voices trail off into muttered insults, scrubbing
industriously all the while. The menacing shadow that had
swallowed my own on the surface of the vat gradually moved
away, the only noise behind me being the faint clink-clink
of well-oiled armour. When the Sherkin was definitely gone,
I sighed with relief.

"That was not bad," Calla murmured. "You catch on
quickly."

I suppressed a grin. Rule One in the code of the Web: if
a Sherkin comes within earshot, pick a fight with the nearest
friend. I suppose they thought if we were quarrelling
amongst ourselves, we could hardly be hatching trouble for
them—or maybe they just enjoyed the sound of a good row.
It was something the Flamens-in-Exile would never have understood.

"I pray by the Lady he didn't hear what we were talking
about," I whispered.

"He couldn't have. Or if he did hear, he couldn't have understood, otherwise we'd be halfway to the south dungeon by now. But Tig—"

"Hmmm?"

"Does Bekri know you can speak Sheranik?"

I peeled at a stubborn encrustation with my fingernail. "Yes, he knows. Strangely enough, he didn't seem very interested, just like the Flamens-in-Exile. They never bothered to teach it to any of the other Scions, you know. And I didn't learn it because of the mission, I studied it on my own long before the Flamens shipped me off to be a hero."

"Why on earth?"

"Out of interest. For pleasure. Perhaps because it was there. I always enjoyed studying languages."

"You have an odd idea of fun."

"That's what Arko always said. It's what I always said to Arko, too."

"Your brother? The one who lost his leg? Tell me about him, Tig."

I rinsed a pair of beakers under the running water, thinking about Arko. Arkolef, the handsome one, the hero, the one who should have come; it struck me suddenly that, but for his accident, I would be working comfortably in the archives at this moment, while he would almost certainly be dead meat and bones. Perhaps back in Exile they were already in mourning for me—after all, I had been gone nearly six weeks, and one week was usually ample to kill a Scion. I watched the water fill the beakers and overflow into the vat. My mother would insist I was still alive, of course, but nobody would believe her.

"Tig? You can put those beakers down now. They're clean."

"Oh? Oh. Yes, of course." I placed the beakers upside-down on the stone draining board. Softly, as we worked, breaking off now and then for sessions of strategic name-calling, I told Calla about Arkolef, about my mother, about Exile, about the delights of the archives and the antics of my training Flamens. Somehow, the long dull hours passed. Believe it or not, I was happy.

Two things, however, hovered unpleasantly on the outskirts of my attention. One was the Sherkin guard; the other, a small door hidden by a cupboard, only a few paces behind and to the right of us. Its existence was marked on the map inside my head; I knew what lay beyond it. And I knew that my mission would truly begin when I opened that door. Tomorrow. The great roasting pans from the feast were the last things we crockers had to wash that day—so heavy that two feeders had to carry one between them, so big that each one filled an entire vat. Calla and I had to bend until our heads were inside the pan to get at the luscious scab of juices and charred meat fibres crusting the bottom. I took a deep sniff, dizzy with the intoxicating smell. Calla slapped my hand away as I reached down.

"Don't sample it," she warned me, "it's punishable."

I watched sadly as she threw the soap in and directed a stream of hot water on to the first appetizing food I'd seen in weeks. By the time we'd finished peeling and scouring and were ready to rinse the pan, my shoulders were creaking with the strain.

Calvo came by as Sibba and Beliso carried the great pan away to the storeroom. There were no Sherank in sight. Pretending to inspect the vat, Calvo whispered urgently to us.

"It went well today. You'll be let in tomorrow without any questions—you must arrange to be the first crockers through the door. I'll set up a diversion first thing, while the guard is still counting the incomers. The cupboard will be pulled away from the wall, just far enough to let you get past it. I won't have time to say this tomorrow—the Lady bless you, Scion of Oballef, and guide you to her hiding place. Good luck!"

He strode off to scream at a pair of crockers across the room. Calla and I picked up the rags we had discarded serially through the day as the temperature in the scullery rose and slowly put them on. My hands were raw from the hot water and blistered from holding the scrubbing stone; my whole body was aching. From the way she moved, Calla was in a similar state.

We joined the pay queue, and received our two miserable

tokens and our parcel apiece of cast-off food. I sniffed mine as we trudged down the rampart tunnel. "Porridge. Ecch. What did you get?"

"Mutton bones, I think. The paymaster must like me."

Which reminded me of Flax, the lecherous Koroskan, who, even as I thought of him, suddenly appeared in the plentiful flesh, standing just inside the street door and counting the scullions as they went out. When he saw Calla, he moved to block the door.

We stood stiffly in front of him, clutching our parcels. He reached out to lift Calla's unresisting hand. "A pity," he said softly, "for these shapely hands to get all rough and red in the scullery. We'll see what can be done, shall we? Goodbye for now, my flower."

Laughing deep in his throat, he stood aside to let us by.

19

WHEN WE GOT home, the kitchen was warm and steamy and full of people. Mysheba immediately put a large bowl of indeterminate stew in front of me. I pushed it aside after a mouthful or two; a vague gloom had been growing through all the weary trudge home, and my belly was full of it. On the other hand, Calla, Sibba and Beliso dug in heartily, chattering to the kitchen's resident mix of the clean and the street-dirty, Sibba with a small child on her lap, Calla performing between mouthfuls a faithful and well-received impression of fat Flax. I sat there for as long as I could stand it and then slipped out, unnoticed by any but Mysheba.

I tramped alone up the staircase, unbothered for once by the creaks and wood-groans and the abyss on my left. On the landing by the council chamber, I stopped for a moment and listened at the crack. Low voices—so Bekri was not alone. I banged on the door and Jebri opened up for me. I was in no spirit for Jebri.

Bekri was lying on his couch, covered with a blanket. Faruli was there, and Corri the Third Flamen and a few others, but I hardly noticed them. "Revered Bekri, I must talk with you," I said. "Alone," I added, with a perfunctory gesture of greeting to the others.

"My lord Tigrallef," Jebri began pompously, but Bekri cut him off.

"You heard the Scion, Jebri." His voice was noticeably weaker than when I'd seen him in the morning. When the others had gone, filing reluctantly out of the little door to the back staircase, Bekri hoisted himself painfully to a sitting position and pointed to the couch beside him. "So, Tig—what's so urgent?"

"Urgent? Nothing. I just wanted to talk with you. And without Jebri."

"Why? Jebri means well."

"I know. But he's a little too much like a Flamen-in-Exile. I couldn't bear it right now."

Bekri grinned asymmetrically. "I hear it went well in the Gilgard," he said. "I've been waiting for you and Calla to report."

"It went well enough. No dishes broken."

"And you talked to Calvo?"

I fingered the bruise on my cheek. "Several times."

"Very good, Tig. So—the end is approaching."

There was enough ambiguity in that to make me stop and think for a few seconds. Bekri meantime picked up a thin sheaf of papers from the floor by his couch and held them out to me. "Since you're here, you may as well look at this. Malviso's report on Lord Shree."

"What's in it?" I was too tired to decipher Malviso's cramped writing, interlined as it was with some sort of Sheranik proclamation. Paper was hard to come by in Gil.

"Oh, in most respects the usual history of a young Sherkin warlord. Born and raised in Iklankish; educated at the war-court. His father was Kekashr's youngest brother, who served in Gil during our beloved governor's first decade of rule—the commander at the third Malvi massacre, indeed. He'll be long remembered in Gil."

"And Shree himself?"

"Said to be a good commander, in Sherkin terms. He won his first honours at the Lamne atrocity nine years ago. You know what that means."

"I know what they give honours for, yes. Anything else?"

Bekri mulled through the paper. "Served under Prince Srinank at the Calloon rebellion—honours; at that hideous temple siege in Tata, when the dissident clerics were wiped out—honours; with the imperial government in Brisian— more honours. Two years ago, he arrived in Gil as his uncle's right hand."

"Honours?"

"Not yet. Strange." He looked at me and pursed his lips thoughtfully. "He's hated, of course, but he seems to have committed no very notable cruelties while in Gil, only the usual ones. Here's an interesting item—his mother's a Gil-woman."

"What?"

"Malviso's marked it as a strong rumour from a usually reliable source. I should think it's true."

"Let me see." I scanned the crowded paper, found the passage. "I see. One of the good old families—not royal, though. There's no chance he's a Scion, thank the Lady. But Bekri, if he's really half a Gilman, how can he—" I hesitated.

"How can he help to oppress his mother's people?"

"Something like that."

Bekri spread his arms. "He was brought up as a Sherkin, Tig. Bloodlines aren't everything. We have good reason to know that."

"You mean me?"

"You?" Bekri puzzled over this for a moment, then chuckled. "No, that's not what I meant. You're not a typical Scion, but you're no disgrace to Oballef's line. Nor to your mother's—you have a fair helping of that good Satheli commercial sense, which is not a bad thing. I was thinking of someone else."

"Who?"

Bekri's smile slowly faded. He poured us each a measure of wine and then withdrew into his blanket like an old scarred tortoise. I shifted uncomfortably on my end of the couch; all at once Bekri looked older and sicker than I liked to see him. His one eye seemed to be fixed firmly on the past.

"Who?" I repeated.

"Did I ever tell you about Myshalla?" he asked abruptly. "My granddaughter, Mysheba's half-sister, the younger daughter of my son? A lovely girl, very bright and beautiful, utterly fearless. She was her father's pride, and mine—she had all the gaiety of the old Gil, and all the craft of the new. An extraordinary girl. Even now it hurts to remember what she became."

"What happened to her?"

"The Sherank captured her in a raid. A handful of others were killed, including my son, but Myshalla was taken. That made her the unlucky one."

"I understand," I said slowly. "But what does this have to do with—"

"Patience, Tig. I'll get to that. We overturned every stone in Gil to find out where she'd been taken. Not that we could have helped her; nobody was ever rescued from the Gilgard, but there was always a chance we could smuggle to her the means of her own merciful release."

I nodded sadly.

"As it happened, there was no trace of her, not so much as a word of where she might be from any of our sources, not for one whole year. She was not among the women kept for the troopers—if she had been, we'd have found out. She simply vanished. Then one day, long after we'd assumed she was dead, she was found wandering in the fields near Malvi, healthy, well-fed, richly dressed, but—not herself."

"Mad?"

"Not quite. She was sane enough to have escaped from the Sherank. But she was *broken*."

"How did she escape?"

Bekri hesitated again. "It relates to a well-known peculiarity of the Sherank. A warlord's concubine is of rather less value than a good horse—a necessity, perhaps, since they are men and their women are not allowed to leave Sher, but nothing more than a tool for their ablutions, like a hairbrush, or a toothpry. Until—"

He stopped again, and hesitated for so long that I began to get impatient. "Until the concubine becomes pregnant," *I* finished for him out of my vast range of reading. The import of my own words hit me a second later.

"Exactly. At that point, the concubine becomes a wife, a Sherkint, the carrier of a warrior-caste Sherkin child, and too valuable to be anywhere but Sher. Myshalla was being carried to Malvi to take ship for Iklankish when she escaped. She was valuable."

"She was pregnant?"

"What else? They wanted her back—her child was a Sherkin, and the father must have been very highly placed, judging by the fuss they made. They turned the island upside-down looking for her. Many Gilmen died, also the guard who had been careless enough to let her escape—the only time a Sherkin enjoyed the Gilman's Pleasure from the inside, as it were. That execution was more happily attended than most. Naturally, there was no question of giving Myshalla up."

"Naturally," I echoed.

"The poor girl's mind was broken; she would tell us nothing of where she'd been, or what had happened to her, or who the child's father was. Oh, there was the odd flash of the old Myshalla, especially in the months after the child was born, and we had high hopes for her at times; but the damage was too deep. She lived on for six years, her own ghost, withdrawing further from us every day, even from her own child. One day she simply lay down and died—murdered by the Sherank just as surely as if they'd hacked her to death in the first place, like the others. But at least we had Calla."

"Calla." I repeated. I don't know why I hadn't seen it coming.

"Yes. Like Lord Shree, she's the child of a Sherkin and a Gilwoman. But unlike Shree, Calla was raised as one of us.

If Myshalla had not escaped on the way to Malvi, Calla would be a proper Sherkint now, far off in Iklankish, and I'd never have known my great-granddaughter. If Lord Shree's mother had escaped, he could well be a Flamen now, or a shull-merchant in the marketplace, or dead of starvation, or taken in the levy. It's strange how the world works out."

"Very strange." After a thoughtful pause, I added, "And Calla knows all this?"

Bekri spread his arms. "Of course she knows."

"That she's half-Sherkint?"

"Hardly that, my lord," Bekri protested gently. "Whoever her father was, she's a Gilwoman."

"You know what I meant," I said, mentally beating myself.

"Yes, of course. It was a fair question. There must be many Sherank in the Gilgard with Gillish blood in their veins as well as on their hands. Many concubines have sailed to Sher over the years."

"Was your granddaughter the only one to escape?"

"Apart from those who died—may their bones bring forth flowers." Bekri poured us both another beaker of wine and became businesslike. "Enough of that. Today was a great and historic day—we should drink to your final success!"

"Or pray for it." But I lifted my beaker and drank. We discussed the morrow then, contingency plans, the between-ways, the upper palace, the finer points of skulking; after a while Jebri poked his head in and clucked to find us still sitting over the wine. Calla did not appear and I was not sure I wanted her to, yet. I needed time to absorb the idea of her parentage. At last I bade the Flamens good night and dragged myself off to my little bedchamber.

I lay on top of the pallet fully clothed, grappling with a strange suspension of my powers of belief. It was not credible that I would rise in the morning hoping to change the world by nightfall; impossible that the grand slow wheel of history could be reversed in a single day; incredible that, after seventy-two years, this very night could be Gil's last under the barbed heel of Sher.

You presume too much, said my inner voice; not Gil's last

night of bondage, more likely your last night of life. That, alas, was all too believable. I rose and went to the window again, to look down on the sleeping city. Not one of my people down there, packed into sorry hovels or squalid tenement rooms, expected tomorrow to be any different: the sun would rise on the Sherank and set on the Sherank, and life would go on as hungrily as usual. If I failed, they would never know it. A few ripples, an old man's disappointment, another Scion taking his turn at failure and at death. Yes, that was depressing enough to be plausible.

A hand touched the small of my back.

"Good Lady in Gil!" I leapt maybe half my own height.

"Jumpy, aren't you?" said Calla behind me.

"I didn't hear you come in." Slowly, my heart climbed down out of my throat.

Calla leaned comfortably against the sill beside me. "So what were you thinking about?"

"I was wondering whether an event can validly be described as anticlimactic before it happens, or if you have to wait until afterwards."

She stared at me for a moment, then sighed. "Oh, Tigrallef. What utter rubbish. I had hoped for something better."

"I'm not feeling witty tonight."

"That's obvious," she sniffed, "but I didn't ask you to be witty."

"All right. What was I supposed to say?"

"That you were thinking about me."

Doom receded a step or two. "You mean, longing for you to come?"

"Yes, that would do."

"Pining for your caress?"

"A bit too direct." She was smiling again.

I smiled back, reached out and traced the smooth arch of her cheek with one finger. Fine, high bones—perhaps a heritage from her unknown father? I searched her face in the dim light, finding nothing in it to suggest Sher, nothing specific that had changed from the last time I looked; except that (and this took me by surprise) every line and curve and hollow in it was now of stunning significance, a marvel and a revelation, as if I'd suddenly recognized in her features the template for everything beautiful in the world. I caught my breath. "You're lovely," I said.

"Not bad, Tig, you're catching on."

I didn't answer. I started to kiss those lines and curves and hollows, seeking each of them out, one by one. Calla slid her arms around me. My resident critic was silent; all thoughts of doom and the morning to come spun away on a wild internal whirlwind. For the second time in my life, I reflected that the romancers were right to make a fuss about this kind of thing. A moment later, I stopped thinking at all.

20

"WAKE UP, TIG."

"Why?" I liked things as they were. Calla's body was nestled along the full length of mine like a silk-lined warming bottle with delightful attachments and her hair spilled across my chest. I had been half-awake for some time, holding Calla as she slept, also holding myself quite still, as if any small movement would launch us down the cliffside on whose brink we were teetering, the cliffside of the day's dread eventualities. Mysheba shook my shoulder gently, but hard enough to jar Calla awake and precipitate the plunge. Calla rolled away from me and stretched. Mysheba tactfully vanished.

Calla sat up and stretched again. I put my hand out to pull her back, but she slapped it away. "Come on, Scion, we have a full day ahead of us. Where's the tray? Pass me my beaker, will you?"

I sat up reluctantly, wincing as the cold air struck my bare shoulders. "I wish you'd put me to bed more," I grumbled, handing her a beaker of broth, "and get me up less."

"We'll talk about it another time." She gulped the broth down—I assume people like Calla have cast-iron gullets—and was pulling her clothes on before I'd taken more than a few sips.

"Is it going to be like this every morning?" I asked.

"I sincerely hope not. Hurry up."

I lay back again and pulled the covers up warmly over my shoulders. "You know, I liked you better when you were sleeping. I watched your face for hours, and you looked beautiful and placid, and you didn't once tell me what to do. Why can't you be like that when you're awake?"

"You should have been sleeping, not looking at me." A smelly wad of clothing hit me in the face. "Get dressed, Tig, remember what Calvo said. We have to be first in line. You haven't forgotten what today is, have you?"

I shut my eyes. No, I hadn't forgotten, I just wanted to defer thinking about it. I opened my eyes in time to see Calla disappearing through the curtain. Sighing heavily, I threw the cover off and started to dress.

There was no farewell blessing this time. The only Flamen in the council chamber was Jebri, talking to Calla in a low voice when I emerged. Sibba and Beliso were rubbing dirt into each other's faces by the door, and broke off to rub some into mine. As they finished, Jebri left, with a hasty sidelong glance in my direction, and Calla strode over.

"Almost ready? Good. Let's get going." Her voice was as calm as if we were setting off on a jaunt to the market. I glanced around.

"Where's Bekri? No blessing today?"

"That was yesterday," Calla said.

"Yesterday we were going out to wash crockery. Today—"

"He's not well," she broke in flatly. "Anyway, how many blessings do you need? You hate ceremonies, and so do I. Let's go." She led the way.

We proceeded down the stairs into the dark, pre-dawn street. There was no sense that anything of significance was happening. Could history really be made with so little drama? It was hard to believe, almost as hard as the singular and perplexing fact that Calla had spent the last two nights in my bed. I mulled over that as we trudged past the statue of the Lady; once might have been pity or aberration or even temporary insanity, but twice could imply that she really liked me. At that, I smiled to myself like a simpleton.

It was at this moment that I suddenly thought of a much more reasonable explanation. I stopped short. The others didn't, so I ran to catch up, my heart thumping. Already, that small awful doubt was growing into a large and equally awful conviction, and I had to know the truth before the question choked me. I grabbed Calla's arm and hissed into her ear, "The last two nights, Calla—were they part of your assignment?"

"What?"

"Part of your assignment. You know, keeping the Scion happy. Making sure I slept well. Keeping the fear away. Was that it? Is that why you came to me?"

"Let go of my arm, Tig."

"Did the council tell you to sleep with me? Will it be part of your next report?"

"Tig!"

Her face was furious. I stared at her, a taste of hurt in my mouth, praying that she would deny it. She only drew herself up proudly and wrenched her arm free. My hand dropped away.

"I suppose I should have guessed," I said bitterly. "Tell me, Calla, did you enjoy your job?"

"Oh, balls of Oballef," she said with disgust, and moved ahead to join the others.

That settled it. Now I was sure.

We were at the rampart gate in excellent time. The Gilgard towered above us, massively foreshortened; an arc of silver traced the edge of the summit, where the early rays of the sun were just striking. A few other scullions were already clumped dejectedly at the head of the street, but we sidled past them, mindful of Calvo's instructions, and placed ourselves as near to the door as possible. There was a pointed quality to the silence in our little group: Calla and myself tight-lipped, Sibba and Beliso puzzled and uncomfortable, like children whose parents have quarrelled. Nobody ventured to speak.

If I thought of the Gilgard caves at all, it was, oddly, without fear. Or at least without the old, familiar belly-twisting terror that I'd lived with since the Flamens-in-Exile first slung me into the fishing boat. Perhaps I was still too angry, or more likely my deep-felt reluctance to be alone with Calla was a more immediate kind of dread. At any rate, while we stood shivering in the chilly dawn, I had to catechize myself: the search for the Lady must come first, the future of Gil must not be jeopardized. What did it matter if Calla and the council, maybe even Bekri, had made a fool out of me? No doubt their motives were the best, their devotion to the quest unimpeachable. This made them no easier to forgive.

I glanced at Calla's cold profile, expecting to hate her. It was a shock, therefore, to find that the sight of her left me drowning again in a rip-tide of tenderness. I badly wanted to throw my arms around her and beg her to make a fool out of me any time she felt like it. The voice in my head clamoured for attention. *She deceived you, fishbrain. You can't possibly imagine you're in love with her, not at a time like this*. I can so imagine it, I told myself sadly. It was true. My symptoms exactly matched what I'd read about in the erotic and romantic literature. And for that, I cursed Calla, and I cursed the council; I was just settling nicely into cursing myself when the rampart door was flung open and the Sherkin guards stepped out. It was not Flax who followed them, but Calvo himself.

"Good morning, shullbait," he growled, surveying the crowd. I remembered to cringe along with the others, but Calla nudged me forwards. Calvo shifted minutely to one side.

"Get to your places," he roared as we scuttled past him, the first through the door, "there's a mountain of crockery waiting, and more to come after breakfast. You! Let me see your hands!" He blocked the way of Sibba, who in her capacity as rearguard was blocking those behind her. Calvo's bellowing and her whines faded into the distance as we dashed for the scullery.

Miraculously, or by Calvo's cleverness, the Sherkin guard was not there when we burst into the scullery. We raced through the clouds of steam towards the hidden door, but as I came level with our vat, a pair of dark figures rose menacingly out of the floor in front of us. I slid to a halt, Calla smashed into my back, we both fell over; breathlessly untangling myself, I scrabbled for the knife hidden in the folds of my cloak. Typically, it eluded me. The figures loomed above us, at least ten feet tall—their hands reached out—

"Hurry, my lord, the guard will be back any second." One of them hauled me to my feet.

"Who are you?" I gasped. "How did you know—"

"We're doubling for you at the vat. Calvo's orders. Don't ask questions, just go."

Obediently, I dived for the cupboard with Calla at my heels. It was now a couple of spans away from the wall, the gap camouflaged by a tall pile of dirty crockery. Another moment, a tight squeeze, and we were behind it, crammed together, facing a small wooden door almost masked by cobwebs.

"Hurry up!" Calla whispered urgently. "I can hardly breathe."

"There's no handle—"

"Just push, stupid, it must be stuck!"

Voices were audible in the scullery behind us. I shoved at the door with my shoulder and it gave abruptly, but not very far, as if something on the other side of it was limiting its arc. Calla and I tumbled through. The door swung shut behind us.

The darkness was suffocating, solid, choked with dust. This was because we were not in the expected passageway, but trapped behind a curtain of some exceptionally heavy dark material, scratchy like goat-hair, closely-woven, impenetrably black. I flattened myself against the door and groped sideways for Calla.

"I'm here," she whispered. "And keep your hands to yourself. What is this? I thought the door led into an old passageway."

"It used to. Obviously it doesn't any more. Do you hear anything?"

"No. Yes."

On the other side of the curtain, and far off to our right, heavy boots echoed on the stone floor. I held in my breath and my belly, thanking the Lady that my paunch had been trimmed, praying that the abundant folds of the hanging would hide us. As an afterthought, I turned my feet parallel with the wall. The heavy footfalls approached, passed us without stopping, died away. We remained frozen for a long moment.

"I think it's safe now," Calla breathed at last.

"Safe, eh? Define your terms," I muttered.

"What? Never mind, let's see what's on the other side of this curtain."

I heard her rags rustle. Light shot up from the floor—Calla was kneeling, holding up the edge of the curtain and peering underneath. "Good Lady . . ." she whispered. The light disappeared as she slid into the open and let the curtain drop behind her.

I followed her example. What I expected to see was the other wall of a narrow passage, just broad enough for two to walk abreast. Instead, we were in a low cloister running along one edge of a vast, high-ceilinged hall, separated from it by a series of graceful pillars. The floor of the hall was tiled in a complex mosaic that I recognized at once.

"Ah. I understand now," I said in a low voice. "It's the Hall of Harps. The passage used to be part of it, but it was bricked up about four hundred years ago when Tallislef Second was remodelling the Lower Palace. The Sherank have opened it up again as a cloister, that's all. It's a bit of a joke, isn't it?"

"What is?" She glanced at me coldly.

"Well, that the Sherank have been using this supposedly secret passage all along."

"I don't think it's funny."

"Do I look like I'm laughing? If they've found this passage, what other secrets of the Gilgard do they know?"

Calla went pale under her dirt. "Why, where does it lead?"

"This one? Nowhere in particular, but there's a panel at the end that gives access to the between-ways. You know about the between-ways?"

"A bit."

"Good. Let's hope the Sherank don't. Come on, we can't stay here. This way."

We crept along the cloister, ready to dive for the curtain at the slightest noise. I became aware of a curious form of double vision as we went: although I was seeing this place for the first time in my life, it was familiar. Of course, I had studied the plans of the Gilgard, and could see them clearly if I shut my eyes—but the sensation went deeper than that. I seemed to have walked this cloister before; the view through the pillars of the Hall of Harps was old and beloved. I stopped for a better look by the last pillar, beyond which the cloister became an enclosed passage again.

There should have been trees flowering in great brazen pots under the tall windows across the Hall; an array of harps of all sizes should have crowded the far end, before an arras the size of a small meadow. The hall was empty now, the mosaic floor littered with dirt and horse-cobbles, the arras probably ripped apart for its golden threads. I clicked my tongue sadly and turned away.

"What are you dawdling for—my lord Scion? Someone could come along at any moment." Calla beckoned impatiently from the shadows ahead.

"I'm coming." I looked at her mildly, wondering where my anger and hurt had gone. "You know, it's very interesting, in a horrible sort of way, to see what they've done with the old place."

"We've no time for sight-seeing," she exploded in a whisper. "Come on."

"I'm coming," I said cheerfully. I caught up with her and we ran on into the gloom towards the end of the cloister, beyond the reach of the light from the Hall.

We were out of sight just in time. There was sudden thun-

der from the Hall behind us: raucous shouts, neighing of
horses, a sound like the clicking of a dancer's fingerdrums
magnified a hundred times. Iron-shod hooves on ancient tiles;
I realized they were using the Hall as a drill ground. This
explained the strew of horse-cobbles.

Calla grabbed my hand and pulled me along. "You are not
going back to have a look," she whispered grimly.

"Of course I'm not. No intention of it. Whatever made
you think I had?"

"Well, you never know. I've seen that look on your face
before. Ever since we came through the door, you've been
like a scholar-child with a new scroll."

"Have I?"

"Yes. You're forgetting what's ahead of us and the danger
we're in."

"I am not. Anyway, we're in no danger from them, if
they're all on horseback. The passage is too low."

"Who says they're all on horseback? And the one we
heard before was on foot, and coming from this direction.
Just hurry, will you?"

I grinned as we scampered along in our soft shull sandals.
Calla was wrong. There was no chance of me forgetting our
mission or our peril, and my fear was still there, a goodly
lump of it; but I was light-headed with the wonder of being
in the Gilgard at last, dazed by the sense of homecoming.
There was a strange sense of power filtering up from the
Gilgard stones as I trod on them.

The passage was darker now, but we dared not risk a candle. We walked more cautiously, hands stretched out before
us. Suddenly we were there: the passage turned to the left,
a long dark tunnel with a dim rectangle of daylight at the far
end. I ignored that and moved to the corner. The transverse
corridor was wood-panelled from that point; I dropped to my
knees and began tracing the outline of the flagstones, counting back, losing my place, starting over again. Calla hovered
impatiently over me.

"Hurry up, Scion. What are you doing?"

"Looking for the right stone. Hush."

She fidgeted as I counted. Three stones forward from the

panel and two to the side. I pressed on the stone with my hands. It seemed steady. Taking a deep breath, I stood up and trod carefully on one corner. It shifted under my foot with a tiny snicking noise. "That's it. Panel's open!" I pulled Calla with me through the wall, into a blacker darkness, an icier cold, into air stale as old breath and silent as a charnel-house. We had arrived in the between-ways.

21

CALLA STRUCK HER flint and lit a candle. We were, as I had known we would be, in a cramped chamber, low-ceilinged, stone-walled, with a narrow flight of stone stairs ascending from a doorway on our left; the far wall was invisible, though I knew it was only twelve feet away. Cobwebs, massed shrouds of them, filled the corners and encroached upon the centre, curtained the stairway, trailed shreds of dusty gossamer across our faces. I kicked at the thick layer of dust on the floor.

"Good," I whispered. "Nobody's been in here for a long, long time."

Calla sneezed. "Quit raising the dust."

"Sorry. Come on, there's a door on the far side of the room—we could take these stairs, but it's better to go up at the other end of the buttery."

"You do sound like you know where you're going, my lord Scion, I'll give you that," she said grudgingly, moving after me. A fragile peace seemed to have been established. "I suppose the between-ways are part of the Secrets of the Ancients, are they?"

I stopped and looked around at her in surprise. "These?

Good Lady, no—there was no secret made of the between-
ways. Not deliberately, anyway."

"What do you mean, no secret? Why doesn't anybody
know about them, then?"

"They dropped out of common knowledge long ago.
Quiet, I'm trying to visualize the plan."

"What were they?" she persisted.

"Just the old servants' passages, built into the walls. I
thought you knew."

"How could I? Bekri mentioned them now and then, but
never explained anything; he made a great mystery of them."

I did not answer at once. We were at the door in the far
wall, and I took the candle from Calla and held it cautiously
through the opening. My memory was correct—the doorway
gave on to a passage leading to our left, dank, narrow and
almost choked with cobwebs. Just at the edge of the candlelight, it made a dog-leg turn that brought it under the line of
the staircase. I grunted with satisfaction.

"So?" Calla said impatiently.

"What's wrong now?"

"If they're not secret, why hasn't anyone heard about them
except you and Bekri and a few other Flamens?"

"They were forgotten—not in use for about six hundred
years, not since the Middle Palace was extended and the
dumbwaiters installed. Bekri learned about them as a young
Flamen, though he never entered them; they weren't important then, you see, they were just one of the curiosities of
the old Lower Palace."

"What about you? How did you learn about them?"

"They're marked on the original plans for the Lower Palace, which are in the Exile archives—fortunately for us.
Please, Calla, trust me."

She shrugged, shut up and followed close at my heels,
both of us batting at the veils of cobweb clogging the passage. Dust billowed around our feet and danced in the candlelight, filling my nose, birthing pallid monsters in the
corners of my eyes. Calla sneezed again, explosively, but the
cobwebs muffled the echoes like a blanket. The passage descended gently for a short distance and then levelled out and

veered diagonally to the right; one wall was masonry, the other native rock. We were below the level of the Lower Palace floors now, below the buttery itself by my calculations. Our feet whispered through the dust.

"I'm confused," Calla muttered behind me.

"Really? Don't worry, I know exactly where we are."

"Fine. So tell me. You said the between-ways run throughout the Lower Palace. They don't run through the Middle Palace, right?"

"Right."

"And the Middle Palace is between the Lower Palace and the Temple Palace up the mountain."

"Right again."

"And the entrances to the Gilgard caverns are in the Temple Palace."

"Right. What's your point, Calla?"

"Don't be so dense. How do we get through the Middle Palace?"

"I don't know yet."

"You *what*?"

"Keep your voice down. Not all the air vents were plugged."

Calla grabbed my shoulder and pulled me around to face her in the narrow confines of the corridor. "Bekri told me you knew exactly what to do," she whispered fiercely.

"Well—"

"Did the two of you make no plan at all?"

"No, not exactly—"

She slammed her fist against my shoulder in exasperation. I sighed. "Listen to me, the Sherank have made numbers of changes in the Gilgard, and we don't know exactly what and where. I'll make a plan when I see what the situation is—in the meantime, the between-ways will get us more than halfway to the caves, quickly and safely. I hope. Understand?"

"I understand, my lord Scion," she said, but grimly.

"And another thing: I wish you'd go back to calling me Tig. I'm not angry any more about—I understand that you and the council were only trying to help."

I had begun to turn away when Calla's face caught my

eye. I'd seen that look before—it was on the face of a rip-percat into whose den the training Flamens had shoved me, with deadpan instructions to be quick and merciful in the kill. Calla was much more attractive than the rippercat, and she did not have fangs the length of my hand, but the effect was astoundingly similar. I stepped back.

"You're not angry any more. That's very nice of you, my lord," she said levelly. "You call me a whore, and the council a pack of pimps, and then you decide not to be angry. You're much too forgiving."

"Calla," I began, but she pushed past me, grabbing the candle in transit, and stomped down the passage. I stood stupidly for a moment, and then hurried after her. I thought she was behaving very strangely for a person who had just been forgiven.

"Wait," I called. The candle was a dim silver glow diffused by the torn spider-webbing and the thick haze of dust. Suddenly it cut off, and I realized Calla had turned the corner into the branching place; I stumbled on through the darkness, one hand groping along the wall, muttering to myself, until I reached the turning. It was a biggish chamber where the buttery passage broke into four: one to the old barracks complex, one to the south stables, one to the law courts, and the fourth a staircase to the old royal nursery, which had been turned into the College of Flamens when the Middle Palace was extended. It was this staircase that I wanted to use, and I was relieved to see Calla's web-frosted form hunched on the lowest step, waiting for me. I started to cross to her. The floor crunched under my feet.

"Here, take the candle," Calla said stonily, "I've seen enough already." Reaching her was like treading across a bed of dry twigs. I took the candle from her hand and knelt to examine the floor.

For a moment, I could not quite make sense of what my eyes told me. Twigs and branches, yes, long and dry and splintered, but not grown on any tree ever rooted in the ground. They were bones, clean and shining in the candle-light, crushed and scattered where Calla and I had heavy-footed through them; the skulls were queued neatly along the wall at intervals of a couple of spans. Something metallic shone below one toothy smile, and I reached across to pick it up—a miniature of the Lady in Gil, in silver, attached to a chain that was still looped through a strew of disarticulated vertebrae. That one had been a Flamen in life.

"They must have taken refuge in the between-ways when the Sherank first entered the Gilgard," Calla went on flatly, "and then died of starvation rather than go out into—into what Lord Kishr was making of Gil." She picked something off the floor and tossed it to me. I caught it awkwardly, a slim curved blade of rib-bone. "The shulls found them, even if the Sherank didn't." I nodded soberly, noting the marks of tiny teeth. Still holding it in my hand, I picked my way across the chamber to examine the bones ranged along the far wall.

"You know, Calla," I said a minute later, as calmly as I could, "someone beside the shulls found these people. Look how neatly these bones over here have been piled."

"What?" She was suddenly beside me, grabbing the candle to play it over the tidy heaps of remains. "But who?"

"How should I know?" I looked around. The dust lay thick and undisturbed in the mouths of all the passages and on the stairs; the cobwebs hung heavy, the produce of decades of industrious spiders. "It was a long time ago, whoever it was."

She shrugged uneasily. "Perhaps a last survivor of the group?"

"I don't know—I wouldn't think so. But it was after the shulls finished with them."

We crouched uneasily amid the bones, listening to the silence. A sudden thundering overhead—Calla started, the candle dropped and went out. I caught her shoulder in the darkness.

"Don't be afraid, the main door to the buttery is just overhead; it must be the troops massing for breakfast."

Light flared as she struck the flint and relit the candle, pointedly casual. "Who's afraid? Noisy buggers, aren't they?" Something crashed above us and we could hear voices, far and thin through the ceiling slabs. "We'd better be going. There's nothing we can do here," she added.

"One thing." I took the candle again and searched rapidly through the piles of bones. There were twelve skulls altogether, including two infant-sized ones, and there were two more silver miniatures of the Lady, signifying two more Flamens among the dead, but what I was searching for was not there. I sat back on my haunches and looked up at Calla. "Three Flamens present, but the Primate wasn't one of them. His pendant was gold, and he wore a pectoral as well."

Calla looked at the three little figurines gleaming on my palm. "What about these? Do we take them with us?"

"No." I carefully replaced the pendants where I had found them. "If the Gilgard becomes ours again, we'll return and give these poor wretches the proper rites; until then, we'll leave them undisturbed. Let's go."

She followed me to the stairs. Neither of us wanted to look back into that chamber of death. We climbed steadily, softly, the clamour from the buttery falling away below us as the stairs led us up through the massive wall, up to the upper storey. As we turned a corner, cooler air hit our faces, and three thin slots of light appeared in the wall. Air vents. The noise from the buttery was suddenly clearer.

We peered through the slots. The wall between us and the buttery was only one stone's thickness here, and we had a good view of the room far below. Long trestle tables creaked under the troopers' breakfast; scores of Sherank, looking almost naked without their helmets, jovially demolished trenchers of roast meat, of quivering raw eggs, of hot bread and rice and toasted grains. A whole roast hog was trundled in, its upturned belly spilling avalanches of baked onions and hot-roots. Not a stewed shull in sight.

I nudged Calla and pointed: Flax, the fat Koroskan underchef, was bustling about the hatchway to the kitchen, directing operations. As we watched, he clouted one of the Gilman servers hard on each side of the head. The nearest troopers appeared mildly entertained. I pulled my eyes away from the slot and sat down on the step, nauseated by the overabundance of lovely smells. Calla remained glued to the slot.

"That was Barri that Flax hit, that great bag of grease. He's in the Web. I wonder what he'd done?"

"Dropped an onion, maybe. Maybe nothing. Who knows? Maybe Flax just felt like hurting someone." My belly rumbled dangerously. "Let's get out of here."

The face Calla turned to me was a mask of anger, but for a change I wasn't the target. "When I think, Tig," she said, "of the number of maggots I've eaten in my life, and thanked the Lady for, I could—" she subsided into mutters.

"Cheer up, Calla." I tactfully ignored the fact she was calling me Tig again. "It'll be roast hog and onions for everyone when we find the Lady, eh? Think of that."

She smiled faintly. "Honey-cakes for the children?"

"Every morning."

"Let's get going, then," she said. We moved on.

22

THE STAIRCASE LED up to the Spine—that was the name it was marked with, in tiny faded script, on the plans of the Lower Palace. The air was fresher and it was gloomy rather than pitch dark; we could see the passage stretching along greyly ahead of us, broader but lower-ceilinged than the passages we'd left behind, pierced at intervals on both sides by air vents like those into the buttery. Something about the visibility jarred on my mind.

"Go softly," I whispered to Calla, "we want them to think we're spiders in the walls, if they hear us at all."

We crept along the dim passage. A light hum of voices floated through the air vents, female voices mixed with trilling laughter. Calla headed straight for one of the vents, but I grabbed her arm at the last moment and pulled her back, pointing at the floor. She was on the brink of a steep staircase that spiralled down into deep shadow, the unguarded well taking up nearly half the breadth of the corridor. Another step and she'd have fallen in—perhaps breaking her neck, but certainly making too much noise to be a credible spider. She grimaced, stepped around the well to reach the air vent, and cautiously peered through. A few moments later she looked back, frowning.

"Why are we so high, Tig? We must be just below the roof—the rooms are below us!"

"Shh. The Spine was built over the central corridor of this wing; you reach the servants' door to each chamber via those stairways. What do you see?"

"Better you look with your own eyes," she whispered with an odd smile, moving aside. I put my eye to the vent, squinting into the daylight.

"The shintashkr," I breathed.

"Shint what?"

"Shintashkr. The sow-sty. Charming language, Sheranik, such elegant metaphors."

"Never mind that. The concubines?"

I shook my head, still peering through. "The concubines wouldn't be crowded together like that; these must be the women kept for the troopers. It's a nice irony, isn't it—those used to be contemplation cells for novice Flamens."

The air vent, set high into the wall, gave a reasonably clear view into the hall below, without itself being obvious. The hall was vast and vaulted, its periphery divided into a maze of little cells by walls just higher than a man; from our vantage point, we could see into most of them. In each was a wardrobe and a pallet, comfortable-looking, though not luxurious. Most of the cells were empty, but in some sat young women, brushing their hair, oiling their skins, painting their eyes, doing all those mystical things that women do to make themselves beautiful. The centre of the hall was taken up by a large square parlour, strewn with divans, cushions, carpets—and more young women.

All kinds of women, from all the slave kingdoms under the mailed hand of Sher. Gilwomen, seductive coppery-

skinned Lucians, little swart Glishoran, moon-faced Tatakils
with straight black brows; a couple of very tall, stick-thin
Storicans, their black skins shining with oil; a cluster of giggling red-haired damsels who could only be from Calloon in
the far west; and, hulking by the doors like mountains covered with snow, a pair of fat white-robed Koroskan ward-
resses with whips coiled in their hands. As I watched, another
pair of wardresses threaded their way through the maze bearing between them a tray piled high with bread, fruit and
meat.

Calla pulled impatiently at my cloak. "Come on, haven't
you seen enough?"

"Just a moment—"

"Certainly, my lord Scion." Her voice dripped with sarcasm. "You're enjoying the view, are you? Perhaps you want
to join them?"

"Not this time, thank you." I turned away from the vent.
"This is probably what Flax has in mind for you, Calla. Not
a bad life—anyway, the girls don't appear to be suffering."
I was joking, but Calla was clearly not amused. I removed
the grin.

She made a face of disgust. "Most of them come of their
own free will. Whores, the lot of them."

Any reply would be a flat-footed leap on to thin ice. I held
my peace and started behind her down the passage, carefully
avoiding the stairwell to the chamber on the other side. She
was quite right, time was passing, and we had none to waste.
Still—had there been a hint of jealousy, even possessiveness,
in her sarcasm? Very unlikely, I told myself, but I grinned
anyway at her stiff back as she stalked on ahead, liberally
coated with cobwebs. Suddenly, the small discrepancy that
had been niggling at me leapt out and identified itself.

"Calla, wait. Did you notice? No cobwebs."

She looked around, lifting the candle to see better. "You're
right. So what?"

"Don't you think it's odd?"

"Oh, I don't know. It's better ventilated up here—"

"Which should mean more flies, more spiders, and
therefore more webs, not fewer. I'm not sure I like this." At

a sudden thought I knelt down and peered at the floor. There was some dust, about as much as a careless servant might leave on a bad day, but nothing like the ankle-deep drifts in the lower between-ways. I frowned up at Calla. "Actually, it's *very* odd. I don't like this at all."

"So what are you going to do about it? Come on, let's just keep moving."

I moved, but my back felt cold. Not far ahead, I could see the end of the Spine, where a narrower corridor turned sideways into the thickness of the old Flamens' Court wall. Beyond that was a large clearing chamber with openings to the rubbish and laundry shafts and just on the other side of that, our immediate goal, the staircase that led up to the final level of the Lower Palace, which was partially set into the mountain, and partially overbuilt by the Middle Palace. At that point, I thought, when we were forced to leave the between-ways, our troubles would really begin; but I was being much too optimistic.

I stopped Calla again in the Flamens' Court passage. "More sight-seeing, Tig?" she asked wearily. I ignored her as I peered through a vent into the old Court. Its mosaic floor was reputed to be the finest in the Gilgard, and therefore the world; Oballef himself, it was said, had laid down the tiles under the guidance of the Lady. I suspected the story was apocryphal, but it hardly mattered now—if the mosaic still existed, it was thirty feet deep under a tip of garbage that rose almost to the level of the vents. Middle Palace garbage, I thought, dumped through the clerestory windows; the grand doorway must have been buried decades ago. The stench through the vent was powerful and appalling, even worse than the stench in the market. I shook my head sadly as I turned away, opening my mouth to say something suitably mournful; but Calla, standing tensely, head cocked as if listening to the gentle sifting of dust motes through the vent, motioned for quiet.

"Did you hear anything?" she whispered.

"No, but I wasn't—"

"Hush. Listen."

I hushed and listened. Total silence, now that the woman-

sounds from the shintashkr had been left behind. I opened
my mouth again, but Calla shook her head and spoke with
her fingers: *let's get out of here.* Her urgency was infectious;
she scuttled down the passage, with me almost treading on
her heels, the dimness quickening with menace. Suddenly
Calla stopped. "Somebody's there," she said softly.

I moved up beside her, my skin crawling. A grey form
was crouched on the floor by the wall, misshapen, motion-
less, poised—waiting. By a miracle, my groping hand located my knife. "Who are you?" I breathed. But Calla, after
her brief hesitation, abruptly dropped the candle and
launched herself at the figure. The candle went out. As I
stumbled through the semi-darkness to Calla's aid, the
sounds of struggle ceased. There was an eerie, ominous silence. Then Calla giggled. Giggled. I didn't know until that
moment that she could do anything of the sort.

"What's happening?" I hissed. "Did you get him? Calla,
where's the damned candle?"

"I dropped it," she said. "And Tig—it's a sack of rubbish."
She giggled again. I found the candle and my flint and managed, after a few nonproductive swipes, to light the wick.
Calla was slumped grinning on the floor, embracing a large
sack with a row of black spiky characters stamped near the
mouth. I was not amused.

"All right," I said, "so it's a bag of rubbish. So who
brought it here?"

"What?"

"Who brought it here? It didn't walk here by itself."

Calla sobered immediately. "Perhaps," she said uneasily,
"it's been here all along, since before the catastrophe."

"Hardly that," I said. "It's labelled 'Second Barracks' in
Sheranik."

She looked blankly at the characters on the sack. "But
who—?"

"Whoever is in the between-ways with us," I said flatly.

We had no choice but to move on, but we walked fearfully
now, knives in hands, ears straining through the dead silence.
We even doused the candle and relied instead on the thin

light filtering through the air vents. This was perhaps my worst moment in Gil up to that time—my illusion of safety was shattered, also my illusion that I knew a trick or two those bastards from Iklankish didn't. The between-ways, supposedly a ribbon of free territory, were after all in the hands of the enemy—and the enemy could be lurking around any corner, laughing at us out of the darkness as we had been laughing at them. Where were they? Were they playing with us, as I'd seen a pack of shulls play with a hen? And if they had stumbled on the between-ways, was it possible they had found the entrance to the caves—?

I shook off the thought. We were at the door to the clearing chamber now, and the silence was still unbroken. No light penetrated there from the corridor. Calla fumbled for her flint; her hands were shaking, and for once she had to swipe twice before the wick caught. The contents of the chamber leapt into existence as the light touched them. We gasped, practically in unison.

I'd seen tidier rubbish-tips, but never richer ones. Two-thirds of the chamber, floor to ceiling, was piled with furniture, with crockery, with sacks, with swords and knives, with ropes, with wooden crates and carven chests and architectural fragments and awkwardly folded carpets and a thousand other things, with here and there a gleam of gold or bronze or tarnishing silver. The remaining third, in contrast, was severely tidy: a bare table, some wooden stools, a neatly made pallet on the floor with a thick blanket folded on top. I put my hand out for the candle, fascinated, but Calla held it out of reach.

"The answer is no," she said firmly. "We're getting out of the between-ways, now. Where are the stairs?"

"Across the room. Believe me, I don't want to linger, I—"

"No." She pulled me after her across the room. Her hand was icy.

"But—"

"No buts, just come on," she hissed.

"Listen to me," I began, elbowing past her to block the

stairs. A tiny rustle behind me—I started to turn. The side of my head exploded. Calla shouted something from a distance of a few miles, and I did my best to make sense of it; but halfway to the floor, I lost interest.

23

SHE WAS JUST *ahead of me in the between-ways, her great stone bowl tucked under one arm. Her marble hips rolled smoothly under a floating cloak of cobwebs as she walked unhurriedly away. I ran after her, crying to her to wait, but I gained no ground at all; she looked back once, incuriously, wiping the paint from her face with the back of her hand. Then she turned a corner and was gone.*

I groaned and rolled on to my side.

"Please, Tig, wake up."

I opened my eyes, blinking. Candlelight. A red glow somewhere behind my eyes pulsated wickedly when I moved my head, so I lay still. Someone's sharp elbow poked me in the back.

"Are you awake, Tig?"

"No. Leave me alone."

"Raksh take you! It's about time you woke up. I almost thought he'd killed you."

"It feels like he did. He—who are we talking about? Who's he?"

"How should I know who he is?" Calla retorted. "You're the expert on the between-ways."

"Well, whoever he is, he's not marked on the plans." Very delicately, I rolled over on to my back. By turning my head gently to the left, I could see that Calla was lying beside me;

her elbow, in fact, was now digging into my side. I observed fuzzily that we were on the pallet in the clearing chamber. Further observations revealed that my hands were tied in front of me, with a line running down to bonds around my ankles. I gulped down the escalating nausea. "Tell me what happened."

"I can't tell you much," Calla said. "As far as I know, there was just one man. He was waiting for us on the stairs. He hit you on the head, and then half-strangled me until I blacked out; when I woke up, we were trussed up like this on the pallet. That's all I know."

"But what was he? Sherkin? Gilman? What did he look like?"

"Hairy."

I waited for more. Calla was silent. "That's all? Hairy?"

"That's all I remember. I hardly even saw him, Tig, I dropped the candle when he grabbed my throat."

"Well, was he in armour? Uniform? Sherkin dress? You must remember something else."

"Nothing." She sounded aggrieved. "It happened very quickly. I can tell you one thing, though—we've been here for hours. That candle's burned down to a stub, and if he doesn't come back soon, we'll be in the dark."

"And if he does come back?"

There was silence from the other side of the pallet. After a brief struggle with the ropes, which convinced me that our captor was undoubtably talented at tying people up, I lay still and tried to think.

"Tig?"

"What?"

"He didn't pick up our knives. They're still on the floor where we dropped them. I can just see them."

Aha, I thought, progress. "Why didn't you crawl over and get them long ago? We'd be free by now."

"Do you imagine I didn't think of that?" she said defensively. "We're tied together at ankles and neck—I nearly throttled us both when I tried. We might manage it now you've condescended to wake up. Can you move?"

"I think so." I lifted my head experimentally; the red glow

throbbed in protest and I groaned, but the pain was bearable and the nausea just under control. "You start, I'll follow."

She wriggled sidewise off the edge of the pallet and I felt the pressure on my neck immediately. Hurriedly, I wriggled after her; with a jar that loosed forks of red lightning inside my head, I bumped off the pallet, half on to the floor, half on to Calla. She grunted.

"Get off me, you great lump. No, better if you roll right over me, so we're on our bellies."

I swallowed a throatful of something vile and heaved myself across her, the jerk of the rope nearly taking my head off, but when the red light in my head stabilized again, we were face-down on the floor and able to rise on to our knees and elbows. At that moment the candle-flame climbed the last of its wick and guttered out; dizzy as I was, I lost my bearings at once.

"This way," Calla hissed. She jerked ahead before I was ready; the ropes at my neck and ankles pulled me off balance and I toppled with the majestic inevitability of a felled tree. As far as my belly was concerned, it was the raindrop that burst the dam; I vomited copiously, mostly on the flagstones, but partly on Calla, who had been pulled over on top of me.

There was a meaningful silence.

"Ecch," Calla said at last. She jerked to her knees again, yanking me after her. "My hair—why didn't you tell me you were going to be sick? Disgusting!"

"It's no more disgusting than what's usually in your hair," I muttered rashly.

This silence was even more meaningful. Then Calla said, primly and dangerously, "The contents of my hair didn't appear to bother you last night."

I groaned. "Forget about last night—"

"Oh, I shall. Indeed I shall. All about it. I hope you do, too. Come on, my lord."

I cursed myself with all the curses I could think of in Gillish and Sheranik and Satheli, throwing in a few from Plav and Tata for good measure. Meantime we humped across the floor in the pitch-darkness, the two of us swinging our bound knees after our bound hands like synchronized caterpillars, occasionally bumping off each other's shoulders. When my forehead crashed resoundingly into the table, I began to curse out loud. Calla took no notice. At last, after what seemed like half the distance to the Archipelago, I felt a cold iron blade under my hand.

"I've got one! Where're your hands?"

"Let me do it," she said coolly, "I don't trust you with a knife." I ignored that and began sawing carefully at the lump of rope around her wrists. She stopped protesting after a bit. Strand by strand, I could feel the ropes falling apart; my own wrists ached with the effort of pressing the knife, and I was starting to feel sick again. Just when I thought I could hold the knife no longer, Calla grunted and pulled her wrists apart, snapping the last few strands. She grabbed the knife and hacked at the ropes yoking us together, then groped for the cords at my wrists.

"Almost there, my lord Scion. And then we're going to get out of here. Back to the scullery."

"What?"

"You heard me. We're going back."

Astonished, I shook my head in the darkness. "No, we're not."

"Yes, we are. Heaven knows how long we've been tied up—if we're not back by the time the crockers leave, we'll be trapped in the Gilgard. And you, my lord Scion, are in no fit state to carry on."

"I'm fine," I lied, "and we must go on; Calvo's count will be correct if he sends the doubles out in our stead, if that's what you're worried about. We've come too far, Calla."

"Then we'll have to hurry to get back," she said firmly.

"No. This could be our best chance—we may not have the same luck getting into the between-ways again—"

"You call it luck, do you?" she interrupted. "Bad luck, maybe. Isn't that lump on your thick head proof enough?"

"Of what? That the between-ways aren't the royal road we hoped for? They're still the best route to the caves, probably the only route."

"We'll go back," she insisted. "Bekri and Jebri will think of another plan. Our orders—"

"Orders? I am a Scion of Oballef, Calla, nobody gives me orders." The little voice in my mind jeered at me: clown, coward, weakling, who are you trying to fool? I hushed it, and went on, "if you don't want to come with me, then you're free to go back; I'll carry on alone."

She stopped sawing at the ropes around my wrists. "Not if you're still tied up, you won't." Her voice was thoughtful.

"Calla!"

She didn't answer. She began to saw busily at the ropes on our ankles, leaving my hands still securely bound.

"Calla, finish freeing my hands."

No reply.

"Calla."

Flinty silence.

"You're planning on carrying me back, are you?"

"If you won't walk," she said calmly.

I gritted my teeth with frustration. "Gilwoman, I am ordering you to free my hands."

"Too bad, Scion, my orders come from the First Flamen. I will free your feet, of course."

"Oh, many thanks." I paused to think. "What about your hairy friend?"

"What about him? He won't take me by surprise again."

"That's not what I meant. He's not necessarily hostile, you know."

"No, no, of course not. He knocks you out and nearly strangles me, and then ties us up like two hens on a spit, but that doesn't make him hostile—can you stand, my lord?"

"I'm not going to move until you listen to me. He's not a Sherkin—if he were, he wouldn't have left us here in the between-ways, he'd have hauled us in front of Lord Kekashr before you could blink, demanding a reward. And do you really imagine a Sherkin would be living here, in the thickness of the walls? It's not the Sherkin style."

"What else could he be? A Gilman? Don't make me laugh." She snorted incredulously.

"Why not a Gilman? Those bones under the buttery were Gillish bones. We should talk to him if we can; he may even be of use."

"But he attacked us, Tig."

"I'm not surprised. See us through his eyes: we skulk through the between-ways looking like the Ghouls of Ghasca in these cobwebs, and then traipse across his bedchamber flashing bloody great knives—what would you do in his place? For that matter, he may have thought we were the Sherank."

"I still don't—"

"Ssh!" Suddenly I could see: nothing much, only the phantom of a glimmer, a faint greyish rectangle projected on to the blackness across the room, strengthening as I watched. A distant candle, I realized, advancing steadily along the passageway towards the clearing chamber. "Someone's coming. Quickly, loosen my hands."

She must have looked over her shoulder and seen it too, for she found my hands and hastily finished slicing through the cords. The rectangle was sharper now, and the quiet rasp of sandals on stone came clearly to our ears. Hand-in-hand, we groped our way in the opposite direction, where I figured the foot of the stairs should be. Miraculously, we stumbled right into it, and just in time; a second later there were low voices in the room, and the candle glowed on the wall. I peered cautiously around the door-jamb. And froze. And then walked out into the candlelight, ignoring Calla's frantic tugs at my cloak.

It was the Lady herself, just as I had seen her in my dream, her back turned to me, her silvery hair limned by candlelight, her marble body silhouetted through a diaphanous cobweb cloak as she bent gracefully over the pallet. At the sound of my footsteps, she straightened abruptly, and whirled around to face me. After a moment, she smiled.

24

DID I TRULY think she was the Lady? I would have to say yes—for a mad few moments anyway, until the shock of seeing her faded and sanity returned. The resemblance was extraordinary, but not flawless: the features marginally less than perfect, the eyes harder than marble for the broken second before she smiled, the smile itself most provocative and unLadylike. I goggled at her like a finny-fish until a shaggy shadow interposed itself and a pair of large tough-skinned hands fastened around my throat. They were just getting a good purchase on my windpipe when the girl spoke.

"Let him go, angel, you can see he's no Sherkin." The thumbs pressed for a moment, then fell lingeringly away. I regained my breath with a gasp, but lost it again as the shaggy personage pressed a knife blade where the thumbs had been. The girl chuckled. "He's just a dirty Gilman, angel, though Raksh knows how he got here—what are you doing here, darling?" Her voice was low and breathy, with laughter threaded through it like ribbon—a bedworthy voice if ever I heard one. She pushed the shaggy one aside and held the candle closer to my face. "Talkative, aren't you? But angel said there were two of you; where's the other?"

A sandal scraped on the flags behind me as Calla emerged from the staircase. "I'm here—Lissula," she said coldly.

Shaggy growled like an animal and surged forwards, but stepped back at once. Calla advanced into the circle of candlelight. The knife was long and sharp in her hand and her face was businesslike. Even without the knife, she'd have looked formidable—I'd have retreated from her myself, and she was on my side. The knives flashed at each other as

Shaggy feinted and Calla matched his move; but Lissula's musky laugh broke the tension.

"By Raksh, it's Calla under all those spiderwebs. Angel darling, put the knife down; meet an old friend."

"No friend of yours, Lissula." Calla's knife glittered warningly, but Angel (it was dawning on me that this was not an endearment, but his name) slowly lowered his. Lissula laughed again.

"Same darling Calla—how wonderful to meet you again! How is the dear old Web these days?"

Calla's hand shook, probably with rage, but her guard remained up. I cleared my throat. "Lady Lissula—" I began. Calla icily cut me off.

"Forget the title, Tig. 'Whore' would dignify that one."

I gulped at the twitch of Angel's knife-bearing hand. Lissula's eyes narrowed, leaving the rest of her smile unaltered.

"You really haven't changed at all, have you, Calla?" she said sweetly. "Tell me, darling, is that puke in your hair?"

Calla drew herself up; I could swear she gained a span in height. The tension became a slender cord drawn tautly between the two women, a strikingly ill-matched pair, Lissula curved and satiny, Calla a gaunt fierce construction of twigs and mud and ravelled string. Half in shadow, Angel shifted uneasily from foot to foot, probably feeling as redundant as I was. Abruptly, Calla tucked the knife back inside her cloak and folded her arms. "You haven't changed either, Lissula— darling," she said pointedly. "Cleaner on the outside, perhaps, but a gutterbutt all the same."

The dimples deepened in Lissula's rounded cheek. "How you talk, Calla. Who's your friend?"

"Who's yours?"

I opened my mouth eagerly, which might have been tactless considering Calla's hostility; at any rate, she cut me off again before I could begin to introduce myself. "Say nothing," she snapped, "Lissula was never to be trusted."

"Don't be like that, Calla," I said, "it's obvious they're not friends to the Sherank."

"Aren't they? Don't you realize what little Goldbottom here—that's what we used to call her in the street—does in that harlot's kit? Friendly! Ha!" She advanced a step towards Lissula, who held her ground. "You're in the shintashkr, aren't you?"

"Of course I am." Lissula tossed her silver curtain of hair and surveyed Calla with a look that said: my, you're dirty. Then she turned to me. "Tig is what my good friend Calla called you; is that all of your name, darling, or is there more?"

"Tigrallef—" I said without thinking. Lissula nodded and held out her hand, ignoring Calla; but Angel, whom we seemed (incredibly) to have forgotten, started violently and moved closer, much closer, until he was practically standing on my toes. He stared into my face.

"Tigrallef," he repeated wonderingly. His voice sounded rusty, as if he didn't use it much; his face, what little of it was visible in the borderless tangle of grey hair and beard, was dead-pallid in the candlelight, and finely wrinkled. His dark eyes were disconcerting—not with madness, exactly, but with something close to it. Somehow I managed not to drop my gaze. "A royal name," he went on haltingly, "for one of Oballef's line—"

"Er—yes."

"A Scion."

"Yes, that too."

Abruptly, he dropped to the floor and pressed his forehead to my feet. Apart from embarrassing me, this was a typical Sherkin courtesy; Calla reacted by kicking the knife out of his hand, then kicking him in the side of the head for good measure, an unacceptable tactic according to the Heroic Code but quite normal in the Web. It was less effective than she was accustomed to. Angel grabbed her foot and jerked upwards, throwing her on to the flagstones with a painful thonk; a second later he was sitting on her stomach with his knife back in his hand, the point poised over the hollow of her throat. I lunged forward to help, but Lissula's dainty hand was already on Angel's shoulder.

"Let her up, Angel, there's my good little man. Really, Calla, you mustn't startle him like that. Poor dear, he's very sensitive."

Calla glowered helplessly from the floor. "She hurt me," Angel said in his flat rusty voice, not moving. "She kicked me."

I squatted so that my eyes were level with his. "Let her up," I said quietly. At once, he nodded vigorously and sprang off her body; and then, with a shy ducking of his head, fell to embrace my feet again. I sighed.

"Please don't do that—Angel." I gagged on the name. He swivelled his forehead on my instep, so that one bright black eye glinted up at me through the facial undergrowth; otherwise, he didn't move.

"He doesn't know any better," said Lissula, helping Calla to her feet. "All his life he's been watching the Sherank through peepholes, and he's picked up a few of their customs. Not the nasty ones, of course," she added, reaching down to pat his upthrust bottom, "in fact he's perfectly sweet."

I looked at Calla, who shrugged off Lissula's hand and turned away. "I don't understand any of this," I said.

Lissula smiled charmingly. "There's no mystery about us, darling, just about you. What's all this about royalty? What's a Scion?"

"You don't know?"

"Goldbottom never took any interest in history," said Calla without turning around. "She's an ignorant little gutterbutt, who never could see beyond the bottom of someone else's purse."

"Please, Calla." I tried to step towards her, but Angel was still firmly planted on my feet.

"I think you have to kick him a little in the face," said Lissula helpfully. It worked—Angel scuttled backwards to watch me impassively from the shadows. It was horribly distracting, but at least I could move. I turned again towards Calla, but found that Lissula had mysteriously appeared in my way, and was looking up into my face with apparent adoration. This was distracting too, but not horrible. She was so close that I could feel her warm scented breath on my chin.

"Er," I said.

She took my arm and wafted me towards the table. "Those Koroskan sows won't miss me for a while," she said. "Why don't we sit down here, darling, and you can tell me all about yourself."

Calla whirled fiercely. "No! I won't allow it! Tig, I demand—" She stopped for a moment, and then continued in a softer voice, "I beg you to come back to the scullery with me now, before it's too late. Please, Tig."

I wavered. Calla knew Lissula much better than I; perhaps she was right. Perhaps I'd be a fool to reveal myself to this troopers' whore from the gutters of Gil. But did Calla realize that if we did not treat with them, we would be well-advised to kill them—if we could? And even if Lissula had been less soft and golden, cold-blooded killing was not an idea I could relish; they were, after all, my own people. I hesitated and then pushed past Lissula to where Calla was standing. "We should at least hear what they have to say," I whispered. "It's probably too late to go back anyway."

"It's a bad idea, Tig."

"Maybe." I hesitated again. "Perhaps, when we've heard them out, you should go back alone and report to the council. You know the way, don't you?"

"Of course I do. But the answer is no."

"But this could be important—especially Angel. I have a strange feeling about him."

"Have all the strange feelings you want. I'm not going back without you."

I sighed. All my instincts told me that to go back would mean the end of the quest; the little voice at the back of my head pointed out patiently that it didn't matter, I was bound to fail anyway, and at least I might exit with a whole skin if I returned now. Calla's eyes caught the candlelight. She was looking at me levelly, pleading with me, a dignified and resolute plea; it was more persuasive than all her blustering. But I shook my head, and signed with my fingers: *I can't go back.*

Then neither can I. Aloud she said, I think mostly for Lissula's benefit, "I'm not leaving you alone with that man-eating shark in whore's clothing. And that's final."

"Marvellous," said Lissula. "Now come and sit down—we have so much to tell each other."

Not daring to look at Calla, I went back to the table and pulled up one of the stools. Calla followed, dragging her feet. Lissula gazed at me expectantly.

"Tell me about Angel," I said quickly.

She looked hurt. Somehow her stool was closer than it had been and one of her knees was delicately juxtaposed to one of mine. "Angel? If it's Angel you want to hear about, so be it, I'll tell you anything you want. But—Tigrallef, is it?" her voice became soft and inviting, "I really wanted to hear about you." Calla snorted. I hemmed uncertainly.

"I can speak for myself, my lord Scion." The words came haltingly from the shadows where Angel crouched. I turned to him in surprise and found him edging forwards, though still on his knees. For the first time I noticed that he was dressed in a dirty, ragged version of what could only be a Sherkin long-gown, the kind the ill-begotten bastards wear when they're off duty. His eyes followed mine. "The long-gown is stolen, my lord Scion," he said.

"All right, all right, it's not important. Just tell me who you are, and where you came from. How on earth did you get into the between-ways?"

"I have always been here, my lord Scion."

"Stop calling me that." I paused. "What do you mean, always? You were born in the between-ways?"

"Yes, my lord Scion. Parali said so. He's dead now."

"Parali?" The name tickled the edge of my mind. There was something familiar about it, something I had read in the archives, or heard from the older Flamens-in-Exile. But I could feel that time was short, and it was vital to hear Angel's story. I beckoned him to the last stool by the table. He came willingly enough, and without further prompting, almost before his rump touched the stool, he began to talk.

25

"THEY HID THEMSELVES in the between-ways when the Sherank came. They—"

"Wait, wait," I said, "who are they?"

"Parali Flamen and the others, my lord Scion."

I sighed. "Who are the others?"

He started to rock back and forth on his stool, staring over my head. "Parali wrote them all down."

"Go on," I said. Why was that name so familiar?

"There were fifteen. Parali and some other men, and two women, and three children. My mother—"

"Yes?"

"My mother was one of the children." Meditatively, he picked something out of his nose. "That was before she was my mother."

I nodded significantly at Calla; this would be the story behind those tidy heaps of bones in the branching place. She shrugged. Angel began to plait the ends of his beard.

"So what happened?" I asked.

"They died."

"All of them? All at once?"

"No."

"Well—did the Sherank kill them?"

"Some. And maybe some others."

There was a long pause while Angel and I looked earnestly at each other and I felt precious time rotting away. "So what happened to them?" I demanded, perhaps more sharply than intended.

He hunched his shoulders fearfully, then pulled himself upright on the stool and shut his eyes. He stopped swaying and drew a long breath, and when he opened his eyes again, they were different. "In the first year," he intoned in a strange, sonorous voice, "Fenri Flamen laid his belly on his pallet and willed himself dead. In the first year also, Telli and Anlivo, guardsmen of Gil, were captured by the Sherank whilst scavenging in the Great Hall, and died under torture in the south dungeon. In the fourth year—"

"Wait, what is this?" I broke in. "I thought you didn't remember their names."

He blinked. "These are Parali's Annals of the Between-ways. Abridged." He blinked again.

"Ah." I remembered then. Parali the memorian, the prodigy of the Gil archives, of whom great things had been expected before the catastrophe. The older memorians in Exile still talked of him wistfully now and then. They assumed he had been killed by the Sherank, along with the rest of the intelligentsia left in Gil. I carefully put a lid on my excitement. "Carry on."

He nodded obediently and let his gaze drift away. "In the fourth year, Mella wife of Canesri Flamen died in childbirth, and the child with her. In the seventh year, Castu Memorian died of old age. In the ninth year, the Trembling Fever struck in the between-ways and carried off Canesri Flamen, Sibbi guardsman of Gil, Nysha wife of Malseri Flamen, and three children born in the between-ways. In the tenth year, Malseri Flamen laid his belly on his pallet and willed himself dead. In the fourteenth year, Tasli crocker of the Gilgard kitchens wasted to death with the burrowing disease. In the sixteenth year, Fasli guardsman of Gil broke his neck in the chute. In the nineteenth year, Shula daughter of Canesri Flamen died of childbed fever, and the child with her. That was my mother and brother," he added in his normal voice. "I was about two."

"Do you remember your own name?" I asked hopefully.

"No, my lord Scion."

"Do you remember Parali?"

"Yes, my lord Scion."

"Do you remember what he called you?"

"He called me Dear Boy."

I groaned. It was no improvement over Angel. I nodded for him to go on, and he straightened his back again.

"In the twentieth year, Raneso and Sorsi sons of Malseri Flamen sought to leave the between-ways, and vanished without trace. In the thirty-second year, Parali Memorian laid his belly on his pallet and willed himself dead—no, my lord Scion, actually he was old and ill, and he drank a cup of poison. There was only me to finish the Annals. May their bones bring forth flowers."

"Quite."

He put his chin down on his hands, on the tabletop, carefully tucking his beard out of the way. "Did I do well, my lord Scion?" he asked.

"You did well." I reached out and touched his shaggy head, knowing that his barren litany of deaths had only just begun to describe the outcasts' desolation. I could imagine it. They would have watched the Sherkin horror through the vents of the between-ways, a matter of survival since they'd have to subsist on what they could scavenge, darting like shulls through the secret doors when they saw that a chamber was deserted. A strange living it must have been, I thought, a narrow slice of hushed darkling life, of tight lips and tight belts, of perilous safety and diminishing hope as the months stretched into years and still the Sherank ruled in Gil. They would not have been unaware of what was happening on the rest of the island, since the between-ways commanded a view into the south dungeon, but they'd have been an audience watching a play, unseen, not directly affected by the action, equally unable to take part. Free men, and yet prisoners, their country dwindled to those dusty corridors, all that was left free of the old Gil—

Lissula pushed her knee against mine. "I don't have all day, darling, I'll be missed soon. It's your turn now." Her voice was a faintly querulous purr.

"No, Goldbottom, it's your turn," Calla said grimly. Angel stiffened again, but Lissula laughed.

"Me, darling? Nothing much to tell. The winter before last a Koroskan named Flax saw me in the market. Of course, he could tell at once that I was different from the rest of you—"

"He knows a whore when he sees one, does he?"

"Say what you will, Calla darling. At least I don't smell."

"Oh, you smell, all right. You stink of Sher," Calla began, warming to battle. I rapped on the table.

"Enough of this," I said firmly. "Lissula, I need to know how you learned about the between-ways. Do the Sherank know?"

"I'm sure they don't." She smiled between her shining falls of hair. "Angel is our secret—the shints' secret. About five years ago, the shintashkr was moved from one of the outbuildings into the new place—much more comfortable, I'm told, though it does get noisy at night without real walls that go all the way up to the ceiling. You wouldn't believe the racket, darling, nights when you don't have a taker and are trying to get some sleep with all that groaning and bellowing and creaking going on all around—"

"I can imagine," I cut in hastily. "But about Angel . . ."

"I saw them through the vent," said Angel, "and I wanted to see what they were. I waited until the Koroskans left, and then I went through the secret door. They're my friends." He tore his loving gaze from me and trained it on Lissula.

"Ah."

"We come with him sometimes when those sows of wardresses aren't around. He steals things for us, and takes us to look through the windows."

"And you say all the women of the shintashkr know about this?"

"Of course, darling. Don't worry, no one's about to tell." She chuckled a silvery chuckle. "It pleases us to have a secret from the Sherank. Anyway, no new shints are told until we're sure we can trust them. If we decide we can't, then something happens to them before very long."

"Honour among whores," said Calla flatly.

Lissula smiled with all her teeth. "You're still as boring as you ever were, Calla darling."

I left them to it and engaged myself in mental calculations. Angel would have been born in the seventeenth year, would now be fifty-five, and would have seen women for the very first time at the impressionable age of fifty. And between

Parali's death and the advent of the shintashkr, he had been alone in the between-ways for thirty-five years. Thirty-five years, my lifetime plus half again. The wonder was that he had remained even approximately sane. However, in thirty-five years he would have learned all there was to know about the between-ways and the daily routines of the Sherank, and how they might be circumvented. His information could be invaluable to us. And there was something else—he had recognized the royal form of my name where Lissula had not; he knew what a Scion of Oballef was, he could well have an accurate idea of what I was trying to do. And if such a memorian as the great Parali had been his mentor, who could tell what other odd treasures of learning might be cached inside his head?

Calla and Lissula had moved on to reminiscences of their shared girlhood. Bloodshed seemed imminent. Angel had prudently left the table and was again crouching in the shadows. I thumped the table and the women swung brittle faces towards me.

"Save your quarrel," I said severely, "we have too many important things to do. Angel!" He came to me out of the shadows, warily skirting Calla, and seemed to be on the point of falling at my feet again. I stuck them hastily under the table. "Angel, you know who I am. Do you know why I'm here?"

He rolled his eyes up and stuck out his lower lip while he considered. "Yes."

"Tell me."

"For the Lady."

"That's—"

"Like the others. The other Scions of Oballef."

I grabbed his shoulder. "What do you know about the others? Did you see them?"

He shook his head. "I heard them talking."

"Who? The other Scions?" My heart thudded.

"The Sherank. When they'd caught one."

By an effort of will, I stopped my teeth grinding with frustration. Sorting out Angel's utterances was like swimming through molasses. "Tell me what they said."

"It was Lord Kekashr and some of the warlords. He said it was a pity he died before the Lady was found. The torturer was punished."

"How long ago?"

Angel's eyes rolled up again. "A long time. I don't know. Before the shintashkr."

More than five years ago. Not Baraslef, Callefiya's husband, then. And it was less than twenty-five years, for that was how long Kekashr had governed in Gil. How many others had come in the last twenty-five years? I tried to count back, but the headache got in the way. All I could remember was my father, and that memory was more painful than the headache. "Were any names mentioned? Do you remember anything else? Tell me everything you can think of."

Back went the eyes. "No names. I don't think they knew. That other. Lord Kekashr talked about that other. He said all was not lost, even if no more came."

"Do you know what he was talking about?"

"No."

I gazed at him helplessly. One more try. I spoke slowly and clearly. "My father's name was Cirallef. He was one of the Scions who came to Gil. He was captured trying to climb one of the towers. Nobody ever heard from him again. It was nineteen years ago. Could he have been the one they killed?"

Angel began to sway gently back and forth again. He looked close to tears.

Calla put her hand on my arm. "It's no use, Tig. He doesn't know anything. He can't help us."

"Hush up." I shook off her hand. This much I had learned—that Kekashr was aware of the game being played by the Flamens-in-Exile, and had been for years. I studied Angel, who had returned to plaiting his beard.

"Have you listened to them talking in the last few weeks?"

He nodded.

"Have they said anything about me? I mean, about another Scion arriving in Gil? Do they know I'm here?"

He nodded again.

"Impossible!" Calla exploded. "We've been too careful."

Angel cleared his throat. "The little spider told them."

"What?" Calla and I demanded together.

"That's what they call him. The little spider. The traitor."

26

WE CROUCHED IN the duct, Angel and I. The wonder to me was that I could fit. Angel, who had looked bulky at first sight in his cast-off Sherkin gown, seemed here to be as slim and jointless as a snake. He had writhed in feet-first and had pulled me along by my hands whenever I faltered in the dripping darkness of that tight, elbow-rasping, stone-lined gullet in the body of the Middle Palace. Now we were head-to-head at a narrow vent and my exhaustion and discomfort were temporarily forgotten.

As the man in the room below us shifted forwards to stir the fire, his face came into the light. Lord Shree, my half-compatriot, the nephew of Lord Kekashr. There could be no mistaking that sharp, dissatisfied profile. His dark hair was brushed straight off his forehead and secured with a gold clip at the nape of his neck. He looked younger than when I'd seen him at the Gilman's Pleasure, and very slim without his armour. The flagon and meat on a small table at his elbow were practically untouched. He sat back and continued to stare into the flames.

The duct vibrated subtly, as if heavy boots were thumping along the corridor below. A breath later, the door directly beneath us crashed open. Lord Shree looked up.

The newcomer advanced into our field of view, a circle of iron-coloured hair with a distinct bald spot in the middle, not more than five feet below the vent. A nose like a bird's beak jutted out in front. He put out his hand, and a great ruby flashed on the forefinger—unmistakably the Stone of Callilef, my six-times-great grandfather. I knew at once that I was, in my unobtrusive fashion, in the presence of Kekashr, Governor of Gil, Lord of the Gilgard, Fourth Warlord of Sher, Hammer of Iklankish. He looked every inch the measure of his titles.

Lord Shree made no move, either to rise or to grovel. Kekashr stood for a moment below us, then strode to the hearthside. Now that I could see his face, it seemed to me that he was furious—or was that the habitual face of a high Sherkin warlord? He picked up the flagon, drank directly from its mouth, and slopped about half its contents into a goblet. Shree looked impassively back at the flames.

"They won't even admit he exists." Kekashr spoke in Sheranik, but slowly and with emphasis, and the smooth stone wall tossed his words up to us with perfect clarity. I had no trouble in understanding.

Shree poured a goblet from the flagon and nursed it in his hands. "What does the spider say?"

"That he may already be in the castle."

"That's impossible. Not a flea entered the Gilgard yesterday without my hearing of it."

Kekashr spat into the fire. "Don't be so sure. It seems there is a way." He laughed. "The spider wants more before he'll tell us what it is."

"Will you pay?"

"Not bloody likely. I had the messenger followed. By nightfall, the spider will be in *our* web." He laughed again, a grating laugh that became even nastier as it echoed.

"Is that wise? It will end his usefulness."

"That's almost finished anyway, and he knows it. Why else would he be so greedy, and so shy of coming forward for his reward?"

"What about Krisht?" Shree asked.

"Well—that's a different story. Nothing for the last few weeks, except that desperate favour. We'll have to wait and see."

Shree did not comment; except, perhaps, by taking a long pull at his wine. Kekashr drained his and tossed the goblet on to the floor.

"Why so gloomy, nephew, when our goal is in sight? Where Kishr failed, we'll succeed; and with the Lady in our hands, we can take Iklankish as well as Gil for our own. Our empire will be greater than Fathan's, and will never fall. To the Lady in Gil!"

Shree lifted his goblet without drinking. Kekashr clapped him on the back and rose to go. "You have the new time-table; don't keep me waiting," he said. Shree nodded without looking up. Kekashr passed under us, stopping directly below, so that (had I been so inclined, and so stupid) I could easily have dropped a gob of spittle on to the beautifully drawn target of his bald spot. He swung around to face Shree. "I expect great things," he said. "Kishr himself never came so close." Shree nodded slowly.

I watched Shree closely when Kekashr had gone. He turned to look into the fire again, the goblet to his lips. Then, without drinking, he pitched the vessel into the flames and rose to wander restlessly around the chamber. I had never seen a more miserable human face, not even on the wretch destined for the Gilman's Pleasure. He was cursing to him-self in a mixture of Sheranik and Gillish, and his command of both idioms was admirable. Finally he stopped in front of the hearth again, leaning towards it as if intent on hateful pictures in the flames. Then he straightened and turned. His face was a mask. He passed under us and the heavy door slammed behind him.

Calla was waiting for us in the clearing place, stretched out on Angel's pallet with her knife by her side. If she were asleep, she recovered very quickly; before Angel and I had half-crossed the room, she was on her feet, knife in hand.

"So? What did you think?"

"It'll work. Angel knows his way around, right enough."

"Where did you go?"

My legs were wobbly; I lowered myself on to the pallet

and rubbed the aching calves. "The air-duct over the governor's chambers."

Calla's eyes widened. "What? Did you see Lord Kekashr?"

"Yes, we saw him. And Lord Shree as well."

She distinctly pouted. "You should have let me come."

Angel made a small, unamicable noise.

"You'll have to make friends with Angel first. But never mind that now. We have problems."

I retailed what we'd overheard of Kekashr's words to Shree. Calla's face hardened as she listened. "They do know you're here, then, in the Gilgard," she said slowly when I had finished.

"I assume, modesty aside, that they were talking about me, yes."

"And the little spider?"

"No names were mentioned. Wait—there was one. What was it? Krisht. Angel, does that mean anything to you?"

"No, my lord Scion."

"Odd—it sounds Sheranik—the feminine form. But that's not possible. The women can't leave Sher." I tried to focus on the puzzle; my head spun.

Calla shifted impatiently. "So what are we going to do?"

"The same as we'd already planned, I suppose." I slumped back on to the pallet, deathly weary of conversation, of thinking, even of breathing. We had talked through the night, Angel and I, before jaunting off to explore his private ways through Sherkin territory. I had patiently drawn out of him the details of ducts and drains, the hidden roads through the Middle Palace, as familiar to Angel as the seams on his wrinkled palms, and the ways through the Temple Palace, not his usual scavenging ground, but he knew enough to get me as far as the sanctuary. After that, I would need no guide. I suspected he had even been into the caves, but when I tried to press him on the point, he became more impenetrable than usual. In fact, it was the toss of a token whether talking to Angel or slithering through the Middle Palace ducts had been the greater strain. My eyes started to close. I shook my head to clear the fog.

Calla looked at me shrewdly, and felt my forehead. Her hand was cool. "You need some sleep," she said. The nagging tone was gone from her voice. "I'm rested, I'll keep watch."

"No. We have to be moving." My tongue was about as thick and responsive as a scrubbing sponge. "I told you what Kekashr said. Once they have the spider, they may learn about the between-ways, and we won't be safe here."

"Kekashr said they'd have him by nightfall," she said soothingly. "It's only morning—we'll be out of here by then. Angel should get some sleep too." She smiled at Angel, with perhaps too many teeth.

Angel looked alarmed, but I was tempted by her offer. Something was bothering me but I could not focus on it. "Only for a little," I mumbled, and collapsed gratefully back on to the pallet, already half asleep, and drowsily felt a blanket thrown over me and heard whispers and light running footsteps and a hissing of more whispers that turned into the steam of a kettle boiling in the kitchen in Exile as I started to slide into a dream. And then Calla was shaking me, and the silvery gleam behind her could only be the candlelight on Lissula's hair. Sleepily, I tried to draw Calla closer.

"Wake up, Tig. Wake up!"

"Hnh? Why? How long did I sleep—?"

"A minute or two." I groaned and closed my eyes, but she punched my shoulder hard enough to shake them open again. "Goldbottom's here. There's going to be a raid," she said tightly. "They're going after the Council of Flamens."

I blinked up at her. Surely this was part of my dream. Lissula's shining head appeared over Calla's shoulder. "It's true, my lord. One of my takers told me last night. He promised me a gold token from his bonus."

The fog thinned inside my head, but the sense of nightmare persisted. I stared up at Lissula with my mouth open.

"They want Bekri."

That woke me. "How do you know?"

"My taker described him. How many men have scars like his? Lord Shree himself is going to lead the raid."

Shree. I remembered his face in the firelight and damned

myself for not putting a dart into his neck. And I damned myself for a drooling idiot, remembering what Kekashr had said; why would the spider's usefulness be finishing unless the Web was going to be torn? Then I would be the traitor's only counter; and the fact that he was also doomed was meagre comfort.

"When is the raid?" I whispered.

"Probably tonight." Lissula daintily shrugged. "My taker told me not to look for him tonight, but tomorrow night he'd bring me a—"

"Tonight! Tig, there's still time to warn Bekri. If we go back now we can save them!"

I looked numbly up at Calla.

"Let's go, damn it!" She pulled me roughly to my feet, knocking a bowl of fruit and meat out of Lissula's hands. I watched apples and pikcherries scatter on the floor around us as Angel retreated into the shadows, his hands and mouth full. It helped me to put off for a few seconds what I knew I had to say.

"We can't go back."

"What?"

"We can't go back. There's nothing we can do, Calla."

Clown, coward, weakling. That's what her eyes said. Her mouth said, "Then what is your plan?"

"To carry on. We must get to the caves."

"The caves!" Calla reared up in her fury. She spat a Sheranik phrase too obscene to have a Gillish equivalent. "The caves, by the (genitalia) of the (procreatively engaged) Lady," she went on, reverting to Gillish. "I'd never seen her so angry. "The Caves be (penetrated from an unusual position)! How can you think of your (coprophagic) mission when those (incestuous offspring of) shulls will put Bekri under torture?"

"We can't help him," I said miserably. "What did you intend to do? Ask the guards nicely if they'd let us pass? Be reasonable, Calla; our only hope is finding the Lady."

"You could kill Kekashr," Lissula lilted, in much the same tone as she might have suggested a picnic. "Angel could help you find him—"

"No!" said Calla forcefully.

"Whyever not, darling?"

Calla disdained to answer, but I supposed I knew. Killing Kekashr, even killing Shree, might gain us valuable time, but if I knew anything about the Sherank, it would release a murderous rage against the helpless citizens of Gil. I thought of how five thousand freemen of Kuttumm had been fed to their own dogs after a failed attempt on the life of Lord Kekashr's grandfather. How much worse would it be for Gil if we succeeded? Bekri himself would tell us to go to the caves if we could, I knew that. And yet, sense and reason aside, the thought of abandoning Bekri and the Web to Lord Shree without even a warning sent a jab of agony through my heart.

Calla clapped her hands together explosively and hurled herself into the shadows where Angel was squatting. He flinched away, but she knelt down and gripped him hard by the shoulders. She pushed her face close to his. "Do you know a way we can get out of the Gilgard?" she demanded.

Still chewing, he nodded.

"Without the Sherank seeing us?"

He swallowed and nodded again. Calla looked up at me. I kicked at an apple. It was madness.

"Oh, all right," I said.

27

"THIS IS COMPLETELY mad," I informed Calla. I peered down the deep, dead blackness of the rubbish chute.

"Scared?"

"I don't like heights."

"You don't have to come."

"Yes I do. Angel won't take you otherwise. He doesn't like you."

At that point, Angel found the coils of rope he wanted within the wild medley of his collection. He tied one to a ring-bolt in the clearing-chamber wall and pitched the rest of that armload into the shaft. It snaked down into the darkness. He kept the second, longer rope looped over his shoulder.

"That ring-bolt," I remarked, "is at least six hundred years old."

Calla tugged on the rope to test it, not listening. Lissula came to my side and gazed with interest into the chute. "How deep is it?"

"Maybe a hundred and fifty feet."

"You know, I once saw a man who fell only a hundred feet. Every bone in his body was smashed, splintered actually, and the splinters were sticking right through his skin, and there were buckets of blood pouring out of his mouth, and—"

"Thank you," I said.

"—his skull was so crushed that his head wobbled like a water-bladder if you poked it—"

"Which of course you did," put in Calla grimly.

"—or like a raw, peeled egg—"

"Shut up, Goldbottom." Calla turned purposefully towards her. Angel seized the rope with all speed and disappeared into the chute. I shut my eyes and thought of the training Flamens as they urged me on to a rope dangling over the edge of an abyss: *a real Hero feels no height at his back.* Big help. My bowels had rumbled then, and they were rumbling now.

"You next, Tig—if you're going, that is," said Calla. I opened my eyes. She was standing firmly in Lissula's way, as if to block any attempt on the latter's part to kiss me goodbye. Lissula may actually have been planning something of the sort, for she was managing to look both wistful and annoyed. Clutching the rope, I shut my eyes again and worked my way over the edge of the chute.

I have consistently tried and failed to block out the mem-

ory of that descent, though it was by no means the worst
few moments of the quest. There was something peculiarly
memorable about clinging to a rope secured to an antiquated
ring-bolt, with my feet flailing for purchase on the top few
stones of a long vertical tunnel. The idea was that I should
"walk" down the shaft, braking myself with a loop of the
rope about my middle; in fact, my method was much more
extemporized than that, and much less dignified. For one
thing, the rope kept swinging me around so that my back
was to the wall; for another, the walls were slippery as glass
with condensation, and the superb workmanship ensured that
few footholds were available in the masonry. I wriggled, I
cursed, I jerked down a few spans at a go; I took twice the
time of either Angel or Calla and landed at last in pitchy
blackness, dazed with elation that I had made it and op-
pressed by the thought that eventually, if I lived that long, I
would have to climb back up again.

I sprawled beside Angel at the bottom of the chute while
Calla made the descent. She landed hard on my shin and
immediately struck a flint for the candle. The walls glim-
mered wetly around us. We were on a platform that sloped
gently to an arched aperture through which wafted a slight
but chilling draft.

"Is that the sewer?" said Calla.

"One of them—the old main sewer under the Lower Palace. There's an outlet into the sea at the north end of the
Gilgard. You can swim, can't you?"

"I'll manage." She pushed past me with the candle,
through the dark archway. Angel and I followed.

The sewer was an arched tunnel through the living rock,
with its floor about three feet lower than the end of the platform. The underground spring that used to feed it had been
diverted long ago to the Lower Palace fountains so that only
the faintest trace of a sewer smell lingered, but the moisture
dripped down the walls and oozed along the floor and the
damp coldness crept like frozen spiders into the marrow of
my bones.

"Which way?"

"That way."

Calla set off at a determined pace, with Angel and I trotting in her wake. Every muscle in my body whined with fatigue. Calla's candle, bobbing along a few paces ahead, seemed to swell and recede, brighten and darken, and at last to take on strange and nightmarish shapes as I fought to stay awake. The world compressed itself into the tiresome necessity of putting one foot before the other, staying upright, moving on, not falling, not stopping; right foot, left foot, right foot, left foot. When we finally halted, it took me some moments to take the fact in. "Are we in Malvi yet?" I asked drunkenly.

"Malvi? Wake up, Tig."

I fought to focus my eyes, partially succeeding. Not dark now; the candle was paled by a source of light from below. The tunnel ended at that point, or rather turned downwards as a steep flume that slid grandly into a vast cavern floored with turgid, gently undulant seawater. It seemed as if we stood on the edge of a well of weak daylight, tinted seagreen at intervals as the swells rose in the outlet to the open sea. It was not, I thought, the most efficient of waste disposal systems, and I was slightly surprised at my ancestors. I started to explain this to Calla, but she cut me short.

"It looks like we'll have to slide down and swim out—try to find the ledge Angel talked about, outside the opening. You go first."

I sat down hard. "Me? This expedition was your idea."

"I can't swim."

"What? I thought you said—"

"I said I'd manage. Where would I have learned to swim? Most Gilmen never even learn to wash. Come on, down you go. There's a rock by the entrance, swim to that and secure the rope." Angel started to say something, but Calla hushed him with a look.

"And then what?"

"I'll pull myself to you along the rope, stupid."

"And then what?"

"And then we'll see. The rock isn't far from the opening, and then there's the ledge. If you can help me to that, we'll be fine."

"And how do we get back up if—when—we return?"

"Angel will stay here with the other end of the rope and pull us up. Now get going."

I gaped at her. She was serious. I could think of no major objection, except that we would probably be killed. Shaking my head, I tied one end of Angel's rope around my middle and sat down to dangle my feet over the brink of the flume. From that vantage point, it seemed nearly vertical and horribly long. I looked back at Calla. She bared her teeth encouragingly. "If I do this," I asked, "will you be impressed?"

"It's possible," she said. "Anyhow, there's no other way to save Bekri."

I nodded gloomily, took a deep breath and slid. There was a lightning impression of Angel stepping forwards to say something, but I dismissed it as improbable. Anyway, I was busy. The stone surface of the flume, polished by centuries of unspeakable drainage, hurtled me bottomwards. Two thoughts flashed through my mind in that tiny scrap of time: first, that we had not stopped to consider what might be lurking in the cloudy waters rushing to meet me; second, that the sea-troglodytes of Miishel actually did this kind of thing for fun.

I slammed into the water with a shocking jolt and then was deep under it and still descending with the runaway momentum built up on the flume. I kicked desperately to slow the downwards plunge and opened my eyes. Strange twisted towers and hillocks took murky shape around me, silhouetted in the diffuse greenish glow from the opening and haloed by long seagrasses that whipped slowly in the surge like the hair of drowned women. Then I was suspended among the seagrasses, surrounded by the weird underwater topography, within touching distance of one of the towers; an anxious message floated up from my lungs—will this take much longer?—and I kicked myself upwards through shoals of little flickering fish-shadows. The surface was an iridescent, unreachable far horizon, right up to the instant when I crashed through and took a burning gulp of air.

I trod water, rocked ponderously by the tide, and oriented myself to the sentinel of rock by the opening. Echoes thundered around me; Calla was shouting, but everything except the timbre of her voice was lost. I wasted no breath in trying to reply, and set off towards the rock in my own free-form version of the Calgornu Flail. It was not easy swimming—the waves pushed me back a stroke for every two or three I took; on the other hand, the cold water woke me up fully for the first time in hours.

Somehow, gasping and choking and fairly clear-headed, I reached the rock. It was a smooth granite finger, slimed with algae, unclimbable, but the tide lifted me so I could slip the loop of rope over the top and pull it lower with my own weight when I dropped in the trough. Then I turned in the water to squint for Calla, but the head of the flume was a black mass of shadow.

"Calla! I'm ready," I shouted. The echoes boomed. There was no answer.

"Calla!"

Her voice came quietly from behind me. "I'm over here. Stop shouting and come quickly."

I twisted in the water and goggled with disbelief. She appeared to be stuck like a fly to the glistening wall about thirty feet away, and a few spans above water level. I remembered the Sheranik obscenity she had used in the clearing chamber, and used it myself, with conviction, several times.

"Never mind that. Just get over here. *Hurry!*"

Gibbering, I obeyed. I told myself it was the only way to get my hands around her neck. Something brushed past me in the water, twined softly around my ankle and drifted away again. I stopped gibbering and swam faster. The next brush was more insistent, and a cluster of little knives swept along my leg. Then Calla had my hands and was tugging me upwards; I found a blessed foothold and used it to catapult myself out of the water. I fell hard on my knees and gasped with the pain, but Calla hauled me bodily away from the edge and slammed me against the stone wall. Her knife was out.

I slowly caught my breath. We were on a ledge a bit wider than I was tall, which curved away around a projection of the cavern. One leg of my britches was shredded and blood was just starting to ooze out of four shallow parallel scratches down the calf. Calla was watching white-faced as something just out of sight over the rim of the ledge churned the water to froth and hurled itself repeatedly against the stone; a sharp, glistening fin-shape rose majestically into view and sank again. There was a louder, more violent explosion of water that slapped down over us both, and then silence except for the leisurely swash of the tide.

"I think it's lost interest in us," Calla whispered after a moment. "Thank the Lady it couldn't reach us here."

"What couldn't reach us here? Where's here? And how, by Oballef, did you get here, anyway?"

She had the grace to look embarrassed. "I took the stairs."

Under my breath, I recited the Zelfic Prophylaxis to Choler. When I had finished, I asked, "What stairs?"

She fiddled with her knife, not meeting my eyes. "There's a staircase from the sewer down to this ledge. Angel showed me, just after you—" she paused "—left."

"You mean," I said, unlocking my teeth, "just after I launched myself down a sheer precipice into freezing water swarming with dangerous man-eating seabeasts. That's what you mean."

"There was only one of them," she said defensively.

I leaned my head against the wall. Calla crept tentatively to my side and draped her cloak over me. It only just missed being as wet as I was, but I was touched by the gesture. When she began to swab at my scratches with the cloak's hem, I gave up entirely on being angry. "Never mind," I said. "We should be getting on. Where's Angel?"

"He wouldn't come."

"Why not?"

"He didn't say. I'd guess he's afraid."

"I can sympathize," I said dourly. Keeping well away from the rim, we made our way along the ledge towards the outlet. To my relief, the ledge continued through to the outside, although it dropped nearly to water level by the time it reached the opening. Indeed, the higher swells washed it a span deep every few seconds. Warily, with one eye on the smooth menace of the cavern waters, we waited for the trough of the next wave and dashed through into the sunlight.

28

THE LEDGE CONTINUED. It was only a couple of spans wide and the rock ballooned above it so that we had to stand slant-bodied with a hand on the clammy wall, but we could see it stretching away from us, almost on the waterline, until it passed around the curve of the Gilgard cliff and was lost to sight. The high-water mark was just above waist level.

"By the Lady, I wish we'd known about this ledge before!" Calla said. "A secret entrance to the Gilgard—"

"Do you think the tide's coming in or going out?"

"How would I know?"

"We'll find out soon enough. Come on."

In fact, the tide was coming in, and fast. It came flush with the ledge, then lapped over it; it licked at our ankles and then tugged at them, gaining power with each incoming wave. By the time a tiny wedge of beach came into sight, the water was halfway to our knees and we had to brace ourselves against the strong suck of every retreat.

The beach was a little pocket of shingle, the first outlier of the flatland that collared the Gilgard on three sides; not much further, and we should encounter the first pickets of the Sherkin guard. But it was enough for the moment to collapse on to the shingle, to rub our soaked and aching calves, to stretch the arms cramped from steadying our bodies against the convex rockface. The mountain loomed over us, sheer and smooth and dizzying; it seemed to extend upwards indefinitely, as if the sky had suddenly polarized into stone and air. Beside me, Calla gasped and covered her eyes with her arm. "It's toppling over," she moaned.

"It does look like that," I agreed, "but it's only an illusion. You see, the—"

"Never mind."

"But—"

"I don't want to know. Come on, we're wasting time."

I sighed. Knowing what was ahead, part of me was quite happy to waste time. But the thought of Bekri was a goad; also the conviction that, were we to stop too long, the cold and the numb fatigue that was spreading slowly through our bodies would paralyse us completely. Shaking ourselves like dogs, we set off over the curve of jagged granite boulders that lay between us and the city.

We came too suddenly on to the edge of the main beach. I had been expecting—dreading—to hear Sherkin patrols long before we got that far. The sea-wall stretched away from us towards the harbour, where the fishing boats and the Sherkin warships lay peacefully at anchor. Too peacefully. It was late afternoon; the fishermen should have been unloading the early catch, or readying the boats for the night-time trawl. At the very least, the menders of nets and cleaners of keels should have been working around the boats pulled half out of the water on to the beach, but not a soul was in sight, neither Sherkin nor Gilman. Only the sluggish susurration of the waves and the whisper of sand grains crawling in a light breeze broke the silence.

Hugging the sea-wall, we crept to the first set of steps and stood listening. The silence was pervasive and unnerving. No feet, no wains on the corniche above our heads. No market sounds. No voices, though I knew very well that a drinking house was located directly across the corniche, and should have been uproarious at that time of day. I looked at Calla, who shook her head. Her eyes were enormous with puzzlement.

"Something's wrong," she whispered.

I didn't bother to reply. Cautiously, we set our feet on the sea-stairs and climbed; as our faces came level with the pavement, we could see that the corniche was indeed deserted. The drinking house was closed and shuttered. Along the street, the stalls of a tiny fishmarket leaned dejectedly together, empty of sellers, buyers and fish. No smoke rose from any of the chimneys, nor from the smokeholes of the hovels festering around the buildings. We climbed the rest of the stairs wordlessly and stole along the corniche.

"I feel like we're being watched," Calla whispered. I could feel it too—as if a thousand eyes were following our progress and a thousand breaths were being held until we had passed. "Nonsense," I said. We turned up the same street I had followed on my first memorable morning in Gil: deserted.

"Two days," Calla muttered. "We've only been inside since yesterday morning. What could have happened in such a short time?"

A plague? I thought. Like Calloon in the Year of Chastening, when three out of four swelled with the poison until their skins burst like rotten fruit? Their memorians had written of silent streets, where the dead lay where they had fallen, and the living fled, and the only sound was the buzz of carrion-flies; and even the flies were silent when they grew too gorged to move. I sniffed the air, but the stench seemed to have no more of death in it than usual. A thin dog drifted out of an alley, saw us, rooted unconcernedly in a pile of rubbish, drifted back into the alley. Nothing else moved.

Calla laid a hand on my arm. "Listen."

A concerted tramp-tramp of booted feet, and at least two horses, maybe three. They were in the next cross-street, still distant, but moving our way. We dived for the shelter of the nearest hovel, pushed past the ragged blanket in the entry— and stopped in confusion. A semicircle of wide eyes, of pinched and nervous faces, surrounded us in the gloom. Calla, recovering first, held her hand in a dusty chink of light, and signed: *friends*. The older woman nodded and we hunkered down on the floor, completing the circle.

With the tramping from the street in our ears, Calla asked silent questions. *What's happening? Why are the streets empty?*

How can you not know? Orders from Kekashr. The name was a claw drawn across the throat.

Why?

When has he needed a reason?

When was the order made?

This morning. The Pleasure for anyone caught on the street. The Claws for the slightest noise. Keep quiet.

The patrol had turned into the street, and was approaching with cruel slowness. The younger woman turned a set face down to her sleeping baby. Three small children with aged eyes sat calm and unmoving and perfectly silent, holding hands. I thought of Callefiya's son, safe in Exile—until such time as the Flamens would send him, disastrously primed, to Gil. As the smart clatter of feet and hooves passed the hovel, I looked down at my hands, and found that the knuckles were white around a knife I could not remember drawing. The patrol reached the end of the street, turned on to the corniche, and faded into the distance. Calla stood up.

We'll endanger you no longer.

The woman raised her hand to reply, but we were already on our way out of the door. Knowing that inside each hovel crouched a circle of terrified innocents, the desertion of the streets took on another dimension of wrongness and despair. We crept along, hugging the shadows at the edge of the pavement, uncomfortably aware that the topmost towers of the Gilgard commanded a view of the whole city.

Calla grabbed my elbow. "Did you hear that?"

"Yes—but I don't think I believed it." It came again, drunken, mournful and woefully off-key; the Lament for the Lady, the unofficial anthem of the new Gil. Just to hum the air meant an appointment with the clawed whips. Mysheba had taught me a few of its countless stanzas, and I had written down as many as I could gather; these lines I did not recognize, a scatalogical and unflattering speculation on Lord Kekashr's personal habits. Despite the circumstances, my fingers itched for a pen.

"He's out of our way," Calla said. "We should leave him, but—"

"If a patrol finds him, he's a dead man."

We looked at each other helplessly, then turned in the direction of the singer. He was not hard to find, sprawled comfortably on a high-piled midden in the centre of a crossroads only a street away, bawling to the sky; but as we started towards him from the far end of the street, a thunder of hooves suddenly echoed off the silent housefronts. I pulled Calla into the shelter of a gaping doorway. "Too late," she groaned. The lament cut off abruptly; then the horses screamed. A shout in Sheranik, also truncated, and a series of almighty thuds and the crashing of metal; Calla swore and stepped into the street before I had time to move, took one look, swore again, and vanished towards the action.

I stepped out. At the end of the street, one horse kicked feebly on the ground. Two others lay like collapsed tents in their billowing caparisons. The bodies of five or six men were spilled around them, dressed in the black, silver and scarlet of Kekashr's crack troops. As I watched, the last survivor fell to his knees, pushed off his helmet and clawed at his throat. The singer rose from the midden and finished him off with one swipe of a heavy club.

I ran up the street in Calla's wake. By the time I reached her, a dozen men and women in Gillish rags had materialized and were silently stripping the dead of their weapons and armour and securing ropes to the horses and dragging them away. Calla and I stood speechless on the edge of this scene of model efficiency, ignored until the singer from the midden came up to us and pulled the hood away from his face.

"Hawelli!" Calla gasped. She recovered herself. "I should have known it was you—you never could carry a tune."

He grinned. "You must admit I can organize. Did you see that? Beautiful! Perfect! The fourth patrol we've wiped out today, and I'll wager old Crockjaw still doesn't know about the first three."

"Crockjaw?" I asked.

"Kekashr, our esteemed governor." Hawelli beamed at me triumphantly—also smugly. "My lord Tigrallef! Still alive. Congratulations. And do you still think we're helpless against the might of Sher?"

"Yes."

His smile stiffened, but remained in place. "Why? You've seen what can be done with clever planning and a few simple dart-tubes. And this is only the first stage."

"How much venom have you got for the darts?"

"At this rate, enough to account for eleven or twelve patrols. It's quick, it's quiet, it's clean, and we can hide any traces before moving on to set up the next trap. They can't touch us—we know every twist in the city, and they don't even know yet they've been bitten."

"Fleabites," I said. "They'll start to wonder soon about these missing patrols. And what happens when you run out of venom?"

"We're the heirs of every Sherkin we kill." He waved at a pair of Gilmen trotting off around the corner, bearing between them a stretcher heaped with captured armour and weapons. The last of the Sherkin corpses, stripped to the skin, was being hauled unceremoniously out of sight into a nearby building. Already the street was empty except for ourselves and one Gilman with a rake, who was busily rearranging the patterns left in the dust.

"I'm impressed," I said softly. "But there are several thousand Sherkin troopers here, and hundreds of thousands in Sher. Will you take all of them on? And didn't you promise Bekri you'd do nothing—"

"Bekri! There's a point. I assumed that you'd have been with Bekri and the council—but of course, I'm very glad to see you. Both," he added after a pause.

"Bekri is why we're here," Calla began. "We've come to warn him. There's a raid planned on the council, and a traitor—oof."

I removed my heel from her instep. "Hawelli Flamen," I said with maximum formality, "we have important business to discuss with the Council of Flamens. May I say that I admire what you are doing, and wish you well, and even give you my blessing, but we must leave—"

"To see Bekri? I hope not."

"Why?"

"Because Bekri is in the Gilgard. You're too late."

29

HAWELLI DETAILED A little Gilwoman, hardly more than a child, to guide us through the deserted streets to what he darkly called his "warbase." It had been a mansion of some importance, judging by the ornamentation and massive spread of the façade, but it was a shell now, the roof and upper floors having long since collapsed into a mountain of matchstick rubble contained by the standing walls. Our guide led us to a well-concealed hole in the forecourt and then pattered off on some other errand; we descended to find ourselves in a long, stone-vaulted cellar that had somehow withstood the weight of the wreckage, cut into segments by a succession of low arches. A busy swarm of revolutionaries, working in near-total silence, greeted Calla with a frenzy of welcoming fingerspeech, and me with curious looks.

Calla and I were installed in a corner and given clean britches, cloaks and tunics in exchange for our damp street-rags. We requested and received two pairs of magnificent Sherkin boots from the latest haul. Some sort of healing muck was smeared on the slashes the seabeast had made in my leg, and a loaf and two beakers of lukewarm, grease-clotted shull broth were produced, tasting at that moment like the finest gourmet delicacy ever to come out of Oballef's kitchens. None of this did anything for my spirits; *too late* thudded like a drum between my temples.

Hawelli appeared, stopped to give orders, and joined us. "I don't have much time—another trap is nearly in place. Have you been well taken care of?"

"Yes," I said, "but—"

"Good. Now, I have some plans about how I can use you."

I blinked at him, surprised. "Me? You want to use me?"

"Yes. You'll be a figurehead—naturally, I shall retain command, but it might hearten the people to know that a Scion of Oballef is in Gil. If they remember what that means, of course. Don't worry, I won't ask you to do anything dangerous."

Beside me, Calla drew herself up with the wrathful dignity that I had come to know too well, since it was usually directed at me. This time, she was glaring at Hawelli. "If you had the slightest idea," she said stiffly, "what the Scion has been doing in the last two days, you would know that he sneers at danger."

I dropped my beaker of broth. Hawelli looked from Calla to me and back again and raised his eyebrows.

"There's to be no more talk of using him, as if he were a shit-hoe or a broom," Calla went on severely. "If anything, you should be laying your weapons at his feet and offering him your loyalty."

Hawelli's mouth twitched at the corners. "Fine," he said. He extracted a dart-tube from his cloak and tossed it on the floor at my feet. "Satisfied, Calla?"

She glowered, but I picked up the dart-tube and handed it back to him. "Don't fight, children, please. Hawelli?"

"Yes, my lord Scion?"

"Tell me about the raid on the council." It was too painful to ask directly about Bekri. Hawelli gave me a suspicious look, then one of his famous shrugs, accepting the switch of topic.

"It was midmorning, while the council was meeting. Lord Shree was in command of the raiding party. They went directly to the tapestry chamber, grabbed everybody in sight and hauled them straight off to the Gilgard. I'm told it was over in minutes. Calla, I'm also told that Malviso and Big Sor were killed."

She bowed her head, and raised it again with tight lips and dry eyes. I put my hand on her shoulder.

"And the curfew?" I asked.

"Instant. Before the prisoners were halfway to the castle, the heralds were in every square in Gil. Kekashr gave us half an hour to get indoors, though he started grabbing Pleasurebait a few minutes early, the pocketing bastard. When I heard about the council, I knew it was time to act."

"Who was taken?" I asked quietly.

"Everyone in the chamber, plus a few others. Maybe thirty altogether. Mysheba and some of the other women managed to get the children away, and Faruli was off delivering a baby—fortunately, for we'll need a healer before this uprising is done. And the Second Flamen wasn't with the council, so he's safe."

"Jebri? But he hardly leaves Bekri's side. Why wasn't he there?"

"Ask him yourself. He's somewhere about."

I looked around. He was not visible in that segment of the cellar, nor through the archway into the next, where the captured weapons and uniforms were being sorted and gloated over. "How did he know where to find you? Did he know about this place?"

"No, we found him. I think Sibba brought him in."

Calla started and asked, "Sibba's one of yours?"

"To the core. Most of the youngsters have been aching for real action. Bekri was out of touch."

"Out of touch? Hawelli Flamen, how can you be so ungrateful? Who was it that founded the Web? Where would we all be without him?" Calla was indignant again, but I was still thinking about Jebri. Why, today of all days, had he been absent from the tapestry chamber, and at the crucial hour? No doubt there was a valid explanation; I badly wanted to hear it.

"Have Jebri fetched," I broke in.

Hawelli appeared glad of the diversion, although he raised his eyebrows again at my tone. He motioned to one of the young boys nearby. "Go find the Second Flamen. Tell him the Scion of Oballef wants to see him." The boy ran off. Hawelli ignored me and turned back to Calla. He sighed heavily, like a man who is at some pains to come to terms with a fool. "This is not a good moment for us to quarrel, Calla. I withdraw my remarks, if it makes you feel better, although I still insist—never mind. What's important is that you're here now, and it's our chance to fight back at last.

Join with me on the next raid; come and strike a blow with me against the enemy."

"What about Lord Tigrallef?"

"The Scion will stay here—however brave you say he is, we shouldn't risk him until we need to."

I sneezed. "I'm touched by your concern for my safety, Hawelli Flamen, but—"

"Don't take it personally," he interrupted. His tone was not very friendly. "I'm just aware of your value to the people."

"As a symbol?"

He looked wary. "Something like that."

"I'm sorry, I don't have the leisure to be a symbol. Thanks for the broth." I pulled on one of the Sherkin boots. It was too big.

"Where do you think you're going?"

"Back to the Gilgard, just as soon as I've seen Jebri."

Hawelli laughed incredulously. "You're mad. How are you going to get into the Gilgard now?"

"I have my ways." I pulled the boot off and stuffed some rags into the toe. This time, it fitted. While I started on the other boot, Hawelli stood up and leaned over me. "What if I don't let you go?"

"Could you pass me the cloak, please?"

He passed it automatically. I crammed the heel of bread into an inner pocket and stood up. Hawelli moved back a pace, shaking his head. "Calla, can you talk to this lunatic?"

She was already on her feet, booted and cloaked. "I'll talk to him on the way to the Gilgard."

Hawelli's lips tightened. He turned his back on me and grasped Calla's shoulders. "Have you forgotten—"

"No," said Calla hastily, "but things are different now."

An icy stare at me, this time over his shoulder. "But we talked about this—what we would do if Bekri were ever taken. You said you'd die fighting by my side."

"I know what I said. But there may be a more helpful way to die."

"By *his* side?"

"Yes." Defiantly.

He stared at her, then abruptly released her shoulders. "You're as mad as he is. Or as stupid." He settled himself down on a crate again, and looked disapprovingly up at us like a Flamen about to scold a pair of recalcitrant novices. "Naturally," he said, biting each word, "what's going on between the two of you means nothing to me."

I took a long breath as the light hit me. He was jealous. I had never been on the receiving end of jealousy before, especially sexual jealousy. The feeling was novel and not unpleasant.

"But I still can't let you go," Hawelli went on. There was satisfaction hidden in his voice.

"How do you plan to stop us?" Calla asked.

"By force. I'll tie you up if I need to. You're not going anywhere."

"Why not?"

"You know the location of my warbase. When you're caught, as I'm sure you will be, Kekashr will have it out of your hero here in no time at all."

My eyes were caught by someone drifting through the next segment of cellar. "You needn't worry, Flamen," I said. "If they were to catch us, they wouldn't ask us about anything as trivial as your warbase." Hawelli's face turned a dangerous red, but I gave him no time to answer. "Anyway, it will make no difference shortly."

"And why is that?"

"Because I believe you've already been betrayed."

The young boy whom Hawelli had sent to fetch Jebri came through the archway and stood quietly behind Hawelli, waiting to be noticed. He waited until his leader's outraged sputters subsided, then touched Hawelli's shoulder respectfully. "There's no sign of the Second Flamen," he said.

"Don't bother us now," Hawelli said testily. The boy shrugged and turned to go, but I put out my hand.

"Where did you look?" I asked.

"Everywhere. He's nowhere in the cellar."

"What difference does it make?" snapped Hawelli. "Why do you want to speak to him anyway? He wasn't even there for the raid."

"Exactly my point, Hawelli Flamen. Why do you suppose he wasn't there?"

"How should I know? Does it matter?"

Calla looked like she was slowly adding things up. "You don't mean—"

"I mean it's possible that Jebri is the little spider, the traitor, and he's gone off to sell Hawelli's secret to Kekashr."

Hawelli shook his head. "I don't believe you."

"Are you willing to take the risk?"

"There's no risk. Why should I listen to you?"

"Hawelli," Calla said softly, "I've found that Lord Tigrallef often knows what he's talking about. I know, it was a surprise to me too, but he's brighter than he looked at first. And if he thinks there's a chance that Jebri is the traitor—"

"But that's ridiculous," Hawelli grated. "Jebri is the Second Flamen. He's been an uncle to us all, especially to you, Calla."

There were tears in Calla's eyes. "I know that. But you should still listen to the Scion. Move your people, at least until you're sure you haven't been sold out."

"But the weapons—the stores—"

"Leave them for now," I said. "If I'm wrong, they'll come to no harm and you can return to them later. If I'm right, then you have no time to move them. Just get your people out."

Hawelli's face hardened. "This is a trick to make me let you go."

"The Lady give me patience!" Calla exploded.

At that moment, an urgent ringing froze Hawelli and the boy beside him. The source was a bell hanging just under the ceiling, on the end of a rope that vanished up through an aperture near the wall. The rope jerked again, frantically, three tense bursts of clangour followed a second later by two more; all through the cellar, Hawelli's revolutionaries picked up the nearest weapons and moved towards the entry. They went calmly and purposefully, as if the bell were a signal that put a well-drilled plan into motion.

"What is it?" Calla whispered.

"Morra, on lookout. She's signalling a large force headed our way. Not a patrol."

I didn't actually say I told you so, but I thought it. Hawelli scowled at me for a moment, and then at the ground. "Calla," he said, "are you determined to go with this madman?"

"Of course."

"There's nothing I can say?"

"You could wish us good fortune."

His face darkened. I think Calla was asking too much. Still not looking at either of us, he caught up a Sherkin sword from the table and tested its edge against his palm.

"Then go," he said bitterly. "Get out fast. Head for the sea; we'll be drawing them the other way, towards the market. Enjoy the Gilgard." He whirled, sword in hand, and was gone.

Calla and I joined the stream out of the hole. Hawelli's people boiled out around us and vanished into the wreckage and the street. I heard a shriek, abruptly terminated, and then a peculiar muted rumbling, like many feet walking across a pallet, and I remembered—when the Sherank wanted to move quietly, they would muffle their boots and horses' hooves with sheepskin.

Calla pulled me over the mound of rubble and through a shadowy gap in the back wall, then we were off and free and skimming through the ghostly streets of Gil towards the corniche. Somewhere behind us, there were screams and the clash of swords.

30

JUST BEFORE SUNSET, Calla and I stood again on the shingle beach under the mountain's looming mass. The tide was on the ebb, but the ledge that would take us back to the cavern was still under water. There was nothing we could do but wait. To the east, on the rim of the sea, a narrow moon was rising. In the northern sky, the first stars of the Crown and the Ladle had just become visible. I pulled my warm new cloak, courtesy of Hawelli and the Sherank, tighter around me and sat down on the pebbles.

"A beautiful night," I said. "These early spring evenings are really the best ones of the year, don't you think?"

Calla flopped down beside me. "You talk as if we're taking a quiet stroll in the moonlight. We failed, Tig. It was all a waste."

I threw a pebble into the sea. "I know. A waste of precious time, a risk of the whole enterprise, and we didn't even manage to save Bekri. You're right—it was a waste. We failed."

"You're very calm about it."

"We can't change the past." I took the bread out of my pocket and pulled it in two. Calla hesitated before she took a piece.

"It was my fault," she said. "You'd have gone looking for the Lady if I hadn't dragged you away—you might even have found her by now."

"Maybe," I said with my mouth full. "And maybe not."

"What's worse, Bekri was already in the Gilgard by the time we set out—"

"Stop it, Calla."

She bit unhappily into her heel of bread, chewed for a

long time and then swallowed. "You blame me, don't you?"

"I blame myself. After all, going back was the heroic thing to do. I should have known better."

There was a pause. "Was that a joke?"

"Only partly," I said.

We sat quietly on the shingle waiting for the tide to go down. Kekashr and the frightened city seemed no closer than the moon itself. The sea calmly carried on receding; the moon-path across the water looked as solid as a marble pavement, as if we could set our feet on it and walk clear over the sea to Exile. I wondered what Arkolef and my mother were doing at that moment; the Flamens, I knew, would be happily and contentiously involved in their favourite pastime, planning their next hero's training, all unaware that I was still alive. Marori, the old Gilborn, would be mumbling in the corner: *trust no one*. Calla stirred at my side, and I reached on impulse for her hand. At least, I told myself, I could trust Calla. She interwined her fingers with mine.

"Tig? What happens when we find the Lady?"

"We win," I said.

"No, no. I mean, what do you do with her if you manage to find her?"

Still holding Calla's hand, I leaned back on my elbows to look up at the spangled sky. "I invoke one of the Wills— they tell me I'll know at the time which one to use. The Lesser, with any luck."

"Why is luck involved?"

I laughed, softly and without mirth. "Because I'm afraid of the Greater Will. Nobody has ever invoked it, not even Oballef when he turned this island from a barren rock in the sea into a paradise. The Lesser Will was enough for even that."

Though I was staring at the sky, I could feel the intensity of her eyes. "So there is danger?" she asked.

"Possibly. There's a Caveat attached, but nobody knows what it means. I wonder if even Oballef knew. Unfortunately, it's in the same forgotten tongue as the Wills are."

Calla pulled insistently at my hand. "So you don't know what could happen." She sounded angry. "The Lady could destroy you even while you're trying to destroy the Sherank."

"No. Never."

"But how do you know? You've just said—"

"I'm a Scion of Oballef," I broke in, sitting up straight. "No direct harm can ever come to one of us from the Lady in Gil. That seems to be woven into the fabric of things. The dangers are of a different order."

"You're not making any sense."

I turned to Calla, enfolding her hand between both of mine. "When a Will is invoked, there is a melding. What the Lady does then depends on what's in the Scion's mind. And that's what frightens me, Calla. That may be what the Caveat warns against. There is such a thing," I said, dropping the words like stones into a pit of sleeping horrors, "as too much power."

The horrors stirred in their sleep. I tightened my grip on Calla's hand, as if she were a protective talisman, or the Lady in Gil in person. She exclaimed softly and curled her other arm around my shoulder, pulling me closer so that our cheeks were pressed together for a few moments. Then she pushed me gently away.

"Thank you," I said.

"What for, Tig?"

I resumed chucking pebbles into the dark receding sea. "For that moment of comfort, for one thing. For everything you've taught me. For volunteering to come with me in the first place." A cherished mental image came into my head. "For putting that wonderful look on Hawelli's face, back in the city. It was good of you to speak up for me."

Calla shifted uncomfortably. "Oh, that. Yes, well. About Hawelli and me—" she began. She stopped.

"What?"

"It's that Hawelli and I—we used to agree on many things. We disagreed on many things, too," she added quickly.

"Oh?"

"You know what I'm trying to say, don't you?"

I thought about it. "No."

She sighed. "Are you really so innocent?" She turned her

face away. "I simply thought you might be wondering about Hawelli and me. After what he said in the warbase."

"About dying by his side?"

"Yes." She hesitated, then went on, "There was a time, not so long ago, when that seemed like a good idea if anything serious happened to the Web."

"Are you lovers?" The Lady roast me if I lie, the words just popped out. Calla went rigid. "We were," she said.

"Were." Past tense. I liked the sound of that. I reached out to take her hand again and pulled her around so that we were face to face. The moon turned her skin to ivory and her hair to ebony, and I was swamped again by that now-familiar deluge of tenderness. "How do you feel about me?" I asked.

Her voice was remote. "Don't you know?"

"Not really. There have been certain signs," I said, "that you find me not totally objectionable, but I have no experience in these matters. And I still can't imagine, hard as I try, why you'd sleep with someone like me unless you'd actually been ordered to."

She pulled her hands away. "You're very dense at times." She looked tight-lipped back at the sea.

I remember smiling. It was a mystery to me still, but the evidence seemed quite clear: nobody had ordered Calla into my bed. She had come to me because she wanted to. I took a deep breath and let it out again, still smiling. Bekri was in the south dungeon, the tide was about to uncover the slideway to danger and possibly death, and somewhere in the mountain at Calla's back, the Lady was waiting—but for these few moments, in the quiet eye of the storm, we could allow ourselves to be happy.

"I love you," I said.

Calla glanced at me and away again. "I'm horrible to you."

"Not as often as you used to be."

"We could die tonight."

"I know."

She looked me full in the face, and said forcefully, "There are things you don't know about me."

"I don't care. I love you."

"If you knew—"

"It wouldn't matter."

"I'll wager it would." She stood up and walked away from me to the water's edge.

"Then tell me," I said, not moving.

She said nothing. I waited for a comment from the critic in my head. Nothing. I stood up and walked along Calla's moon-shadow. She turned as I reached her and flung her arms around me, as if she were drowning and wanted me, not to save her, but to drown with her. I was willing. No whispers this time, no fumbling or uncertainty; only a fusion and a sinking together, beyond fear and the reach of reason, into dark rhythmic waters.

"Time to go." Calla shook me. "The tide's well down."

I stared straight up at the Ladle. My bare legs were freezing and the hard pebbles were digging into my back, even through the thick cloak, but I was still too full of wonder to think of shifting. "If I die in the next few hours," I said dreamily, "I will not feel my life has been entirely wasted."

"Stop that." She kissed my forehead and helped me up and into my clothes. The moon was not much higher, but it felt like a long time had passed. At the far side of the beach, the ledge was visible just above the waterline.

"May the Lady in Gil help us now, if she never helped us before," breathed Calla. She edged her way on to the narrow strip of rock. I sidled along after her. Our Sherkin boots were squelching within seconds, but we looped our beautiful new cloaks up out of danger. There had never been a quieter night, nor a glassier, more silent sea; though my muscles knotted from sliding crabwise along the slippery ribbon of path and my back ached like it was carrying the whole weight of the mountain, I found myself savouring that stillness. The Sherank, the Web, the Lady herself, all seemed like a bad dream. Or a bad joke. If only the ledge led nowhere! If only, I thought, we could drop into the sea and swim away from the Gilgard's awful prospects, together, into a world where Gil and Iklankish were as dim and legendary as long-fallen Fathan. But the ledge did lead somewhere, and it was somewhere I was obliged to go; right foot, left foot, right foot, left foot. All at once we were at the mouth of the cavern and Calla was bracing herself at the bulbous edge of the turning. A moment more and she had vanished inside.

I breathed deeply and took a last look at the brilliant moon, balanced like a bubble on the points of the Crown, then turned and slithered around the treacherous corner after her. She was waiting for me a few feet along, where the ledge sloped upwards to an entirely relative safety.

It was not as dark in the cavern as I expected, even before Calla lit her candle. Not only did moonlight wash through the opening, but the depths of the water were alive with phosphorescence that outlined the submarine towers and tors and swirled around the little fish and—notably—a long, dark, finned and tentacled shape the size of a Storican trunk-beast that cruised the cavern purposefully just under the surface.

"You see?" said Calla. "There is only one."

"One would have been enough. Thank the Lady we don't have to swim. Let's go."

The stairs were narrow, worn and absolutely straight, slicing like a swordcut through the solid rock. They ended in a high arched opening just ten feet from the top of the flume. Angel was not there; the rope, neatly coiled and with one frayed and worried end where something had bitten it through, was the only visible artefact. I slung it over my shoulder—on the principle that you never know when you might need a good rope—and gazed into the blinding blackness of the sewer tunnel. From far, far away, there was a whisper of an echo of a sound.

Calla didn't seem to hear it. "What now?" she asked.

"We try to find the right rubbish chute and climb back up into the between-ways. With luck, Angel will be waiting for us there."

"You told him to wait here."

"No, Calla, you told him to wait here. Maybe he didn't like being alone."

She sniffed at that. "He's been alone most of his life."

"Never mind." Again, that distant ghost of sound. Calla didn't react and I began to doubt my ears. We started down the tunnel. My ears strained as we hurried along, hand in hand, but the fearful darkness that lay ahead of us was silent now.

Calla stumbled and fell, pulling me with her, but she managed to keep the candle alight. "What was that?" she asked in a puzzled voice. "I tripped on something."

"Rubble—no, bricks," I said, sitting up and rubbing my knee. "They're all across the tunnel."

"They weren't here the first time we passed," Calla said decisively. "This tunnel was as bare as a Gilman's cupboard." She lifted the candle higher and drew in her breath, shook my shoulder and pointed at the wall. Her eyes were huge.

I turned. The smooth rock-cut wall was broken by a square opening, which someone had, at some time, blocked with brick masonry. About half of this had now been torn away, leaving a jagged hole large enough for a man to crawl comfortably through; on the floor near the hole was a knife with a broken blade. The knife was familiar. I had last seen it in Angel's hand, at Calla's throat, during one of their minor disagreements. Of Angel himself there was no sign.

Calla hesitated. I took the candle and pushed myself halfway through the opening, holding the light into the darkness beyond. Upwards, there was nothing but more darkness, higher than the feeble light could reach; downwards, a rippled, water-polished surface of dark stone, tufted here and there with whitish fungus. At the edge of the light, a flick of movement; a roach as big as my thumb, white as a grub, scuttled into visibility and stood waving its antennae wildly for a moment, then flashed clear across the circle of candle-light, almost faster than my eye could follow. A broken second later, with a clicking of tiny claws, a snow-white bat hobbled after it across the light, looking, with its wrinkled face and folded wrinkled wings, like a little old blind man on crutches. It, too, disappeared into the darkness, and a second later a scrabble and a crunch marked the end of the miniature drama. I withdrew the light and sat down with my back to the sewer wall.

"Well?" said Calla. "What is it? Where does it go?"

I handed her the candle. "I had a feeling he'd been in there, you know. Though why he was afraid to mention it—"

"What? Who?"

"Angel, the Lady bless him. This hole—"

"Yes?"

"—leads straight into the mountain. Into the caves."

31

"DO YOU KNOW where you're going?"

"No. Well, not exactly. Generally upwards."

"I thought you knew the caves. I thought the Secrets of the Ancients—"

"The Secrets assume you're starting from one of the proper gates, up in the Temple Palace."

Calla stopped short. "Then we could get lost."

"We're already lost, in a way."

Calla made a sound of exasperation, which echoed along the passageway to become a full-throated chorus of nonconfidence. We had left the chamber where Angel had broken through and followed a rather grand, gently spiralling corridor that suddenly narrowed into a writhing natural cleft in the rock. We rapidly discovered that this was a common pattern in the Caves, particularly the lower reaches, but it was disconcerting the first time it happened.

It was equally disconcerting to find, nearly by catastrophic and intimate personal experience, that the floors were fissured here and there by broad, sharp-edged cracks, or by sudden pits that ranged from shallow scoops to unfathomable wells of still, black water. We were not alone; the caves housed a simple life-chain of their own, the white bats feeding on the white roaches, the roaches on white antlings, the antlings on the ubiquitous white fungus, and the fungus, presumably, on the rock itself.

While these little stumping and creeping denizens gave us the occasional nasty turn, they were also company of a sort. Imagine a small, dry rustle magnified by echoes and ambient silence into the scratch of a behemoth's belly-scales right at your heels; there is a certain comfort in knowing it is the roach you didn't step on a minute ago, or one of the diminutive, flightless bats lurching along in pursuit. We became inured fairly quickly to the soft sighs and whispers, the busy clicking of claws, the delicate whistles and squeaks—but even so, I was uneasy; there was a feeling of sleeping powers all around, as of other presences, or as if the twisted intestinal tunnels of the Caves were indeed the gut of some immense, dormant creature. I did not mention this to Calla.

Of course, I didn't really need to. "Do you get the feeling," she asked as we scuttled along, "that we're not alone?"

"Not really," I lied.

Calla sensibly discounted the lie. "Maybe it's Angel."

"I don't think so. Why would he hide from us? Anyhow, there's nobody there."

She did not answer, but stopped again to listen. I realized that we were not just holding hands now, but were more closely linked, my arm tight around her shoulders, her arm warm around my waist. She jerked suddenly.

"Listen! Did you hear that?"

"A bat," I said.

She raised her head, nostrils wide as if she were trying to smell the trace which the sound had left on the air. "Do you remember the legends about the caves?" she breathed.

"That's all they are—legends."

"You don't believe them?" Her voice was unsteady.

"They're legends, Calla. Primitive superstitions from before Oballef came: never observed, never authenticated, no more real than—than the steam dragons of Calloon, or the Ghouls of Ghasca. No, I don't believe in them."

She cocked her head at me suspiciously. "You don't believe in those either?"

"I'm a memorian, not a priest. I'm not obliged to believe in things that can't be documented."

"You believe in the Lady in Gil."

"She can be documented. Her—" The same sound came again. A sliding sound, not loud, but with size built into its timbre. The squeaks and whispers hushed for a few seconds, then gradually resumed. Calla and I looked at each other over the candle. We walked on quickly.

Decision time came again. The tunnel branched into three, two of them broad and smooth and climbing, the third no more than a rough pipe, wide enough for us to squeeze into, but furred all over with fungus. Calla sniffed with distaste and started to move past its mouth, but I found myself held by it.

"Come on," said Calla impatiently, "which is it to be?"

Feeling strange and light-headed, I took the candle and held it into the white-crusted opening. Within reach of the light, the pipe twisted downwards and to one side. Calla peered in beside me. "Not that one, thank the Lady. You said we should keep going up."

Only half of my head heard her. The other half was preoccupied by an entirely novel sensation.

"This way," I said.

"You're joking. In there?"

"Yes." I tucked my knife in my belt, dumped my cloak and Angel's rope on the ground and climbed in.

"Tig, you fishbrain, it turns downwards!"

Under my hands and knees, the fungus yielded spongily, then popped like blisters, releasing a viscous liquid that smelled like rotting onions.

"Tigrallef!"

"It's all right," I called back. There was a scramble in the darkness behind me, followed by a small explosion of heartfelt disgust. I grinned and crawled on; however reluctantly, Calla was following.

She caught my foot and held on doggedly. "You've finally gone mad," she snapped. "Why in Oballef's name choose this one? There are two perfectly good passages back there that don't involve swimming through hogbile, or whatever this muck is. You come back this instant."

"They're dead ends, Calla. This one will get us there— the others won't."

"How can you be so sure?"

"I'm a Scion of Oballef, aren't I?"

"So what? You come back here."

I kicked my foot loose, but she grabbed it again and started to pull. "Calla," I said, "trust me. I know where we are. We've reached the parts I memorized."

That knocked the wheels off her wain. "Why didn't you say so in the first place?" she said. Her voice still dripped with suspicion, but she released my foot. Onwards we squelched, onwards and downwards, pulling ourselves along on our elbows and knees. It became as tight a fit as any duct in the Middle Palace, but the malodorous fungal slime had the advantage of oiling our progress.

I had lied, of course. For all I knew at that point, we were still miles from any landmark described in the Secrets. I could hardly explain to Calla (not fully understanding myself) that some impalpable certainty had poked its paw through the mouth of this stinking hole, and beckoned me in—that I knew no closed doors lay between us and the Lady now, only an unbroken pipeline of passage and cave, tortuous but unmistakable, as if I held one end of an unseen cord, the other end of which was tied around the Lady. This was not something mentioned in the Secrets, this pull between Scion and Lady; however, I could think of no other time when the phenomenon might have revealed itself.

The pipe turned sharply downwards, but I could see that it opened out about three feet beyond, just on the edge of the candlelight. I started to ease myself forwards, but it was not easy head-first, especially since I was greased crown to foot with fungus-blood; I lost my grip and slid the rest of the way, landing with a thud on a hard stone floor. The candle went out. A second later, a solid, weighty object slammed into me from behind. Calla had arrived.

"Give me the candle." She sounded upset. I groped for her, caught her hand, pushed the candle into it. A dull scraping noise was repeated several times, followed by a memorable Sheranik curse.

"Is the flint giving you trouble?" I asked.

"Yes." She packed more sheer deadly expressiveness into that one little word than into the preceding several, rich as they had been. "It's wet," she added in the same tone.

This is what it's like to be blind, I told myself.

"I am also wet," Calla went on accusingly, "and mucky, and my cloak is mucky, and everything in my cloak is mucky, up to and including our last bit of bread. And we're lost—"

"We're not lost," I interrupted.

"You know where we are?"

"I know where we're going."

"Really?" Judging by her voice, she had pulled down her eyebrows and stuck her chin out an inch or two, and badly wanted to hit me.

"Really." I found her hand again and pulled her upright. I closed my eyes—unnecessarily, in fact, given how dark it was—and felt for the tug of the invisible line. It drew me unerringly through the darkness to a wall where, to Calla's surprise but not to mine, there was an opening and the foot of a stairway just beyond. "See?" I said. "Everything's fine."

The higher we climbed, the drier the air and walls became, and the sparser the population. Calla made me stop now and then while she tested the flint, but for a long time it sullenly refused to spark; from the powerful clutch she maintained on my shoulder it was clear that she found the dark oppressive. Often she would stop just to listen, digging her fingers into my arm, shushing me fiercely if I even breathed, muttering about being followed. To me, nothing mattered now, neither the darkness nor the strange noises, nothing except the sureness of every step I took, the sensation of utter certainty. I was exhilarated, Calla glum and fearful; I chatted to her softly, she answered in monosyllables or did not answer at all. At last, on about her twentieth periodic attempt, the flint produced enough of a flame to light the candle. The light

bounced off the crazed coating of slime-residue on her hair
and face.

She held the candle between us and gripped my arm.
"What's wrong with you, Tig? You've been babbling like a
madman for the last half-hour or so. And stop smiling at
me."

"Was I smiling? Sorry. But we're very near, Calla, I can
feel it."

"What do you mean, feel it?"

"The Lady's very close." I looked around and the details
of the chamber clicked into place on my mental map: the
placement of the narrow archways breaking three walls, the
particular curve of the broad-treaded staircase we had
climbed to get there. Without knowing, or without bothering
to know, we had reached those labyrinthine stretches of the
Caves that were laid out, span by span, in the Secrets of the
Ancients. "If you look at the floor, Calla," I said airily, "you
will find a nicely executed mosaic of the Plavipern cosmog-
ony."

She dropped to one knee and cleared the dust from a small
patch of floor. "It's a tortoise," she said coldly.

"That's right. Tortoises are worshipped in Plav."

"Oh." She got slowly to her feet.

"Through that doorway," I went on, "is a corridor decorated
with a mural of Oballef's Scions—the first seven generations,
anyway; the rest, down to my great-great-grandfather, are on
the far side of Lyksolef's Folly, so we won't get to see
them."

"I don't want to see them. Where's the Lady?"

"Precisely? I don't know yet. Come on."

She shrugged resignedly and followed me through the
archway. Faces lined the passage walls, wise, calm faces in
themselves, but decidedly unnerving in their habit of
springing unheralded into the candlelight and then back into
the shadows as we moved past. Curallef the Versifier, Oballef Third, Tilislef the Harpist, Oballefiya the Beautiful—I
murmured the names as we passed, feeling the power rising
inside me and the exhilaration, the oneness with and heri-
tance from a thousand years of wise, powerful ancestors. The

Lady was close, so close; the knowledge that hauled me along was nothing like an invisible rope now, more like a whirlpool centred on the spot where the Lady waited. Up the stairs at the end of the corridor, off at the second landing, through the Septagon, almost running by that point; down the small spiral ramp with the gemstone inlays, along a short whitewashed passage with a startling golden light spilling on to its floor from the further threshold—and there it was, the Lesser Chamber, directly under the sanctuary. (The Flamens-in-Exile had decided, after much debate on the old Primate's state of mind, that it was the last place I needed to look.) I leaned against the jamb, bent almost double, panting to catch my breath. Calla moved fearfully up beside me.

The Lady was there, all right. Shining, coruscating, she lit the whole chamber, not steadily, but in bursts and ripples like sunlight through shifting leaves. The form was indistinct, lost in the bright, blinding core. Calla choked and moved closer to me. "Who's holding it?" she whispered. A hunched figure in a green robe and heavy green cloak, unmoving, one hand outstretched with the light balanced on the palm. Two green shadows knelt in front of him, and they were not moving either.

"It's the Primate and the senior Flamens," I said softly. "They were trying to work the Will, poor fools. Interesting how they've been preserved."

With Calla lagging a few steps behind, I walked into the Lady's radiance. The Primate's mummified face, illuminated behind her, showed no signs of pain, just the beginnings of a profound astonishment. The light welcomed us, bathed us. I was within a few feet of my destiny—and Gil's, and Sher's—when something rustled behind us.

The first arrow slammed through my shoulder and spun me around and on to the floor. The second hit the old Primate, who exploded into glittering dust, robes and all. The Lady fell, turning gracefully in the air, and rolled away from me towards Calla. I tried to crawl to her, but a flood of crimson darkness rolled past my eyes and I collapsed back on to the flagstones. Calla dove along the floor, caught up the shining object in both hands and started in my direction.

"Krisht." A voice from the shadows. Calla froze.

"What are you waiting for?" I hissed. "Calla! There's still time!"

She stood like a stone figure just out of range, staring at the entrance, frowning. I reached out with my good arm—my fingertips brushed the hem of her cloak.

"Krisht—give it to me."

One of the shadows at the door stepped forward into the Lady's light, slime-streaked, filthy, but familiar. Calla stared at him. I cried to her despairingly and she half-turned, her face haunted and confused. Then Lord Shree reached her and gently disengaged the Lady from her hands.

Calla came to me then, too late, dropped to the floor, took me in her arms, cradled my head in her lap. "I'm sorry, Tig," she whispered. "I'm so very sorry."

32

IT TOOK SHREE, obviously a bright bastard, about five heart-beats to figure out that the counterweight system on the far side of the chamber was worth a try. He pushed gingerly at just the right place, then leapt back as the beautifully balanced machinery, gritty with decades of dust but still functional, rumbled into action. Slowly, smoothly, the great altar from the Sanctuary sank downwards into the Lesser Chamber; two Sherkin helmets peered over the edge of the gap in the ceiling, appearing more startled than helmets can usually manage on their own, then vanished. Lord Shree shook his head ruefully.

"Seventy years we searched that damned room," he said in Gillish.

I rolled my head off Calla's lap and edged painfully away

from any contact with her. "The way is opened from a different chamber, not that it matters now."

"That's true," said Shree, "it doesn't matter now." His voice lacked the triumph one might expect from a man who had just conquered the world. The Lady was tucked carelessly under his arm, still lambent, but dimmed by the bright light pouring down from the Sanctuary. There was a distinct air of anticlimax. I lay bleeding quietly on the flagstones; Lord Shree and his beslimed guardsmen waited in awkward poses near the sunken altar, hardly more animated than the two senior Flamens. I did not look at Calla, so I have no idea what she was doing.

Such was the end of the quest for the Lady in Gil.

A whole array of helmets appeared in the ceiling, looking like a frieze of gargoyle cutouts pasted around the opening. With them was another familiar face. The shadowy eyes moved from Calla to me to Lord Shree and what he carried; the thin lips curved. "Well done, Nephew," said Lord Kekashr in Sheranik. And he added in Gillish, "Is that you, Krisht? Well done, Daughter."

They treated me tenderly, by their standards. After all, they needed me. I was carried to a small room with a good fire in the grate and laid on a comfortable pallet. A Koroskan healer, grander than the one who had inspected the levy, was brought in to cut the arrow out of my shoulder and tend the wound. This was followed by a wash, and then by a platter of steaming meat and vegetables, which I rejected, partly because the rich smell turned my stomach, partly because I had some notion of wilfully starving to death before they could use me to work the Will. That aim was frustrated; when I would not eat, several of them held me down and forced a good measure of beef broth down my throat. No maggots for Kekashr's honoured guest. When I vomited back most of what they had poured into me, they simply sat on me again and repeated the process. This time the broth stayed down. After that, I was left alone—alone, that is, except for two well-armed troopers in full battledress, who never took their eyes off me.

Failure, betrayal, doom, the downfall of all hopes. My mind shuttled busily back and forth among those four like a shull on a griddle, not daring to settle too long on any one thought. The searing pain from my shoulder—the Sherank do not believe in soothing ointments—was like a refuge. I dived into it, wallowed in it, savoured the way the physical distress blotted out the other anguish, but always the thoughts returned. Calla had betrayed me. Everything that had happened between us was no more than good acting on her part, and insane foolishness on mine. The Lady was lost, Gil was lost; there was a good chance that the League of Free Nations would start grovelling once they knew the fabled Lady in Gil was in Sherkin hands, and eventually the whole world might be lost. And I, Tigrallef, Scion of Oballef, had led them right to her. I groaned out loud, occasioning snide remarks from the guards about the Gilman lack of *shrikk*, or balls.

The door swung open. I looked up with dread, expecting to see Lord Kekashr; but I would have preferred him to the woman who stood there. A strange and dazzling woman, heavily robed and rouged, hair shining and piled high, body tricked out at every possible point with feathers and furs and golden doodads and assorted lumpen jewels. Typical Sherkin lack of taste, I thought, though I'll admit she looked magnificent in a barbaric sort of way. I stared at her for a moment, and then closed my eyes. "Go away, Calla."

"Tig, I need to talk to you."

Her robe rustled closer to the pallet. Her cool fingers touched my cheek and I turned my face away.

"Please, Tig. We should talk."

"I don't see why. Go away."

"Do you think I planned what happened back there?" She sat down on the pallet beside me. Helplessly I opened my eyes. Beyond her, the Sherkin guards watched with frank interest.

"Well," I said, grinning sourly, "look at you."

She grimaced and yanked at the tight bodice. "Damned uncomfortable, if you must know. It's those pocketing Koroskan handmaids."

"Zealous, are they? You know, the Sherkin style of women's dress is designed to slow you down. They're a little afraid of their womenfolk."

"I can believe it." She hesitated for a long moment, obviously nerving herself. "Tig?"

"What is it, Calla?"

"Don't hate me for what happened."

I smiled. The slyness of her! I wanted to throw up again. "It's not going to work this time, Calla. Don't even try."

"You think I'm a traitor, is that it?"

"It's hardly a matter of opinion." I could hear my voice hardening.

"Please listen, Tig—"

"I suppose I should call you Krisht now. How long have you been betraying the Web, Krisht? Are you the little spider?"

"No! That was Jebri, you were right. But I didn't know until you figured it out."

"Was it you who sold Bekri?"

"No! No! I never told my father anything. And he never asked me—it was a pact between us."

"A pact with a warlord of Iklankish. Brilliant." My anger was starting to choke me. "I suppose it was on *his* orders that you slept with me."

"What?"

"I'll tell him what a good job you did, if you like—maybe he'll give you a bonus. You'd make a fine whore, Krisht; Flax read you rightly, you do belong in the shintashkr. You really had me believing for a while that you—" I had to break off then. The beach, Calla's face silvered by moonlight, rose to mock me.

She reddened with outrage or embarrassment, or both. "Will you listen to me?"

"Do I have a choice?" I stared up at her, loathing her—all the more bitterly because I had loved her the day before, and had a sickening suspicion that part of me was unable to stop loving her. "Say what you must, Krisht, and then go away."

"Stop calling me Krisht. Listen. About three years ago, I

was captured on the road to Malvi Point. Nobody in the Web ever knew about it—I'd been sent out alone to do some reconnaissance in the countryside and nobody expected me back for days."

"Very convenient. Who sent you on this mission?"

She looked startled. "It was Jebri. So even then—"

"Go on."

"I was taken straight to my—to Lord Kekashr. He knew who I was, or at least who my mother was. Myshalla. Bekri told you about her?"

I nodded.

"He told me I was his daughter, a Sherkint, no matter what my rearing had been. He was kind to me, Tig. He hoped that someday I would leave my mother's people and take my place as his daughter, but he was willing to wait until I did it of my own free will. He felt he owed me that." She was talking rapidly now, urgently, pleading with me to understand.

"Actually," I said, "you were of more use to him where you were. Surely you saw through that."

"But he never asked me to betray the Web! He never asked me about it at all—in fact, he may not have known I was part of it."

"Oh, Calla," I said with feeling, "that was naïve."

She jerked angrily at her ridiculous gown. "He kept me for a few days that first time. Not in the dungeons, you understand, but in a chamber in the Temple Palace, a beautiful place. He came to see me every day and just talked—little things, tales about Sher, about my half-sisters in Iklankish, things he had seen in his travels. At first I tried to attack him on sight, every time he came, but then I began to see him differently—"

"Don't tell me. The father you never had. But what about the great-grandfather you did have? What about Bekri?"

She shook her head sadly. "I can never make you understand, Tigrallef. They're both my people. My father let me go after a few days, but he begged me to see him when I could, and told me how to contact him in secret. I didn't for a long time, but something pulled me back in the end."

"And so you became a traitor. And now Bekri's in the south dungeon."

"I did not betray the council! How can you even think that?"

"You betrayed me, why not others?"

She flounced angrily to her feet. "I saved you. When you were taken in the levy, I saved you. I went straight to my father and asked him to have you released. If I weren't Kekashr's daughter, you'd be grubbing in a mine in Iklankish this very minute."

"Did you tell him then who I was?"

She sat down again, with great dignity. "No, or he'd never have let you go. I told him you were my lover."

That struck me as the best joke I'd heard all day. I exploded into laughter. "So you even betrayed your poor father! I'll bet he won't like that when he finds out. You should have given me to him then, you know, and saved us all a lot of trouble."

"Stop it, Tig! How can I explain? Calla and Krisht are two separate people; I had to make it so. Remember, whatever is done by half of me is treachery to the other half. Can you understand that?"

I was too strangled by rage to try—to my later, bitter regret. "Why," I asked, "did you choose this particular time to betray your Gillish side? Why not a minor bit of treachery to practise on?"

"I didn't mean to," she said. "When I went with you into the between-ways, it was to help you find the Lady and overthrow my own father, I swear it—but when the moment came, I could not decide." She was genuinely pleading by now. "Don't you see? I was going to put the Lady into your hands, but Shree called me by my other name and I—I got confused. I didn't know what to do. And then Shree came and took the Lady from me, and I didn't have to decide any more. If you had reached me first—"

"Stop." I turned over on the pallet so that my back was to her and concentrated ferociously on the pain in my shoulder.

"Nobody can understand except Shree," she said, half to herself.

"Shree?" I rolled back to glare at her. "So he's another in your stable, is he? I should have guessed."

"There's been nothing between us," she retorted. "His mother was a Gilwoman, that's all. He's riding the same dragon's back as I am."

"So you want me to pity you?"

"No." Her face changed. She leaned over me. "Listen carefully, and I'll tell you what I want. You told me only a few hours ago that you loved me."

"Don't remind me."

"Well, you can have me. We can be together. And on the throne of Gil." Her hands were twisted together.

"What in the Lady's name are you talking about?"

"Listen. My father will be happy to make an alliance between us; he'll make you the Priest-King, Tig, he'll sail away and leave you to rule in Gil. You'll have won after all, you'll have liberated the island."

"And what does he want in return?"

"Don't be such an idiot." She was definitely the same Calla, Sherkint baubles or not. "Some small favours, that's all."

"Would these small favours happen to involve conjuring the Lady for him?"

"Well—yes. But not to use against Gil. He promised me that."

"He promised? What a relief."

She leaned closer to look into my eyes. "So you'll do it? You'll accept?"

"Never. Not even to save myself from the Gilman's Pleasure. I know what he wants—Gil's just a stepping stone. He wants Iklankish. He won't give up Gil and he'll gain the whole empire, plus the League of Free Nations in the end. He wants the whole world. I will not help him to get it."

"But he promised me—"

"I suppose he sent you here with this obscene offer?"

She drew herself up proudly. "It's a good offer. He'll break you if he has to, to get your cooperation, but he doesn't want to. And I don't want him to, either. I love you, Tig."

"You love me?" I gaped at her.

"That's what I said, isn't it?" she snapped. "Nobody ordered me into your bed, not my father, not Bekri, not the council, not anybody—I'm not a whore, I came to you because I wanted to, and I love you. Please believe me."

I stared up at her, speechless. Her face twisted with desperation.

"Tell me that you believe me."

I searched my soul. Suddenly, try as I might, I could not find the blinding fury that had been there only a moment before. Anger, yes. Sadness, loss, longing—plenty of those. The main ingredients, however, were a deathly weariness and an overwhelming sense of futility. Nothing mattered any more. I turned my back to Calla and muttered into the rough blanket, "I believe you."

Her voice quickened with hope. "Then you'll do it? Say you'll do it, for your own sake and mine. For Gil's sake."

Laughter bubbled up bitterly from somewhere deep in my entrails. I crushed it with difficulty. "I can't."

"Why not? Have you got any better ideas? You can't save the world now, Tig, I'm sorry, but you can't. At least save us."

"There's nothing left to save."

"Then what are we going to do?" An anguished cry.

"There is one thing," I said softly, turning back to her. She looked at me with a resurgence of hope. I hooked my fingers into her awful bodice and pulled her face close to mine, as if meaning to kiss her. Very quietly I murmured, "You could put a knife in Kekashr's throat."

The light died in her eyes. "I can't do that. He's my father." Her face hung over me, a tear dropped from one of her eyes and rolled down my cheek. Not very gently, I pushed her away. I had known it was useless; each of us was asking the other to do the impossible.

She swiped at her tears with an angry gesture, as if they irritated her, and said harshly, "You must accept my father's offer."

I held my fingers in front of her face and curved them in the *no* that cannot be withdrawn nor negotiated nor mitigated by changed circumstances, the rarely used *no* that means for ever. She went pale.

"I told you on the beach there were things you didn't know about me," she whispered. "You said they didn't matter."

"I was wrong."

"You said you loved me."

"So I did. But it means nothing now."

She looked at me long and hard, her face becoming strangely calm.

"I'll never see you again anyway," I said. "Once your precious father knows you can't subvert me, he'll send you packing on the first ship to Iklankish. You're a Sherkint now, your place is in Sher."

She shook her head. "He promised he wouldn't send me away from Gil."

I sighed, infinitely weary. "Another promise. You never learn, do you?"

Her mouth tightened. "It's no use talking to you when you're like this. I'll come later." She rose to go.

I watched her walk away from me towards the door. The first heat of a fever shimmered in front of my eyes. For a moment Calla was nameless, faceless and doomed; the door was the maw of a high-masted black ship, bound for Sher— or worse. Choking, I sat up and called her name. She turned eagerly at the door, took a pace towards me, halted, hovered. "What is it, Tig? Have you changed your mind?" As soon as she spoke, the hallucination dissolved.

I lay back. The sight of her was agony. She looked small and distant, on the far side of a desert of impossibilities; we were already lost to each other, youth was soured, all hopes were false, love was suffering a sort of living death. I searched my soul again, this time for one kind word to be the last I'd ever give her, but the futility of it drained my strength. I closed my eyes.

"Tig?"

Tight-lipped, wet-eyed, I raised my hand in the air and sketched the sign of final goodbye.

The door slammed behind her.

33

"POOR FOOL." THE voice grated out of the air vent near the ceiling. The guards jerked like puppets and became upright and very severe. Seconds later, part of the wall pushed open and Lord Kekashr, followed by the omnipresent Shree, stepped into the room.

"Wonderful invention," Calla's father said in Gillish, "these between-ways of yours—I wish the little spider had told us about them long ago. Remind me, Shree, to reproach him for that, among other things. Are you comfortable, Scion?"

"Not really." I looked up at him, repelled. His face was an exercise in sharp edges and hard flat surfaces, dominated by the dagger nose, meshed with razor-slash wrinkles, ornamented with a livid scar that started near one ear and sliced across his chin. He had enviable teeth, most of which were visible. I remembered a similar smile on the jaws of a Storican river-devil, in the bestiary on Sathelforn—as I recall, the creature had just eaten a tourist. Lord Kekashr's smile had precisely that air of self-congratulation.

"You're quite right about sending Krisht to Iklankish. It's easy to see you're an intelligent young man," he said pleasantly, settling himself on the same bit of pallet that Calla had recently vacated, "more intelligent, anyway, than your half-witted relations. If not for Krisht, you might even have beaten me to the prize. I'm sure you're far too intelligent to oppose me now."

"Intelligence has nothing to do with it."

"Really? Then how about pain?" He watched my face intently. "Fear? Loyalty to friends? Yes, Shree, I think we'll try loyalty first. That is, when the Scion has had a chance to consider." He laid one hand heavily across my forehead. "He's already feverish. Good."

I closed my eyes and pulled away from his hand. Kekashr chuckled.

"Don't fret yourself, Scion. We won't really start chatting until the fever is higher—just a few easy little questions for now. You are Tigrallef, Cirallef's son? Eh? Don't be stupid, young man, save your spirit for the questions that matter."

"Where is the Lady?" I asked.

The Stone of Callilef, flashing on Kekashr's finger, made a more effective weapon than my ancestor could have known. Even a light blow drew blood. "All in good time. Now tell me—who is the man with the beard?"

"The what?"

He opened up the other cheek. "You do know who I mean. The hairy one who was cutting a way into the caves for you when my nephew interrupted him."

"Hairy?" I opened my eyes in time to see Kekashr's hand smashing down again. The direct hit on my mouth hardly registered—Angel must be free, or why would Kekashr be asking?

"Uncle," said Shree quietly in Sheranik. Kekashr paused with his arm raised, and looked enquiringly at his nephew. "He could be telling the truth, my lord Uncle. The bearded man escaped into the caves long before the Scion and Krisht came along—there's nothing to say they know him."

"Nothing," Kekashr retorted, "except the long tongue of coincidence. Would it not seem odd to you, Nephew, if he and the hairy man should be in the same forsaken arsehole of the Gilgard within a few hours of each other, and yet be strangers? It would seem very odd to me."

"But Krisht confirms it, my lord Uncle."

Lord Kekashr smiled grimly. "That means nothing. Krisht has not quite decided whose throne she's behind. She could lie to us as easily as she did to this Scion."

"But she's your daughter."

"All the more reason to mistrust her. You know me, Nephew." He shook with mirth.

"Yes," said Shree impassively.

Kekashr stopped laughing and bent on his nephew a sharp and contemplative look—not the sort of look I'd fancy receiving myself, although Shree seemed unperturbed. What was more disturbing to me was the sudden, short-lived shadow of Calla in Kekashr's barbed features, especially in the set of the eyes and the long-lipped cut of the mouth, leaving no question about her parentage. The look continued for a long few moments before Kekashr returned his face to me.

"Yes, she's a tricky one, my Krisht," he said, switching to Gillish. "A credit to her old father. Don't you agree, Tigrallef? What a pity you turned her down! Don't you want to be Priest-King in Gil?"

"Not really. Anyway, that title is not in your gift," I mumbled. My lips were already swelling.

Lord Kekashr bent closer to examine his handiwork. "The whole world is in my gift. I have the Lady."

"Go ahead and use her. I'd love to see that."

The Stone of Callilef descended again. "I'm sure you would. I saw what happened to the old Flamens."

I licked the blood off my lips and said nothing.

"That's right, save your voice for later. Look at him, Shree! Whatever can Krisht see in him?"

"I wondered that myself, Uncle, when I took him to her in Malvi." Shree's calm face appeared above me, flickering a little around the edges as my fever took hold. "Of course, we didn't know at that point who he was."

The beast-smile again. "Naughty Krisht. I'll give her a fatherly talking-to about that." The Hammer of Iklankish brought his eyes to within a few inches of my face; they approached me slowly, slowly, like the iron spikes of the Pleasure. "Never mind," he said. "I have him now—and the Lady—and absolutely no mercy. Under the circumstances, I can forgive my erring child."

He left me with the promise, or threat, of a quick return. The guards relaxed after he departed and began to swap what passed for jokes in Sheranik, very raw and with little in the way of punchline. Little, anyway, that a non-Sherkin would laugh at.

Angel was alive and free. Kekashr was mystified about him, and uneasy. Calla had not (yet) betrayed Angel; nor, it seemed, could she have told her father about Lissula and the other shints—for if she had, then Kekashr would not have needed to question me about the mysterious hairy man. These were the only crumbs of comfort I had, and they made up far less than a feast. Where was Bekri? What was happening to him and to the others? What was my future? I hated to think. Calla having failed to tempt me, Kekashr would not dare put the Lady into my hands until I was well and truly broken; speculating on how he might do that (based on my extensive reading on the subject of Sherkin atrocities) was a high road to panic. My body began to shake—only partly fear, I realized; partly also an omen of the rising fever. I lay on my back and stared at the ceiling, breathing hard, trying to think of nothing at all. The pain was much like Sherkin music—a deep, throbbing drumbeat from my shoulder, a shrill and discordant note from my lacerated cheeks.

High on the wall, immediately below the well-camouflaged vent into the between-ways, something moved. I squinted up at the vent, trying to decide whether what I was seeing was real, or merely signifying the onset of true delirium. A dark stroke was painting itself down the masonry, pausing momentarily in the runnel between blocks, spilling over, branching into a clutch of smaller trickles like the fingers of a hand, lengthening into slender claws as I watched. According to the coolest part of my brain, it had to be a liquid of some sort, looking like tar in the firelight but moving too rapidly, dividing too readily. Blood would run like that. I held my breath.

One of the guards was well into an anecdote featuring two Gilwomen, one Sherkin and a large bowl of raw eggs. I've often wondered how it ended; he stopped in mid-sentence, leaned against the wall and slid gently to the floor. Even before he came to rest, the second guard toppled forwards and landed neatly in his colleague's lap. Aside from the clatter of a falling helmet, their collapse was silent.

I gulped and sat up. My head spun for a moment, then came to rest. There was a faint rustle from behind the wall and, for the second time that hour, the secret door swung open. Nobody appeared. "Who is it?" I whispered. Behind the door, feet distinctly shuffled. "Calla? Is that you?" No reply. "Angel?"

"Yes, my lord Scion."

"Good Lady in Gil," I breathed fervently. "Help me, Angel, get me out of here, I'm not feeling very well."

He emerged shyly, still holding a dart-tube, helped me off the pallet and half-carried me through the secret door. It swung shut behind us. At the top of the stairs, a third guard, helmetless, was crumpled against the wall, the blood from his crushed head pooling on the sill of the air vent and oozing out through the narrow opening. Angel lowered me to the floor beside the body. The wall was cool against my burning skin.

"Where are we, Angel?" I asked. "What's happening?"

He peered woefully at me out of his complexity of hair. "They got in. The little spider told them how."

"What else?"

"We're not safe here now. They found my sleeping place."

The gymnastics recommenced inside my head. I held it with my good hand to stop it spinning. "I'd guessed all that—Kekashr himself was right here on this spot, not an hour ago. It won't be long before he finds the guardsmen you killed, and he'll know I'm in the between-ways. We have to hide."

Angel nodded. Without another word, he hoisted me to my feet, pulled my good arm around his shoulder, and trotted off down the corridor. I leaned heavily on him, fighting a desperate battle against head and belly and fever. My arm transmitted waves of shocked protest at every step. The pain began to feel like a personal insult; by extension, so did Angel's supportive shoulder.

We staggered around a corner into a stretch that seemed familiar. I searched for words in the hot red slurry between my ears. "Angel—where are we going?"

"My lord Scion?"

"Where. Are. We. Going."

"Somewhere safe."

"Safe? Nowhere's safe."

"I know a place."

"Where?"

"Quietly, my lord."

The contents of my head sloshed angrily about. "You dare to hush me? I'm the Scion of Oballef, you know, a hero, a great hero. Today I gave the Lady in Gil to Gil's greatest enemy—"

With characteristic directness, Angel pulled a rag out of his robe and stuffed it into my mouth. Thus gagged, I whimpered with outrage—Angel became not the man who had saved me, but the latest in a long series of tormentors, denigrators, inquisitors, obstructors. The sense of grievance swelled alongside the fever; I was desperate to win at least one argument before I died. At the next air vent, I pulled violently away from Angel and fetched up against the wall with a thud. I tore the rag out of my mouth and peered through the vent. "You idiot," I cried, "that's the Flamens' Court—we're too close to the clearing chamber. Are you going to betray me too?" He retrieved me with difficulty (I remember with shame that I yanked out a handful of beard; not that it made much difference) and hauled me, struggling feebly, along the corridor and into the Spine.

Noises far ahead penetrated even the thrumming blood-beats in my ears. Angel hesitated, then launched us both forwards. Suddenly we were half-scrambling, half-falling down from the dim corridor into the dark shelter of a stair-well, and Angel was stuffing the rag back into my mouth. I think I fought him—but my chief memories are of a heavy weight pressing me painfully against the edge of the stone riser, a hand hard as iron fettering my wrist, a clicking and clumping of many boots along the stone floor of the corridor above us. Then silence, and the weight lifting, and the red-shot darkness folding around me like a heavy woollen blanket.

"Are they gone?" The voice was mine, although it seemed to come from an immense distance away.

"They're gone, my lord Scion." He rustled away from me. When I reached out, he was not there. I laid my forehead on the beautiful cool of the stairs and earnestly wished the rest of the world into nonexistence. It didn't work, alas; moments later Angel reappeared and lifted me off the friendly stones.

"It's clear, my lord Scion. I looked through the vent."

"What's clear? Nothing's clear." In front of us, a long vertical line of light suddenly sliced through the darkness. I watched it with interest, waiting to see what it would do. It grew wider. Angel, carrying me in his arms, lurched into it and through it; neither I nor the light offered any resistance. This was also interesting, as was the burst of sunlight, of exotic fragrances, of soft music, on the other side. Hazily, I identified the timbre of a Tatakil woodwhistle. I started to tell this to Angel, but was diverted by a vision of the Lady's gold-and-white face hanging over me, unreproachful, concerned, ineffably beautiful. It broke my heart that I had failed her.

"What did those shullturds do to him, Angel?" the Lady said. It was strange that she looked so much like Lissula. Even the voice was similar.

"Forgive me," I whispered.

"What's he saying? Never mind—we've got to get you both out of sight before those bitch Koroskans come sniffing around. This way, quickly!"

34

THE NEXT TWO days I don't remember at all. My body, battered, lacerated, shot, starved of food and sleep, pushed beyond its limits and burning with fever, finally decided it had taken quite enough, thank you, and refused to take any more. If the shints had asked me at that point, I'd have told them to let me die. Begged them, even. After all, with the Lady lost and the whole world about to become Lord Kekashr's private playground, there would have seemed little point in waking up at all. As it happened, they didn't ask me. They were having too much fun.

I awoke on the third day, feeble but clear-headed, also hungry and mildly puzzled. It wasn't Exile, it wasn't my cold little bedchamber in the Gil slums, it most certainly wasn't the south dungeon, not with all those cherry-coloured satin bed cushions. I closed my eyes again and began to remember, fragment by fragment. The odd thing was that the memories were barren of emotional content, as if I were recalling remote history of purely academic interest; even Calla's treachery and the loss of the Lady evoked no more than vague regret. So that's that, I said to myself; the game's over. Now where can I get some breakfast?

I opened my eyes and turned over. There was something on my head, presumably a bandage. A woman with a mane of bright auburn hair was hunched on the floor beside the pallet, draped in a loose yellow robe. There was something familiar about the ungainly set of her shoulders. I reached out to touch her, and she raised her head. The face was not familiar, except for the eyes, which were unmistakable. "My lord Scion," she said. The voice clinched it.

"Angel! Angel? Is that you?"

Angel clawed a wisp of fiery hair out of the side of his mouth. "Yes, my lord Scion," he said.

"Good Lady in Gil! What's happened to you?"

"They shaved me." He scratched morosely at his stubbled chin. "I'm in disguise."

"Ah. I see." There was nothing else to say. Anyway, I was losing my powers of speech. The more I looked at him, the more he resembled a hound my mother used to own, the kind with exuberant hair over a face that was entirely jowls and sad brown eyes. I held my breath, resisting an attack of hilarity.

"What's wrong, my lord Scion?"

"Nothing, Angel." That finished it; in combination with

the face, the name was too much. I covered my mouth and tried to strangle my laughter as circumspectly as possible. He watched me mournfully from under the glorious wig, which only made matters worse; and when he knocked the wig askew to scratch at his shorn head, the effort not to burst nearly killed me. "I'm sorry," I gasped finally. "I don't mean to criticize, but the wig isn't very convincing. You look— you look—"

"You're in disguise too," he said flatly.

"Me?" I felt the thing on my head—not a bandage, a mass of ringlets. The one I held in front of my eyes was brassy blonde. I was still adjusting to this when Lissula and another woman, a dazzling Tatakil, floated through the curtained doorway and stopped to look us over. Expressions of intense enjoyment spread across their dainty faces. I sat up and tried feebly to bow, and my wig slipped, which threw them into muffled convulsions. After some moments of this mirth, pointedly not shared by Angel and myself, Lissula composed herself. "Oh, my darling," she said, "you'll never make a decent shint."

"Thank you," I said.

"You should see yourself."

"No, I'm sure I shouldn't." But the giggling Tatakil produced a copper hand-mirror from nowhere and held it in front of me. What stared back from the polished surface was a stranger's face, thin, hollow-eyed, papery where the skin was drawn tightly over the bones, etched with new lines and jagged scores from Callilef's ring. The saucy curls were as fitting as a party crown on a corpse.

"What's the point?" I asked, handing the mirror back.

"My lord?"

"What's the point of the disguise? Neither of us could fool a blind man."

Lissula coiled herself decoratively on the end of my pallet. "You're not meant to be seen close up, darling. It's just a precaution, in case anyone's watching from the between-ways."

Involuntarily, I raised my eyes to where the air vent should be. It was hard to pick out unless you knew it was there, but

I could remember the panoramic view it afforded of the shin-tashkr. The disguises already seemed less ridiculous.

"What about the Koroskans?"

"Those moustached lumps? Don't worry about them."

"But surely—"

"Tigrallef, my dearest darling, we have them well under control."

"But I thought they had you under control."

"They think that, too." Lissula and the Tatakil exchanged amused glances. Angel nodded sagely, as if he knew all this already and could substantiate it with volumes of evidence. "Don't worry," Lissula went on, "we've kept you well-hidden for three days. It's the most marvellous joke, my dearest—our masters are looking for you everywhere else. They say Lord Kekashr himself is shitting parth-asps." The Tatakil giggled with her.

I boggled at this image of Lord Kekashr, then passed over it. "But the Koroskans have access to the whole shintashkr. Where did you hide me?"

"Well, darling, the whole shintashkr, so to speak. We have fifty pallets to choose from—we've simply been moving you to wherever those bitches weren't likely to come, and making sure they stayed away. And when you were raving, we just sang, or fought, or took turns getting hysterical—the ward-resses think we're highly-strung, you know."

"But what about when you had," I paused, "visitors?"

She stretched prettily. "Duty hours? We put you under the bedclothes of any shint on her week off. You could rave at the top of your voice then without anyone noticing, since our masters are so noisy at their pleasures."

I lay back on the satin bed cushions. "You're good," I said, "maybe as good as the Web."

"Maybe better," Lissula retorted, "seeing as they're all in the south dungeon."

For a moment I didn't like her, but it passed. "You'll be in the south dungeon yourselves, or worse, if the Sherank find me here. I should go."

"Don't be foolish, darling, you're welcome here for as long as you want to stay." The Tatakil whispered something to her and they both guffawed delicately. "Silka likes you, but she's too shy to say so."

Good Lady in Gil, I said to myself, one thing Silka didn't look was shy. "That's very nice of her, but I should still go. I'm putting all of you at risk."

"Where do you think you'll go? You're still weak as a baby, and Kekashr has every trooper and spy in Gil out searching for you. Anyway, there's trouble in the city, some kind of silly uprising. You'd be dead or captured in minutes. No, darling, you're much safer here. We want you to stay, we really do." She managed, at one and the same time, both to pout seductively and look firm.

I stared at her helplessly. Of course she was right. It occurred to me that, firstly, I did not know where to go; and secondly, I did not know what to do when I got there. Kekashr had the Lady. Unless I could steal her back, which seemed about as likely at that moment as dying of old age, it hardly mattered where I was. Thoughtfully, I tossed the ringlets out of my eyes.

"Darling, you're like a skeleton. Have some more gravy on that roasted beef." Or, "Still feverish, poor dear. I'll just sponge you down." Or, "Dearheart, are you in pain? Let me rub your back." Or, better yet, "Move over, my love." I began to think that, given an adequate supply of books and paper, I could live quite happily in the shintashkr for the rest of my life. Angel also seemed to be quite at home, though as impenetrable as ever, whereas the shints were clearly having a wonderful time. Hide-the-Scion was the best game they'd played in months.

But all the while we were playing on the lip of an abyss. Angel knew it, the shints knew it, and I knew it. News arrived nightly in the form of pillow talk, all of it bad—strict curfews in the city, house-to-house searches, packed dungeons, the Gilman's Pleasure set up indefinitely in the great market; my description had been circulated and a handful of look-alikes pulled in and never released. The Gilgard had been scoured for me, until they were fairly sure I'd somehow been smuggled out into the city, then the search had widened

and become more brutal. The harbours were closed and
Malvi was also under a strict curfew.

My disappearance was not the only factor, however. There
were also reports of resistance, of traps set and sprung on
increasingly wary Sherkin patrols, of pitched battles in the
tenements and bloody streets. A few faces vanished from the
shints' clientele, not all of them unmourned, though the re-
ported counts of Gil's casualties were far higher. Behind
much of this, I thought I could see Hawelli's fine, futile
hand—his pinpricks, that is, countered by great whacks of
the Sherkin cleaver. By all accounts, Kekashr was quite as
outraged as Lord Kishr had been when my forebears escaped
to the Archipelago.

By the fifth day, I could feel my strength returning, such
as it was. Rasam, one of the Glishorans, a skilled midwife
as well as a talented whore, dosed me very effectively with
a powder used to alleviate menstrual cramps and build
strength after childbirth. The shints giggled at this, but my
damaged shoulder and scarred cheeks healed the better for
it. Even the wig became more flattering once my face filled
out. I learned a surprising amount about cosmetics.

Altogether I had never in my life been better amused, fed,
cosseted or regarded. While I was able to keep my mind
shuttered, I was the king of this closed little castle; but when
I thought of what was happening outside the shintashkr, it
was like looking at a firestorm through the windows of a
straw house. Much of the time I managed not to think at all.

On the afternoon of the seventh day, I was sitting with my
back against the rear wall of the shintashkr, one of the few
spots invisible from the air vent, sharing an enormous basket
of pikcherries. Angel and Lissula were there, and Mbuha, a
Storican; Lissula was uncharacteristically quiet. Silka had
been sitting in my lap, but had gone off to take her turn as
lookout. I was happily pumping Mbuha about some of the
lesser-documented Storican fauna, a childhood interest of
mine, when Lissula broke in.

"You've never told me what happened to Calla," she said
bluntly.

It was a shock—like having cold water poured over my brain. Calla was one of the matters I had strictly avoided thinking about. I was silent for so long that Mbuha shrugged and went back to describing the ngor, a tall beast with a neck like a spotted tree-trunk, which I had assumed to be mythical, but which she claimed to have seen many times. Gently, I put my hand over her mouth.

"Calla betrayed me."

Lissula nodded, unsurprised. "That bitch; I thought she might. She's really half-Sherkint, did you know?"

"Yes, I did know." Sadly. The pikcherries tasted sour. The others were quiet now, the cheer had vanished. I think they were peering out with me at the advancing flames. Finally I asked, "What happened after we left to warn Bekri?" (Stab of remorse—what was happening to Bekri while I filled my face with pikcherries?) "Did you wait for us in the between-ways?"

"No, thank the Lady. When I could hear nothing more from the chute, I came back to the shintashkr—and not long after lunch, the secret door crashed open and a mob of troopers burst in from the between-ways, shouting and waving their swords."

"What did you do?"

"We told them to leave, of course. It was out of hours."

"And they left?"

She bridled. "Naturally they left. They know better than to upset us."

I shook my head, marvelling at this new-found facet of the Sherkin character. Obviously the Web had erred in not planting a few doxies of their own among the troopers' women. "So that was all that happened?"

"Yes, until Angel brought you in."

"And there's nothing more you can tell me?"

Reflectively, she popped a pikcherry into her mouth and spat out the stone. "Lord Shree was leading the troopers when they burst in on us. Now there's an attractive man. When I see him, I could almost wish to be a concubine." Mbuha chuckled, but I don't think Lissula was joking. She went on, "They must have found the rope hanging down into the chute—I can't imagine how else they could have tracked you. Such bad luck, darling!"

"They came into the sewer while I was opening the way for you," said Angel. "I hid in the caves and they lost me."

I put my hand on his shoulder. The scenario was clearer now in my head, from Jebri's disclosure of the between-ways, to Shree and his troopers crouching near Angel's breach of the Caves, waiting to follow whoever would appear. Calla and I appeared—and Krisht and I arrived at our objective, the Lady, with Shree and the world's doom close on our heels. For the first time since awakening in the shintashkr, I forced myself to look squarely at the chaos outside.

Lissula poked my shoulder. "What are you going to do, my darling?"

"I don't know yet—but I can't stay here much longer."

"That's obvious," she sighed, "but what are you going to do?"

"I'm going to get the Lady back and destroy the Sherank."

I laughed as if I'd just made the best joke in history. Only Mbuha laughed with me.

35

"IT'S SUCH A pity you can't risk the between-ways," Lissula said. It was at least the tenth time.

"I know."

"Now, if you could use the between-ways—"

"I know, I know. Everything would be easy. You've already pointed that out. But we can't risk it, and anyway, you're wrong."

"I was going to say," she said coolly, "we wouldn't have to go to all this trouble for the uniforms. You don't have to get nasty, darling, even if you are pissing with fright."

I sighed—she would never have believed me if I had told her, but I had moved beyond fear into fatalism. "I'm sorry, Lissula. You know I love you all for what you're doing."

"All of us, my lord? No one in particular?"

"All of you," I said firmly.

Lissula shrugged. "A few of the shints will be disappointed."

"But not you?"

"Don't be silly, darling."

After that we lay side-by-side, not talking, for what seemed like a long time. In the dim light, Lissula's face was a pale golden oval on the pillow, close beside mine. There were no takers for her that evening, since she had, with the help of one of Rasam's preparations, faked a fever, but the nightly cacophony panted and yowled all around us. I amused myself by composing the abstract of a treatise on Sherkin sexuality, a hitherto neglected field, although it seemed highly unlikely that I'd ever get a chance to write it.

Surprisingly, Sherkin males appear to be sexually timid and easily manipulated by any female who can legitimately be viewed as an object of desire, this extending even to their non-Sherkint shints and concubines. Perhaps it is to compensate for this timidity that they generate extraordinary volumes of noise during the sexual act, thereby assuring themselves and the listening world of their potency and aggressiveness. It is even possible that their nation's obsession with conquest is intimately bound up—

A rapping on the wall close to my ear, almost inaudible, but I could feel the vibrations.

"It's time, Lissula."

I crawled across her under the bedclothes, feeling a twang of desire in my loins; but my idyll in the shintashkr was ending. As I slipped off the pallet, Lissula caught my face in her hands and kissed me—not for the first time, you understand; the shintashkr was nothing if not hospitable, but never before so tenderly, with so much of actual affection. Perhaps she felt it was for the last time—I know I did.

"Good fortune, Tigrallef," she whispered.

I pulled her hands gently away and held them for a moment between mine, thinking *damn* the Sherank, *damn* the Lady, *damn* Oballef and all the Scions and Flamens, *damn* the life that made Lissula a stamped-in-the-selvedge slut—and then turned away from her without a word and crept out of the cubicle.

Next door, Silka was half-sitting on her pallet, the streak of black brows startling in the white moon of her face. She rolled off the pallet when she saw me and began to tug at the bedclothes. I helped her.

The Sherkin under the blankets was still warm, and there was no blood; the Tatakil have a neat trick involving a long pin into the base of the brain, very quick and quiet, although it takes much practice. Sometimes I wondered about pretty little Silka.

Together we hauled the body over against the wall and covered it with a dark cloak so that it was invisible to a casual eye—for example, that of any other Sherkin taker who entered the cubicle that night. "But what will you do with the bodies in the morning?" I'd objected when the plan was being worked out. "Never mind about that, dearheart," they'd said, and there was something about the Storicans' smiles that made me reluctant to press for details. With the luckless Sherkin laid temporarily to rest, I sorted out his discarded uniform from the jumble on the floor and got myself dressed, with much fumbling of complicated buckles and straps. Even the helmet was there, since the deceased, a man of habit, came directly from guard duty on alternate nights. With this predictability he had written his own death-warrant.

When the last buckle was in place, I hastily kissed Silka goodbye. There were tears running down her cheeks. "Don't worry, little Silka," I whispered into her ear.

"I'm not worried," she sobbed, "I was quite fond of poor Karesh, that's all, he was one of my best regulars. He always brought me presents."

I clapped the helmet on to my head, making very sure it

covered the back of my neck, before embracing her again. I
asked myself how Tatakil men would ever dare to quarrel
with their women. Silka released me lingeringly, and I threw
back my shoulders and swaggered out of the cubicle in the
confident Sherkin gait I had rehearsed for the past two days.
Angel was not yet at the agreed point near the centre of the
shintashkr, so I leaned against the wall and tried to look as
if I belonged there.

With the din of Sherkin passion, I failed to hear the Koroskan approaching. Suddenly she was there, a glacier of
womanhood, towering above me in her vast white robe. I
jerked like a fish on a hook. "Well, trooper," she boomed in
Sheranik, "finished your fun? What are you waiting for?
We're busy tonight."

"I'm waiting—" I squeaked, coughed, then started again
in a deep growl that threatened to rend my vocal cords, "I'm
waiting for my guardmate."

"Taking his time, is he? No consideration, some of your
lot. How much time do you need for a little storm-the-
gateway, hey? Here!" She bent down to peer at my helmet,
and my heart, what was left of it, froze solid. On the other
hand, the Koroskan seemed to melt. Her face puddled with
pleasure.

"Hoy, it's you, Karesh. Thought I knew the helmet.
Sounds like you've caught a cold—and you've lost some
flesh this week as well, haven't you? Not surprising, seeing
how Old Claw is pushing the troops these days."

She nudged me with an elbow the size and general shape
of a Sherkin battle-club. I oofed faintly. Leaning companionably against the wall, the wardress excavated a pouch out
of the mighty battlements of her bosom and offered me a
plug of something that looked and smelled like the cud of a
dead cow. I accepted it without thanks, in the Sherkin manner, and pretended to push it through the mouth-orifice of
Karesh's helmet. Then I dropped it discreetly on to the floor
and stood on it.

"It's rough times for us all, you know," the Koroskan went
on, practically shouting to be heard. "You troopers have been
working the girls too hard lately, what with all this trouble

you've been getting in the city. The last week alone, we had three shints die on us, just floated off in their sleep, not a mark or a day's sickness among them. I call it exhaustion, that's what I call it."

I nodded sadly. Silka's pin, that's what *I'd* call it, or something choice from Rasam's extensive Glishoran herblore. Lissula had told me the shints had methods for dealing with potential problems, but she did not tell me they'd been applied in my defense. The golden days in the shintashkr lost slightly in lustre.

I became aware at that point that the Koroskan had started to breathe on me. She was definitely closer. "They're all like that, these skinny girls," she said. "Now if you had a real woman, Karesh, someone with some sinew in her thighs, you wouldn't need to ride those poor splinters so hard, hey? Am I right?"

I nodded dutifully. She edged closer.

"I mean, think about it—would you rather have an armful of bones or an armful of good solid meat, hey?"

"Yes, quite," I said vaguely.

A trooper in off-duty whites turned the corner and strode towards us. I was almost glad to see him. "Ho, Karesh," he grinned as he went by, "water first, wine after, is that the plan?" He chortled off down the corridor, the Koroskan simpered and blushed, and I began to sweat. The strain was weighing on me, as was the damned uniform—how did the bastards manage to fight so well, dressed like that?

"You're not very sociable tonight, Karesh. Surely that stringy little Tatakil can't have worn you out, a good strong man like you?" She moved even closer. She overhung me like a cliff.

"It's my cold," I mumbled.

"Ah, yes, poor lad. Here, take off your helmet."

"What?"

"Take off your helmet. Let me have a look at your throat."

"Thanks, but—"

"Come on, trooper. Happens I have a remedy in my bed-chamber that might just help you." She grinned vastly and reached for the helmet, and I took a desperate step backwards.

"Mistress!" A wail ending in a gasp—Lissula lurched out of her corridor and tottered towards the Koroskan. Just short of us, she swayed gracefully and dropped; the Koroskan leaped to catch her, grumbling ferociously under her breath. "You see what we have to put up with?" she demanded, swinging Lissula over her shoulder like a lovely sack, "these fragile flowers, no stamina, a few good pocketings and they're finished for the night."

"Not in my experience," I mumbled.

"What's that?" She swung back to face me.

"Nothing."

She poked me genially in the chest. I blessed the Lady for the Sherkin breastplate. "Don't go away, Karesh, I'll be right back—and then we'll see what we can do to make you feel better, hey?" As she marched away towards the infirmary, the floor vibrating to her tread, Lissula's dangling hand waggled a delicate obscenity.

I collapsed against the wall. Where in the Lady's name was Angel? Lissula had bought me a little time, but I would rather have faced Kekashr and all the hordes of Iklankish on my own than be waiting when that amorous mountain came back. I turned towards the exit and bumped squarely into another helmeted Sherkin.

"Had a good one?" he asked.

"Yes, thank you, very good," I babbled, then realized that I had just been given the password, composed (naturally) by the shints. "Angel? The Lady be thanked. Let's get out of here."

We turned and marched side-by-side through the maze of cubicles. "You took your time," I muttered, "where were you?"

"What's wrong, my lord Scion?"

"I was practically raped, that's what."

"The Koroskans?" A curious sound issued from behind Angel's helmet.

"It isn't funny, Angel."

He seemed to be thinking this over. "Yes it is, my lord Scion."

"What do you know about it?" I asked crossly as we stepped into the little entrance enclosure, where a handful of troopers played at fingersticks while they waited for a shint to be free. Another Koroskan wardress sat at a desk beside the door. She glanced up at us without interest and made a couple of notes on a list in front of her. "Next two," she called out.

The shints had told us what to do at this point—we walked past the desk without comment, tossing a couple of tokens into a bowl near the Koroskan's elbow as we went by. The great doors of the old Contemplation Hall of the Novices swung open before us and closed behind us, and the final phase of my quest began.

36

A FAIR-SIZED PARTY of troopers came out of the shintashkr just after us and followed us down the Spine. They were not far behind us—I could hear their voices and the tired clumping of their boots on the stone floor—but they made no attempt to catch us up. Angel was as stolid as ever; I used every grain of willpower I owned to keep from breaking into a run. We walked the long, long length of the Spine that way without meeting another soul—not surprising, since it was only a couple of hours before dawn. The Spine brought us out into the colonnades of the old Inner Garden, where the queens of Gil had raised flowers and herbs, and where generations of little Scions had played.

Legend held that unwelcome seeds never sprouted there, which presumably saved my ancestresses the trouble of

weeding; now weeds were all that remained, and there were
pitifully few of those. A rough stone pavement had been laid
over the rich soil. Horse-stalls had been built among the por-
ticos on two sides. Of the original five fountains, only one
survived, now reincarnated as a watering trough, and the statuary group that once graced it (Oballef's children frolicking
in the spray) was gone. Amazingly, some of the delicate
wrought-iron brackets designed to support garlands of flowering vines were still affixed to the columns, now holding
flaming torch-poles that stank of grease.

The courtyard was unexpectedly crowded with dark figures, milling busily around by torchlight while a light rain
glazed the stone pavement. We walked along in the shelter
of the raised south portico without attracting attention, although I was worried by Angel's tendency to shamble when
he should have been striding. It was hard not to hurry, hard
to remember that we were effectively invisible, just two of
a crowd of uniformed troopers, identical except for small
details of helmet and sword. There, of course, lay the greatest
danger; I expected any moment to be hailed with the name
of Karesh, or to have some friend of my late benefactor (may
his bones bring forth etc.) swagger up jovially to slap me on
the back. But nobody even glanced our way—all attention
was on the rain-slicked centre of the courtyard, where four
great black horses were being hitched to a black-and-gilded
carriage and mobs of ostlers were saddling up a troop of
cavalry mounts.

"Here! You lot!"

I turned, my hand moving involuntarily to the grip of my
sword. A harried-looking officer stood by the door to the
Queen's Vestibule with his helmet under his arm. He was
addressing us—but not just us, also the straggle of troopers
who had followed us out of the shintashkr. "Over there, the
top of the stairs," he snapped, "and hurry! That means everyone, Roshek. And I don't give a Gilman's fart if you're off
duty or where you've just come from, you randy buggers,
I'm short-handed and Old Claw wants an honour guard for
this. So jump!"

We jumped. He pointed to a broad strip of carpeting that

snaked down the flight of steps from the portico to the court-yard, so we jumped in that direction. Then I noticed with panic that Angel had not moved, so I jumped back, grabbed him and hustled him over. The others, muttering, were already lining themselves up along both edges of the carpet, one on each step. I planted Angel at the top and myself on the second step. The officer strode down the steps and up again, dressing the line fiercely; he halted in front of me and my heart stopped.

"Great Raksh," he groaned. He extracted a rag from his sleeve, spat on it, polished a spot on my breastplate, moved on to straighten Angel's helmet. "Now nobody move!" He vanished inside the vestibule.

We stood like a frieze of statues. Several minutes passed, then several more. There were too many troopers around for us to fade discreetly away, and holes in the honour guard might have been conspicuous. My knees began to ache. More minutes passed. The trooper one step down from me muttered a colourful expletive, one I hadn't heard before, and I committed it to memory. Almost half an hour passed.

At last the same officer dashed through the vestibule door. He shouted—I risked moving my head, and saw the troopers in the courtyard running to form up their lines. Within seconds the honour guard was complete, an unbroken double file of snarling helmets and wind-whipped cloaks stretching from the vestibule to the carriage waiting in the courtyard. A measured tramp of boots sounded from the vestibule. A phalanx of officers swept grandly through the open doorway, followed by Shree under his red crest, Kekashr himself—and Calla.

She was even more gloriously gowned than when I had last seen her, to the point where one could hardly tell there was a flesh-and-blood woman under all those tiers and rigid billows of metal-laced gold satin, the bodice that could have turned a sword, the filigreed headdress that rested on her hair like a towering, bejewelled birdcage. But there was nothing decorative about the iron fetters on her wrists, joined by a short, solid-looking chain, and her face was one to make the nervous or unarmed keep their distance.

That much I gathered with a quick glance. Then it was eyes to the front and arms stiff by my sides, in imitation of the trooper facing me across the carpet; thus, I heard rather than saw a brief and energetic struggle just outside the vestibule door. A second later, Kekashr appeared in my field of view, looking exasperated. He stopped just below me on the stairs, but turned to look towards the vestibule.

"Come now, Krisht," he said softly in Gillish, "this is not seemly behaviour for the daughter of a lord of Iklankish. Nor will it affect my decision."

"You promised me—"

"I know what I promised. Perhaps I was not entirely frank with you, my beloved child, but I suspect you have not been frank with me either. We will not discuss it."

He turned to continue down the stairs. Calla followed, after a fashion. She was flanked by two troopers, who were not so much hustling her along as trying to channel her natural energies, but without great success. Just in front of me, one of them grunted and folded up, gasping for breath—really, from Kekashr's point of view, it was a mistake to dress Calla in a gown that was virtually a close-combat weapon. Tearing free from the remaining watchdog, she crashed resoundingly into the trooper across from me. Her bodice proved to be not quite a match for his breastplate—she ricocheted off and fell forwards down the stairs, a dozen arms reaching for her as the Sherkin line broke. But Calla was not finished. A howl from one of the troopers below, and she reappeared in the crush, swinging a heavy sword in her fettered hands and working her way up the stairs again.

"Stop her!" That was Kekashr's roar, and the troopers closed in, but they were obviously unsure how to proceed. She was a Sherkint and the daughter of a great warlord, and she was not cooperating. I stepped forward, forgetting myself, tugging at my own sword—no matter whose daughter she was, whatever her treachery, she was Calla, and in that insane moment I knew that I still loved her—but the flat of her sword thwacked into the side of my helmet and tumbled it off my head, and then she went down under a tide of rather apologetic troopers, and I returned abruptly to my senses.

Fervently blessing the confusion, I scrabbled around for the helmet—it had rolled into and partly under the writhing knot of bodies that represented Calla and her retinue. With horror, I watched it disappear. I dropped to my knees and shouldered into the mêlée, feeling blindly for the helmet in its last known position while somebody stuck a boot in my nose. Then my hand found a face, actually a mouth, which bit down hard on my fingers and shook them like a shull shaking a chicken. I was too desperate even to cry out, being drawn well into the scramble by then, with my cloak twisted around my neck and threatening slow strangulation or a quick snap of the vertebrae, and someone grinding a knee down on to my other hand—and then the struggle just stopped, and muttering troopers were picking themselves up and dusting off their armour, and Calla was lying panting on the stairs, her face a few inches from mine, her eyes looking directly into mine, her teeth still clamped on my fingers. I truly believe my heart stopped for a long few seconds.

Then she opened her jaws to release my fingers, closed her eyes, and rolled away from me on to her side, as if exhausted. Hopelessly, I knelt beside her waiting for the denunciation, for the second betrayal—and when it didn't come, I reached out for the helmet lying beside her and pulled it over my head. As I staggered to my feet, I caught a small flicker of her fingers. *Goodbye.* The forever variety.

I hung over her like a slack-jawed imbecile until Lord Kekashr himself pushed me aside. Somebody, perhaps Angel, hauled me backwards into line by the scruff of my cloak. Kekashr whispered to one of his attendants, who ran into the vestibule. Minutes later the Koroskan healer who had tended me rustled out and bent over Calla, kneading and prodding her where he was able through the obdurate gown, while she lay passively at her father's feet.

"The lady is not injured, Lord Kekashr," the healer said at last. He looked up for instructions.

"Make her sleep," Kekashr murmured, "I've had more than enough excitement from my poor misguided daughter."

Calla rolled on to her back to look up at him, and laughed.

"Misguided, Father? By Oballef, you've just spoken a true word."

"A slip, daughter," Kekashr grinned. Calla did not resist as the healer lifted her head and poured something into her mouth from a bottle. She drank obediently. Her eyes passed along the line of helmets, stopping at each one, but with no flicker of recognition, not even when they rested briefly on mine. Then they closed. Kekashr himself unfastened the shapeless mess of wires and gems that used to be her headdress and picked her up, not ungently, and carried her down the stairs towards the waiting carriage.

I stood beside Angel, stiff with shock. Gratitude? Not really. Grief? Not yet—that was for later. The carriage door slammed shut, the horses clattered off through the gate in the west arcade, and Calla was gone, leaving nothing behind her but the broken headdress, a few dishevelled troopers, and the toothmarks on my hand. It was disbelief that paralysed me. It had happened too fast. I shot a quick glance down the row of troopers, noting the signs of Calla's passing—and ran full into the intent, level gaze of Lord Shree.

His face was blank, but he was staring straight at me. There was no mistake about it. Disbelief gave way to a form of controlled panic—how long had he been watching? I gulped and snapped my head around to the regulation position. Had he, alone among the Sherank, recognized me while the helmet was off, or caught Calla's fleeting reaction? Of course not, I told myself, or he'd be doing more than just staring at me, he'd have me in fetters by now and on my way to confer with the hot irons.

Maybe. A memory stirred: eons ago, standing miserably beside Calla in the marketplace, waiting for Gil's butchers to notice that a wretch in the Pleasure was dead—and all the time, Shree knew, Shree saw and did nothing. Slowly, I turned my head and met his eyes. He was still watching me.

"Well, that's done, Nephew."

A muscle twitched in Shree's cheek—no other reaction. Lord Kekashr preceded him slowly up the stairs, inspecting the damage to the line of troopers as he passed.

"What a little firecat I sired, eh, Shree? Almost a pity they'll knock it out of her in Iklankish."

"If they're able."

"Come now, she won't be the first vixen they've tamed. Look how they broke your mother."

"True." Shree dropped a gauntlet on the stair by my feet, and stooped to retrieve it. When he straightened, he looked me full in the eyes and slammed my helmet so hard with the mailed glove that my ears rang. "You," he snapped, "your boots are a disgrace."

I stared straight ahead. "Yes, sir," I said. It was plausible—certainly, I had not stopped to clean Karesh's boots. This could have been the reason he was staring at me, but somehow I didn't think so.

Lord Kekashr called irritably from the doorway. "What are you doing, Shree? Leave discipline to the officers."

"We need a few extra hands, Uncle—I'm going to teach this one a lesson with some punitive duty."

"Fine, just come along. I want to get started."

Shree was still standing in front of me. I stared at him. A hundred factors balanced themselves in my mind, fifty risks versus fifty reasons to hope, and I made my decision. Keeping my eyes fixed on Shree's, I jerked my head the thickness of a fingernail in Angel's direction.

Shree's jaw tightened. "You too," he snapped to Angel, "fall in with the others—and next time," he shoved Angel back a pace, "polish your boots!" He strode on up the stairs.

Numb, almost breathless, I motioned to Angel and we joined the tail of Kekashr's retinue. I was still not sure what I had done.

37

IRONICALLY, LORDS KEKASHR and Shree took us exactly where we needed to go. Left to ourselves, we'd have made the disastrous assumption that the Lady was in Kekashr's own chamber or in the sanctuary, and wasted valuable time and run unthinkable risks nosing around the Temple Palace. Instead, Lord Kekashr turned left from the Queen's Vestibule and took the long bare corridor that led towards the south dungeon. In my ignorance, I was dismayed.

The broad staircase Kekashr led us down was twisted around a central shaft where, in better days, a great cage on a woven-iron cable was used to lower wine amphorae and casks of honey for storage. Naturally, there was no dungeon in the old Gilgard—no crime in Gil, and no war, and therefore no prisoners. The north dungeon used to be a mushroom plantation. The south dungeon was the old wine-cellar, adapted by the ever-ingenious Sherank once the Vintage of Gil was exhausted or shipped off to Sher. This happened rather quickly, the news reaching the Flamens-in-Exile only a few months after the catastrophe.

I knew what the cellar used to look like, from a painting by a long-dead Flamen-in-Exile who remembered the wine of Gil with special fondness. The painting was superb, range upon range of silver-braced amphorae, each with a polished silver label that twinkled in the torchlight until the cellar resembled the night sky, strewn with constellations of fine rare vintages—his words, not mine. Quite irrelevant anyway; the wine racks were long gone, the amphorae long since emptied and smashed, the silver melted down and sent as ingots to Iklankish. The dignified silence of aging wine had been given over to a low, continuous roar, which I thought at first was the sea echoing through some trick chamber of the mountain until I rounded the last turn of the stairs and the cellar lay open before us. It was voices, perhaps a thousand of them, blending into one terrible massed moan of anguish and despair.

The chicken market at Sathelforn is rebuilt daily out of little openwork wicker cages, stacked two deep to a height of six feet or more, each holding three doomed but cheerful fowl. The south dungeon was superficially similar, but the cages were made of iron bars and were hideously more crowded, and the inmates may likewise have been doomed but they were certainly not cheerful. Four tiers of cages within a clearance of about twenty feet; long rows of cages separated at floor level by narrow aisles, linked at higher levels by catwalks paced by silent guards. Faces crowded the bars, dirty stubbled glazed faces; claws reached out towards us, cracked voices begged for water. The guards, perhaps anxious to impress Kekashr, sliced at the bars with short lengths of chain, driving the miserables back and eliciting more than one shriek of agony, more than one crack of bone and spurt of blood. It was Hell by torchlight, as conceived by the bloody-minded Lucians with their doctrine of divine judgement.

I tried to stare straight ahead, as the other troopers were doing—these horrors held no novelty for them. We marched along the central aisle just out of range of the imploring hands on either side, and I felt my shock turn to a terrible pity, the pity harden to a rage like a jagged lump of metal in my throat. It was too late to save, for example, that wretched woman whose remains were pulled from an upper cage while we were passing and tossed down like a bag of slops to be loaded on the body-cart in the corner, a sodden thud behind me to be remembered sometimes in nightmares—but there could be a chance for the rest, and for Gil, and vengeance for her.

I fixed my eyes on the enemy himself, striding along at the head of the column beside the cloaked enigma that was Lord Shree; it seemed incredible that Kekashr could not

sense the heat of my anger, that my radiant hatred did not
pull him up and force him to look over his shoulder at the
sure approach of his doom. I, Tigrallef the short and cautious,
was outraged enough to feel that I couldn't fail.

"Raksh take you, Karesh, get off my heels." The trooper
ahead of me poked rearwards with his mailed elbow. I fell
back a pace, back into step with Angel, who glanced sideways at me but held his tongue.

A wall of rough masonry marked the end of the dungeon
proper—a Sherkin innovation, since it was not in the archive
plans. Lord Kekashr swept through the doorway with us in
his train. The enclosure beyond was perhaps fifty feet by
thirty, with a large table and several torture frames set up
near the entrance. There were troopers there already, formed
up and ready to be relieved.

There were also prisoners, but they were harder to see at
first, since the cages that held them were set against the far
wall. As my eyes adjusted to the light, their battered faces
emerged out of the gloom. Some were faces I knew: Corri,
Namis, Farano, Sorvi, all Flamens of the Council-in-Gil, and
also Calvo the scullery-master, bruised and bloody and minus
the comfortable paunch. And isolated in a small cage at the
end was another familiar face: Jebri, alias the little spider. It
seemed the Sherank were repaying his treachery with more
of the same. His eyes were closed. There was blood on his
forehead, and in a wide stripe from the corner of his mouth
to his chin. He looked dead at first, but he shifted and
groaned while my eyes were on him, and one of his plump
hands pushed at the air as if repelling something in his
dreams. There was no sign of Bekri.

While the first lot of troopers marched smartly out and my
lot took their places, Kekashr inspected an impressive array
of torture tools laid out on the table. Angel and I were left
standing awkwardly on our own until Lord Shree barked at
us to stand on either side of the door. We jumped to obey.

Kekashr studied a paper taken from the table. "So the old
one's still alive?" he said to Shree.

"Yes—very much so. The healer came in to look at him."

"Well?"

"He's tough. Xilo says he could survive another questioning, if it were carefully done."

Kekashr grunted. "Well, well—and most Gilmen die so easily. We'll make him the first."

"Why, Uncle?" Shree made no move. "He's too valuable to waste in such a chancy experiment. Anyway, even if it did work, he'd be the last to cooperate."

Kekashr's face darkened, but cleared after a moment. He laughed without warmth and clapped Shree's shoulder. "I'll overlook your impertinence, Shree, since you may be right. We'll need the old man when Tigrallef's back in our hands. The spider said there was a bond between them."

I realized then that they were talking about Bekri. Relief that he was alive mixed with a sick realization of what he had suffered, and what Kekashr planned for him. Loyalty to friends. Those were Kekashr's words, and the tool he intended to use—not my agony but Bekri's. If he caught me, that is. Uncomfortably, I wondered about Shree's intentions— if he were planning a dramatic exposure, this moment would be ideal. I peered at him, half expecting him to stride over and pull the helmet triumphantly off my head, but he was watching his uncle.

"And what of our star prisoner, Nephew?"

Shree sorted through the papers on the table, pulled one out. "Xilo's report. The man's mind is quite gone and he's still unable to form words. Xilo's been working on him, but he holds out little hope. He's bringing him down just after dawn, whatever state he's in."

Kekashr suddenly slammed the table. Everybody in the room jumped, even Shree. "It's damnable, Nephew. For years we have a Scion in our hands and no Lady, now we have the Lady and no Scion, or not a usable one."

"Damnable," Shree echoed flatly. For my part, I was rocked on my heels; Angel was right. There was another Scion in Gil.

"And that scrawny whelp-of-a-shull that poor Krisht was so weak about," Kekashr went on, "he'll suffer, Shree, he'll suffer for this before he conjures the Lady for me, make no mistake."

"I make no mistake, Uncle."

Kekashr gave his nephew another of those thoughtful stares. "Well," he said at last, "we've wasted enough time. Bring the first subject—but not the old man. I think we'll have that young firebrand who made so much trouble in the city. He owes us a few favours."

The cage door clanged open and Shree motioned to a couple of troopers. They parted the prisoners roughly before them as they pushed to the back of the cage, emerging a moment later with a limp half-naked Gilman hanging between them. It was Hawelli, though it took me a horrified moment to be sure of this, so gaunt he'd become, so bent and torn and pitiful, all the pride and strength beaten out of him. He could not walk; one leg looked to be broken and was glistening black under the tatters of his britches. He moved his head feebly and blinked at the torchlight as the troopers half-carried him towards Kekashr. Miserably, I steeled myself for the torture that was to follow.

Except that it didn't. Hawelli was not strapped into a torture frame—he was brought before Kekashr, sagging between his supporters while the warlord studied his face.

"Yes, he'll do for a start," Kekashr said. He reached under his cloak and pulled out a long cylinder of dark cloth, which he proceeded to unroll.

Even before the radiance came, I knew what the cloth held. I stepped forward a pace, caught Shree's eye on me and stepped back again, but my veins were pounding with heated blood. As the last fold of cloth fell away, a dazzling light burst in the dim chamber, the torches paled.

Kekashr chuckled. "Beautiful, isn't it, Nephew?" He held the coruscating brilliance, the Lady, high in one hand and shouted across to the cages, "Is this what you were looking for, old man?"

The cages were well illuminated now. I saw a stir among the Flamens, Corri reaching behind him to help a hunched figure from the back of the cell to the bars. Bekri straightened himself painfully; his face was golden with the Lady's light.

"You have not won yet, Lord Kekashr," he said in a strong

voice. It may have been a trick of the shifting light, but I
felt sure he was smiling.

The warlord strolled to the cages. "By Raksh, you are a
tough old rooster," he said in Gillish. "I suppose in the end
we'll have to put you in the Pleasure, just to see if its spikes
can pierce your thick hide. As for winning, I have the Lady
in Gil, haven't I? It's only a matter of time before a Scion
comes my way."

"I'm sure one will," said Bekri. "Even in this place, we
hear whispers. The Scion Tigrallef slipped right through your
fingers."

"Just temporarily—and my daughter tells me he's a simpleton." I could not see Kekashr's face, but his voice was
like a saw-blade labouring on granite.

"A simpleton? And he's eluded you for ten days? What
does that make you, my great Sherkin lord?" Bekri laughed,
quietly, but with real amusement. He turned his back on Kekashr, still chuckling.

Kekashr stood for a moment and then turned back to poor
Hawelli. His face was dark with rage, his gauntlet clenched
around the Lady. I honestly wondered if Bekri was trying to
get himself killed.

Shree was watching me again and I asked myself: what
was I to him? A prisoner? An ally? A trooper with dirty
boots? Had I imagined that glance of silent conspiracy in the
courtyard? Inscrutability was all very well, but it gave me a
poor basis for planning. And if he knew who I was, what in
Oballef's name did he expect me to do? I could, I suppose,
have jumped through the torture frames, scrambled across
the table, made a dash for Kekashr and grabbed the Lady—
but I'd have been cut to dogmeat before I was halfway there,
and conjuring the Lady is no instant matter anyway. So I
stayed where I was and watched Shree, and Shree watched
me, and both of us bided our time. The dangerous game,
whatever it was, went on.

Kekashr wrapped Hawelli's hand around the Lady. Their
faces were washed almost to invisibility by the glare and I
had to squint to see. Hawelli sagged and his hand dropped,
and Kekashr snapped at one of the guards holding him, to

steady the Lady. Then Kekashr stepped back—well back.

"Repeat after me, Gilman," he said. Hawelli raised his head. "*Aro elian calos pilian*—say it!" I jerked as I recognized the words. The Lesser Will. More of Jebri's treachery.

"No, Hawelli!" Bekri was back at the bars, pressing desperately against them, not laughing now.

Hawelli shook his head in confusion. I think he was barely conscious. One of the guards reached down and twisted the gangrenous leg. Hawelli screamed.

"Aro elian calos pilian," Kekashr repeated gently. Hawelli whispered the words after him. "Calos milaf aro elian . . ." The Will went on, Kekashr echoed faintly by Hawelli—I closed my eyes, knowing what would happen and powerless to stop it. The Heroic Code yammered in my head, urging me forwards. But if I did, Kekashr would win. It was as simple and deadly as that.

They reached the end of the Will. For a second, nothing seemed to be happening, the light was growing so slowly. Then it soundlessly exploded, and I threw my hand over my eyes; faint tremors in the floor, hardly perceptible at first, built in violence as if the mountain were arching in pain. The stone walls seemed to writhe for a few seconds, then gradually solidified, and the Lady's light faded back to no more than its normal brilliance.

Oddly, the room was undisturbed, the torture tools still in good order, the table upright, Hawelli and his guards frozen in the same postures. But when Kekashr moved closer and picked the Lady out of Hawelli's hand, all three men crumbled into dust.

38

"WHAT A PITY," Lord Kekashr sighed. "Well, Shree, we have no end of Gilmen, if it comes to that."

"It was a little hard on the troopers," said Shree, frowning at the three heaps of dust.

Lord Kekashr shrugged. He strolled back to the cage and stood in front of Bekri with his arms crossed and his head thrown back triumphantly. "You see, old man?" he said in Gillish. "You should have waited before laughing."

Behind the bars, Bekri raised his head wearily. "I can't imagine what you think you're doing."

"Exploring an option, Flamen. I grant you, we've had bad luck with Scions, though we'll continue down that path as well—but I'm told that all we really need is a Gilman with a drop of Oballef's blood in his veins."

Bekri laughed, this time bitterly and unamused. "It will be a long search."

"But worth it in the end—of course, we may succeed with Tigrallef or the other before then." Bekri looked uncertain at the mention of the other, and I remembered—this would be the first he'd heard of another Scion in the Gilgard. Lord Kekashr moved closer to the bars and I had to strain to hear him. "You could shorten the search for me, old man. You must know if any by-blows of the royal line remained in Gil after the invasion. Tell me; you could save many lives."

"While causing many deaths."

The warlord spread his hands. "Everyone dies in the end."

"So I've learned. But why should they die to your profit?"

"You're a boring old bastard, you know," Kekashr said evenly. "You should have died yourself seventy years ago, along with your brother priests. Just consider what I've said."

He swung around and paced back to the table.

He set the Lady carelessly down and stood by her, pondering, drumming his fingers. I gauged the distance—it was just possible I could make it that far without a bolt in the back, but what then? It seemed unlikely that Kekashr and his troopers would be kind enough to wait while I intoned the Lesser Will, and I was not sure enough of Shree's intentions to trust him for help. Angel would do what he could, but what would that be against the eight remaining troopers, not to mention the hordes in the next room? A vagrant thought wandered through my head: Arkolef would not have hesitated—but Arko had no sense of timing. I sighed, and clenched my fists, and waited.

Everybody waited. Kekashr did not suggest another of those obscene experiments, somewhat to my surprise. The troopers stood silently at attention, the Lady glowed on the table, Kekashr contemplated the Lady, Shree contemplated Kekashr. Now and then Shree's eyes flickered towards me, and there was the shadow of a smile on his face as if he were enjoying himself. The only sounds in the chamber were suppressed groans from the cages, although the room was far from silent. There was always the threnody from the outer dungeon, a lamentation as performed by waterfall or tidal race.

At last, the sound of booted feet. Lord Kekashr looked up; in the cage, Bekri rose unsteadily with Corri's aid. Four Sherkin troopers marched through the door and fanned out, followed by a pale Koroskan with an even greater paunch and heavier silver chain than most. He was followed in turn by two troopers carrying between them a blanketed figure on a stretcher, with four more troopers bringing up the rear. These last also spread themselves about the chamber, one of them practically on top of me. The room was getting too crowded for my liking.

The Koroskan grovelled formally, and Kekashr delivered a token kick to the head, but he seemed impatient with the courtesies. "Tell me quickly, Xilo," he growled, "what progress have you made?"

The Koroskan heaved ponderously to his feet, but gave a

clear impression of continuing to grovel. "My lord Kekashr, mighty Hammer of Iklankish, his condition remains almost the same. He has said nothing."

"Almost the same?" Kekashr asked, leaning forwards.

Xilo hesitated. "He stood again, with assistance. And once his lips moved, but there were no words that I could make out."

"Did he seem to be hearing you?"

"Perhaps, great lord, but one cannot be certain—" The Koroskan's voice faltered. If ever a man that massive could be said to squirm, he was squirming. And no wonder—Lord Kekashr's infamous temper, already in a poor state, looked to be getting worse. He strode to the stretcher and coldly examined the face above the blanket. I turned my head as far as I dared, straining to see the same face, guessing that it was my kinsman, going over the possible names in my mind. Tension spread throughout the chamber; the trooper beside me was taut as a harp-string after tuning. Nobody was safe when a warlord of Iklankish felt an itch under his armour.

Of those outside the cages, only Shree appeared unaffected. He joined his uncle beside the stretcher and gazed down at the still figure. "It takes time to bring back the dead, Uncle. After all, he spent nineteen years in the dark with only shulls for company, and—"

Nineteen years. I missed the rest of Shree's no doubt reasonable argument. Nineteen years. *Tell your father when you find him that I'm still waiting.* It hardly seemed possible, but there it was. The husk on the stretcher was (or had been) Lord Cirallef of Gil, of the line of Oballef, son of Arrislef, grandson of Callef, father of Arkolef, and my father as well. Suddenly the inside of my helmet was wet, and I wondered bemusedly whether the tears would drip down my chin and give me away—the Sherank were not known to cry—but nobody was looking at me, not even Shree.

"But we have no time," Kekashr was saying when I began to hear again. He was biting his words, which appeared to taste progressively worse. "Iklankish is already impatient about the insurrection—and you know I had to send news

of the Lady with Krisht's vessel, in case the princess should
hear from another source that it's been found. Why, they'd
suspect me of treachery then!"

"With good reason, you must admit," Shree said mildly.

Kekashr's voice was low and dangerous. "If you were not
my brother's son—never mind. Of the three paths, this is the
surest. We'll force the Scion to notice us."

"How, my lord Uncle?"

Silence while Lord Kekashr glided back to the table, ca-
ressed the Lady, turned to look gloatingly at the watching
Flamens behind their bars. He said, "Put him in the frame."

Without a second's hesitation, Shree nodded to Xilo.

I swayed forwards, reaching for my sword. It was not the
Heroic Code that impelled me, it was blind revulsion—whatever the risks, whatever the consequences, whether Kekashr
conquered the world or not, I could not let this happen. I
could not let my father, dead for nineteen years though his
body still breathed and his heart still pushed the blood
through his veins, be wakened from his long sleep by Lord
Kekashr's terrible little tools; my fingers tightened on the
sword. I felt my muscles gathering for the spring, and a snarl
forming on my lips under the snarling helmet.

"Wait!" Shree's voice was sharp. He was speaking directly
to me. I froze. His eyes were wide, and there was a clear
message in them. *Please. This is necessary. Trust me. Do
nothing yet.* After an endless moment, my hand dropped from
the sword.

"What is it, Shree?" Lord Kekashr's voice came testily
from a great distance.

"Nothing, my lord Uncle." Shree turned a blank face to
Kekashr. "I thought I saw the Scion move." Truthful but
ambiguous: Shree's style.

"Xilo?"

"I saw nothing, great Hammer of Iklankish."

"Then get on with it."

With blurred eyes I saw my father lifted off the stretcher,
stripped of his blanket and strapped naked into the torture
frame. I had a moment's uncertainty—my father was not
much past forty, whereas this man was old, old and scarred,

bony with an old man's boniness, sunken and withered. A sudden memory encompassed me. Myself at four years old, high in the air in a tall man's arms, Arko's five-year-old face upturned far below, then the short descent to my mother's arms and her voice in my ear while the tall man walked away from us through an archway of flowers, *don't worry, little man, you'll see your father again*. I choked and the memory dissolved. The man in the frame was open-eyed and staring at nothing. I could not mistake his face.

It is strange but true, that small discomforts can sometimes distract the mind from horrors that might otherwise break it. Throughout my father's torture, I was desperate to blow my nose.

Xilo was skilled, but the Hammer of Iklankish was impatient. After a long, anguished time during which I smothered helplessly in my own snot and my father continued to dangle like a dead man from his wrist-straps, Kekashr shoved the Koroskan aside. "Have the box fetched," he snapped to Shree.

I had once read about this instrument with some interest, naïvely wondering if it might have benign possibilities—just a box fitted with a crank handle and a couple of long copper wires, but the peak achievement of Sherkin magical research. When the wires were glued to the victim with hot wax and the handle was cranked, mysterious blue sparks crackled along the copper, the body jerked, the throat laboured to scream. Very satisfying from the Sherkin point of view, especially as it did no fatal damage if intelligently used.

When the box was brought, Kekashr ruminated for a moment and then pointed to my father's temples. Cirallef did not flinch as the hot wax dripped on to his skin. I felt it in my own temples. Kekashr himself turned the handle, not too fast, just enough to make the wires seem to shimmer. My father hung limply. The handle speeded up, and my father's body twitched, then convulsed in a crazy wooden dance. Kekashr stopped cranking.

"A response of sorts," he said thoughtfully. "Put in the protector, Xilo, we need his tongue intact." Xilo slipped something into my father's mouth and the cranking resumed, as did my father's grotesque ballet. I was afraid those frail arms would snap in their leather restraints, but Kekashr knew his business, judged his speed, watched my father's convulsions with the intentness of a dance critic. A lowing began behind the tongue protector and built up to a roar. Kekashr stilled the handle.

"That's much better," he beamed. "You see, Xilo? He's starting to take notice." He stepped up to the frame and slipped the protector out of my father's mouth. "Cirallef, my friend," he said gently, "speak your name."

My father stared straight ahead. There was no sign that he had heard. Kekashr slapped his face hard, and he shook his head, something of awareness surfacing briefly and then vanishing again. Back went the tongue protector; back went Kekashr to the box, and the whole painful process was repeated. And repeated, and repeated again, until my fists ached with clenching and my heart burned with the shame of letting it continue. Finally, after the fifth measure of the dance, my father raised his head at Kekashr's approach.

"You have something to say to me?" Kekashr enquired pleasantly, as if my father were a supplicant on the Day of Appeals. My father's jaws worked silently for a few seconds before the sound emerged.

"Dazeene—"

"What's that? Dazeene? That's not your name, idiot."

Disappointed, Kekashr turned back to the box, but Shree caught his arm. "It's a Satheli name, Uncle, not Gillish," he said helpfully, "his whore, maybe, that he kept in Exile. A good sign."

By the Lady, it was hard to forgive Shree for that. Dazeene was my mother, a princess of Sathelforn, and she was no whore—a woman who kept herself to herself for all the years of her prime, because her man had ridden the storm on a soap-bubble and never come back. And whose fault was that? The guilt was shared by so many, even by my father. Something exploded inside my head. It was rage.

Oh, that was a good rage, a strong rage! I recognized it suddenly as an old companion, incubated in Exile, hatched in Gil—an anger at wasted lives, at throwaway heroism, at treachery and cruelty and the lust for power. It had broken through before, this rage, but not like this; I suppose I had never welcomed it before. Fortunately, it also strangled me for the moment. I stood silently, a model trooper, letting the rage spread throughout my body until it became a second entity sharing my skin.

In the meantime, I had missed something. Kekashr was standing by my father, looking rather pleased. "What do you think, Shree? It needn't be loud as long as the syllables are clear."

"Right as always, Uncle," said Shree. He loosened the wrist-straps, and my father immediately collapsed. Shree added thoughtfully, "He'll need to be held—but there could be some danger."

"What danger? He's a fullborn Scion."

"A fullborn Scion who's lost his mind. We don't know that the Lady will answer in the way we hope. Didn't the little spider mention a Caveat?"

Kekashr waved off this trifle. "I leave it to you, Shree," he said. He picked up the Lady; his hands vanished into the light.

The thin smile was back on Shree's lips. He was very pale, except for a blotch of colour high on each cheek. He looked around and seemed to notice me for the first time. "You, trooper—the one with the dirty boots. Yes, and your friend. Come over here. If you live through this, you'll remember to clean your kit."

I floated over on the wings of my glorious rage, poking Angel to follow as I passed him. Under Shree's direction, we hoisted my father to his feet and lugged him past the drift of dust that marked Lord Kekashr's previous experiment. How light he was! No more weight than a four-year-old child. I saw Bekri and Corri and a few other Flamens huddle against the bars in mute despair. I saw Jebri, awake now, cover his face. I saw Shree gazing through my helmet with eyes that said: *your waiting is over, Scion, here is your chance, use it in good health*. I saw the Lady approaching in the hand of Lord Kekashr. The radiance was almost unbearable at this range—my poor father moaned with the pain of it, and screwed up his face.

"You'll need to help him hold it, trooper. Wind your fingers around his—that's good. Now, Lord Cirallef—repeat after me . . ."

39

"ARO ELIAN CALOS pilian."

My father's lips moved. So did mine.

"Calos milaf aro elian—is he saying it, trooper? Can you hear the words?"

"Yes, Great Lord." He was actually murmuring my mother's name, but Kekashr did not need to know that. The Lady was cool and glassy under my fingers—the statues were a sham, she was a featureless cylinder concealed in her own nimbus, warming and quickening as I whispered the Lesser Will.

"Milaf solor calos pilian."

I knew the words, I did not need Kekashr to prompt me in his barbarous Sheranik accent, but it was a pleasing irony to repeat the lines after him and let him take part in his own doom. The power was gathering—I remember the Lady purring and pulsing, and streaks of jade fire playing along the surface of the light. My grip tightened.

"Calos pilian aros elian."

That was the key line. Oballef's glittering fog rolled out of the light and filled the chamber. Kekashr moved closer, his face washed ghastly pallid by the incandescence, but avid, triumphant. He reached for the Lady.

I laughed. I knocked off my helmet and showed him all my teeth, and his hand jerked back. He stared at me with his mouth wide open. Then he cried, "Kill him!" and the troopers reached for their swords and found fangs instead, serpent fangs. Parth-asps, probably; I had no chance to look and they were swords again by the time the troopers hit the floor, but parth-asps had certainly been in my mind.

Kekashr glanced around wildly during the brief screaming. He backed away until his mailed rump hit the table. I gently disengaged my father and transferred his whole pitiful weight into Angel's arms, keeping my eyes on Kekashr. I barely registered Shree unlocking the cage, but it must have been while his back was turned and my attention was focused on Kekashr that Xilo slipped unnoticed through the door.

The warlord's arm was almost too fast to follow. A little scalpel from among the torture tools flew towards me, aimed at my exposed throat. It slowed in the golden haze, flashing like a minnow in a sunlit pool, and dropped at my feet. I shook my head chidingly at Kekashr and moved closer to him by a step.

"Scion! The door!" Shree's voice.

I spun around, and so the knife took me not in the exposed nape as intended, but in the shoulder, the same damned shoulder as before, bouncing off the mailed sleeve but cruelly jarring my old wound in the process. I hardly felt the pain—only the rage. Troopers spurted through the doorway, their swords flaming in the mist. I held up my hand, and the flames were real, the troopers were victory bonfires on jerking feet that carried them on a step or two before the flames reached their faces. I dropped my hand again and the conflagration died. The troopers lay where they fell, blackened and stinking of burnt meat, charred leather. From the outer dungeon, a hush—in the chamber, only Jebri's sobbing and my father's incessant murmur, Dazeene, Dazeene.

Lord Kekashr recovered himself quickly. He surveyed the carnage with every sign of critical appreciation, also noting Shree, judging him, cursing him, and passing on to more urgent matters with little more than a narrowing of the eyes. "Very impressive, Tigrallef," he said. "My grandfather Kishr was right about your Lady's potential."

I did not answer. My shoulder was making itself felt, and

the room was in slow but sickening rotation. I shifted the
Lady to my stronger hand and tightened the fingers. In the
outer dungeon, the locks burst on all the cages. A brief dis-
believing continuation of the hush, and then a babble of
voices, followed by a hesitant scrabbling of feet. In the
chamber, Shree was carrying the last of the injured Flamens
out of the cage.

"Such power was wasted on Oballef," Kekashr went on.
"Peace and the pursuit of beauty, pah! Music and poetry.
Milk-piddle and shit. Without the Lady, your fine overbred
forefathers collapsed like a house of sand."

"Into the cage," I said.

"Now you could be different, I see you have the makings
of a conqueror in you. Between us, we could—"

"Into the cage."

"—take the whole world, you and I—" He broke off with
a squawk of surprise as an invisible hand took him by the
neck and dragged him into the cage. The Lady pulsed in my
fingers. The door slammed, the lock fused in a flash of green
fire. In the other cage, Jebri whimpered and pushed himself
into the furthest corner.

Taking a deep breath, I staggered towards Bekri, holding
the Lady out to him like a trophy. He pulled away from Corri
and toppled to meet me. When we met, it was debatable who
was supporting whom, but somehow we didn't fall over and
I didn't drop the Lady. Bekri leaned away from me far
enough to sign the ultimate in respectful greetings to the
Priest-King in Gil.

"Not me, Revered Bekri," I said, smiling, and he opened
his mouth to answer, also smiling, but only a soft sigh
emerged. He crumpled slowly to the floor, dragging me with
him to my knees. He was already dead.

I cradled his head on my good arm. Shree cursed and
started to draw his sword, but I had already seen the dart-
tube at Kekashr's lips. It turned white-hot in his fingers. He
dropped it hastily. I eased Bekri's head down and advanced
on the cage, the Lady in hand.

The rage was upon me; every detail in the chamber had
an icy clarity. Kekashr's face seemed chiselled out of solid

defiance, but that was no more than a patina on his fear—
oh, yes, he was most certainly afraid. "Was the first dart
intended for me?" I asked softly.

He rose to meet me, still defiant; his hands, though, were
shaking. "Indeed it was—what a pity the old man moved.
And the next would have been for my well-beloved nephew.
You should have given me another second, Scion of Oballef,
for your own sake. Do you really imagine he won't betray
you too?"

"You're the one who taught me about treachery, Uncle."
Shree came to my side and gazed impassively through the
bars.

"That's enough," I said.

I turned to look behind me. Bekri's dead face was flushed
by the venom, his scars painted on in paler ochre. Kekashr
squawked and thudded to his knees. Dazeene, Dazeene,
whispered my father; Kekashr began to make small sobbing
noises. I turned again to look at him. He was bleeding from
a thousand short, deep wounds, like those made by his own
torture tools; blue sparks bearded his face and writhed along
his arms. "Perhaps a few boils," I murmured, and a moment
later he was the very image of a beggar I'd seen in the Great
Market, but otherwise not really human. A moment after that,
his heart burst and he was dead.

That was my first deliberately vicious act; but, unlike the
things that happened later, it never caused me a broken moment's regret.

What to do now? I had effectively captured the Gilgard,
though the Sherank hardly knew it yet and might whip about
like the body of a beheaded snake for some time; but even
when the island was wholly ours, there would still be Iklankish to reckon with. That was where the real danger lay. I
closed my eyes and looked deep into my own mind.

The Lady in Gil was there. A mass of silvery hair crackled
about her head but the features were Calla's. She spoke,
though her lips didn't move. *The Greater Will, Scion of Oballef. You must use the Greater Will.*

It's never been used before.

It has, you know—but not recently. She laughed with Lissula's voice and Calla's face, that eerie resemblance to Kekashr surfacing again around the lips.

And the Caveat?

The Caveat has nothing to do with the Wills, Scion. Has so much knowledge been lost? Flames rose around her. The filmy robe fluttered without catching fire.

But what will I do?

She laughed again. *Whatever comes to mind. You're the Scion. You'll know.* The flames roared around her. She evanesced, fading into the flames of my rage, until only Calla's smile, Kekashr's smile, remained. I opened my eyes.

I was standing over Bekri's body, still clutching the Lady. Shree was shaking my shoulder—rather gingerly—and the surviving Flamens were watching me with awed faces. "Dazeene," whispered my father, still in Angel's arms. I reached out to touch him. The room wavered one more time and became solid.

The Lady was right. I would know. The knowledge was already there, inside my head, a smooth black egg waiting for the right moment to hatch. But before that moment came, there was work to do.

Screams erupted in the outer dungeon.

"Damn Xilo," Shree muttered, "he must have raised the alarm. Are you there, Scion? Can your Lady take on the whole castle?"

"Oh yes," I said dreamily. Things. Things of legend, terrible creatures of the dark. Marori's words. Not that I believed in them, of course, but all things were possible with the Lady, and even nightmares had their uses. I roused myself.

"Angel," I said. He took off his helmet and looked at me with doggy reverence. "Go to the shintashkr. Use the between-ways, I guarantee no one will stop you. Tell the shints to stay where they are, no matter what happens; until I come, it will be death to step outside the door. Stay there yourself. I'll give you five minutes—go!"

He passed my father over to Corri and made to prostrate himself. "Never mind that," I snapped at him, "just go!" He went straight to the correct flagstone, stamped once and disappeared into the narrow gap that revealed itself. When he was gone, I motioned to Shree to follow and the others to stay, and marched through into the outer dungeon, not looking back.

The prisoners were milling in panic among the ranks of cages, cattle in slaughter pens, gaunt and pale and confused. At the foot of the great spiral stairs, a few fiercer souls were using the spears left by their late guards to hold off a Sherkin sortie, and not doing badly, although they were slowly being pushed back. I spoke, and the Sherank on the lower stairs burst inside their armour, with a noise like overripe apples splitting in a hot sun. Those above turned and fled, but I knew they'd be back soon, and in greater strength.

In the dungeon, there was shocked silence—until they saw us. A terrible outcry of fear and loathing went up at the sight of Shree, but I kept him close by my side and raised the Lady over my head like a beacon.

"I am Tigrallef, Scion of Oballef," I cried. "The Lady in Gil is back in our hands!"

There were sparse cheers, and many puzzled faces.

"The Lady in Gil," I repeated. "With her power, we can drive the accursed Sherank from our shores!"

There was a slightly better response to that, but the concensus was plain bewilderment. I lowered the Lady. "What's the matter with you?" I cried. "She makes us invincible—you've all seen what she can do. What do you think this light around my head is, you pocketing clots?"

Vacant eyes, suspicious eyes, eyes that knew too much misery to trust in miracles. Shree nudged me. He said, rather kindly, "They've forgotten the Lady. Never mind, Tigrallef; you can still save them."

The Gilborns parted before us as we hurried to the stairs and picked our way over the Sherkin mess. At the first turning, I stopped and faced that wretched multitude again.

"Listen to me," I shouted, "stay in the dungeon. You'll be safe here—but until I return, there is death at the top of the stairs. The Sherank will not attack you again."

Still the uncertain faces. I beckoned to Shree and we went

on, wrapped in the Lady's haze. As we reached the final turn, I stopped; I could sense that Angel had reached the shin-tashkr. A few low words, and all through Gilgard Castle the screaming began.

"What's happening?" Shree grabbed at my arm.

"Things of legend, terrible creatures of the dark," I quoted.

"What?"

"Things of—"

"I heard you. But what do you mean?"

"You'll see in a minute. Don't worry, we'll be safe."

"You're insane."

"I read a lot." We reached the top of the stairs and started along the corridor. Something shadowy and many-headed paused politely to let us go by. Most of its mouths were full. Strewn around it were the remains of what would have been a major Sherkin offensive on the south dungeon. Shree kept very close.

"The falorsiirth," I explained as we hurried down the corridor, "a mythical beast from Miishel, closely related to the steam-dragon of Calloonic mythology but with three or four more heads. And it doesn't make steam. Would you like to see a steam-dragon? There's one here somewhere."

"No," said Shree.

"You won't get another chance, you know. They don't actually exist."

He walked faster. "That what-you-said looked real."

"Falorsiirth. The Lady can make them real, for a while. For long enough."

We came to the Queen's Vestibule. Nothing was moving except a gaggle of wispy things in floating white shrouds, off in the far corner; we could not see what they were clustered around, but the slurping noises suggested feeding time in a sty.

"Ghouls of Ghasca," I remarked.

"Do they exist?"

"Only in legend, warlord. I told you, I read a lot."

He started to answer, but broke off with a gasp, staring past me. I turned my head. Xilo, the Koroskan who had tortured my father, was lurching in through the portico door, his fat hands stretched out in front of him, his fat mouth perfectly circular in a silent scream. Shree raised his sword, but I put my hand on his arm.

"No need," I said, "he's all but dead already."

Xilo crashed into a pillar and stumbled backwards, falling to the tiles with a thud that shook the room. His eyelids fluttered open, but there were no eyes behind them—only motion, the kind of seething you see in an eel-basket as it's hauled out of the sea. What was seething wasn't clear until a few of them spilled out on to Xilo's cheek and began at once to burrow downwards into the pallid flesh. Xilo screamed silently; a few more crawled out between his open lips.

Shree made an untranscribable noise of pure disgust. "Maggots," he added. Moved, I suppose, by an impulse of mercy, he leapt forward and thrust his sword into the Koroskan's quivering bulk, to give him a quick death. A kind idea, but not necessary. The belly burst open as he sliced into it, loosing neither blood nor entrails, just an agitated mass of the things, like squirming rice or live porridge, boiling up over the edges of the rift. Shree made another of those interesting noises.

"Burrowers," I said, "from one of the Lucian hells. Reserved for gluttons, I think. Nasty minds, the Lucians. Let's go."

We went. A Zainoi harpy waddled past us down the stairs as we went up, its brazen wing-tips clacking behind it. It seemed intent on the problems of walking on its awkwardly barbed feet, and took no notice of us at all. The remains of its dinner were still scattered on the first landing.

The harpy was the last of my miscellany of horrors that we actually saw, although we heard many others. I led Shree up through the Middle Palace, quiet except for odd thumps and creaks and roars that I stopped bothering to identify after a while; up through the Temple Palace, where desperate pockets of Sherank were still holding out, but my business was not with them, not directly.

Higher we climbed, to the topmost chambers of the Temple Palace, bare low-ceilinged rooms cut into the rock, with narrow slits for windows. And in the highest of these chambers was a door, quite ordinary to look at, but leading out of the castle and on to the virgin mountainside. Shree and I stepped together into the open air.

40

THERE WAS NO path, only a stretch of broken rocks and minor screes rising steeply towards the summit, tufted here and there with patches of tough pale grass and bright wildflowers, flanked by sheer cliff-faces. It was perhaps two hours past dawn and the air was still cool on the lee of the mountain, but the sky arched blue and cloudless above us.

I climbed easily, steadily, never faltering, never looking back. Shree kept pace, or so I assume, since he was almost on my heels when I pulled myself over the lip of the mountain and on to the bare rock-strewn tableland of the summit. We stood together on the edge, looking down at the city. Its scars and squalor were masked by the residual grace of Oballef's design; beyond it swept the green crescent of the island, fertile and prosperous-looking, prettily dotted with hamlets and small towns, meshed with a fine tracery of roads. From this distance, it was unsullied—the sores that festered under the illusion needed sharper eyes than mine.

"Krisht is on that ship." Those were the first words Shree had spoken since we left the Lower Palace. I followed his pointing finger. There was a flotilla perhaps an hour's sail out of Malvi harbour, faring eastwards in the direction of Sher. One ship was larger than the rest and glittered in the sun as if silver-plated, which it might well have been. I postponed thinking about Calla—there would be time later; I

could not afford to be distracted. I hissed to Shree to keep
quiet and began to raise the Lady.

Shree grabbed my arm. "What are you going to do?"

The golden motes still danced above my head. Shree's
hand flung itself off my arm with such force that he whirled
towards the brink and teetered for a second before I reached
out invisibly and pulled him to safety.

"I'd rather you didn't talk just now," I said.

He was shaking, but he planted himself in front of me like
a boulder before a plough. The hectic colour was back in his
face. Behind his eyes, I saw a rage at least as great as my
own. "Whatever you do," he said, holding my eyes, "it can't
be half measure."

The rage whirled inside my head. I grinned. "I'll sink the
whole damned continent into the sea if that's what it takes,"
I said. "Now move back and be quiet." I forgot him immediately.

I raised the Lady and began the Greater Will. The words
flowed out of my mouth, slowly at first and at my volition,
but gradually, seductively, taking control of my tongue and
palate and breath. I can't remember those words now, as if
the act of speaking them wiped them out of my brain; but I
remember the wind that rose around me, the live throbbing
crystal in my hands, the dazzle in my eyes that collapsed to
a shining splinter on a background of black nothing in the
moment when the last word was spoken—and then the
power came, enfolding and enfolded by the rage, the two
marbling together like two clays under the potter's hand,
melding, billowing into the great golden shape of a woman
the size of a mountain who towered over my head. This time
the Lady had no face. She cocked her massive head towards
me, waiting. The black egg cracked open, the wind screamed
a monstrous magnification of something terrible inside my
mind. I screamed too, quite separately. A hole into darkness
tore open under my feet; then silence.

Mysteriously, my cheek was cushioned on one of the summit's rare clumps of grass. I opened my eyes. The last golden
motes were winking out around my head. I watched the long
grass blades swaying, a beetle of some sort rooting about in

the junction of stalk and blade. A booted foot moved into my field of view, crushing the grass and the beetle. My grief focused on that tiny murder. I was drained of rage. A hand pushed at my shoulder and I flopped on to my back.

Shree looked down at me. His face was pale but composed. I shook my head, trying to dislodge the pain behind my eyes. "What happened?" I whispered, "what did I say?"

He squatted and handed me a small silver flask. Distilled fith-beer. I choked on it, but it gave me the strength to sit up. The golden mountain was gone; the Lady lay among the sharp pebbles a few feet away, beaming palely in the sunlight.

"What happened?" I asked again.

"Damn me if I know," said Shree. "A big bright cloud blew up all around you, and then tore away across the sea. You howled and fell over. That's all I saw. What was supposed to happen?"

"I really don't know," I said shakily, "I'm not sure anyone ever invoked the Greater Will before, no matter what the Lady says. Tell me—where did the cloud go, which way?"

He pointed to the east. "Towards Sher," he said.

Nothing was visible in that direction, except a vague smudge on the horizon like a line of distant hills. Not Sher itself—Sher was too far. Out on the sea, Calla's flotilla moved serenely onwards, her ship gradually diminishing to a blur of silver surrounded by bobbing grey dots. Far beyond it, the smudge darkened and swelled and became more distinct.

We sat tensely among the rocks, Shree and I, waiting. The island was invisible from where we sat—the world comprised only that stony tableland, the expanse of sea, the ominous growth billowing on the horizon. The sun looked somehow wrong, as if the air between us and the sky had thickened and was slowing the passage of light. I plucked and ate a series of grass stems. Shree offered me his flask again, and I took a long, burning drink.

"Why, Shree?" I asked, to break the silence.

"What?"

"Why did you help me?" I handed the flask back.

He took a long pull at the flask, then grinned companionably, quite unexpectedly. "They made a bad mistake with me, Scion," he said.

"Obviously—but what was it?"

His grin faded. He picked up some pebbles and sifted them through his fingers. "My mother was a Gilwoman, did you know? Nothing unusual about that, Tigrallef, the war-court was full of imperial half-castes, but they let me see too much of her when she was still able to whisper into my ear. They thought she was already broken, you see, but she wasn't, not until after I was taken away from her."

"How old were you?"

"I was five. Oh, they did let me see her afterwards, but she had nothing more to tell me. She was broken right enough by then."

"How?"

He snorted. "You don't want to know."

I picked another grass stalk and put it in my mouth. The tumid mass to the east was growing. The air was dying around us, heavy and gelid and still. Shree lifted his head as if listening for thunder.

"I didn't give her a thought for years after that. I was made into a good little warlord, Scion, and I did what I was told; and later, when what I was doing began to revolt me, I thought it was only weakness and hid it even from myself. But the damage, if you can call it that, had already been done."

Far away to the east, lightning flickered.

"When they posted me to my mother's country, it was the beginning of the end. I was split down the middle, Scion, I became two people, Sherkin and Gilman, and I thought I was going mad. Maybe I did go mad. And I'll tell you honestly," he shot out a hand and clutched the straps of my Sherkin breastplate with sudden violence, "it might have gone either way this morning. I could just as well have given you to my uncle at the last moment, the way Krisht gave the Lady to me."

I gently disengaged his fingers. "That possibility had occurred to me. Why didn't you?"

He was silent for a moment, then grinned again. It gave him a different face. "I decided I wanted to die as a Gilman. That would please my poor mother—may her bones bring forth flowers." Then he jumped to his feet, the grin freezing, and drew his sword and flung it, really an astonishing distance, in the direction of Sher. "Raksh take you all!" he screamed.

At that moment, a giant finger tapped the tight membrane of the earth. A burst of light in the east, as broad as the horizon, washed the sun out of the sky; then came the rumble, not thunder, but a thousand thunders crashing in unison with a thousand immeasurable surfs. The mountain shuddered, tumbling us sideways towards the drop; Shree recovered first, grabbed my swordbelt and pulled me after him, away from the edge. Together we crawled through the rocks to safety, the ground undulating under our bellies. I raised my head and looked to the east where a lurid glow was building in the sky.

My fingers closed around the Lady. The mountaintop, the glassy sea, the burning sky, instantly wavered and became indistinct, like a picture painted on a gauze curtain. Behind it was another world—a world seen, as it were, from a great height, higher than the jagged mountain in the middle distance, much higher than the towers of the city in the mountain's shadow. Not Gil—this city was built like a wheel, with a dark, forbidding castle at the hub, and beyond the mountain a grey desert stretched to a distant southern sea.

Iklankish. It had to be. It looked no bigger than the cities I used to build in the sand when I was a child, adorning them with shells and pebbles and feathers that would whirl away with the scum of the next tide. There was a tide here, too: a massive swell of water that swept under me as I watched and broke at the shoreline, its crest elongating into a great green slab that overhung the city for a moment before collapsing, rolling over the mountain, sweeping across the desert to meet another wall of water advancing from the south. The earth seemed to fall away; the sea boiled over Iklankish. I cried out and let the Lady drop from my hand, and immediately that other layer of vision disappeared.

"By Raksh and Oballef," Shree whispered, "what's happening to the sea?"

I stood up unsteadily, bracing myself against the fading aftershocks. The sea was still a pearly mirror halfway to the eastern horizon; beyond that was a tortured landscape of silver hills and mountains and ephemeral towers that rose and collapsed and rose again in seething turbulence, surging ever closer on a broad front. I watched with mounting horror as the specks of Calla's flotilla sailed helplessly into the edge of the ferment and vanished among the shifting peaks. Nothing could survive that sea.

"Calla!"

Frantically, I scooped the Lady off the ground. No vision this time, no sensation of throbbing life in that shining cylinder of glass. The power was elsewhere, and too busy to bother with my feeble personal will. I cried out anyway to the Lady, I prayed, I willed, I cursed her in as many languages as I could remember, and in the end I sat down on the ground and put my head in my hands, knowing that it was too late to stop what I had started.

Shree was shouting, but his words were lost in the thrum of blood in my ears, the roar of approaching chaos. He pulled me to my feet and dragged me to the edge of the cliff to see the first waves slam into the side of Gil, hammering the lower ramparts of the Gilgard—but the ramparts held; and then the immense spumes and billows of the first assault were past Gil, washing along the seaway to the Archipelago, and the second and third assaults were already weaker, and the fourth was scarcely higher than a spring tide. To the east then were calmer waters, clear of ships; to the west, a series of vast ripples, perhaps mast-high, spreading majestically as far as the horizon.

"What was it?" Shree shouted. I could hear him again. "What have you done?"

"I gather," I said gravely, "that I've sunk Sher into the ocean."

I looked at the Lady, glowing innocently in my hands.

Such a small thing. All the towers and courts, the black fortresses and dismal mines, the warlords and armies, slaves and merchants, Sherkints and shints, innocent and guilty, Calla and her silver ship, I had sunk them into the sea. I was the greatest conqueror in history, the destroyer of Iklankish, the hero of Gil; and I was a greater killer than Kishr himself.

"We're damned," I said to the Lady.

I raised the shining cylinder and dashed it against the hard ground. And again. It seemed my arm would break first, or maybe the mountain. But on the third blow, the cylinder shivered and cracked in a hairline, half across its thickness; on the fourth, the far half snapped free and tinkled away across the pebbles. The last of the glittering clouds poured out of the shards and rose into the air around my head.

When I came to, Shree was loosening my breastplate with one hand and slapping my face with the other. When he saw my eyes open, he stopped slapping me and poured about a quarter-flask of fith liquor down my throat. This felt like a small building falling on my head.

"Are you all right?" He slapped me again.

"I'll be fine if you stop helping me," I said crossly. "What happened this time?"

"You broke the Lady."

"I know that. But what happened then?"

He met my eyes squarely. "You fell over. Are you sure you're all right?"

"Yes, I'm sure."

"Quite sure?" He was looking at me oddly—perhaps the oddest of all the wide range of odd looks I'd received in my life, and I'd received more than my fair share. I stared back at him.

"Let me see. I'm guilty, grief-stricken, and I think I'd throw myself off the mountain if I didn't feel obliged to suffer some more first. Why?"

"Just asking." He hoisted me to my feet. "You've finished here—we'll go down now. Can you walk?"

"One more thing."

I searched among the pebbles for the shards of the Lady.

They were there, two ugly jag-ended tubes of muddy grayish glass, no longer shining. I flung them one by one over the side of the cliff, my eyes losing them well before they hit the water. Then I turned to Shree.

His face was still cautious, but not disapproving. He raised the silver flask in a salute, took a deep draught and offered it to me. I waved it away. Together we found the slope that led back to the castle and descended, side by side, into the new Gil.

EPILOGUE

I AM FINISHING these memoirs seated on a bench in the Great Garden and once I am done, I will go home and file them safely and inaccurately away where the Flamens will never find them.

It is a garden again—that is one small thing to the Primate's credit. New grass grows thickly on the fertile ground, the young trees are in bud. Children are playing on the spot where the Pleasure used to stand. The statue of the Lady is still here, twice life-size, clean white stone luminous in the sunshine, the damage plastered over, the obscenities scrubbed away, and she smiles over the children with a kind of remote, benign blankness. The adults sometimes scowl at her when they think no one is watching. It is five years to the day since she and I sank Sher into the ocean.

Would I still have done it, had I known what it would lead to? Possibly—given that this is an imperfect world, and an exchange of evils now and then may be the best we can hope for. But I was younger when it happened, and I think that in the core of my heart, behind the terrible deluging rage, I had hoped only for good; I could not have foreseen the curious truth that Sher, for all its appallingness, had been the glue that held the old order of the world together.

This truth became manifest at the next congress of the League of Free Nations, held in Luc some two months after the destruction of Sher. The opening ten minutes or so were spent in expressions of thankfulness that the Sherkin menace was removed, which was the first, last and only point upon which the conference agreed. The Lucian envoy then started the entertainment with a long speech claiming special privileges for Luc on the grounds that, naturally, it had been the Lucian Monotheus, on the urging of the Lucian priesthood, who had at last prevailed over Sher.

The Zainoi envoy rose graciously to correct his esteemed Lucian colleague—it was, in fact, the Pantheon of Zaine which had wrought the miracle of the world's deliverance, and Zaine expected the world to show its proper gratitude in the form of certain territorial concessions on the eastern edge of the Great Known Sea.

At this, the envoys from Grisot and Miishel both shot to their feet and made determined efforts to outshout each other: Zaine was talking arrant nonsense, the islands in question belonged by rights to noble Grisot/glorious Miishel, and anyway Iklankish had been swallowed up by the inexpressible might of the Grisoti Numen of War/Miisheli Great Ones, as every right-minded nation must surely recognize—or else. Then they stopped shouting and started glaring at each other, and the festivities began in earnest.

It was all talk; the Lady's role was no secret, the story had spread almost as rapidly as the news of Sher's downfall, but the truth was irrelevant because nobody had anything to gain from it. Indeed, I suspect that the Lady's destruction was as much of a relief to the nations at large as Sher's had been. I didn't mind. I didn't want the credit, the guilt was quite enough to handle. And I don't even remember why I was surprised at what came next. Power struggles, shifting alliances, broken treaties, flare-ups of old grievances that Sher's threat had overshadowed for seventy years—the League itself did not survive that congress. In time, great holes were torn in the fragile web of trade, and wars, famines, plagues followed on as implacably as winter follows autumn. The new Compact of Nations may offer some hope, but I'm afraid the study of history has made me a pessimist. Time will tell.

Naturally, Gil has had its own catalogue of troubles—although, since we are a poor and backward nation now, bereft of the Lady and not as interesting as we used to be to the rest of the nations, our woes have remained largely internal. At first, after the liberation, the people were happy to have the Scions of Oballef back in the Gilgard; but it took less than a year of the Primate's behind-the-throne high-handedness to disenchant them. Without the Lady, the people began to ask themselves, what right had the Flamens to take power? What right had the Scions of Oballef? What claim had the Exiles? Who were the invaders now? The Primate's

only response was to borrow three full regiments from Sathelforn, after which the murmurs continued, but became harder to hear, and every so often fresh obscenities had to be
scrubbed from the statue of the Lady.

There was, and is, nothing I could do. The Flamens-in-
Exile were not pleased with me. It was bad enough that I
had broken the Heroic Code; worse than I had broken the
Lady. They explained this to me, time and again, in the
months that followed their coming to Gil. How, they demanded, were we to rebuild Gil without the Lady's help?
And how to regain our place as the wonder of the world, a
race apart, the garden of the arts, the treasurehouse of learning? They were not interested in my answers.

Therefore, I kept my peace. When my brother Arkolef was
installed on the throne of Gil, I paid allegiance and kept my
peace. When the factions formed around Arko, around Hawelli's spiritual heirs, around the Flamens, around the
mushroom-bed of new cults, I kept my peace. My part in
history was played out; I retired to my natural place in the
audience.

The old First Memorian, may the many new gods of Gil
rest him and his bones bring forth flowers, died of the Gil-
gut fever within a week of his homecoming. I mourned him,
just as he (alone of the Flamens-in-Exile) had grieved for me
when he thought I was dead. Then, since scholarship was
the last thing on anybody else's mind, I appropriated a corner
of the Temple Palace and began the long slow job of pre-
serving the greatest treasure left to us, the archives.

I was helped in this by Angel and Shree—not surprising
in Angel's case, for he had been reared by Parali, the fore-
most memorian of the old Gil; but Shree was a pleasant
shock. I kept him close to me for his own protection at first,
but he rapidly showed a real talent for scholarship. Under
the circumstances, the monograph he is writing on the folk-
ways and history of lost Iklankish will be the definitive work
on the subject.

Apart from acting as recording memorians, we have been
able to keep well out of politics. Quietly, unobtrusively, we
have spent our time searching out and sorting the caches of

old papers, mildewed books, sodden scrolls, crumbling tablets of clay and stone, which the Sherank had tossed into corners and mercifully forgotten. A surprising amount had survived. In due course I was also able to take custody of the archives from Exile, although the Primate left them to moulder on the quay for nearly a month first, out of simple spite.

We've even been gathering pupils. Lissula's little daughter, for example, comes daily for lessons—Lissula wants her to know more than the whorehouse, however brilliantly the business is doing. And my mother often comes to sit with us in the evenings, knitting underbritches for my father as she listens to us reading aloud from the recovered riches of the past. My father must have the largest collection of underbritches in Gil, but my mother can't seem to stop. After nineteen years of freezing in the dark, she says, he can't have enough underbritches now. He began to speak again three years ago; his nightmares have gone away.

My nightmares will never go away. No matter that I can look down from the Gilgard and see Gil being rebuilt, not on the brittle foundation of magic, but with toil and sweat and craft. No matter that children are playing on the blood-nourished grass of the Great Garden, and that not one of them will go home to a meal of maggots and shull. No matter that, from the confusion and struggle of these first hard years, I can see a new Gil emerging. I know what the Flamens planned for Gil; this is no worse, and probably better, and the Primate will not live forever. No, I do not regret destroying the Lady. My nightmares are not concerned with Gil.

My nightmares are of the Pleasure, and the crash of waters. I dream of towers crumbling and deserts flooding, of waves rolling over mountaintops; I dream of the cries of the dying, and then of a great silence. I dream of a child, a fairheaded boy, and I know from his face whose child he would have been. I dream of a golden mist and a silver ship and Calla, my other Lady in Gil, whom I also destroyed.

The millions, the child, Calla: the dead and unborn will be with me always. Such is victory. May their bones bring forth flowers.

DENISE VITOLA

MANJINN MOON 0-441-00521-7/$5.99
Ty is a twenty-first-century detective on an Earth choked with corruption, violence and greed. When she investigates the deaths of three intelligence agents, she uncovers an assassin with strange powers and deadly cunning: the Manjinn

Now she must rescue the man she loves from the grip of an enemy more dangerous and terrifying than any she has met.

OPALITE MOON 0-441-00465-2/$5.99
Winter grips District One like a steel fist. Even the most basic resources are stretched to the breaking point And Ty Merrick, weathering the psychological ravages of her lycanthropy, is busy. Three members of a secret sect—known as the Opalite—have been murdered

Now, under the suspicious eyes of the government, Ty must venture into the frozen fringes of a bankrupt society where the Opalite keeps its secrets. Where the natural and supernatural collide. Where only a lycanthrope would feel at home...

QUANTUM MOON 0-441-00357-5/$5.99
In the mid-twenty-first-century, the world as we know it no longer exists. The United World Government—with its endless rules and regulations—holds an iron fist over the planet's diminished natural resources. But some things never change. Like greed Corruption And murder.